"Of the four volumes thus far, Su[...] most cohesive, certainly the most [...] was well-chosen; every author rep[...] telling, and every conclusion (ever[...] continuing narratives) inevitable and, at the same time, wonderfully surprising."
—Dr Michael R. Collings

"Very enjoyable and well worth reading."
—Hellnotes

"This anthology takes what's expected from the genre and turns it into the strangest, most bad-ass mix of military horror stories in the best way possible."
—Horror Review

"... a great taste of what military horror can achieve."
—Horrortalk.com (SNAFU: Heroes)

"... every single story holds its own and it's damn difficult to pick a standout as they all leave a mark."
—Horrortalk.com (SNAFU 1)

"... Geoff Brown and Amanda J. Spedding deserve immense credit for both the consistent quality and extraordinary variety..."
—This Is Horror (UK) (SNAFU 1)

"I've read the entire SNAFU series and I can wholeheartedly recommend 'em — every one of them delivers the goods."
— Tim Miller, director of Deadpool

Also From Cohesion Press

SNAFU: An Anthology of Military Horror
– eds Geoff Brown & Amanda J Spedding

SNAFU: Wolves at the Door
– eds Geoff Brown & Amanda J Spedding

SNAFU: Survival of the Fittest
– eds Geoff Brown & Amanda J Spedding

SNAFU: Hunters
– eds Amanda J Spedding & Geoff Brown

SNAFU: Future Warfare
– eds Amanda J Spedding & Geoff Brown

SNAFU: Unnatural Selection
– eds Amanda J Spedding & Geoff Brown

SNAFU: Black Ops
– eds Amanda J Spedding, Matthew Summers & Geoff Brown

SNAFU: Resurrection
– eds Amanda J Spedding & Matthew Summers

SNAFU: Last Stand
– eds Amanda J Spedding & Matthew Summers

SNAFU: Medivac
– eds Amanda J Spedding & Geoff Brown

SNAFU: Holy War (2021)
– eds Amanda J Spedding & Geoff Brown

SNAFU
SURVIVAL OF THE FITTEST

Publisher's Note:
This book is a collection of stories from writers all over the world. For authenticity and voice, we have kept the style of English native to each author's location, so some stories will be in UK English, and others in US English.
We have, however, changed dashes and dialogue marks to our standard format for ease of understanding.

SNAFU
SURVIVAL OF THE FITTEST

Edited by
Geoff Brown & Amanda J Spedding

Cohesion Press
Mayday Hills Lunatic Asylum
Beechworth, Australia

SNAFU
SURVIVAL OF THE FITTEST

Geoff Brown and Amanda J Spedding (Eds)

Anthology © Cohesion Press 2015/2021
Stories © Individual Authors 2015
Interior Art © Montgomory Borror 2015
Cover Art © Dean Samed/Conzpiracy Dean 2015
Internal Layout by Geoff Brown
Proofreading by Sarah Bentvelzen

Set in Palatino Linotype
All rights reserved.
No part of this publication may be reproduced, stored in a retrieval system or transmitted in any form by any means without the prior permission of the copyright owner. Enquiries should be made to the publisher.

This book is a work of fiction.
All people, places, events, and situations are products of the author's imagination.
Any resemblance to persons, places or dinosaurs, living or dead, is purely coincidental.

Cohesion Press
Mayday Hills Lunatic Asylum
Beechworth, Australia
www.cohesionpress.com

Contents

Foreword ix

Badlands - S.D. Perry 1

Of Storms and Flame - Tim Marquitz & J.M. Martin 51

In Vaulted Halls Entombed - Alan Baxter 73

They Own the Night - B. Michael Radburn 103

Fallen Lion - Jack Hanson 121

Sucker of Souls - Kirsten Cross 147

After the Red Rain Fell - Matt Hilton 177

The Slog - Neal F. Litherland 193

Show of Force - Jeremy Robinson & Kane Gilmour 221

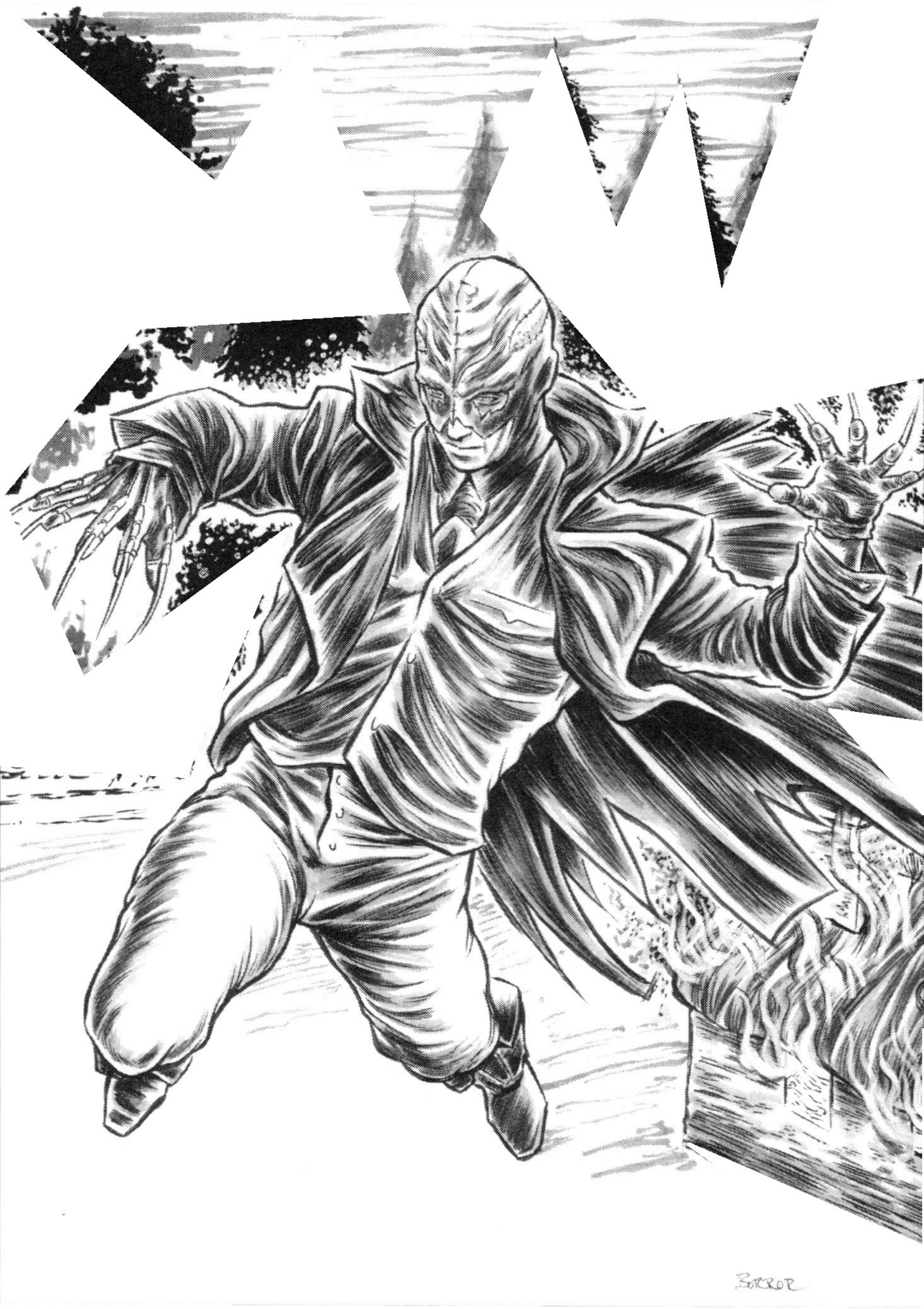

Foreword

SNAFU

Situation Normal, All Fucked Up.
That, I think, says it all when it comes to military horror. Soldiers fighting for their lives, and at times for the lives of innocents, against supernatural or unearthly creatures.

Military writing has been around for as long as the written word, and likely for longer, although we only have a few surviving examples of such.

The idea of military speculative fiction (specfic) may seem like a subject not worth spending a whole lot of time talking about. After all, doesn't it seem rather self-explanatory? It's about the military, any branch, and it's about horror, fantasy, or science fiction. However I believe military specfic is deeper than that. While it may very well be escapist literature to characterise all of the romanticized visions we have of the military, it can also be a hard-hitting commentary on current events and politics.

Beowulf and Homer's *Odyssey* are both examples of early recorded military speculative fiction, although I'm not sure they were designed to be this. The cultures of the time believed in the gods, and sometimes the monsters, of *Odyssey*.

Precursors for military specfic can be found in 'future war' stories dating back at least to George Chesney's story 'The Battle of Dorking' (1871) which was a speculative fiction piece, describing a successful German invasion of Britain.

Other works of fiction followed, including H.G. Wells's 'The Land Ironclads'. Eventually, as science fiction became an established and separate genre, military science fiction established itself as a subgenre. One such work is H. Beam Piper's *Uller Uprising* (1952). Robert A. Heinlein's *Starship Troopers* (1959), more recently a series of films, is another work of military specfic, along with Gordon Dickson's *Dorsai* (1960), and these are

SNAFU: SURVIVAL OF THE FITTEST

thought to be mostly responsible for popularising this sub-genre's popularity among young readers of the time.

The Vietnam War resulted in veterans with combat experience deciding to write specfic, including Joe Haldeman and David Drake. Throughout the 1970s, works such as Haldeman's *The Forever War* and Drake's *Hammer's Slammers* helped increase the popularity of the genre, as did Harry Harrison with the Deathworld series. Short stories were also popular, collected in books like *Combat SF*, edited by Gordon R. Dickson. This anthology includes one of the first Hammer's Slammers stories as well as one of the BOLO stories by Keith Laumer and one of the Berserker stories by Fred Saberhagen.

This anthology seems to have been the first time specfic stories specifically dealing with war as a subject were collected and marketed as such. The series of anthologies with the group title *There Will be War* edited by Pournelle and John F. Carr (nine volumes from 1983 through 1990) helped keep the category active, and encouraged new writers to add to it. I wanted to add more.

When I started Cohesion Press, I already knew I wanted to publish *SNAFU*. It was in my mind before anything else. I've always loved this style of book, with a strong emphasis on plot and action.

Our first anthology, simply titled *SNAFU: An Anthology of Military Horror*, was released just over a year ago. I asked four writers I repected. Four writers whose work mirrored my vision. A year later, Jonathan Maberry, Greig Beck, James A. Moore, Weston Oche, and a great collection of emerging writers made up that inaugural volume. We hoped it would do well when we set it free in the world, and it did. Now, three SNAFUs later, comes *Survival of the Fittest*. I hope you enjoy it.

I'll leave the series co-editor to talk about the stories within.

Geoff Brown – August 2015

* * *

FOREWORD

As far back as I can remember I've had a fascination with monster stories, of the things that hide in the shadows waiting to pounce. I loved that rush of fear, of being forced to push past it to discover what lay ahead and whether the protagonist would defeat the monster, whether they would survive. Who would be the victor?

When you add a keen interest in military documentaries and military fiction, I jumped at the chance when Geoff asked me to come on board as co-editor for the SNAFU series. Who wouldn't want to work with authors on stories that combined two of the best genres of fiction that would have readers wondering 'what fresh hell is this?'

Wars and conflict are a part of our world, of humanity's history whether we like it or not. No matter your culture or creed, combat sits and weighs heavily in our past. Even before the written word there are pictorial and oral records of battles, some of which are woven through our mythos.

SNAFU: Survival of the Fittest takes the warfare between monsters and military to the next level. Being reduced to that heart pounding, sphincter-clenching fear when facing a monstrous unknown; with your ammo dwindling and next-to-no options... how do you survive? At what cost?

The monsters here have been pulled from the abyss, summoned by dark magic, or are those that have lain dormant just waiting for the opportunity to wreak havoc. Pitched against elite forces and your (not-so) ordinary grunts, what will some sacrifice to save themselves, their brothers and sisters in arms, humanity? That's the soul of the stories that lay ahead.

Each takes a different look at war, police actions, black ops and para-military, but with each taking place in different eras (epochs even). It's both modern warfare and historical hostilities that make up this edition, of the finality of an epic battle when there is seemingly no way out... or back. It's that thread of determination and sacrifice that binds these stories together. Whether it's fighting one's way through a gamut of nightmares made real, the horror-filled realisation of battling against an inconceivable and perhaps indestructible creature, or finding yourself up against something you thought was a work of fiction, it's the fealty of the combatants, their courage and vulnerability, that highlights the best of humanity (regardless of how 'human' those soldiers are).

Now don't get me wrong, the monsters in these tales hold their own, often with their own stories to tell, and our authors have taken these horrors from all spectrums of imagination and mythos – so much so that like the warriors facing off these foes, I was unsure what awaited me. What you think you may know, what these soldiers think they may know pales in comparison to the truth of what lurks in the shadows, what hides beneath your feet, or what awakens when the bell tolls.

And toll it does. SNAFU: Survival of the Fittest is just that. The question you have to ask yourself, is that soldier or hellion?

So sit back, keep your weapons close, and let our authors unleash their monsters...

Amanda J. Spedding – August 2015

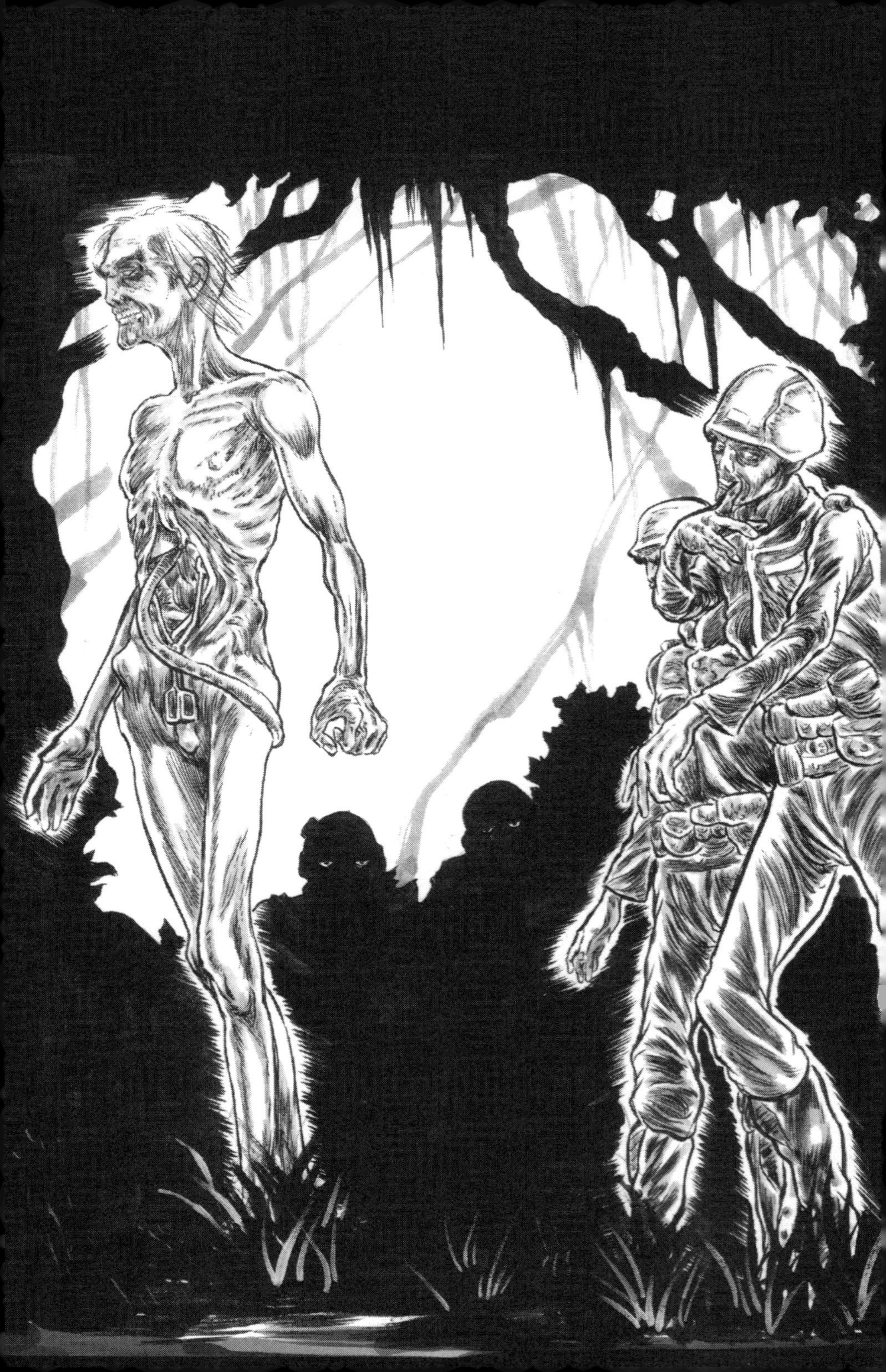

BADLANDS
S.D. Perry

October, 1952

In Korea, October was the only month that didn't eat a bag of dicks, in Sergeant Edward West's humble opinion. Between the sweltering deep green of the monsoon season and the icy slide into brutal winter, there were a few short weeks of relief. The leaves start to change, the humidity drops below fifty per cent, the days are mild. The ever-present stink of kimchi and human waste seem to ebb. It was only West's second October in Korea, wasn't like he had a whole lot of evidence, but he thought two was enough to say. He'd be out before a third, thank Christ, FIGMO whether the talks went on or not – the big R was scheduled for January.

And then what? Factory work? Management? Car sales? He walked slow, his handful of boys strung out in front of him. The gung-ho young West who'd proudly signed up for WWII was long gone, mislaid in the cold winter and spring of 1945 somewhere between Marche and Mauthausen. He'd gone home broken, an old man still in his 20s. Civilian life was a depressing horror show; blind, idiot smiles everywhere he looked. He lost a couple of jobs, drank too much. When Uncle Sam had called him up in '50 with a better pay grade for a little police action over in Korea, he'd listened. Like a fucking idiot.

At least here you're doing something useful. Keeping his guys in one piece, that had to count for something.

Burtoni held up his hand and everyone froze. West listened, scanned the stand of trees to the north, the low foothills east; it was rocky, hilly terrain anyway, but this close to the mountains there were spider holes and tunnels. He heard a scratching, rustling sound, low and close...

Young grinned, pointed two o'clock, and then they were all grinning.

"Mole?" drawled Cakes. His real name was Earl Dupree but everyone called him Cakes, short for Jonnycakes. The kid was a hillbilly. He was also a mouth with a temper, and built like a tank. He never got shook, and was a bear cat with an M1 Garand.

Burtoni took a step back, peered at the small, furry ass of whatever creature was clawing into a rise of leaf-strewn dirt near a stunted maple. "Shrew."

Private Young wrinkled his nose. "It's a vole."

"What the fuck's a vole?" Cakes glared at Young. "You're shittin' me, a *vole*?"

"I shit you not," said Young, holding up two fingers. If anyone was still a boy scout, it was Davey Young. "It's a gray red-backed vole."

Burtoni chuckled. "You made that up." His accent was all Brooklyn. *That* was *dat*. The voice matched his narrow face and quick eyes. West liked him out front for the walk. "It's gray an' red, anybody coulda come up with that."

The medic, Kelly, raised his eyebrows at Young.

Young shrugged. "My girl sent me a book."

Addison spoke up. He rarely did, a family man counting the days. Addy had two children already and a third on the way. "A book on voles?"

"On nature of the Korean Peninsula," Young said. "Like, wildlife and trees."

"Aw, you and your gook thing," Cakes sneered, and thumped him on the shoulder.

"Alright, dry up," West finally interrupted. "We're standing here like targets."

They started walking again. West heard birds, the rustling of trees, the shuffle of their feet. Thoughts of the future were set aside; he'd been lulled by the season, the routine, an hour's walk north and back, uneventful for months. They were reserve and currently too far from the DMZ to have to worry about the hordes attacking, but he should have been paying attention. The commies were a sneaky bunch.

BADLANDS

Brilliant red leaves scattered by from a stand of maples a quarter mile away, on a breeze that smelled like smoke. Behind them, a sound, a patter. Footsteps.

West turned, brought up his rifle. Three people had suddenly appeared at the top of a low, rocky rise southwest of their position, not fifty feet away.

Goddamn Korean topo!

"Backs in," West said. "Burtoni, Addy, watch our six."

It was two old people and a boy, maybe eight or nine years old. They carried sagging, tattered packs and were filthy, hatless and sunburned. The boy was skinny as a slat cat. When they looked down and saw the soldiers, they froze.

"Hey, Mac," the boy called, holding up a hand. He spoke briefly to the old people. Grandparents, looked like. They raised their hands, both of them stepping closer to the child.

West relaxed a little bit, trusting his instincts. North Joes sometimes dressed up like refugees, but not these people. "You speak English?"

"Number one, Mac," said the boy. He lowered his hands slightly. "South Korean. KATUSA, Mac, ROK number one, USA!"

"Anybody see anything?" West said, keeping his voice low, and got a mumbled chorus of negatives. "Keep watch. Cakes, keep these fine people covered. Young, you're with me."

"Hooah," another gentle chorus. Heard, understood, acknowledged. Cakes moved out to flank them.

The threesome hadn't moved, which meant they had to walk up a slight rise to meet them. West kept his own carbine easy. He smiled up at the boysun, watched him smile back. The kid's smile was wide but didn't touch his eyes.

"Sarge, if you think I can talk to them..." Young began.

"Zip it. You're who we've got." Young was always practicing with the kids in the village southeast of the 33rd's base camp. They'd been waiting for a new interpreter since they lost Billy J to Seoul in August, and West couldn't bring himself to tap one of the ROKs, not with Cakes on the walk.

They stopped in front of the trio. West looked at the elderly couple. The old man blinked. The old woman's mouth quivered. They looked a thousand years old.

"Where are you coming from?" West asked the boy, gesturing back the way they came.

"Keigu at MASH, GI Joe, eighty-leven," the boy said. "Clean for you? Take out trash, laundry? All the officers I do. Cheap, Mac, good deal. The best."

"You know where the 8011th is?" West asked Young.

The PFC shook his head. "They're supporting 5th Division and that regiment from Australia," he said. "North of Yanggu, maybe? They could be closer."

Long walk. "Where are you going?" West asked the boy.

He raised one bony arm, pointed northeast. "Ch'alu'un. Home."

West knew there were a couple of small villages out that way, goat herders or something, locals who'd gradually filtered back since the talks had stalled.

The old man looked over his shoulder, back the way they'd come. He sang his strange tongue at the boy, his tone anxious.

"What's he saying?"

Young frowned, listened. "Uh, he says they have to go, they have to hurry... they have to get home before the light of... before the moon rises? I think."

"Where's the fire?" West leaned down a little, smiled at the boy again. The kid's shining dark eyes seemed fathomless. "Why now?"

Boysun didn't answer, and the old woman started talking. West didn't need an interpreter to catch her desperation, her fear. Her old voice broke as it rose and fell.

Young was frowning. "Something – about a bell? Then, you have to let us go... Jabi, jabi... Mercy? I think mercy."

West's adrenaline machine started back up. They were in a hurry, all right. What were they running from?

Young stammered his way through a sentence. The old man said something, Young said something. The old man repeated himself, slowing his words down.

"Come on," West said, starting to feel impatient. They'd been standing still for too long.

BADLANDS

"I don't know," Young said. He tilted his helmet back, wiping at his brow. "He says that the priests are waving their lanterns, something like that. Then... *gangshi*? I don't know the word. He says we should go home, too."

"Try again."

Another stilted exchange, and Young shook his head. "I'm sorry, Sarge. He just keeps saying it's not safe and you have to let 'em go."

"Some superstitious thing?" It sounded right, home before dark, priests waving lanterns. West remembered when one of the ROKA kids back at base had flipped his wig over someone whistling at night, saying that it attracted spirits.

"You got me, sir."

Behind them, Burtoni. "Hey! We got—"

The rattle of a burp gun drowned him out and West ducked and spun, saw Kelly go down, saw Addy fall. West raised his weapon, searching. Next to him, Young grabbed his gut and fell to his knees, and then Cakes and Burtoni were firing back, *there*, two-hundred feet and ten o'clock, movement at the top of a low rock formation. Rock chips flew. West yelled for everyone to get down but his voice was lost to the old woman's scream, a terrible high wailing, and the deeper rattle of return fire.

Again, that flash of movement, a head bobbing up – and then the rocks spat up blood, a distinct spray of gore rising into the air. Cakes or Burtoni had gotten the fucker, taken the top of his head off. Cakes fired once more and the Garand's clip popped, *ping*! In the ringing aftermath there was only the sound of the old woman, sobbing. Nothing moved but the wind.

"Call it in!" West shouted, and then Burtoni was on his knees next to Addy, pulling at the radio. Addison wasn't moving. Kelly had his hands clapped to his throat, blood gushing through his fingers. Cakes grabbed for Kelly's medkit and dumped it out, his thick fingers rummaging. If there were more shooters, they were all fucked.

West dropped to his knees next to Young, saw the pool of blood at his gut. Young turned panicky blue eyes up to him, breathing in choppy little gasps. Burtoni babbled their position into the radio, his voice breaking... medevac... three wounded. Cakes cursed, a steady stream of expletives as he held a stack of red gauze to their medic's throat.

"Hurts," Young said.

"I know it does," West said, pulling off his shirt, balling it up to press to the kid's stomach. "Don't talk. Choppers are coming."

The old woman had stopped crying, at least. West looked up and saw that the travelers had disappeared, like they'd never been there at all.

* * *

After the eggbeaters came and went, Sarge ordered them back to camp, his face grim. Him and Cakes were both blood-spattered and didn't talk much, which was a good thing, since PFC Peter Antony Burtoni was point back to base and he didn't want to miss a mouse farting. They'd been flanked by four gooks without even knowing. Addy and Kelly were dead and who knew about Young? Burtoni was clanked up, edgy, and the whole way back he was bugging his eyes out at everything. How many more lone Joes were out there, creeping behind the low hills, clinging to the shadowy rocks?

The only conversation was between Cakes and Sarge, about what had happened. Cakes said it was a setup with the kid and his grandparents but the sarge didn't think so, he said they were running from something. Seemed like a pretty big coincidence in Burtoni's book, but he was too busy straining to hear and see and smell everything to think too much on it. He was glad that Sarge and Cakes were with him. They were both hard-boiled, but by the time they got back to camp, Burtoni was out of gas.

He got a shower and ate, and drank enough coffee to give him the squirts, but he couldn't get his mojo back. He was actually making plans to hit the sack as soon as it got dark but Sarge came over just when the shadows were getting long. Young had made it out of surgery at the 8011th MASH and was doing fine. Sergeant West and Young's best buddy, PFC Kyle McKay, were heading out in twenty, Cakes was driving... Did Burtoni want in? And how! If anyone deserved to see a few familiar faces when he woke up, it was Young.

Young was always good for a smoke and a joke, he was always smiling. He was real smart, too, but he wasn't no high hatter about it. This one time, they'd all been sitting at mess talking about how shitty Korea was and how they never should have come in, and Young had started explaining all the politics, like with Korea being so close to Japan and what the Soviets wanted to do, and how bad that would be for the rest of the world. Burtoni had stopped giving a shit if the commies took over about ten minutes after he'd set foot on Korean soil. The gooks could all take a flying fuck as far as he was concerned, but the way Young told it... He said what they were doing was important, stopping the Reds, and he really believed it. Burtoni still hated the fucking place with his whole heart, and prayed every day to go home. No conversation was going to change that, but it had made him feel a little better, like at least it wasn't all for nothing.

Besides which, Burtoni had heard that the MASH units were nice, clean, lots of drafted doctors and support personnel with no interest in mitt flopping to the brass. Decent chow, hot water, less horseshit... and nurses. American women of the Army Nursing Corps. He'd never been to one of the mobile hospitals but the fellas talked, saying that for every battleaxe stomping around there were three Doris Days looking to hold hands and kiss it better. Plus a Jane Russell or two thrown in, for thinking about later.

Burtoni needed to see a pretty face, some baby-doll ready to hear some sweet talk from a well-mannered Catholic boy like himself. There had to be at least a few lookers in the pack, but he was entirely prepared to compromise. War was hell. He got his kit together, his exhaustion turning to a kind of wired giddiness. He was famous back home for having a way with the ladies. Maybe he could salvage something from this clusterfuck of a day.

Full dark and Cakes drove them along a beaten track headed south and west, headlights illuminating a sea of nothing but trees and hills and rocks. The night was cold and damp. The wind whistled through the Jeep's buttoned flaps, and the heater didn't work. McKay, a skinny redheaded guy, sat in the back with Burtoni but kindly kept his phiz shut for most of the trip, an hour and a half of ass-cracking potholes and Cakes snapping his cap about them. Sergeant West stared out into the dark, thinking whatever it was he thought about. Burtoni focused himself on the promise of talking up some split-tail Sheba, trying not to see what he kept seeing in his head – Addy, falling, shot in the face, never to see his rugrats again. Kelly bleeding out into the rocks a million miles from home.

Finally, they crested a low rise and there were lights ahead, lights and shitloads of tents and Quonset huts tucked between two hills. Burtoni studied the place through the smeary window. There were some beat up crash wagons just north of the camp, the white-outlined crosses they wore flocked with mud. He counted three copters parked some distance away. Cakes swung around south, past a couple of long barracks buildings to the motor pool in back. Farther south was a camp village, dark hooches stretching out of sight.

A short corporal with peepers and a baby face signed them in and gave them the dope on the place, pointing to a hand-drawn map on the wall – mess, guest quarters, post-op, NCO club. The sarge asked where the honcho was and the corporal, name of O'Donnell, said he'd still be in his office; CO was a bottle-cap colonel called Sanderson. The sarge got a sour look at the name. He hid it quick, but Anna Burtoni hadn't raised no knuckleheads. If Sarge didn't like the guy, neither did Burtoni.

Sarge said he was going to talk to Sanderson and sent them ahead to see Young. McKay led the way through the tent town, and Burtoni quickly surmised that the 8011th pretty much beat the living snot out of their Company base. It didn't smell like shit, for one thing, but also the walkways were packed and smooth, and most of the tents had real floors. Buzzing lamps, swarmed by moths, sent down smooth planes of yellow light, cutting cleanly through the shadows. Someone had planted flowers along the bases of the Quonset huts. Most of 'em were

BADLANDS

dying, but still. Some of the guys walking past were regular army, tucked and spiffy, but there were some real slobs, too, and no one saluted. He even saw a pair of Joes walk by wearing nonreg civvies, cackling like hens.

"Where's all the gooks?" Cakes asked, and Burtoni finally noticed the most obvious difference. The Koreans who lived in the 33rd's little camp town went to bed early, but there were always workers and sellers hanging around, kids running errands, the occasional slicky boy looking to boost anything that wasn't nailed down. At the 8011th, he didn't see a single Korean face.

"You got the eagle eye, Cakes," he said, and Cakes laughed, started to say something back, and then just stood still, his mouth hanging open. Dames, dead ahead.

Burtoni got an eyeful of the pair. The one on the right was blond but older, probably in her thirties, and had a sharp look to her, like she was just waiting to dish out some knocks. They got closer, passed beneath one of the buzzing lights, and Burtoni caught the gold leaf. Jeez, but she was a major!

The other one, though. The gal walking with her was soft and curvy and doe-eyed, her dark hair pulled back in a ponytail. She was a second looey and a bona fide honey.

"Fazangas," Cakes breathed, just when they got in earshot.

"Go chase yourself, Private," snapped the pretty one, hardly looking at them. Her voice was music. Major Blondie gave them a shriveling glare as they passed.

"Forget about him, ma'ams," Burtoni said, turning to call after them. "His mama dropped him on his head."

The gals kept walking but the angel glanced back. Burtoni smiled his best smile and her lips were twitching when she turned away.

"What are you, stupid?" Burtoni asked Cakes, who was inspecting their departing back sides, his mouth still hanging open. "You gotta be a gentleman you wanna make time."

"I got time UTA," Cakes said, in his ridiculous accent: *ah got tahm*. "All I need's a share crop."

Cakes was disgusting. Burtoni shook his head. He'd make a point of asking around about the dark-haired angel, though

9

they'd likely be on their way back to camp early in the morning. Even seeing her again was a long shot.

"Fazangas," Burtoni muttered darkly, and slapped the back of his hand against Cakes' chest. "You should shut up more, you know that?"

"You shut up, ya wop," Cakes rumbled.

McKay had stopped and was waiting for them, his face somber. Right, Young. Burtoni sighed and started walking again. His heart had been stolen away for a minute, but he was recovered. There'd be more nurses in with the patients and it was still early, barely 19:30. After they saw Young, he'd ditch Cakes ASAP and see if he couldn't make some magic happen.

* * *

Admin was behind the surgery at the southwest corner of the compound and West headed that direction, wondering if Sanderson had changed. Anything was possible. He wasn't keen on seeing the man again but wanted to ask about the refugees they'd run across earlier. Common sense told him that Cakes was right; either the whole thing had been a setup or the North Joe had threatened the ragtag family, made 'em target bait... but his gut still said something else. If he didn't ask, he wouldn't sleep. Addison and Kelly had been his guys, they'd been good men.

Robert Sanderson. Eight years before, West had been a PFC to Robert's silver eagle for a brief but memorable push in the first weeks of 1945, taking territory back from the German army after their Christmas offensive. More than half of the guys West had started out with were KIA by then and the rest of 'em got assigned to a command under Captain Sanderson, who'd had his ranks blown to shit on Boxing Day. Thanks to the captain, West lost three more buddies on a frozen street in some nameless little village east of Weiler. Sanderson ordered them to check the bodies of some dead soldiers and *blammo*.

West could understand a mistake – could sympathize, even, having made a few of his own – but Sanderson hadn't owned up. In fact, he had fallen all over himself to pass the buck to one

BADLANDS

of the dead men, a sergeant called Richie Mullens. West had respected the hell out of Sergeant Richie, who'd been with him since near the beginning, who'd literally kept him alive when he was still Johnny Raw. Sanderson had insisted that he'd given the order based on the sergeant's advice, which everyone knew was applesauce; the Sarge would have known better. Before anyone could get too worked up, Captain Sanderson had discovered some pressing business at the rear line and West had been folded into an infantry division headed southwest.

The camp lights hummed, illuminating the few people he passed in murky yellow-white – a young man on crutches with his left lower leg missing, a trio of nurses, a slouching doctor in a Hawaiian shirt. The cool air felt good, waking him up a little, but it smelled like ashes.

Admin was in the last Quonset hut, ahead and on his right. As he approached, a tall, balding man in fatigues stepped out, a tiny silver leaf pinned to his collar. He had the same broad, clueless face that West remembered. All the lines were etched deeper.

West stopped in front of him and saluted.

"At ease," Sanderson said. "What's your name, Sergeant?"

"West, sir."

"Did you need something, son?"

Sanderson wasn't ten years older than West, which put him at forty, maybe. He was still a big time operator, all right, real officer material.

"Sir, I'm over at the 33rd under Colonel Swift. We were on a patrol today and ran across some locals, said they came from the 8011th. A boy and his grandparents. We were ambushed and one of my guys ended up here, shot in the stomach."

Sanderson nodded. "You'll want to talk to Captain Anthony, he's our chief surgeon. He oversees all of the patients."

"Yes, sir. I was wondering if you noticed them leave the camp, though. The boy said he did cleaning for the officers."

Sanderson made an impatient sound. "They're all gone, son. The whole village bugged out two days ago. Every last one of 'em."

West blinked. "Why?"

Sanderson shook his head. "Why do these people do anything? They said there were lights on the hill, they packed their kits and started walking."

"Lights? Sir?"

Sanderson gestured to the north. "The trees, up on that ridge. Last few nights there have been lanterns up there, those yellow paper jobs, swinging back and forth. I sent some of the boys out to look-see, but all they found was footprints in the mud. HQ says it's nothing, a superstition."

The priests are waving their lanterns.

"Did they say what the superstition was?"

Sanderson looked at his watch, his demeanor telling West that their reunion was almost over.

"Oh, some gobbledygook about going home," Sanderson said. "Seems like it worked."

The lieutenant colonel looked at West, seemed to see him for the first time. He narrowed his eyes. For the briefest of seconds, West imagined punching his teeth in.

"Well, I hope your boy makes it," Sanderson said, dismissive, gave a brief, false smile and then walked past him.

"Yes, sir, thank you, sir," West said automatically. He didn't fully trust himself to turn around and follow Sanderson so he kept walking south, past the last camp structures, a storage unit, a supply shed. The village behind the MASH was close, less than a quarter mile away.

West passed the last string of security lights and stepped into the dark but went no further, studying the sad clusters of huts. No fires burned beneath the little houses, no lamps were lit; nothing stirred. Empty doorways yawned like black eyes. Scant light from a rising moon cast an eerie, pale ripple across the thatched roofs.

He turned and looked north – and saw the lanterns. There were at least a dozen specks of dim, glowing yellow on the dark upslope in front of the hospital, maybe a half mile away. They were spread out at different heights and distances. The way they swung and shifted, they were being carried. Easy targets if anyone got nervous.

A warning? A curse? Sanderson was no help, big surprise,

BADLANDS

but there had to be someone around who knew what was happening. He thought about the kid, his unsmiling eyes, the grandmother's frantic speech. What had the old man said, the word that Young hadn't known? Gangshi, something like that.

West walked back into the light of the camp. It was nothing, sure, a nothing little mystery that he'd locked onto because he was dog-tired and heart-sore... but then, why did the perfectly clear night have that electric, unstable feeling that preceded action, or a storm? Something was coming.

Maybe he'd see if he could find a ROK with some English, to explain what had scared the villagers away.

* * *

Fourteen-year-old Lee Mal-Chin was sanitizing bedpans when the three soldiers came in, two PFCs and a single stripe. Of the sixty beds in Post-Op 1 only a third were taken, mostly ROKA enlisted from a small skirmish near the DMZ the day before. Lee saw the trio stop and talk to Doctor Jimmy, who spoke at length before gesturing them towards one of the beds... the American man who'd been shot in the stomach, brought in by helicopter in the afternoon.

Lee went on with his work more slowly, listening to the soldiers talk as they made their way to the cot. He understood most of what they said. He had spent the last two years learning English with anyone who would talk to him. Mostly he talked with Father Maloney now. The father was a good teacher. There was also Corporal Timmy with the ordnance, he told Lee what Father Maloney would not say – the bad words. That Timmy was *jaemi*, a real gas.

The big soldier towhead was full of bad words (*shit* and *asshole* and *fuck*) and loudly told his buddies how he bet these gooks had never had it so good. Lee wiped out a pan with bleach water and kept his expression perfectly blank. It did not pay to draw attention, for any reason. Many of the UN *gun-in* hated Korea, and didn't much like Koreans, either, for their poor and simple ways. Lee could even understand, a little. He had grown up near Seoul, the son of a shopkeeper, and his father had taken pains to see that his children were educated. Out here in the hills they didn't have radios or newspapers. They worked the land and told traditional stories to explain the world. The village behind the 8011th had bugged out only two days ago, when they'd seen lanterns on the hill. Choi Yeo, a man from the village, had come to warn them, telling stories of *gangshi* and the bad temple to the north. Nearly everyone laughed. Lee had laughed, too. The villagers were *smisin-ui*, they believed in magic and ghosts. Was it any wonder that the Americans treated them like children?

The three soldiers settled around the bed of the wounded man, speaking gently. The injured soldier opened his eyes and managed to smile at them. A single tear leaked from his eye. Lee was so struck by the simple joy of their meeting that he didn't realize the big soldier had turned and was glaring at him.

"What are you looking at?"

Lee immediately looked away, lowered his head, backed up a step. He was still small enough to seem a child and could usually avoid conflict with the *deungsin*.

Another soldier told him to cool it. Lee didn't look to see if the big man became cool or not, he got lost fast. Nurse Miss Jenny was taking blood pressures at the other end of the room and he found a stack of blankets that she might need.

He liked Nurse Miss Jenny – he liked all of the nurses, but Jenny had a big round bosom and a smile like sun on the river – and spent a few minutes translating for her when a ROKA soldier woke up and started asking questions. His name was Yi Sam and he didn't remember being shot and was confused. Miss Jenny spoke slowly and clearly so that Lee could explain where he was and what had happened. Lee didn't show off his English, but he always helped the nurses. They were kind to him in turn, they brought him rolls and sometimes chocolate. Chocolate was the best.

"*Gangshi*," someone said loudly.

Miss Jenny had gone back to blood pressures, was talking at him about the upcoming movie night – it was the 8011th's turn to see Treasure Island – but Lee didn't hear her anymore. A man

BADLANDS

had joined the group with the angry soldier, a tall sergeant with a hard jaw and a raspy voice. He was looking around the tent, his eyebrows raised.

"Anyone? *Gangshi*? Kim, you know what that means?"

A ROKA soldier three cots away who'd had his testicles and most of his right thigh blown off by a cart mine was half-sitting, staring at the sergeant. "What is he saying?" he asked, in Korean. A couple of the soldiers he'd come in with stirred. Lee had spoken with the man earlier, he was Pak Mun-Hee from north of Pusan. "Did he say *gangshi*?"

"*Gangshi*," the American sergeant said again. "You know that word?"

Pak Mun-Hee managed a weak salute when he realized the sergeant was talking to him. One of Pak's friends looked frightened; two others grinned.

Nurse Miss Jenny spoke up, looking directly at Lee. "Lee, isn't that what you said when you were telling us about the bug out? *Gangshi*? That's the word you used."

Lee froze, and the tall sergeant focused his attention, stepped away from his group. "Your name is Lee? You speak English?"

"No," Lee said. "Number ten."

"He's putting you on, Sergeant," Miss Jenny said. "He speaks English real well. He told us the villagers left because of those lanterns. Because they're calling all of the dead men home." She smiled prettily. "Only I remember because I wrote a letter to my mother last night, and told her about it. It's so *spooky*."

Pak Mun-Hee had been speaking with his friends, and now raised his voice, calling out, "This man asks about *gangshi*. What is the situation here?"

Another soldier laughed, and Lee tried to smile, it was all so stupid. But there was a tension now, many of the injured talking amongst themselves, laughter and anxiety quickening the air.

The sergeant seemed to feel the urgency. He walked right up to Lee and crouched in front of him. "What does it mean, *gangshi*?"

Playing dumb had become so deeply ingrained that he almost didn't answer, but the man was looking into his face, asking him, and Lee had been taught to speak right.

"The belief is that a man who die away from home, he do not rest," Lee said. "His soul is homesick. A family hires the priest to call the man home. He... *jeompeu*. Jumps?"

Lee stretched his arms out in front of him, stiff, and hopped forward.

The sergeant stood up, his shoulders relaxing. After a moment, he smiled, showing all of his teeth. "So a *gangshi* is a jumping dead man?"

Lee nodded. "The farmers believe this old story."

A patient cried out from across the room, a boy who was likely from a farm. His voice was high, hysterical. "We must guard against them, before it's too late!"

Miss Jenny stood up at once, starting towards the shouter. "Now you calm down, there's no reason to be shouting like that."

"*Jinjeong yeomso saekki*," snarled another. "It is grandmother talk!"

"*Ulineun jug-eul geos-ida!*" the farm boy cried.

"*Dangsin-eun muji!*" another said, laughing at the boy's ignorance.

Miss Jenny called out to the other nurse on duty, Miss Claire, told her to go get someone. Doctor Jimmy was nowhere to be seen, and two of the regular evening nurses were assisting with a surgery in the OR next door.

The sergeant put his fingers to his mouth and whistled, loud. The injured ROKA soldiers all dried up at once, turning to look at him. "Calm down, boys," he said loudly, a snap in his voice. "It's a *story*."

He was an American soldier and therefore every ROK's superior, but it was his clear tone of dismissal that calmed them, even the shouter. Nurse Jenny looked at the sergeant with bright eyes and thanked him warmly as everyone settled down. Lee wished that he could earn a look like that, from any of the nurses.

Faintly, from somewhere to the north, he heard a bell toll, a low, carrying note, and froze. He looked at Pak Mun-Hee, who looked back at him with an expression of disbelief. Of fear.

The tall sergeant chuckled, shook his head. "Jumping dead men," he said, and turned back to his group, and from the OR came a scream of pure terror, and the sound of metal hitting the floor, then more screams.

* * *

Captain Steven 'Stitch' Anthony started his shift in a fine mood. The mail had brought a funny, chatty letter from his mother, he'd tagged Jonesy out in the afternoon scratch game – twice – and all of the boys he'd fixed up were doing fine and dandy. He'd been joking around with one of his patients when Claire had called him over to see the Korean kid.

"Read me the chart," he said, pulling the blanket down. The ROK's belly was distended and solid.

"Twenty-year-old male presents posterior entry wound at L-1, bullet entered left of mid-sagittal and fragmented off the left lateral process of L-1, no anterior wound, fragments removed—"

"Get him prepped, I want him in the theater five minutes ago," Stitch said. The nurses moved, God love 'em. The kid was intubated and Anthony had a scalpel in hand before he had time to notice how rotten his mood had become.

Goddamn Gene, you sack of shit excuse for a surgeon. The major had missed a bowel cut and the kid was in trouble, peritonitis or ascites or a bleed, maybe all three. Gene had learned how to cut from a coloring book; he'd taken care of the mesenteric bundle and called it good.

Good enough for a ROK, anyway. If it had been an American kid, the major would have checked his work; he'd had the time, he just hadn't bothered. Gene Fowler was a menace, an unskilled, humorless hack.

Lieu Jackieboy was the anesthetist, Sheryl and Linda assisted. Anthony told them to get the towels up and opened the patient's abdominal cavity, cutting smoothly. As soon as he was in, pink water poured out and the girls sopped it up, mostly lymph and interstitial fluid but there was a nice bleed, too. *Thank you, Major Gene!*

Linda got retractors on the opening. It took a minute to suction out the fluid and when they were down to sponges,

Anthony saw the seep of fresh blood. He couldn't tell where it was coming from.

He pushed the viscera aside. "Linda, hold this, I want to take a look at the liver."

Linda didn't hesitate, reached into the kid and held his guts out of the way. Sheryl kept sponging. Stitch gently slipped his fingers beneath the rubbery meat of the liver and lifted. Blood spurted out in a jet, splashing the front of his gown. *Motherfucker!*

He set the organ down immediately but the open cavity began to fill with blood. Significant laceration of the common hepatic, and he'd apparently just made it worse. He reached under and pressed his thumb against the artery, felt it slip and slide.

"BP is a hundred over fifty," Jackie said.

"Hemostat," he said. "And hang another bag."

The only reason the kid hadn't bled out already was that there had been three pounds of liver sitting on top of the cut. Stitch kept up the pressure as Sheryl slapped a clamp into his hand, but blood kept coming. Another laceration, maybe the celiac—

"Seventy over forty," Jackie said, his voice strained.

Stitch cursed under his breath, placed the clamp and called for another one, but the blood wasn't spurting anymore. Weak pulses of it washed against his hand.

"BP," he snapped.

Jackie pumped the cuff and Stitch placed a second hemostat, feeling less blood, less pressure beneath his clever fingers. Jackie pumped again, his expression grim.

"Can't get it," he said. "Doesn't register."

Stitch felt a moment of incredible frustration, of anger and despair. The kid's heart still beat, the big, dumb muscle unaware that the body it served was already effectively dead. He looked at the kid's face, pale and waxen, imagined the brain cells dying by the hundreds of thousands, the systems shutting down one by one, robbed of blood and oxygen and purpose. Such a fucking waste. Gene was a prick and he had screwed up but it was really the war, the goddamned war that Stitch hated, an exercise in futility paid for in young men's lives.

BADLANDS

He looked at the clock on the wall, and heard a bell toll somewhere, as though the world mourned the loss of the boy. A distant, plaintive sound.

"Time of death, 19:53," he said.

Linda eased her hands out of the boy's gut. "His name was Hei," she said, and her voice caught. Linda had been at Frozen Chosin back in 1950, she had been to hell and back, but she still cried sometimes when they lost one.

Again, Stitch heard the lonely sound of a bell, clear and haunting on the cool October air.

"Does anyone hear that?" Jackie asked.

"It sounds like a gong or something," Sheryl said.

Captain Anthony snapped off his bloody gloves, looking again at the boy's lifeless face. Gene was going to be cheesed that Stitch had operated on his patient, he would be petty and defensive and wouldn't even care that he'd killed someone. The kid had deserved better.

Hei. His name was Hei.

Hei groaned, a deep, guttural sound, and started to sit up.

Sheryl screamed and reeled back, knocking the instrument tray to the floor. Stitch automatically reached over to push Hei back down, confused, he'd heard stories of bodies contorting in death but why were his arms coming up, how was he turning to look at Sheryl with his flat dead eyes? His intestines slithered out onto the drape that covered his lower body.

Sheryl screamed again as Hei swiveled towards her, his arms straight out in front of him. She stared at the dead boy, shrieking, her eyes wide and shocked – and the skin of her face seemed to shrivel, to pucker and wrinkle around her eyes, her cheeks hollowing beneath her mask. Her screams became a breathy teakettle sound, rising, going higher – and her entire body visibly shrank. In the space of two seconds, she was shorter, smaller, as pruned as an old woman, her eyes going as flat and dead as the Korean's.

At the same time came a sound so deep that it was a vibration. Stitch felt his bones quake.

She collapsed and the vibration stopped. Stitch saw that Hei's skin was now quite nearly glowing, the moldy greenish-white of foxfire. Hei swung his unbent legs off the table, stiff and uncoordinated, and then he was standing, like a sleepwalker in a cartoon, his arms still straight out in front of him, his head angled so that his blank, dead expression was aimed at his own feet. His hands drooped in loose claws. The bloody drape fell to the floor and he was naked but obscenely, his viscera slapped down to cover his genitals, hitting him mid-thigh. The retractors still held the wound open and the stink of hot blood and feces filled the room. Stitch backed up a step, horrified, as Hei turned his whole body towards him.

Hei's head hung, his eyes unseeing, and he hopped forward without seeming to bend his legs. Stitch felt it then, a sensation that he associated with giving blood, a sense of being drained, but the feeling was so much stronger and there was pain now, sudden and shocking, and he heard Linda screaming and Jackie screaming but he couldn't look away from the boy and no longer had the strength to scream and then he was gone.

* * *

West had his personal sidearm out and was moving towards the screams even as the patients started cutting up again, their voices querulous with fear and dread. The screams were coming from behind a set of doors in the east wall. Cakes was a half-step behind, unholstering his own weapon, an M1911 pistol. West darted a look back.

"McKay, Burtoni, stay with Young," he called. "Nurse, get some MPs in here, pronto!"

"What's the play?" Cakes asked, just as the doors burst open and a figure in a mask and scrubs stumbled out, a man. He tripped on a cot and went sprawling, but was on his feet again in a second and running for the exit.

"Hold up!" West shouted, but the man was only interested in getting the fuck out, he didn't look back or say boo as he charged through post-op, crashing through the door and out into the night. The screams had stopped but the patients were all talking, shouting, some of them getting up and limping after

BADLANDS

the masked man, others muttering prayers, the hysterical ROK shrieking like a girl.

"*Joyong!*" West shouted, the word for quiet, but no one was listening. He and Cakes had reached the doors to the next room. West looked through the window and saw a small room with sinks and towels, a bench on one side. Empty, but it looked like a scrub room. There'd be a surgery past that.

"Lee! Tell them to dry up!" he shouted, and a beat later, the kid was talking loudly, his tone harsh, chiding. Whatever he said had some effect, the din of the scared ROKs dying down. Something had definitely happened, but West was betting on a North Joe attacking his doctors. There'd been no rounds fired and the screams had apparently come from the OR. The talk about the *gangshi* had gotten everyone riled up, which was his own goddamn fault.

There was no noise except for the muttering patients, but for a second he felt a strange tension that was almost like a sound, one that made his back teeth clatter. He pushed through a door guarded by a tent flap, into the scrub room. It smelled like bleach and sweat and Army soap. Him and Cakes both kept their weapons aimed at the next door, moved in slow, crouching. The door was thick canvas with a window tied open. A smell of shit and blood wafted out.

West signaled for Cakes to stay put, that he was just going to look-see, and Cakes nodded. West stood and looked through the tied flap – and saw a Korean's naked backside, the skin all over his narrow, gangly body glowing green-white, blood running down his thin legs. There was enough of an angle that West could see a loop of his intestines hanging out of his belly.

What. In hell.

The glowing man jumped at the far wall and rammed right through it, tearing down canvas and wood, shaking the whole building. The noise was terrific and West pushed through the door and fired twice at the retreating figure through the hole, the naked man hopping forward and then south, out of sight in a second.

Cool wind blew in through the ragged opening. West took in the OR, blood everywhere, the two old people on the floor,

21

eyes dead and staring. A masked figure had pushed into the far corner, a woman on her side, curled up like a baby, her knees hugged to her chest.

Cakes stepped to the hole in the wall and leaned out, looked both ways. "I don't see nothing. What was it, Sarge?"

West didn't answer. He went to the nurse, crouched at her side. Behind him, he could hear the calls of the MPs or whoever had come to back them up.

"He was dead," the nurse whispered, and then there were people outside screaming, running, and beneath it all West could hear the ringing note of a bell.

* * *

Basin, soap, water, clothespins. Major Helen Underwood was all set to wash out her personals. She'd taken to doing her own, after a couple of the girls had had some of their underthings go missing from the laundry a few months back. Some disgusting creep was probably pawing through them even now.

Underwood sneered, picking up her bra, thinking about Private Fazangas. It was revolting, the way some of them acted. Her nurses were good girls, they didn't run around.

Her own status as a good girl – as a good *woman* – made her think of Captain Steve Anthony, which was confusing. They'd worked together for over a year. She respected him as a surgeon but they didn't get along well – he was practically a protester, the way he talked, and was always turning everything into a joke. She was a married woman, and besides, she didn't think of the men she worked with like that. Or, she hadn't.

They'd been thrown together one night a few months ago by circumstance, traveling back from a village, caught in a firefight, shells dropping to either side of them. Their driver had been killed. She and the Captain had taken cover in an abandoned hut not far from the wreck, shaken but not injured, except the shelling didn't stop, it had closed in. Convinced that they were going to die, they'd made love on the dirty floor, holding each other through the endless, thundering night. They hadn't

BADLANDS

spoken of it since, not a word, but she thought about it sometimes, just before falling asleep – how they'd both trembled and wept, whispering their fears in the dark, comforting one another. How he'd felt inside of her, warm and alive. She'd made love with a man who wasn't her husband. Was she bad now, because of what had happened?

Outside a man screamed.

Underwood dropped her soapy bra and stepped to her desk, wiping her hands on her pants. Her holstered pistol was on the card table she used as a desk. She slid the semi out of the worn leather, checked the action, and strode for the door of her tent.

Someone ran past just as she opened the flap, looking back with wide eyes. It was Corporal O'Donnell, his chubby cheeks flushed, his glasses sliding down his nose, his expression one of absolute terror.

"Run, Major!" he shrieked, and turned back to look where he was going – just as a man hopped out from behind one of the nurses' tents, directly in front of him.

Underwood's mouth fell open. The man was dressed in ROKA fatigues, there was a gaping hole in his chest, and she *recognized* him – DOA from yesterday, shot in the back – and his face and hands were glowing, the sickly light green of a night-blooming fungus. Its arms were out stiff in front of him.

O'Donnell screamed and managed to veer away but the dead soldier pivoted after him, its arms pointing at the short corporal. O'Donnell ran, and the dead man hopped towards him, its legs hardly bending. It shouldn't have moved as fast and as far as it did but O'Donnell was getting away and then the thing was right next to him, close enough to touch him.

Underwood blinked. It had jumped forward like a grasshopper, almost too fast to see. It was stiff, its body straight, arms parallel to the ground, not shaking or wavering. It was a monster, a demon out of hell. She braced the M1911 and took aim.

"Oh, gee!" O'Donnell got out, and then he was screaming, and she fired, once, twice. The dead man was in profile, and the first shot was high but she saw the second round hit its ribs, the fabric of his shirt blown open, blood and flesh and bone pattering to the dirt on the other side. He should have gone down, why was he still standing, why was O'Donnell still screaming? There was some kind of deep vibration in the air and O'Donnell crumpled. His face had changed, his slight body somehow slighter. The dead man glowed brighter.

It sucked the life out of him.

The creature flexed its feet and was suddenly facing her. It hopped forward like a tin soldier that had been picked up and moved, its arms outstretched, its dead gaze unseeing.

She emptied her weapon, five more .45 caliber rounds, hitting it in the throat and again through the bridge of its nose. Tatters of skin and cartilage flew and she saw the goddamn holes open up in its body yet it hopped again, and a third time, and impossibly, it was right in front of her. She could smell the dead man rotting and the fresh wounds were sticky with clotted blood, almost black against the white-green skin. She could smell the heat of the rounds she'd fired, wisps of seared, decaying flesh. It stared past her with no expression, not seeing her, its jaw slack with death. It was a void.

Underwood screamed. She felt it pulling at her, drawing her life away, and she couldn't move, trapped by whatever it was doing.

—eating me... it's eating my life—

She could feel her body dying, the tendons and muscles tightening, shrinking, the breath being pulled from her lungs, the will to draw another one falling away.

Stitch, she thought, and was gone.

* * *

The sarge stood up and looked at Cakes. The dame in the corner was shook, all curled up in bloody whites.

"I may have seen a hopping dead man," West said.

"No shit?"

The sarge shook his head. "I saw something." He picked up a blanket and covered the nurse.

Cakes' hand tightened on his weapon. The gooks were trash

BADLANDS

people, it made sense that they'd have some creepy crawlies they could hoodoo up. That stuff was for real, he knew it was, there were dark places and devils in the world. The hills of Kentucky were full of 'em, why not a godless country like Korea? Outside, there was shouting. He heard what sounded like the blast of a .45, then another and then five more. Someone had emptied their pistol.

Two MPs charged in with their weapons drawn, barking questions. Before anyone could explain anything, the nurse with the big titties burst in and saw the dead geezers and got real upset, crying and talking about how they looked old but they weren't, something had happened to 'em.

"The kid, where's that kid?" Sergeant West asked. He started back to the room with all the gook patients and one of the MPs yelled at him to stop, he needed to answer some questions. The MP had jug ears and buck teeth and a peeling sunburn on his chunky nose. He looked like he'd fallen off an ugly tree and hit every branch going down. He looked like someone's butt.

The sarge turned around and laid it out fast. "You've been infiltrated, you understand? Report to your CO ASAP and tell him to push the panic button, now. Where's your armory?"

Armory. Cakes felt something inside of him light up while Buttface stuttered out directions. He surely did love to prang a motherfucker, and how! Maybe the slant demons blew up or caught on fire or something.

Nurse Bazooms was helping the shook girl and the MPs finally clued in that something was happening outside – a man let out a yelp like he'd seen death coming, another weapon discharged, twice, then once more. People ran past the hole in the wall, going either way. Cakes could feel himself heating up, a strong, positive feeling that made his muscles twitch and his dick go half-mast. Korea was a dump and he hated Army life but clobbering gooks, that was good times.

Back in post-op it appeared that the doctors and nurses had run off. Half of the gooks were gone, too. The ones too sick to skedaddle were jabbering away at each other in their squawking, whining language. Burtoni and McKay were flanking Young, both armed and alert, watching the doors. McKay was a broke-dick dog, less fight than a Frenchman, but Burtoni was all right.

The sarge spotted the kimchi brat and called him over. He met them at Young's cot. Young was passed out again and sawing logs.

"What happened?" Burtoni asked. "We heard shots—"

"No time," West said. "I don't know what's going on but I want us armed. Me and Cakes are going to the armory, or at least to get our rifles. I want you and McKay to stay here with Young. Lee, you tell these men everything you know about the *gangshi*."

The kid's eyes widened, as much as they could. "The old story? Is it true?"

The sarge shook his head. "I don't know. Could be."

One of the gooks hong-yong-songed to the kid.

"He says to tell you we heard the bells," the kid said.

"Hey, I heard a bell," Burtoni said, looking all serious, and McKay nodded. "Right before the screamin'. Like two, maybe three times."

Cakes hadn't heard shit, but he didn't hear so good anymore, not since the last time he'd pulled combat time. Goddamn mortars.

"They ring the bell to let the people know it is time, to keep inside," the kid said.

"Who does?" the sarge asked, reloading. He carried an old Victory Model 10, a .38 revolver from WWII. "These priests?"

The kid nodded.

"So if we stay inside, we're safe?" Burtoni asked.

"I – don't know," the kid said. "My family did not believe these things."

"Ask around," West said, snapping the cylinder home. "If anyone shows up to evac the patients, bug out with them. If we're not back and the situation gets worse—"

He didn't get to finish. The doors flew open and two enlisted guys ran in, their eyes wild. One of them, a corporal, had wet his pants. They scrambled to pull the doors closed, shouting out useful information.

"There's something out there!" The one guy yelled. "It killed Major Underwood, I saw it!"

26

BADLANDS

"There's more than one!" Yelled Pee Boy. His eyes rolled in his fool head. "They're everywhere! Bullets don't stop 'em!"

We'll just see about that. Cakes had yet to meet anything that could survive a .45 to the face, and it just so happened he was a crack fucking shot. He led the way to the door, pushed past the two fumbling ladies. He held up his M1911, still fully loaded. He had one more loaded box magazine in his right leg side pocket. A total of fourteen rounds.

He looked to the sarge. West was nodding at him, holding up his revolver. The ugly MP had said southeast. Opposite corner of the camp, back by where they'd come in.

"At least you didn't shit 'em," Cakes said to the corporal, and pushed open the door, ready for anything.

* * *

Burtoni watched Cakes and the Sarge run out and swallowed, felt a dry click in his throat. He didn't like this one tiny skosh. Liked it less when he heard more weapons firing and somebody yelling for help. He thought he heard Cakes' voice and then *bam-bam-bam*, close enough to make his ears ring. There were maybe ten ROKs still in the tent, three of them out cold, the rest getting more and more clanked up. What the fuck was happening?

Young was still sacked out, his eyes barely fluttering when the building had shook. Except for a tiny smile when they'd first arrived, he'd stayed unconscious.

"Ask one of 'em if we're safe in here," McKay said to the kid, Lee.

Lee raised his voice and talked over the other Koreans. Burtoni had thought he was still a little kid but he acted older than he looked, repeating himself loudly until they heard him. Sounded like *ooh-dee in-yo gi on da-naga*.

One of the ROKs gabbled back at him. They went back and forth a couple of times, and two other ROKS joined in, then a third. None of 'em were laughing no more and Lee listened carefully to each man before turning back to McKay.

"They say the *gangshi* will walk through walls to go home.

They will steal a living animal's *chi* – the life flow – to keep moving. In the day, they hide, they lie in caves or in the ground until the moon rises. No place is safe, unless you have... *boho*." He scowled, searched for the word. "Ah, defense things?"

"So what are these defense things?" McKay asked, freckles like bloodspots on his young-looking face.

"Many things. They all say rice chaff. Ah, it must be sticky rice. *He* says mirrors will scare them away. *He* says the blood of a black dog or chicken eggs may stop them." The kid pointed at each man as he spoke. "And he says you can kill them with fire or with an ax."

"Swell," said McKay. He was starting to look feverish. "And all we got is guns. This is a joke, right?"

"What do you do with the rice?" Burtoni asked.

"Outside, on the ground," Lee said. He made a scattering motion with one hand.

"What, around the whole goddamn building?" Burtoni asked, and the kid nodded.

Burtoni reflexively fingered the small gold cross around his neck that his *nonna* had made him swear to keep on the whole time he was in Korea. This shit was way above his pay grade. "Unless one of you guys has got a half ton of rice in his pocket, that's no good. What else?"

"What else nothing," McKay said. "This isn't for real."

Outside, the cascading thunder of a half-dozen weapons fired at once. At least someone was getting organized while they were in here talking about zombie vampires and black dogs and rice. What the fuck was rice going to do, anyway? Burtoni couldn't even imagine.

"If we can stay safe until morning, a rooster's call is said to drive them away," Lee said.

"So, what, only ten, eleven hours to go, right?" McKay asked, grinning. "No problem. We got enough of us here for poker."

"Catch a clue, Freckles," Burtoni said. "Something's attacking, ain't it? Lee, ask 'em what else they got."

More shots, and then that weird thing from before, like the air and the ground seemed to buzz for a few seconds. The ROK

BADLANDS

who'd flipped his wig before really started having kittens, he actually rolled off of his cot and tried to crawl for the door. One of his arms was in a cast, so it was slow going. An emergency air raid siren was blaring outside. The two guys who'd run in had retreated all the way across the long room and were holding each other like it was the end times.

"It's a story, like the Sarge said," McKay said, desperately looking around the room, and then the wall crashed in and everyone was shrieking.

* * *

West stepped out behind Cakes into a strung out parade of running soldiers, doctors, support staff, and a few ROKs. They were all headed different directions, shouting orders and questions at each other in passing, some saying it was a bug out, others that the North was attacking. Most of them weren't panicking, yet, but it was a goddamn disorganized mess and it wasn't getting better. No one was in charge. He heard the crack of a rifle, heard a woman cry out *no, no*, heard a Jeep start up and speed away. He looked to the hill in the north. The lanterns were gone.

He had a decision to make – step up to lead or focus on getting his own out – and no time to consider the pros and cons. He brought his fingers to his mouth and let out a sharp whistle, looking for attention. "Eyes over here, sweethearts!" he yelled, channeling his old drill sergeant.

The two or three men who even looked in his direction wore the bright blank eyes of the lizard brain… they were running and they were going to keep running. There was no decision to make, after all.

"Chogie!" he snapped, and Cakes got moving. They made it half the length of the tent before they saw the first one, jumping down a path that branched out from theirs. It was following a panicked guy who appeared to be wearing a ladies church hat, one of those pink pillbox jobs. A matching pink scarf was tied around his neck, and he had the unlit stump of a stogie clenched in his teeth. West just took it in, not arguing with what he was seeing anymore.

The lady-dressed Joe hit the main pathway and tore south, really jiving, arms swinging, nearly knocking down a pair of clerks, and West got a good look at the dead man when it jumped out into the intersection and hop-turned to follow its target. It wore the tattered remnants of a North Korean People's Army uniform and was at least half rotten, knots and pools of black slime breaking up the pale glow of its remaining skin. Through the ragged, decaying holes in its clothing, West could see bone draped in rotten strings of meat. He could smell it, the rich, throat-clotting stench of a human body decaying in wet ground. It hopped again. The *gangshi* didn't move like a man at all – it was like the kid's pantomime, stiff, its arms held up and out, legs not bending. Other than a flex at the ankles, it didn't seem to move a muscle but was somehow closing on the running man, a hop and then a blurry burst of impossible speed.

"Aw, what's this hooey?" Cakes muttered, raising his sidearm.

In a second, the dead man was at the corporal's side. The guy shrieked, tumbled and fell, his lacy topper tumbling to the dirt. He stared up at the monster.

"Go back to hell, ya gook devil!" Cakes yelled and fired, *bam-bam-bam.*

All three were head shots and West felt a surge of triumph, *nobody like Cakes!* Rot and flesh exploded, and the back half of the thing's skull actually fell off, landing at the feet of its victim. A gory mass of shattered bone and rancid flesh and matted hair was all that remained where its head had been, a misshapen, dripping bag sinking down to hang in front of the creature's chest – but it was still standing, unwavering, its rotting arms stretched out and aimed at the howling cross-dresser. The man literally shriveled up, his cries rasping to silence, his skin wrinkling, and the air hummed and then the *gangshi* turned and was hopping west again, the bag of its head flopping against its breastbone, spilling gore like a paper bag full of sick. It was all over in seconds.

BADLANDS

"Go!" West pushed Cakes, got him moving. Its *head* had gone, and it still got to the sad sack in the pink hat. It had eaten him up and hopped away. This was shit for the birds. "Try the knees next time!"

They ran, stopping at the open spaces, pushing past panicking soldiers. Weapons were discharged from all areas of the camp. The men were sloppy, disorganized, terrified, and West spared a dark thought for Sanderson. The doctors might be topnotch, but the CO obviously hadn't run drills or maintained any level of training.

Somebody shouted that there was one by the mess and a small surge of stumbling enlisted and low-level officers nearly knocked them down trying to get away, stampeding like cattle. He saw a sergeant leading a handful of armed men west towards the center of the camp, two with combat shotguns, one with a rifle and a belt.

Praise Jesus, someone was putting up a defense!

West's optimism was short lived. As he and Cakes passed the wide opening where their paths intersected, he looked down and saw three *gangshi* moving towards the soldiers, coming from the west. One was the man he'd seen busting out of the OR – thin and gangly, naked, his guts swinging in the breeze. Some kind of surgical vise had been secured in his belly, holding the flesh open. His face was the blank of death, and his whole body glowed that otherworldly green. The other two wore ROK fatigues and weren't visibly disfigured but couldn't be mistaken for living, with the pallid glow of their skin and their dead eyes and their weird puppet postures. As he watched, all three hopped forward as one.

"Fire!" The captain pointed his own standard issue at the closest creature and opened up. Then they were all firing, and the *gangshi* hopped closer, oblivious to the damage, homing in on their targets. Their drooping faces showed no pain, no awareness, no mercy, not even hunger.

West didn't wait to see what happened, he knew what was coming and they had to get armed and back under cover before the compound cleared out. They ran ahead, chased by screams from the soldiers.

SNAFU: SURVIVAL OF THE FITTEST

The motor pool was lit up, Jeeps revving, gears grinding. A captain was organizing a handful of people to evacuate the patients, but he was mostly drowned out by the engines.

"Holy cow!" a private cried, his voice cracking. "Look at 'em all!"

West turned and looked, out into the dark behind the compound. There were a dozen, two dozen of them, glowing, hopping dead men coming from every direction, heading in every direction. He thought of crickets, or locusts. They moved erratically, a small hop, a bigger one – and then a sudden blur of motion and the thing was twenty feet away from its last position. It hurt West's mind to see them move. East and west, they hopped over the hills or behind the trees, in and out of sight. A handful filtered through the deserted village, stumbling right through some of the little hooches, their arms straight in front of them. Some were moving south; more were headed for the MASH.

"Armory," said Cakes, and pointed to a small crowd in front of a Quonset. A corporal and three privates were handing out arms, mostly M2 carbines and boxes of cartridges. They were blocking the door. The air shook again with that deep, physically unpleasant sound. West thought maybe it was the *gangshi* feeding.

West pushed to the front. "We need something bigger. What else have you got?"

The corporal's voice shook. "I don't know."

"What do you mean, you don't know? What's your armament?"

"I drive an ambulance," the young man said. "Look for yourself, we're bugging out."

He and a handful of the soldiers took off running towards the deserting Jeeps.

West and Cakes pushed into the unlocked room. Inside were two long, cramped aisles maintained for shit – empty racks next to over-packed ones, boxes stacked on boxes in no order. Outside there was screaming and shouting and more of that terrible vibration.

"Find us something," West said, and Cakes started hefting and tossing.

BADLANDS

West saw a rack of shotguns and went to investigate. A half-dozen 20-gauge Ithaca 37s, and seven cases of 28-gauge shells. Useless. Someone had stuck a captured Soviet burp gun behind a stack of dented helmets. He was hopeful for a split second – the PPSh-41 was shit at any distance but up close it could spray a lot of lead, fast – but the sole long box magazine was empty.

Does it matter, anyway? He hadn't wanted to think about it, was planning to assess after he'd seen their firepower options, but that one that had killed the man in pink – it didn't have a *head*. No head, and just as lively as a square-dance. Unless the kid could come up with some folk magic remedy, West wasn't hopeful at their chances.

"I got us three working M1s and a shitload of Willie Petes," Cakes said. "M15s, though, they don't explode."

White phosphorous signaling grenades. Maybe. Fire killed everything. He reached for the heavy, clinking bag of .45 rounds that Cakes had filled, shouldered it, and took two of the M1s. "Bring 'em, whatever you can carry. Maybe these things will burn."

Outside, someone had finally had the presence of mind to hit the air raid siren, and the rising, falling wail of it drowned out the world.

* * *

The *gangshi* burst in through the corner of post-op near the scrub room, directly in front of the two men who'd run inside, and then everyone was screaming. Broken wood and bent metal framed the glowing dead man, clothed in the peasant garb of a farmer. Its body had bloated in recent death; the creature looked swollen, puffy, the man's face as round and shining as the moon. Dust rained down from the ceiling. One of the two men who'd run in – Lee knew he was with the motor pool but didn't know his name – tried to get away and could not. The *gangshi* had already fixed its lifeless attention on him. The man shrieked in fear and then agony as the *gangshi* absorbed his *chi*. His body withered and dried and shrunk as his energy was stolen away and Lee could feel the shudder of shifting balance, imagined that the terrible vibration was the sound of distortion in the universe.

The ROKs cried out and somehow found legs, falling, running, crawling beneath cots. The farm boy on the floor kicked his feet, shrieking, and the *gangshi* turned its whole body towards the movement. Farm boy screamed. He'd pulled out the stitches in his side in his struggles. Fresh blood seeped through his bandages.

"No! No!" he yelled, as the *gangshi* hopped closer, and then the sounds he was making changed, from fear to terror to pain. The *gangshi* had connected with him. As the farm boy's skinny body depleted, the bloated man shone more brightly, rich with *chi*.

If it is full... No one had suggested that the *gangshi* could get full, but surely they could not absorb more *chi* than a body could hold.

"Be still," Lee said to the Americans. "Don't make it see you."

The dark haired man – the tall sergeant had called him Burtoni – immediately froze, his eyes cast down. The other one with *jugeunkkae* on his face, McKay, tried to hold still but he was so afraid. He shook and he could not look away from the *gangshi*, could not make himself calm. Lee didn't want to die but thought that McKay was going to crack and bring the *gangshi* to them. Lee closed his eyes and thought of his family.

Pak Mun-Hee chose the moment to cry out to God, *tongsung kido*, to plead forgiveness for his sins. The *ganshi's* feet shifted, and it hopped towards Pak. The ROK cried out and fell back, unable to get up from his cot. He knocked over a tray of syringes that Nurse Miss Jenny had been preparing and the polished metal tray clattered to the ground. Glass broke. Overhead light splashed across the tray and Lee was up and moving. One word was in his head. *Mirror.*

Lee scooped up the metal tray as the bloated gangshi connected to Pak Mun-Hee from an arm's distance away, stilling his frantic movements, trapping him in the unnatural exchange. Lee

BADLANDS

thrust the tray up in front of the gangshi, breaking the connection, forcing the gangshi to confront his own reflection. The tray seemed to vibrate in his hands. Lee did not look at the creature or at Pak Mun-Hee. He squeezed his eyes shut.

For a moment nothing at all happened, and Lee felt sweat break out all over his body. And then a horrible, high-pitched keening erupted from the *gangshi*. Lee risked a glance. There was no change in the dead, bloated face but the keening cry went on and on, the sound of fury and hate and fear spilling from its lifeless throat. It was a terrible sound.

The *gangshi* shifted on its bare feet and hopped back outside, moving almost too quickly to see. It was there and then it was gone.

Lee felt his knees give out and collapsed. Pak Mun-Hee sobbing, thanked him, thanked God. Burtoni was with him in a second, pulling him to his feet, dragging him back to their friend's cot. Outside, men screamed and fired weapons.

"The story of the mirror, it is true," Lee said. What a terrible cry! Thinking of it made his knees feel weak again.

"Okay, okay, this'll work," Burtoni said. "There's trays all over the place. We can put 'em on the patients, maybe hang them from the walls—"

McKay laughed, a high-pitched, rising sound. His gaze darted back and forth, back and forth. "Right, they're scared," he said, and laughed again. "They're scared! They're not real, but they see themselves and they run away!"

He couldn't control his laughter now, holding himself, tears leaking from the corners of his eyes. Burtoni looked at Lee, met his gaze. Lee could see his thoughts, and agreed. McKay was *michin geos*. Shook.

Burtoni turned a scornful eye on McKay. "Get ahold of yourself, or I'll slap you in the puss. What are you, a girl?"

"They'll be scared," McKay whispered, wiping his eyes, still grinning. "But they're not even real."

"Yeah, that's a laugh riot," Burtoni said. "Come on, help me push the cots together. Lee, get as many of those trays as you can carry."

35

Lee nodded and McKay at least got up to help Burtoni, still chuckling helplessly. Lee ran for the bins of sterilized trays, unable to believe that he'd been able to act. Perhaps because he was still unable to believe that the villagers had been right, that the dead had been called home.

The building shook and another *gangshi* crashed into the room through the south wall. The cabinets there fell to the ground and broke, scattering bandages and suture kits. Lee snatched up the trays and headed back for where the Americans had shoved several cots, Pak Mun-Hee, the wounded American, and two of the unconscious men. He looked back over his shoulder, afraid that it was fixing on him but it only stood there, stupid and dead. They would hold up the trays and be safe, they would —

Lee realized what he was seeing. The *gangshi*'s eyes were gone, dark holes where they should have been. Its whole face had been gnawed and picked at, as though it had been outside on the ground for a long time. A splinter of cartilage was all that remained of its nose. Its cheeks and lips were gone, chewed down to a wide yellow grin. Its tattered shirt was full of new holes. Lee skidded to his knees next to the cots and passed out the trays, sick with new fear. How would it see its reflection without eyes?

Through the holes in the building they could see men running, they could hear trucks driving away.

The eyeless *gangshi* pivoted towards Lee, and the injured and the cots, huddled together in a great obvious lump, trays sliding to the floor and clattering. Burtoni was whispering a Hail Mary, holding a silver tray over his face. McKay shook, his expression a frozen grin, his eyes full of tears.

The doors to post op slammed open and the doctor, Captain Elliott, came running in with two orderlies and Nurse Miss Claire. They saw the *gangshi* and stopped, backing towards the door. One of the orderlies made the sign of the cross in the air.

Lee saw what McKay was going to do a second before he did it, but was too late to try and stop him.

McKay stood up, his metal tray falling to the ground, pointing his weapon at the faceless creature. "You're not real!" he yelled, and then fired and the *gangshi* hopped once more and was with him, ignorant to the fresh holes in its head and body. McKay screamed and was caught, staring into the chopped mask of flesh. His body began to change, to shrivel up.

"Fire in the hole!" someone called out, and Burtoni pulled his unconscious buddy's cot over on top of them, slapped an arm around Lee, and slammed them both to the ground.

There was a clatter and then a soft pop and then the air was alive with snakes, with the smoking hot glow of burning phosphorous. The heat was sudden and searing, the light blinding. The *gangshi* was enveloped in a hissing, electric white shower and Lee had to look away. It was so bright he could see it through his eyelids, and then there were curses and screams and he felt burning particles settle across the backs of his bare legs. He pulled them in, made himself small beneath Burtoni's heavy arm.

The hissing went on seemingly forever and as it died away Lee dared to look up. Coughing, he waved at the thick, burnt-meat smoke and saw a pile of burning flesh and bone and fabric where the *gangshi* had been. The doctor and the orderlies were running around and putting out small fires. The holes in the building let out the worst of the smoke but the chemical stink was terrible, like bad garlic, and Lee's eyes burned and his nose ran.

The two big American soldiers were back, the sergeant and the private with the bad words. The private was spinning a ring around his finger.

"Looks like fireworks," he said loudly, and coughed.

* * *

The GIs helped the doc get the patients loaded into a personnel carrier, Young and five others, plus a handful of camp workers who'd been injured in the attack. All around them chaos reigned. Groups of soldiers ran and fired, yelled and died. A goodly number were getting out, trucks and jeeps heading in all directions. Cakes kept up a steady screen of Willie Petes, the white-hot burning chemicals keeping the *gangshi* away from them. They wouldn't jump through one, anyway. Burtoni helped the orderlies carry the patients out, while Lee and the medical officers ran supplies. West watched their backs toward the north, the black hill where the lanterns had been. Outside the brilliantly lit corridor of hissing phosphorous, dimly glowing *gangshi* hopped and darted silently across the dark land.

There were hundreds of them now, tearing through the MASH buildings, demolishing the tent town on their way to wherever. Main power went out – the generators were dying – and the wailing siren finally wound to a stop. West saw a Jeep whip by with Sanderson peering out the back, dull confusion on his useless face. West didn't salute.

The doctor made his last trip out of the sagging post-op building holding a clinking duffel bag. Burtoni ran alongside him, holding up a metal instrument tray like a shield.

"We're bugging out, Sergeant West," the doctor said. "Get your men in the truck."

"Yeah, Sarge, we gotta go," Burtoni said, nodding emphatically.

"What about the priests?" West asked, gesturing vaguely towards the dark hill north of the camp, where he'd seen the lanterns. "If we don't stop them, they'll keep calling up more of these things, won't they?"

"I don't know anything about any priests," the doctor said. "I'm getting these men out of here, now. We're going south to the 124th."

The Korean kid was looking at West. "The man from the village, he said the temple is rotten. He said the priests follow a bad man."

"Bad how?" Burtoni asked.

"He is *michin*," Lee said. "Ah, wrong in the head. Stark staring bonkers."

"You know where this temple is?"

Burtoni was shaking his head. "It doesn't matter about no temple, we gotta go, Sarge. We should stay with Young, right?"

Lee pointed. "North, they said. High on the hill, in the woods."

BADLANDS

West imagined bugging out with the doctor, with the other MASH refugees. Maybe it was safe at the 124th, maybe not. The way these things moved, where was safe? And how long would it take, to convince someone with the authority to call in a strike this far south?

And then hope we hit the bad temple with the bad priest, and hope that actually stops the dead from hopping around. For Pete's sake, he was looking at the goddamn things and he didn't believe in them. Who would listen? How many more people would die before they could talk the brass into believing ghost stories? They had a chance to stop this here, now.

"Burtoni, Cakes, bug out with Young," he said, making the decision as he spoke. Fuck Sanderson, anyway. The buck had to stop somewhere.

"I'm going with you," Cakes said. West had known he would.

"I'll go with Young," Burtoni said.

"Aw, don't break a heel running," Cakes sneered at him. "We're going after 'em, aren't we, Sarge? Gonna prang those hoodoo gooks!"

Cakes' enthusiasm was both disturbing and welcome. "We're closest and we've got the news," West said. "May as well be us."

"I go with you," Lee said.

"Forget it, kid," West said. "You bug out with the captain."

Lee shook his head. "You need me, to talk to the priest. To stop the *gangshi*."

The kid gestured at the darkness beyond the stuttering Willie Pete. "It is wrong to make them walk again."

The simple words seemed to resonate with all of them. Two years of men dying for scraps of territory, to be on the side with the most when the agreements were finally signed. It was all so pointless, so crazy.

Burtoni gripped his metal tray and his M1 and looked between West and the truck, the kid and Cakes. His struggle was clear on his hang-dog face, stark black and white by the light of the hissing grenade.

"Don't go bleeding all over everything, making up your mind," Cakes said.

"Fuck you, Cakes," Burtoni said, then sagged. "Okay. Okay, I'm in."
"Let's get a ride," West said.

* * *

A tiny little fleck of white phosphorous had landed on Cakes' right leg when he'd blown the shit out of that monster in the hospital ward, and that little piece had burned deep. It wasn't bleeding but it hurt like hell. Cakes was limping by the time they snagged a Jeep, lighting their way to the motor pool with Willie Petes, dodging the blindly hopping gooks through the ruined MASH. Sarge made him sit in the back with his leg up and had Burtoni drive. The gook kid was the only one small enough to fit in the back seat with him.

The kid pointed them along a steep road north that cut back and forth through the woods. As the MASH fell behind them, Cakes dug through their bags, seeing what they had left to work with. It could be worse. He found the loose box mags for the M1s and a carton of rounds. Wincing at the pain in his leg – it was swelling, too – he started loading.

"You been to this temple before, Lee?" the sarge called back.

"No," said the gook kid. "Only the villagers told us about it. It is by the road north."

Cakes looked at him. "Ain't you a villager?"

"No." The kid gazed at him with flat eyes. "I am KATUSA, with the MASH."

Korean Augmentation To the United States Army. Cakes snorted. Bunch of starving refugees digging shitholes and hauling sandbags.

"You have family with you?" the sarge asked, raising his voice to be heard over the grind of the Jeep's lower gears. The grade was steep and bumpy as hell. Burtoni was a shit driver.

"No," the kid said. "No family."

He didn't sound whiny or look all heart-broke about it, just said it, matter of fact.

"What happened to 'em?" Cakes asked.

BADLANDS

"We were on the Hangang Bridge two days after 625," the kid said. "In the early morning. Our army blew it up to stop the North from advancing into Seoul. I would have died, too, except my father sent me ahead to find out why no one was moving."

Cakes wasn't sure what to say to that. He tried to imagine all his relations, his parents and sisters and cousins and grandparents, all blown up at once. He couldn't do it.

"After that, many of us walked all the way to Pusan," he went on. "I was there in September 1950 when the first UN soldiers landed."

"Fuckin' marines," Cakes said, and shook his head. "Think their shit don't stink."

The kid smiled a little. "Hey, I got a Marine joke."

"*You've* got a Marine joke?" Cakes snorted. "Let's hear it."

The kid nodded, smiling a little more. "A dogface and a marine are walking down the street, and they see a kid playing with a ball of shit. The dogface says, what are you making? The kid says, a dogface. The dogface says, why aren't you making a marine? The kid goes, I don't have enough shit."

Not enough shit to make a marine, that was a good one! Cakes laughed. The kid had more hard bark on him than Burtoni, anyway.

"You getting an inventory?" the sarge called back.

Cakes kept loading. "We got eight signal grenades left, four extra mags of .45 ACP for the M1911s plus about forty rounds, six full clips of thirty-aught-six for the M1s plus a carton loose."

"There are the silver trays," Lee said. He held a stack of them in his lap. "We saw one run from its reflection."

West looked back at them. "We're going in ready but we're gonna talk to them first, okay? See if we can't persuade these guys to stop what they're doing..." He trailed off, staring out the back.

Cakes craned his head around and looked.

A pale green glimmer far back on the road was suddenly closer, close enough for Cakes to see the outstretched arms, the hanging face. It hopped forward and then was falling away, standing still as they drove on.

SNAFU: SURVIVAL OF THE FITTEST

"Hey, I think this is it," Burtoni said. "There's some hooches up here on the left—"

Cakes was watching the devil recede, and it was some strange trick of the eye, that its narrow hands were suddenly pressed to the back flap of the moving Jeep. They'd left it behind but now it was right on them, its mouth hanging open drooling and stupid, one of its eyes stuck closed, its skin glowing like radium.

* * *

There was one of them right in front of the Jeep, out of the goddamn blue. Burtoni swerved, fighting the machine for control and then they were slamming to a stop, almost rolling, settling back to the rocky dirt with a jaw-slamming bounce. Burtoni felt the steering wheel stomp on his chest and he gasped for air. The Jeep died, leaving them in the dark.

"Move out!"

Burtoni grabbed his rifle and stumbled out of the Jeep, looking everywhere, holding on to one of the MASH's metal instrument trays. There were two, three of the things closing in. One of them hopped closer to the sarge, fixing its lifeless attention to him like a moth fixed to a light. It was a young ROK with a big dent in one side of its head. The eye on that side had bulged out, giving it an almost comically lopsided look.

"Head for the buildings!" West said, falling back. Cakes ignored him, aiming his M1 at the creature's legs. He opened up and put all eight rounds of Springfield through the thing's knees, the Garand's clip ejecting with an audible *ping*.

The *gangshi* hopped forward on its broken, shredded legs, shorter by a foot and a half but still holding its arms out, leering up at the sarge with that bulging eye. It was almost close enough to the sarge to touch him.

"Catch!" the kid yelled, and swung one of the surgical trays at Cakes.

Cakes caught the tray and pivoted with it, smashing the *gangshi* in the face, knocking it backwards.

"No, use it like a mirror!" Burtoni screamed. He held up his own tray, shook it. "Like a mirror!"

BADLANDS

Cakes didn't seem to hear, banging the tray into the creature's face again and again. Another of the things moved in. Cakes gave up on the tray, dropping it, taking a Willie Pete out of his shoulder bag. The Sarge waved them all back.

"Fire in the hole!" Cakes yelled.

Burtoni stumbled backwards, *yeah, burn that mother,* he thought—

—and then his thoughts were strange, running together, and Lee was shouting and dancing around, something was wrong.

Burtoni turned and there was a middle-aged man with a bad haircut and a bullet hole in one temple in front of him, staring at him, its peeling white fingers brushing against the front of his shirt.

"No," Burtoni breathed, unable to believe it, unable to move or think anymore because the thing was pulling him away, stealing him from the world and it wasn't fair, it wasn't goddamn fair, he should have bugged out when he had the chance.

* * *

"No, no, *no!*" West screamed. The monster had Burtoni and it was already too late, the kid's long, wolfish face was collapsing inward, his quick eyes rolling back in his head. In a few seconds he was a husk on the ground.

Cakes pulled a pin, threw, pulled another one. The world exploded in a fountain of bitter white and West shielded his eyes, his heart torn up. The *ganghsi* burned, hopped and melted, collapsing silently as the fire ate their rotten skin.

"The buildings, chogie!" he shouted, ducking away from the brilliant light, running for Lee. He never should have let the kid come, he wasn't thinking straight.

Cakes ran with him and they caught up to Lee, flanked him, heading for the hooches. Behind them, the phosphorous hissed and muttered. Dim figures flitted through the trees, flickered through plumes of white smoke and the dull orange of burning fat. More of them were coming.

They reached the first raised shack and ran past it, West pointing them north, there was a clearing past another of the small buildings – and there were people in the clearing, ten, a dozen of them, men, sitting around a fire. They wore homespun robes of dull brown. Behind them was a tall, narrow building, presumably the temple.

West looked back and saw more of the creatures hopping after them. They'd be dead ducks in the time it took for one of the things to do its impossible jump. No time for recon or diplomatic talks.

"Back us up, Cakes," West said. It was all he had time to say as they ran into the clearing, chased by the *gangshi*. West moved in front of Lee and stopped at one of the sitting men. He pointed his revolver at the man's head.

The man was older, his face lined and careworn. He stared into the fire. All of them just stared into the fire, completely ignoring West, not moving an inch.

"Lee! Tell them to stop these things or I kill this one!"

Lee shouted at them, his voice harsh, threatening. The men didn't look away from the fire, but one of them spoke briefly. A man about West's age, sitting on the other side of the fire. His voice was a monotone.

Lee blinked at West. "He says go ahead. He says they are already home."

"Sarge!" Cakes' voice was an urgent stage whisper. West turned and saw that a half dozen of the *gangshi* had gathered behind them, at the outermost edge of the fire's flickering light. They clumped together, dead and stinking, their arms outstretched... but they didn't come any closer. Couldn't, maybe.

West looked helplessly at the circle of men, still aiming at the older man's head. He didn't want to shoot the guy, didn't want to kill anyone, only wanted them to stop whatever it was they were doing.

"Ask them why," he said. "Why are they doing this?"

Lee asked, and another of the men spoke, not looking away from the fire. Lee translated as the man droned, his voice steady and toneless, firelight dancing in his blank eyes.

"In every war for a thousand years people have died here, victims of needless slaughter. Innocents, monks and priests,

BADLANDS

healers, men who have refused to take up arms. The stones are washed in their blood. They called the Master, who speaks for them now. He is their channel. They cry for the killing to stop."

West shook his head. "So... you sent out dead men to kill more people?"

Lee spoke for him, and another man took up the narrative. "The Master tell us that when everyone has gone home, the wars will end. There will be no more bloodshed, here or anywhere."

West stared at the circle of motionless men, unable to believe what he was hearing. "That's what you believe? That what you're doing here will stop war, forever? That we're all just going to *change*?"

The men didn't answer when Lee stopped speaking, staring into the fire, but one, two of them shifted, breaking their perfect stillness. West looked back. The gathering *gangshi* edged closer, as though the circle of protection cast by the firelight had shrunk. Cakes held up one of the grenades, looking to West for a signal.

"You don't understand," another of the men said finally. "You don't belong here. You should go home."

"Jesus please-us, are these gooks numb in the head?" Cakes muttered.

"Have you been out there?" West asked, not realizing how angry he was until he heard it in his voice. "Have you seen what you've done?"

He jabbed a finger at the *gangshi*, still edging closer. There were three more of them, their dead faces staring, their arms reaching. More of the sitting priests shifted. He could see that their concentration was breaking. One of them stole an uneasy glance at the dead.

"You made monsters out of your own people," West said. "You called up their sad sacks of bones and turned them into killers."

More of the priests were looking now. The firelight flickered, painting the dead faces in strange light. One of the *gangshi* hopped forward a tiny step and two of the priests were suddenly on their feet, backing towards the narrow temple building.

One of the sitting men snapped at them, his voice urgent,

but neither responded, still backing away. He repeated his command, added something in a rising shout.

"He tells them return to the circle," Lee said. "Return or we are all lost!"

One of the sitting priests pushed up on his knees. From under his loose shirt, he pulled a small hammered blade, held it up. *"Naneun nae insaeng ui maseuteo leul boho!"*

Before he'd finished speaking a second man was doing the same, a third, their words overlapping, two more knives held up.

Lee was pale. "I protect the master with my life."

"Oh, shit," West said, as all three of the men cut their own throats and fell, blood spurting out into the ground. One of them hadn't cut deep or far enough and was pumping a narrow stream of blood across a few of his fellow priests. He flopped around on the ground, spraying like a fountain. Blood hissed into the fire.

Most of the priests were on their feet and many held knives but they didn't seem to know what they wanted to do, whether to join their suicidal brothers or run for it. West looked back and saw the *gangshi* hopping forward, entering the clearing. Whatever the priests had been doing to keep the dead men at bay, they weren't doing it anymore.

* * *

"Here they come!" Cakes shouted, and threw the M15. Lee saw it hit one of the *gangshi* in the chest and turned away, saw his own shadow black on the ground against the sudden brilliance of hissing white light.

"Move, move!" The sergeant shouted, pushing Lee towards the temple. Lee ran. Three of the priests ran with him. He saw a knife on the ground and scooped it up, pushing past one of the priests who'd frozen, who hadn't decided to stay or go.

The temple door was open. The trio of robed men ran inside, calling for their Master. Lee stopped outside and turned back, searching for Sergeant West and Cakes in the chaos, fountains of light and smoke and the silent, glowing dead, hopping and freezing, blurring as they darted forward.

BADLANDS

Around the fire, two of the three men who'd killed themselves rose, their bodies stiff, their arms stretched out. The third rose a moment later as the first vibrations shook the world. The priests unable to choose were falling now, fed upon by their dead brothers. Lee held his metal tray out to the grisly scene, blocking it from view.

Lee heard Cakes before he saw him, cursing more than Lee had ever heard anyone curse, taunting the *gangshi*. Lee saw how far away from the church they were and felt his chest go tight. It was too far.

The sarge fired his revolver into the crowd of *gangshi*, trying to cover Cakes as the private threw more grenades, but the bullets did nothing. The *gangshi* were too close and there were too many of them and Cakes was retreating too slowly. Lee opened his mouth to cry a warning but then there was a blur of green light and it was too late.

"I got this one, Sarge!" Cakes shrieked and stepped into the creature, popping rings on the M15s in his arms. He reached out and grabbed a second dead man, his grenades spilling to the ground.

Sergeant West turned and ran for the temple, his face a mask of hard-jawed determination, his eyes anguished. Behind him, Cakes screamed, enveloped by white light. Smoke billowed over the *gangshi*, the clearing, the world.

Two of the priests tried to close the door but Lee kicked at them, brandished the cheap knife he'd picked up, and then West was pushing through, knocking one of the priests to the ground.

Lee turned and looked at the church, finally. It was a single room, bare except for some rolled mats. It was cold and smelled of decay. At the far end, an old man was lying on the floor, lamps burning by his head and feet. The priests hurried to him, casting frightened looks back at West and Lee. There were only three of them now.

"Is that their master?" West said, starting after them. Lee had to run to keep up. Behind them, the door was crashed off its hinges. A *gangshi* stood in the jagged frame, white, choking smoke pouring in all around its stiff body.

47

SNAFU: SURVIVAL OF THE FITTEST

The priests called for their master to wake, whining voices full of fear. When they saw West and Lee approaching, West holding his revolver, all three of them stood.

"I protect the master with my life!" one of them shouted, and they all ran at West. He shot the first one in the chest but the others crashed into him, all of them collapsing in a tangle of limbs. The revolver went off again.

The building shook as another *gangshi* thundered through the wall. It was one of the dead priests. Fresh blood oozed from its glowing neck, its head hanging. It hopped forward and was halfway to where the sergeant struggled. Behind it, a third *gangshi* hopped inside through the ragged hole, a very old and rotten one.

Lee knelt by the old man, the mad master. He didn't look special or important. His eyes were open, staring at the air, but he was alive, Lee could see the rise and fall of his chest.

"This has to stop now," Lee said, and drove the cheap knife into the man's wrinkled neck, deep, pushing as hard as he could.

The Master made a choking sound in his throat. Awareness flooded back into his eyes, and he looked at Lee, who saw depths of madness in his tired old face; suffering and loss and despair twisted into something dark and consuming. When he pulled out the knife, blood poured onto the dirt floor.

The three *gangshi* inside the church crumpled, suddenly boneless. For a moment there was a sound in the air like the fluttering of wings, but perhaps it was only the last, spluttering hisses of the white phosphorous burning itself to death outside.

The sergeant held his revolver by the barrel and hit the last struggling priest in the head with the gun's grip. The man groaned and fell away, holding his skull.

West sat up and looked around, taking in the scene. The fallen *gangshi*. The dead master. The bloody knife in Lee's hands.

"Good," he said, and nodded. "Good deal. You okay?"

Lee started to say yes but then shook his head. It was terrible, the thing he'd done, but he wasn't sorry. The man's blood was still warm on his hands and he was glad that he'd killed him, he wished he could kill him again, for making the dead walk. He

BADLANDS

tried never to think of it but the idea that his own family might not be at rest haunted him. Sometimes, it was all he could do not to think about it.

"I don't know how to feel," Lee said.

The sergeant looked at him for a long time. "Yeah," he said finally. "Yeah, it's like that sometimes. Let's get out of here, what do you say?"

Lee nodded. The church was cold, the air heavy with blood and smoke and maybe ghosts.

The ground outside was littered with corpses. The *gangshi* had lost their glow, were only dead now, heaps of skin and bones and clothes. They passed what was left of Cakes and then Burtoni, but the sarge didn't look at them, and told Lee not to look, either. He said they were good guys, and his voice broke a little.

Lee thought they might talk on the long walk back to where the MASH had been, but neither of them did. As they came down out of the woods, the sky opened up over them, clear and beautiful, and they walked on in silence, occasionally slowing to look at the stars, to breathe in the air.

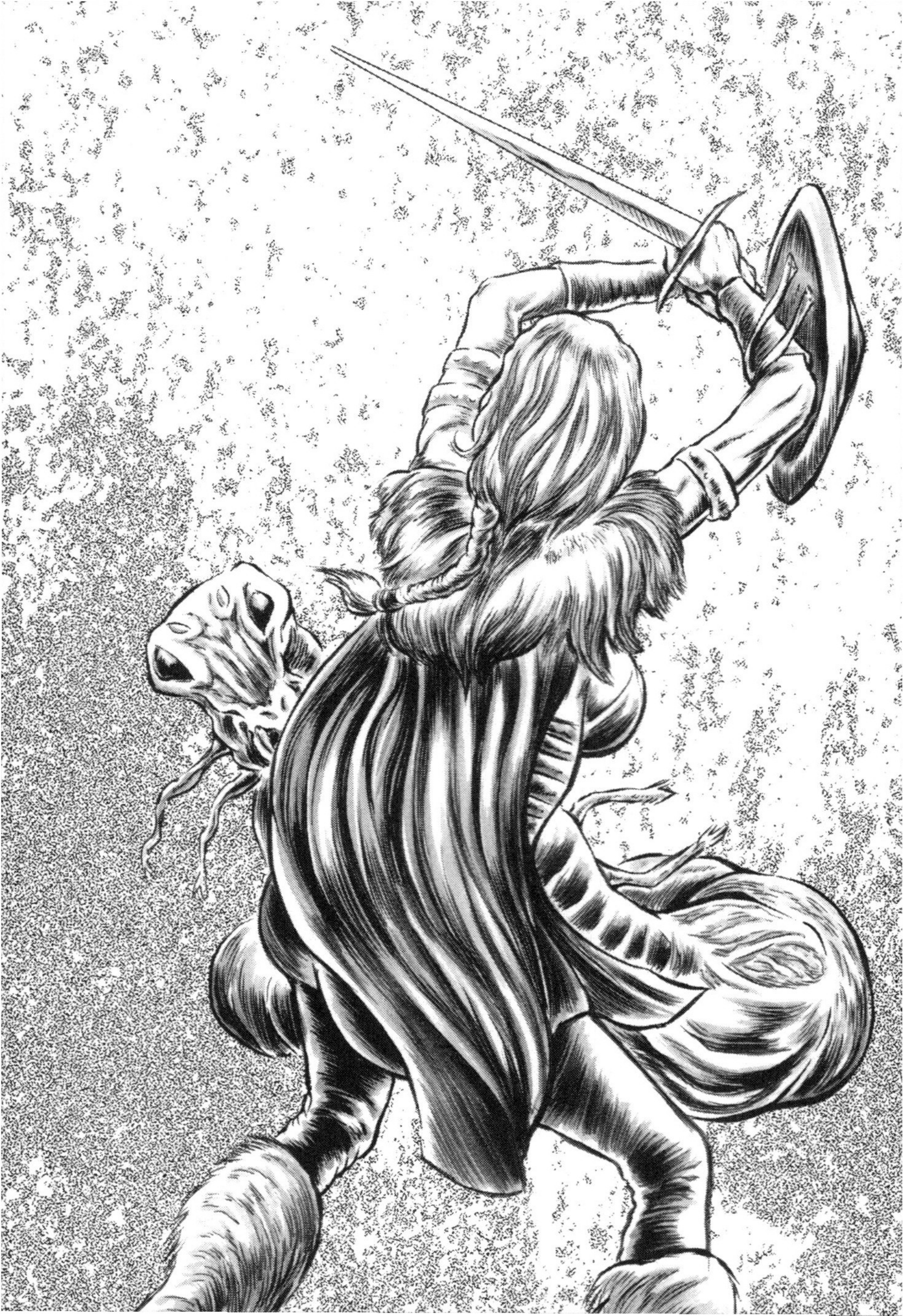

OF STORMS AND FLAME

Tim Marquitz & J.M. Martin

AD 955
Island of Frei, Norway

Fog suffocated the light.
Bard clung to his axe as a drowning man to driftwood. His fingers throbbed, pinpricks of fire erupting across his skin as the numbness crept in, no mercy in its arctic crawl. The blood of his enemies – the Austmann who'd met them on the field of Rastarkalv – dripped from his hands. The gore dulled the shimmer of his blade, its cloying wetness magnifying the chill, but the tang of Eiriksønnene's defeat infiltrated the frigid air. Bard had followed his young king, Harald Greycloak, into battle, and now he wondered if he would soon see Greycloak's father, King Erik the Bloodax, in the halls of Valhöll.

They had been routed by Haakon's forces, especially his circle of detestable witches, the spastic, chanting *völur*. And though Bard had slew many warriors and his limbs ached from the doing, a swirling mass of unnatural grayness now washed over him, clawed at his throat, and he held his breath for fear of its dark magic befouling his lungs.

Witchery, this was. The product of an invoked *galdr*. And Bard went to one knee, clenching his teeth against the mist. But it caressed his defiant lips, a foul lover, perilous in its kiss. He knew it would not be long before he would drink it in, and he feared the fog would obscure his lifeless body. Would his spirit make it to the Golden Halls? Or had the Norns of old another fate in store for him? Even if he did somehow find his way to a warrior's afterlife, how could the Allfather accept an offering as poor as this?

Death had thus far left Bard unscathed. Even as armies clashed amid the witches' fiery *galdrar*, and Haakon's beasts,

51

summoned from the very depths of Hel, tore flesh from the bones of his brothers-and sisters-in-arms, Bard knew there was no honor in such an end – to merely slip away into the cold silence, unremembered by the gods.

No.

The word filled his skull.

No. It strengthened with every whispered echo.

No. He would not succumb to the treachery of Haakon the Good's sorcerers, whose abominations had slain so many this day. The scion of warriors would not meet Death on his knees. Bard tightened his grip upon his ax, stood, urged his feet forward.

"No," he growled through clenched teeth. The direction no longer mattered. The familiar swell of the sea had long since faded in the distance. Only the empty gray greeted his senses, and in its embrace, with enemies all around, one way was just as good as any other.

His muscles ached as he pushed on, bones creaking in their joints. The dead grass was slick beneath his boots, and the muffled *squelch* of his footfalls built to a careful rhythm as he bulled forward. Bard cursed the noise of his passage as only silence came back at him through the mist. Spiders of fear crawled along his spine. A tribe of *jötnar* might well loom just paces ahead but he would never know it. Not in this murk. He swallowed hard at the thought; set one foot in front of the other.

Bard traveled for a thousand beats of his heart, ax gripped tight, scowling, his eyes narrowed and searching for someone – some*thing* – to kill, until a shadow materialized, and another beside it a moment later, and yet another. But this was no enemy.

Runestones.

Bard tapped the first with his boot to test its certainty. He ran a cautious hand across its graven surface. *Futhark* stood out from its smoothness. The meaning of the script leapt clear to his mind before his eyes could pick them from the stone. The runes read: *Honor. Peace. Memory.* The words sang against his fingertips in turn. *Haraldr Hárfagri ræisþi kumbl þausi æftiR Øyvind eR vaR*, he read on the nearest stone, equal in height to himself as it manifested from the gloom.

OF STORMS & FLAME

Harald Fairhair raised these monuments in memory of Eyvindr the Valiant.
His pulse stilled in his veins, a curse withering on his tongue. He'd come to Freiøya's long barrows. Far from where his fellow *víkingr* had come aground, the burial site was a grim landmark, and one he had prayed never to visit; still, for all its sanctity, there lurked hope within its hallowed fields.

Who but a fool would seek life in a barrow?

Bard had heard stories some years prior of Eyvindr's exploits in the west, as well as his hand in slaying one of Harald Fairhair's own brothers at the behest of the Norse king himself. Bard snorted, but he did not linger – he needed shelter with more substance than these accursed stones, some sanctuary before Haakon's völur called back their mist and revealed him.

The ghosts of his enemy's forefathers lingered in the air. Bard could feel their presence bearing down upon him as he crossed the stone boundary. With a willowy breath he muttered apologies, despite his lineage, for his trespass. He'd no intention of befouling this resting place, but it was what the living Bard had to contend with for now. The dead would have their turn with him soon enough.

It seemed an impossible task. The barrow stretched out before him in desolation, but just when he'd begun to despair he might be trapped there forever his outstretched hand struck something solid. A reverberating *thump* resounded and his hand throbbed at the impact. The cold sent the pain bone deep, but he ignored it and examined the object. Smooth marble greeted his touch. He inched closer and the towering form of a warrior slipped loose of the fog, looming above. Bard's heart threatened to burst but reason took hold before it could beat its way free of his ribs. The monument of a Víkingr king stood bold in his path. Might this be the monument of Harald himself?

Bard let out a slow breath, choking back a nervous laugh only to go rigid at a muffled susurrus in the wet grass behind him. He ducked as a whirl of smoke and steel hurtled over his head, crashing into the statue with a *clang* and sending chips of stone flying.

The vague shape of boots appeared and Bard lashed out, driving the point of his ax toward where he believed the enemy came at him. Metal sang out. A sharp gasp followed as needling stabs reverberated up his forearms. His blow had done its work. The boots toppled backward, barely visible, and Bard scudded forward to keep on the move. A pained grunt slipped loose of his assailant as he struck hard earth. Bard closed without hesitation, his left hand seizing the warmth of his opponent's throat. He growled and hefted his ax to rain down a blow but then his arm went stiff as a familiar face formed beneath him.

"Gods, Hilde," he cursed. "I nearly killed you." He released the woman's neck and lowered his weapon.

"Don't be so certain," she answered, grim humor in her voice as two slivers of steel crept from the gloom and wavered before his face.

He grinned as twin shadows took shape – brothers he'd thought dead coalesced from the fog, their own smiles a radiant sight to behold.

"We found her smirking atop the bloodied remains of a great, horned mare, its head split asunder and its brains gouged from its skull," Devin boasted, gesturing to the woman. "If ol' Hrimgerd herself couldn't bring down Hilde, I doubt a *fifl* like *you* could."

"At least that's how she'd tell it," Arndt said with a chuckle.

Relieved laughter spilled from Bard's throat and he rose, pulling Hilde to her feet. He embraced her quickly and did the same to the others in turn.

"We'd thought you dead," Arndt told him with a clap to the shoulder, his plaited red beard darkened and congealed with blood. His helm boasted a respectable dent, and a shallow cut ran across the bridge of his broad nose but Bard had seen the warrior worse off.

"As did I." Bard slapped a hand over the warrior's meaty shoulder and gave a reassuring squeeze. "As did I." He let his gaze wander over the others; having been separated rather quickly on the battlefield, he reveled in their unexpected presence and found his mettle buttressed by their good company.

OF STORMS & FLAME

Hilde looked much as she had when they'd disembarked: her long blonde hair pulled so tight against her scalp as to appear untouched by chill wind or her wretched battle against the strange beast. Her big blue eyes stared back at him as he appraised her. Her buckler hung on her arm, and her breastplate was painted with the crimson stains of those who'd dared stand before her – only the slight indentation from his own ax marred the steel of it – but no visible wounds other than a shallow cut or two proved she had given more than she got. A subtle flicker of amusement played at her pale lips and a hint of rose colored her freckly cheeks, then she bent and retrieved the sword Bard had knocked from her grasp.

He watched her, grateful he'd not buried his ax in that fair skull of hers, for he was sure that would provoke the goddess not to mention her aunt, Queen Gunnhild. Bard's gaze flickered to Devin, a wiry Thuringian who stood blade in hand, and gave Bard a solemn nod. The man's frame made Hilde look almost masculine, but Bard knew deceptive strength lurked within the warrior from his long years as a galley slave pulling oars on a Byzantine *dromon* before his liberation at the hands of Bloodax's longships. Dev's sharp features peered from the gloom like an eagle's, barely shadowed by the growth of fuzz at his chin. He'd lost his shield somewhere along the way but he looked no less fierce for it.

"If we don't find sanctuary Óðinn might yet catch us in his hall," Hilde said, the ghost of her smile having passed on. Thunder rumbled somewhere above as if to punctuate her point.

Bard nodded, the pleasure at finding his companions alive fading at the return of their unfortunate reality. For all their company, they were no less safe from Haakon's witches than when they'd been divided.

"The ships?" Arndt asked.

"Likely put to the torch or set adrift by now," Bard said. "We're a long way from shore."

"Then north is all we have, brothers. North to the far shore where we might stumble across those who slipped away... should there be any, that is." Devin spun in a slow circle, eyes growing narrow as he surveyed their surroundings. "Of course, it might help to know which way that is first."

Hilde grunted agreement, and Bard peered through the fog after Devin, eyes settling at last on the hazy statue that hovered nearby. He let out a quiet laugh, drawing the attention of the others. "Were you a monument to a king of old, would you stare at the land behind you or the way your spirit pushed on?"

Hilde stood quiet a moment and followed his gaze, her eyes gleaming crystalline in the murk. "To the sea," she answered with a grin.

Bard nodded. "Then let us pray Haakon's forefathers had some sense in their skulls the day they set this stone." He trailed down the statue's right arm and pointed the direction it led.

"We've our path, it seems," Devin said.

Arndt shrugged. "The *Valkyr* will find us no matter where our carcasses collapse, so lead on, my friends."

"Such optimism, brother." Hilde chuckled low in her throat, yet didn't hesitate scything through the fog as she marched on. "Stay close," she warned, though she need not have wasted her breath. Bard and the others hounded her heels, near to tripping over her. For all their bluster, the trepidation that wafted from his companions soured Bard's tongue, but his own fear tasted no less bitter.

Every step was plagued by thoughts of the corpses beneath their feet, and time slipped past unknown as they made their way through the crowded necropolis. Thunder rattled the heavens, a somber serenade to their uneasy flight. Bard had lost all sense of direction not twenty paces after the statue had faded behind them, and he prayed Hilde steered them true, but he could not tamp his growing nerves that festered with each step. Bard expected *draugar* – the animated bones of those long accursed – to step out from the fog, and his nostrils flared as he strove for even a hint of the unmistakable stench of decay. He glanced about wildly, certain he felt more than just the virulence of the dead upon them, only then realizing he could see his brothers without having to strain to do so.

"Wait," he whispered, raising a closed fist. The others slowed and gathered about him, expressions uncertain.

OF STORMS & FLAME

Hilde grasped his concern first. "The mist lifts."

Her proclamation seemed to rally the fading tendrils of gray as they drifted toward the lightening sky, the clouds thinning. A frigid wind crept in as if to fill the wound left by the departing fog. It sent a chill scurrying along Bard's arms.

"They'll be coming for us." No sooner had the words left his mouth than a gargled hiss cleaved the air. A dozen more followed it. He tightened his grip on his ax as recognition of what wended toward them sunk home.

The first of Haakon's beasts cleared the edges of the retreating fog. Bard held his ground despite the terror that urged him to flee. With a crazed howl it charged at them. Sleek like serpents, Haakon's creatures were preternatural; *nidhoggr*, they were called – the name given them springing to Bard's mind of its own accord – summoned from the bowels of Hel, and though they came only up to the víkingr's knees, their bodies slithered out for yards behind, while feral, bear-like mouths with row upon row of jagged shards comprised their ill-shapen snouts. Four milky-white eyes glared at them with malevolence, deformed lumps of hate bubbling from the hairless skull of the closest beast. Their multitudinous legs scrabbled while their sharpened claws *clacked* a dirge along the packed earth.

An instant later, the beasts were on them.

Hilde was first to draw blood. She slammed her buckler into the mouth of the nearest nidhogg and drove her blade beneath its slathering chin. The sword broke through the hardened bone and pierced its skull, severing its unnatural ties to this world. Hilde booted its corpse aside and met the next, but Bard could watch no longer; he had his own to contend with.

The nearest nidhogg crouched as if it might go for his legs, but Bard had seen the creatures' tricks. He ducked low as the creature changed tack and leapt high. It sailed overhead and Bard thrust the point of his ax into the beast's belly, spun it about, and drove it back to earth with a sickening crunch. Its ribs shattered within its chest and it shrieked in agony, a dozen claws slashing at empty air, but there was no time to revel in one monster's defeat.

Bard drew back a few paces and swung his ax as another serpent-beast flew at him. Steel and bone collided and the creature fell away, its head cleaved in twain. A third beast caught the haft upside its skull on the backswing and *thumped* senseless to the grass with a muffled whimper. Bard took rapid breaths and glanced from its twitching form to see Devin cutting a swathe through a trio of nidhoggr, their rancid blood and severed limbs cavorted in the air about him like some knife juggler's morbid finale.

Arndt lacked Devin's grace. He grunted and frothed as he swept his greatsword two-handed in wide, arcing swings. Muscles bunched beneath his sun-scarred skin as the warrior put the whole of his strength into every blow. Nidhoggr flopped at his feet in pieces, howls and ragged grunts slipping from their foul mouths as they curled in on themselves and died. Yet more came, as if they knew Arndt's ferocity would prove his undoing when the warrior's strength flagged.

One found truth in that presumption.

Arndt batted aside a nidhogg that had gotten too close, but the movement sent him stumbling backward, off balance. Before he'd the chance to right his feet, the squirming front half of a beast he'd left to die latched onto his ankle. Bone *crunched* like a dry branch and Arndt screamed. He screamed again as his foot ripped free of his leg and he landed flush on the squirting stump. The warrior crumpled, his eyes rolling white.

Bard leapt across the intervening distance, but for all his effort, he was too late.

Arndt snapped to alertness as a monster buried its muzzle in his armpit. A wet rasp spilled from the warrior's throat as the creature feasted, tearing at sinew and bones as it likely had worried at the very roots of Yggdrasil in its earlier days. Blood sprayed from the wound and rained crimson on the ground, as a black pool formed beneath Arndt.

Hilde reached his side first, driving her sword into the nidhogg's gnashing maw, killing it before it could gorge further. Devin came up behind her, clearing the space of the dying beasts that thrashed in the grass. Bard did the same on the other side, facing off against the last of the monsters that had yet to be put down. He cut through their ranks, grinding his blade into their corpses until he was sure they were dead. He turned back to check on Arndt.

The fallen warrior trembled, gasped like a landed fish, stared off at nothing. Hilde held him to her breast, but it was clear he knew nothing of her presence. She shook her head at Bard's unspoken question, meeting his gaze. "He's done."

Before Bard could think to reply, Hilde dragged the edge of her blade across Arndt's throat, spilling the last of his life between the limp braids of his beard. He shuddered and slipped away without a sound.

Even with all the death surrounding them, Bard felt the warrior's spirit writhe. This was a warrior worthy of the Golden Halls, and he cast about for a sign of the coming of the Valkyr.

Hilde laid Arndt's head on the ground with careful reverence and climbed to her feet. Though there was little time left to them before the rest of Haakon's minions found them, Bard knew they could not leave their brother with nothing. Perhaps the Shield Maidens would come soon, perhaps not. They could not return him to the womb of the goddess, but...

"*Lo, jeg ser her min far og mor,*" Devin started, making the decision for them.

Bard drew a breath and nodded. They could honor Arndt in this way, and so his tongue wove the rest of the prayer in little more than a whisper: "*Lo, nå ser jeg all min død slektningsbordsetning. Lo, det er mitt hoved, som er å sitte i Paradis. Paradis er slik vakkert, så grønn. Med ham er hans menn og gutter.*"

"*Han kaller til meg, så fører meg til ham.*" The last of the words danced from Hilde's lips, and Bard repeated them in his head.

He calls to me, so bring me to him.

As the prayer faded, Bard collected Arndt's sword and placed it in the dead man's hand, laying the blade across his massive chest should his brother need it on his journey. Then, without another word, the survivors marched on, leaving their companion behind as the ominous gray slowly melted into the violet tones of the failing sun. Bard shivered, though not from the cold. He stared into the distance, watching the clouds devour the light and knew they'd only traded one horror for another.

The others seemed of similar mind. Their pace quickened, milking the last vestiges of illumination to see them free of the boneyard before the darkness returned. They'd only just made it to the barrier of stones when the sun slipped from sight, shadows dancing a tribute to its demise.

"This way." Hilde's whisper was the mooring upon which Bard cinched his hope.

They huddled close while the blackness leeched the color from the world, the gods' twinkling eyes yet to awaken. Distant howls were met with savage rejoinders, the song of predators growing closer as Bard and the others shuffled on. For all his earlier desire to die in battle rather than the firestorms born of the witches' loathsome *galdrar*, he found himself craving life above all. He did not wish to perish on this foreboding isle, its taint so wretched as to profane the spirit of any who struck upon its shore. He gnashed his teeth and cast a prayer to the heavens in Arndt's name before marching on with renewed vigor in his step, vowing to scrape the mud of this place from his boots.

Strange, guttural sounds dogged their heels as the party trudged north, the hours rolling by in a leaden crawl, fear clawing at their feet. It wasn't until the stars alighted that Bard spied the deeper darkness of something looming ahead. He brought his companions to a halt, motioning to the shape that sat along their path. They waited in silence for several long moments, willing their vision to resolve.

"Another barrow?" Devin asked.

Bard shook his head, though the warrior couldn't see the gesture, standing before Bard as he was. "It's a hut."

"Aye," Hilde confirmed, not waiting for the others before she started off again, Bard and Devin following.

Shortly after, they stood hunched outside a rocky pit house, ears pressed against its cold wall. Nothing stirred within. Bard pulled away and circled the home to find its door left open. He peered inside, heart aflutter, only to find the tiny hut empty.

"There are others," Hilde said at his back, drawing his

eyes to where she pointed. And, true enough, a dozen or more similar homes were spread out behind the first, each separated by a few horse-lengths of open space and little more but weeds and thorns. No lights or sounds greeted the trespass of the three Norse warriors.

Bard drew in a lungful of brisk air and crept to the nearest of the huts to find it, too, deserted. He went to each in turn, Hilde and Devin at his back, but there was no one to be found. When the last of them also proved empty, Bard turned to his companions. "We've a choice."

"Live or die?" Devin answered, a crooked smile on his lips, but no light reached his eyes.

Hilde ignored them and stared off, her thoughts tormenting her features. Bard followed her gaze to see the hazy flutter of trees a distance further north. Their leaves danced serpentine in the gloomy starlight, the barest whisper of a rustle reaching Bard's ears.

"The woods are one of our choices, eh?" Devin said. "I'd much rather dig a hole and wait for morning."

Bard agreed. He looked back to the nearest of the huts and was made wary by its emptiness, but the lure of shelter, after battle and wind had pecked at his marrow since he'd set foot upon the isle, was undeniable. He caught Hilde's stare as he scanned slowly about.

"If you had a choice...?" he started.

She sighed. "If nidhoggr roam the land in the open like sheep, I'd prefer sunlight on our necks before setting foot in yonder woods."

"Then a hole it is," Devin said. He motioned for Hilde to enter the nearest of the huts first. "Never thought we three would share a warren on a cold winter's night." He winked at Hilde. "Don't tell your *faðir*, now."

She grinned and grabbed at her armored chest as she went inside. "It'll be my blade you need worry about should you try making a nest of these pillows, boy."

Devin glanced to Bard, an eyebrow raised.

"You'll find no love here, either. Keep your hands on your

own sword tonight," Bard told him, stepping in behind Hilde. Hilde's throaty laugh welcomed them, and Bard eased the door shut, setting the bolt.

"Damn Freiøya's eyes. Leave me to spend my final hours with a swollen sack and two old maids with shuttered arses," Devin muttered. "I could have stayed home with my wife had I wanted to die with a limp *kokkr* between my thighs."

Hilde dropped into the corner furthest from the door, wiping the grin from her lips. "If we make it home, brother, I'll let you take Dagny for an eve."

"Your goat for a whole night? How generous."

Bard sat near the door, muffling his laugh against the stiff sleeve of his tunic while balancing his ax across his knees. The other two prattled on in quiet voices as he settled in, resting his head against the cool stone of the wall, letting its chill sink into his fevered flesh. He blinked once, twice, resting his eyes, the quiet murmur of his companions blurring, and then darkness pulled him under.

* * *

"They'll be here soon."

Bard snapped upright, eyes flying wide at the familiar voice. Arndt stood before him. Blood had crystallized upon his chest, and the wound at his throat pulsed – a gaping black crevice in his pale skin, as though it clasped at the air, trying to draw breath.

"How…?" Bard asked, barely able to get his tongue moving in the dry well of his mouth.

"No time," Arndt answered, drawing Bard's gaze to his friend's face. It was there that Bard found his answer as to how the warrior he'd thought dead could be there beside him.

Eyes a deeper blue than Lake Votka stared back at him. Bard's gaze sank into their abysmal depths, will o' the wisps drawing him deeper with every passing moment. He shook his head to clear the sluggishness from his limbs and scrabbled to his feet. Though his gaze never left Arndt, he avoided the warrior's eyes, focusing instead on the man's broad nose.

"Why have you come?"

"The hounds are loose. They have come upon your scent." His spectral hand swept the room, motioning first to Devin, and then to Hilde. "Flee now, but beware the roan that has shorn its coat."

"Arndt?"

Hilde's questioning voice cut through the gloom. Bard looked to her as she clambered up from the floor, and then back to the warrior spirit only to find he was no longer there. Only the barest scent of grave dirt remained in the wraith's stead.

Hilde pawed at the space where Arndt had just been, fingers stirring empty air. "Was he truly...?" The question was devoured by the bestial roar that set the night to trembling.

"Merciless Hel," Devin muttered as he came to stand alongside Bard and Hilde. "What was that?"

"We need to leave." Bard retrieved his ax and went to unbar the door.

"No," Hilde called out. "We can't just—"

But Bard had no ears for her. When the dead warned of doom, those who wished to live heeded their words. He shucked the bar free of the door and yanked it open, charging outside, ax leading the way. Only the empty village greeted him, but there was no mistaking the corruption that wormed its way amidst the darkness. It set his skin afire.

Another guttural roar thundered, this one nearer than the last. Whatever Haakon had loosed would be upon them soon. The sound faded, and he heard Hilde's and Devin's shuffled motions over the last of it as they followed him, their reluctance nipped in the tail. He spun about, his companions but a blur to his side, and instinct made his choice for him. Bard sprinted for the trees.

Though the darkness crowded about, the stars lent him their sight. He cut straight across the grassy terrain, doing nothing to hide his presence from whatever witchery dogged his heels. Neither stealth nor subterfuge would serve him now. His companions followed where he led, their huffed breaths keeping pace.

They reached the line of trees just as something crashed at their backs. Wood splintered like shattered bones and stones clattered, heavy thumps sounding as they rained down from the force of the blow that had demolished the hut they'd only just fled. The ground shook beneath Bard's feet, but it did nothing to slow his headlong flight. He barreled through the clustered trees, branches and leaves slashing at his face, each fresh sting spurring him on.

"This way," Hilde called as she darted past, her long legs slicing away at Bard's lead. She ducked low and veered left, and Bard turned after her. He heard Devin do the same just behind.

Trees whipped past as they ran, humus crunching beneath their boots. Whatever hounded them stayed the course, malevolent shrieks peppering their spines with sharpened knives of terror. Branches snapped in discordant rhythm as the creature entered the woods.

Bard set his eyes on the back of Hilde's head, her blonde hair a beacon in the darkness, and matched his pace to hers as best he could. She ran as if Fenrir himself chased after them, and that was not far from the mark.

"*Lindvurm!*" someone yelled, and Bard glanced back at the outline of the enormous monster, for it was indeed a lindvurm of sorts, a massive serpentine shadow that parted the trees and crushed the undergrowth as it came slithering and grunting.

Bard turned to keep running but before he could spot Hilde, or spy where Devin was behind him, he collided with something that gave way with a howl of pain – albeit a howl from a human throat. They both hit the hard ground, and Bard found himself sprawled alongside a man in mail who wore the sign of King Harald Bluetooth on his coat. The man spared him a brief glance, then looked agape at the lindvurm as it came on. He left his sword and helm among the leaves and scrambled to his feet.

"Wait," Bard growled, fetching his ax and clambering upright, but the man dashed into the darkness of the woods.

Bard cast about, noticing more of Bluetooth's raiders fleeing in the same direction. *Toward the sea*. Had they been coming this way to join the battle? Perhaps decamped here at the coming of early night due to the völur's accursed fog? Mayhap the sea was closer than he thought, and mayhap Bluetooth's ships awaited.

OF STORMS & FLAME

A scream grabbed Bard's attention before he could sort his thoughts, and he looked to see a warrior snatched within the massive lindvurm's jaws. The man's howls were cut off as the monster's snout snapped shut. It swallowed the warrior down, tossing its head back, and shafts of white moonlight illuminated the beast. Atop its snake-like coils swiveled the head of a dragon and a spiky mane of bleached spines. The bulk of the monster was seemingly made from a motley transgression of slain nidhoggr, patched in spots with rivulets of grave dirt, while here and there jutted the moldy bones of the long-dead, as well as much fresher, battle-fallen corpses.

Bard started as something gripped his shoulder, raising his ax before seeing Hilde and Devin standing there.

"What are you doing?" Hilde looked at him as if he were a fool.

"Bluetooth's men…"

"Aye," Devin hissed. "Let's move!" He jerked his head toward the men fleeing northward, or at least Bard believed so.

"Get down!" Hilde suddenly yelled, shoving Bard.

"Too late. It's spotted us," said Devin. "Go!"

The lindvurm, glaring at them from two nacreous pairs of eyes atop its scaly skull, barked a croaking howl. Chewed up corpse-meat dropped from its maw as it slid toward them, snapping saplings and scrub beneath its daunting bulk.

Bard was yanked backward as the lindvurm's maw clacked shut where he'd only just stood. He felt the air of its passage, a fetid stench hammering against his nose. Hilde's hand was a vice about his wrist while she tugged at him, pulling him along with her, but Bard knew it to be futile. In close, the vurm was just too quick to be outrun, too powerful to be faced down. If there was to be any hope, it lay in wit, not brawn.

"Separate," Bard shouted as he shook Hilde free and shoved her aside. "Find a way to get behind it, out of its line of sight."

Hilde stumbled, hesitant, but Devin seemed to see the sense in his words. The warrior bolted between two large trees that had grown clustered together, leaving his companions to stare down the monster.

SNAFU: SURVIVAL OF THE FITTEST

Bard gave the creature no time to choose between him and Hilde. He snatched the sword left behind by Bluetooth's man and hurled it at the beast. It rang out against the lindvurm's skull, bouncing harmlessly aside, but it had done its duty. Hilde was forgotten as the vurm reared up and loosed a fearsome roar, its blood-red gaze latching onto Bard with flash fires of fury burning inside. Ragged claws tore at the trees that separated them, clearing the way.

But Bard was already gone. The moment its attention was solely on him, he had run. For any of them to survive, he needed the lindvurm's focus. He stomped and screamed and struck out at the trees as he fled. His breath scorched his throat at every exhalation while he pushed on, the monster tearing up the ground between them. Though every footfall was a minor victory, it would be on him soon, and he envisioned much more than a momentary reprieve.

Then, just ahead, an unfortunate hope appeared.

Huddled in the trees, steel helms poking up from the ground like rigid mushrooms, cowered dozens of King Bluetooth's soldiers. Their eyes went wide upon seeing him leading the vurm in their direction. Curses rang out and chaos took hold, the warriors scrambling from the path as Bard plotted a course through the trees. There was no avoiding them, scattering as they had. He growled and dug his boots into the soft earth to turn away from the men. He'd hoped to find a ravine or someplace he could duck into and hide as the creature stormed past, not sacrifice his allied king's own liegemen.

The Norns evidently had other plans. His foot caught an errant root, and Bard crashed face first into the ground. Bitter dirt filled his mouth and clouded his vision. He rolled onto his back, wiping at his eyes, just as the vurm slithered to loom over him, putrid slime raining down from its mouthful of sword-like fangs. Bard raised his ax, turning its edge toward the lindvurm. It would do nothing to kill the beast, of course, but he would hack and saw as the creature swallowed him down. Bard would not be devoured easily, nay.

His Thuringian friend, Devin of Nordhausen, clearly felt the same.

OF STORMS & FLAME

The warrior leapt from the trees and drove his sword into one of the lindvurm's pale eyes. It sunk in to the hilt, and the creature shrieked and thrashed its head to be rid of the offending steel. Bard jumped to his feet as the vurm reared up, taking Devin with it as he clung to his blade.

"Let go!" Bard screamed.

Devin did just that, but the creature twisted aside. Before the warrior had fallen but a hand span, the lindvurm grabbed Devin's torso in its maw. A symphony of *snaps* erupted all along his ribcage as the monster clamped down. He gave one last scream, and went silent, the two halves of his body dangling at unnatural angles on either side of the creature's mouth.

Bile filled Bard's throat at seeing his brother so defiled, yet there was nothing he could do to free him from the clutches of the beast. And though the decision would haunt him for however many moments remained to him upon Midgard, Bard spun and ran, leaving Devin's corpse to the lindvurm.

He said an oath to the Allfather and to the Thunderer both, wishing his brother well on his way, yet despairing that Devin's sacrifice was not enough to see Bard clear of the hellish abomination. The lindvurm screeched, and Bard heard it resume its chase, trees giving way to its insistence. The sound set a trail of Surt's flames to Bard's posterior, and he marshalled every last vestige within as he flew through the woods. Death came next for him, and there was naught else he could do. A warrior might make a final stand, but the crack of Devin's bones echoed in Bard's head, and the sharp salt of the sea was on the wind and gave him wings.

Then, the din of hundreds of voices and the familiar ringing of metal joined the vurm's blaring. The trees parted before him and a yellow-white field hove into view. Greycloak's and Bluetooth's soldiers spanned the length of the winter-washed meadow, all locked in combat with Haakon's forces, warriors and beasts alike.

Bard stopped at the forest's edge and gawped not at the battle, despite a nidhogg atop a nearby man, screaming as it tore into his guts, but at the stupefying vision of greedy flames cavorting amidst their longships. The wrath of Surt himself leaped between the vessels on black pinions of distorted smoke. Bard roared in desperate fury. Their way home was well and truly gone, for Haakon had set his völur bitches' magic loose upon the víkingr fleet, razing their ships in one fell blow, setting them to bright white flame like funeral pyres atop the water.

Bard's heart *thrummed* a mournful dirge, but the beast at his back offered him no time to grieve. It burst from the trees with a savage howl, Devin's steel still buried in its eye, the warrior's blood still staining its maw. The ground shook beneath the lindvurm, and Bard nearly lost his footing, but terror lent him renewed strength. He realized he'd lost his ax in his flight from the beast, so he skirted a fighting throng of soldiers, took up a fallen sword, and jabbed it into an enemy who had spun on him but then paused upon taking note of the lindvurm bearing down on them. The warrior fell with a peculiar expression of awe and pain, and Bard bellowed and struck a leaping nidhogg, the bloody-hafted sword ripped from his grasp as it wedged in the writhing monster's scales. Behind him, the lindvurm struck the ranks like an angry storm, men flung wildly about on the sharpened ends of teeth and claws.

Bard fought on, heading away from the vurm and into the hue of battle, seeking his doom while wielding steel against men rather than in the belly of that crazed, Hel-spawned abomination. His lungs billowed like forge bellows as he kicked an enemy warrior in the back and snatched his spear away. He turned and barreled toward the sea, toward where he saw the chanting völur raising their blue-painted arms to the sky, waving their knotted staves as they beckoned more storms of monsters and flame.

Every step rattled his jaw as he made his way toward that chanting circle. Behind him he heard the cries of his brethren as they fell, but he never once tarried, and just as he felt he could run no further, his feet struck the sandy beach, kicking up gold in their wake. He loosed his stolen spear with foul intent.

Focused as they were on their task, the ring of nine völur saw nothing until it was too late. The spear took the first in the chest. She grunted and fell back into her companions, pulling several down with her in a tangle of thrashing limbs. Bard crashed into another before they could gather their wits about them, fists flailing. Blue lips exploded with red as Bard waded into the group, but there were simply too many to keep track of.

Pain cut across his lower back, the smell of his own charred meat filling his nostrils a heartbeat later. He spun to see a lone *völva* holding her crooked staff in Bard's direction. Wisps of fire sputtered at the tip. More flames crackled, and Bard was alight with witch fire. He screamed and beat at the flames but they would not be denied. Still more of the völur closed while he battled the conflagration he'd become.

Hooves thundered close by and amidst the whirling chaos Bard saw a half-dozen riders. He recognized Haakon leading them, and the Good King pointed at him with a bloodied sword. "Kill that man!" he ordered his warriors, and the others kicked heels to flanks, urging their mounts toward Bard, spears lowered.

Disarmed and aflame, Bard turned from the charging riders and Haakon's blue-skinned she-demons, and ran for the sea as gouts of fire roared past. A moment later the frigid water caressed his ankles, and then his knees. Waves lapped at him, and he dove into their midst. Still the fires pecked at his flesh, steam hissing off his blackening skin, but Bard denied them their victim.

He stretched above the waves and drove into deeper water, swimming toward open sea until the flames sputtered and died. Not long after, his arms gave way and he was forced to embrace a remnant piece of wood. He gathered a few more as he drifted through a field of wreckage, desperate to collect enough to hold his weight afloat so he might rest his scorched and weary arms, but there was little of substance to cling to.

He was fast growing weary, hands benumbed in the cold swell. He cast a glance at the shore he'd left behind. He saw the lindvurm prowling the beach, its prodigious size diminished by distance, a frantic shadow cavorting about the field of its slaughter. And he saw the riders had returned to the slaughter as well, while the völur resumed their chanting, minus one of their nine. Bard wished his brothers glory in the next life; for certain, he would join them soon.

SNAFU: SURVIVAL OF THE FITTEST

He watched as the island of Frei was swallowed by the darkness. Bard felt a pang of muted joy at having escaped despite every wave that carried him further from shore, and once the isle slipped from view, so did Bard slip into the ocean, the last of his strength sapped from his limbs.

Darkness encircled him. He took one last breath of glorious air before he plummeted toward the bottom of the sea.

Then came light.

He opened his mouth to greet the Valkyr, but choked and spit water from his lungs. Strong hands clutched him. Pain speared through his veins, and Bard cursed the god who would be so cruel as to not extinguish his agony before ferrying him to Valhöll.

When at last he could squint through cataracts of brine, he saw the wide-set blue eyes and freckly cheeks of the Valkyr who'd collected him. "I'd thought the choosers of the slain...might be hideous to behold," he muttered, pressing a weak smile to his lips. "I thought...*true.*"

"Aye," Hilde answered, drawing him higher onto the makeshift raft of splintered boards with a quiet chuckle. "And I thought I'd caught a fish worth keeping."

Bard coughed and hooked sea sludge from the corner of his mouth. "Seems we're both wrong," he said, and clasped his blistered hand about hers.

She gave his a firm squeeze in return, both going silent as thunder serenaded them from above.

Bard's stomach knotted at the sound. He stared over Hilde's shoulder at the dark clouds boiling overhead, choking the flickers of dawn in their sullen advance. He spied dots of cankerous blackness growing in the distance, looming over the swell, riding its building fury toward them. Bluetooth's ships or Haakon's? They would know soon enough.

Bard gripped Hilde's hand tighter, an oath to the Aldaföðr – *the Allfather* – playing at his lips. It seemed Óðinn's hounds, ever ravenous and slaughter-greedy, had yet to give up the chase, and the halls of Valhöll still called.

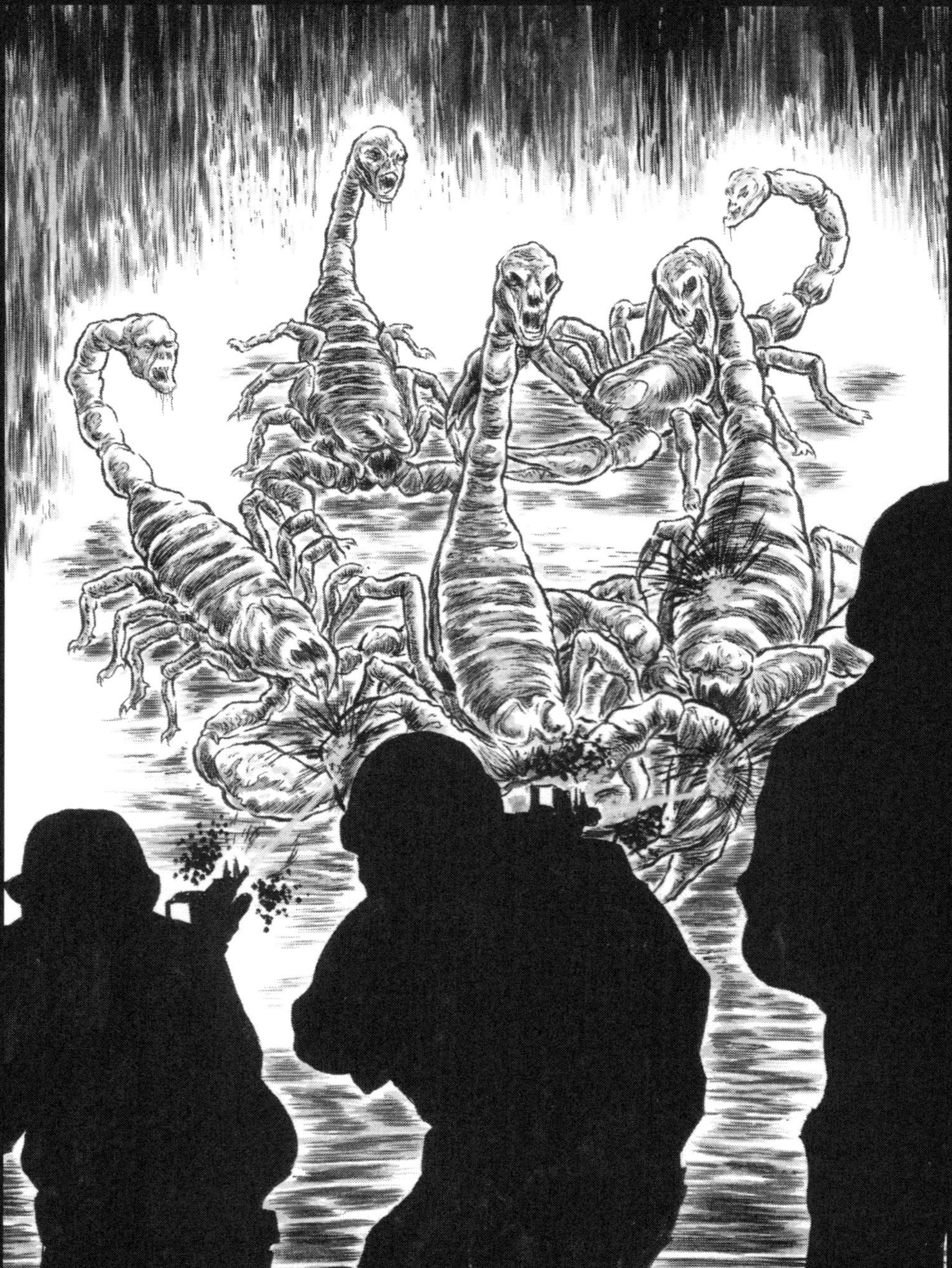

IN VAULTED HALLS ENTOMBED
Alan Baxter

The high, dim caves continued on into blackness. Sergeant Coulthard paused, shook his heavy, grizzled head. "We're going to lose comms soon. Have you mapped this far?" he asked Dillman.

"Yes, Sarge."

Coulthard looked back the way they had come, where daylight still leaked through to weakly illuminate the squad. "Radio it in, Spencer. See what they say."

"Yes, Sarge." Corporal Spencer shucked his pack and set an antenna, pointing back towards the cave entrance. "Base, this is Team Epsilon. Base, Team Epsilon."

The radio crackled and hissed, then, "Go ahead, Epsilon."

"We've followed the insurgents across open ground to foothills about eighty clicks north-north-east of Kandahar, to a cave system at... Hang on." Spencer pulled out a map and read aloud a set of co-ordinates. "They've gone to ground, about eighty minutes ahead of us. We'll lose comms if we head deeper in. Orders?"

"Stand by."

The radio crackled again.

"They'll tell us to go in," Sergeant Coulthard said.

Lance Corporal Paul Brown watched from one side, nerves tickling the back of his neck. They were working by the book, but this showed every sign of a trap, perfect for an ambush. It would be dark soon, and was already cold. It would only get colder. Though perhaps the temperature farther in remained pretty constant.

He stepped forward. "Sarge, maybe we should set camp here and wait til morning."

"Always night in a fucking cave, Brown," Coulthard said without looking at him.

"You tired, possum?" Private Sam Gladstone asked with a sneer.

The new boy, Beaumont, grinned.

"You always a dick?" Brown said.

"Can it!" Coulthard barked. "We wait for orders."

"I just think everyone's tired," Brown said. He shifted one shoulder to flash the red cross on the side of his pack. "Your welfare is my job after all."

"Noted," Coulthard said.

Silence descended on the six of them. They'd followed this band of extremists for three days, picking up and losing their trail half a dozen times. He was tired even if the others were too hardass to admit it. Young Beaumont was like a puppy, on his first tour and desperate for a fight, but the others should know better. They'd all seen action to some degree. Coulthard more than most; the kind of guy who seemed like he'd been born in the middle of a firefight and come out carrying a weapon.

"Epsilon, this is Base. You're sure this is where the insurgents went?"

"Affirmative. Dillman had them on long range scope. Trying to shake us off, I guess, going to ground."

"Received. Proceed on your own initiative. Take 'em if you can. They've got a lot of our blood on their hands. Can you confirm their numbers?"

"Eight of them, Base."

"Received. Good luck."

Spencer winked at the squad. "Received, Base. Over and out." He unhooked his antenna and slung his pack.

"Okay, then," Dillman said. He shifted grip on his rifle and dug around in his webbing, came up with a night sight and fitted it.

Brown sighed. No one was as good a shot as Dillman, even when he was tired and in the dark. But it didn't give much comfort. "We're not going to wait, are we?" he said.

Coulthard ignored him. "Pick it up, children. As there are no tracks in here," he kicked at the hard stone floor, "we move slow and silent. Spencer, you're mapping. I want markers deployed along the way."

"Sarge."

"Let's go. Beaumont, you're on point."

"Yes, Sarge!"

"Slow and steady, Beaumont. And lower that weapon. No firing until I say so unless you're fired on first."

"Yes, Sarge."

The kid sounded a little deflated and Brown was glad. Youth needed deflating. They fell into order and moved forward. Spencer placed an electronic marker and tapped the tablet he carried. It began to ping a location to help them find their way back.

It became cooler and the darkness almost absolute. The light that leaked through from outside couldn't reach and blackness wrapped them up like an over-zealous lover.

"Night vision will be useless down here," Coulthard said. "We're going to have to risk torchlight. One beam, from point. Dillman, go infrared."

"Way ahead of you," Dillman said, and tapped his goggles. He moved up to stand almost beside Beaumont.

The young private clicked on his helmet lamp and light swept the space as he looked around. The passage was about five metres in an irregular diameter and as dry and cold as everything else they'd seen over the last few days. Dust motes danced in the torch beam, the scuff and crunch of their boots strangely loud in the confined space.

"All quiet from here on," Coulthard said and waved Beaumont forward.

They fell into practised unison; moved with determined caution.

"I'm a glowing target up here," Beaumont whispered nervously.

"That's why the new boy takes point," Coulthard said. A soft wave of giggles passed through the squad before the sergeant hushed them.

Dillman patted Beaumont on one shoulder. "I got your back, Donkey."

Beaumont's torch beam shot back into the group as he looked around. "Don't call me that!"

75

Laughter rippled again. Brown grinned. Poor sap. Caught petting a donkey back in Kandahar, just a lonely kid far from home taking some comfort by hugging the soft, furry creature's neck. Of course, he'd been spotted, photographed and by the time he got back to barracks the story had him balls deep in the poor animal.

"Enough!" Coulthard snapped. "Are we fucking professionals or not?"

Their mirth stilled and they crept forward again. The ground sloped downwards and Spencer paused every fifty yards or so to place a marker. After about three hundred yards the passage opened out into a wider cavern. Something was rucked up and definitely man-made on the far side.

Weapons instantly trained on it and Beaumont moved cautiously forward. "False alarm," he called back after a moment, his voice relaxed and light. Relieved. "Someone's been here, there are blankets, signs of a fire, an empty canteen. But it looks months old, at least."

The squad relaxed slightly as Beaumont shone his torch in a wide arc, illuminating the cave. Nothing but rough, curved rock. A few small fissures striated the walls on one side, black gaps into the unknown, but nothing big enough for even a child to get through. On the far side, a larger gap yawned darkly, a tunnel leading away and down. Large rocks were scattered around the opening.

Coulthard nodded the squad forward.

"Looks like these have recently been moved," Gladstone said.

Brown moved in to see better. "Looks like this passage was blocked up and those fuckers cleared the way."

Dillman kicked at a couple of broken stones. "I guess they weren't so keen to ambush us here and are looking for a better option."

Brown shook his head. "Why would this passage have been blocked? And by who?"

"Emergency bolt hole they knew about?" Coulthard mused. "Move on."

IN VAULTED HALLS ENTOMBED

The tunnel beyond was around three metres in diameter, sloping down again. Beaumont's was the only light, but in the otherwise total blackness it made the tunnel bright. Shadows flickered off the irregular surface.

Beaumont took his flashlight from his helmet and held it at arm's length to one side. "If they do ambush and shoot at the light..."

After a couple of hundred metres, Brown, bringing up the rear, paused and looked back. "Hold up," he said quietly.

Coulthard glanced over his shoulder. "What's up, Doc?"

"Kill the light, Beaumont."

"Gladly!"

There was a soft click and the tunnel sank into blackness. Within seconds, their eyes began to adjust to something other than the dark. In crevices on the walls and ceiling of the passage, even here and there on the floor, a soft blue glow emanated. Almost imperceptible, easier to see from their peripheral vision, a pale luminescence. No, Brown thought. Phosphorescence. He crouched and looked closely into one crack. He pulled out a pocket knife, flicked open the blade and dug inside the crevice. The blade came out with a sickly blue smudge on it.

"Some kind of lichen," he said. "I've heard of this kind of stuff, but always thought it was green."

Gladstone pulled his googles down and flicked the adjustment. "Doesn't matter what colour it is, it's giving enough light for night vision."

"Lucky us," Coulthard said. "Goggles on, people. Keep that light off, Beaumont."

"Thank fuck, Sarge."

Brown pulled his own goggles down and watched the squad move forward in green monochrome. He was glad they didn't need harsh torchlight any more, but the glowing blue lichen gave him the creeps. He stood and followed before they got too far ahead, shifting his heavy medical pack as he moved.

They continued silently for several minutes, Spencer periodically dropping markers. At a fork they tried the left hand path and quickly met a dead end. Backtracking to the main passage,

77

they travelled further and found a small cave off to one side, too low to stand upright. No passages led from it.

"Looks like this one tunnel is gonna keep heading down," Beaumont said. His voice had lost some of its excitement.

Coulthard raised a fist bringing them to a halt. "How far?"

Spencer checked the tablet that shone in their night vision even though its brightness was down to minimum. "Seven hundred and eighty-three metres."

"Three quarters of a k in, really?" Dillman whispered.

He sounded as nervous as Brown felt. The strange lichen continued, scattered randomly in cracks and fissures. Occasionally a larger patch would glow like a bright light, but for the most part it was soft streaks like veins in the rocks.

"Move on," Coulthard said.

After another couple of minutes, Spencer whispered, "That's one kilometre."

Before any discussion could be had about that fact, Beaumont hissed and cursed. "Sarge, got something here."

The squad sank into fighting readiness and crept apart to cover the width of the tunnel.

"Bones," Beaumont said. "Just a skeleton."

Coulthard turned. "Doc, go check."

Brown went to Beaumont and looked down on the bones scattered at the curve of the tunnel wall. Streaks of the blue lichen wrapped the skeleton here and there, like snail trails. He crouched for a closer look. "Male, adult. No discerning marks of trauma that I can see at first glance."

He took a penlight torch from his pocket and lifted his goggles. "Mind your eyes."

The squad looked away as he clicked on the light and had a closer look. The bones had no flesh or connecting tissue remained to hold them together. "There's a kind of residue," Brown said quietly. "Like a gel or something." He took a pen from his pocket and dragged the tip along one femur. It gathered a small wave of clear, viscous ichor. It was odourless.

He put one index finger to the same bone and gently touched the stuff. It seemed inert. As he brought it close to his face to inspect he frowned, then pressed his finger to the "This is warm."

Tension tightened the squad behind him.

"What's that?" Coulthard asked.

Brown swallowed, heart hammering. He looked at his fingertip then gripped the bone, felt the heat in his palm. "This skeleton is warm. And too clean to have rotted here."

"What the hell?" Beaumont demanded, his voice quavering.

"You shitting us?" Gladstone asked. His voice was stronger than Beaumont's but with fear still evident.

Brown held one palm over the skeleton, only an inch or so away from touching, moved it back and forth. "It's warm all over," he said weakly. His mind tried to process the information, but kept hitting dead ends. The cold rock under his knee seemed to mock him.

"Warm?" Coulthard asked.

Brown's heart skipped and doubled-timed again as he spotted something beneath the bony corpse. "Hey, Dillman."

"What?"

"When you scoped those fucks we were following, what did you see that you thought was funny?"

A tense silence filled the space for a moment. Then Dillman said, "One of them had a big fucking gold dollar sign on a chain around his neck. Fancied himself a rapper or some shit."

Brown used his pocket knife to hook up a chain from where it hung inside the stark white ribcage. With a toothy clicking, he hauled it up link by link. Eventually a metal dollar sign emerged from between the bones, its surface no longer gold but a tarnished, blackened alloy.

"What the actual fuck?" Beaumont asked in a high voice. He shifted from foot to foot, looked wildly around himself.

"These bones are too clean and white to have decayed to this state," Brown said. He shone his penlight among the bones to show coins, a cigarette lighter, the half-melted remains of a cell phone, belt buckles. Two automatic pistols, both with traces of the gel-like slime, were wedged under the pelvis.

Coulthard stepped forward, leaned down to stare at the

pse like it was a personal insult. "You trying to tell me this is one of the guys we're chasing."

Brown shrugged, hefted the pen to make the dollar sign swing.

"Fuck this," Spencer said. "What the hell can do that to a person?"

Brown shook his head. "Who knows?" He played his torchlight around the walls and ceiling of the tunnel.

"And where did it go?" Gladstone asked weakly.

"Go?" Coulthard asked.

"I think it's pretty clear someone or something did that to him and is no longer here, right?" Gladstone said.

"Some kind of weapon?" Beaumont asked, still agitated.

"What kind of weapon does this?" Brown countered.

Coulthard stood up straight. "Can it, all of you. We have a mission and we'll keep to it. We'll find answers on the way."

"It's still warm," Brown reminded him. "This happened very recently, I think."

"Then we move extra fucking carefully," Coulthard said.

A burst of gunfire and distant shouting echoed up the tunnel. Epsilon squad froze and listened. A scream, another burst of gunfire then a deep, concussive boom.

"Grenade?" Dillman asked quietly.

Silence descended again.

"Lights off, mouths shut," Coulthard said. "Brown, up front with me in case we come across any more bodies. Beaumont, rear guard. Move out."

Brown nodded as he pocketed his knife. He wasn't happy about it, but that was a smart move by the sergeant. Beaumont had sounded very spooked by this encounter and understandably so. His nerves were like an electric current through the squad. Best he go to the back and have a chance to calm down. Reluctantly the squad fell into place. Brown glanced once more at the skeleton on the tunnel floor and shivered as they moved almost silently away.

They travelled in silence for another ten minutes before Spencer whispered, "Two clicks."

A distant scream rang out, cut off equally fast. Several bursts of gunfire. They froze and listened, but heard nothing more.

"Move on," Coulthard said tightly.

"Are you sure, Sarge?" Brown asked, but the sergeant's only answer was a shove in the back.

Several minutes later, Spencer said, "Three clicks."

Brown pointed and Coulthard nodded. Two more skeletons were lying on the tunnel floor. Brown crouched and felt the warmth rising off them, stark against the cold rock all around. Two AK-47s and a variety of other metallic objects littered the ground.

"What the fuck, man?" Beaumont said, his voice still high and stretched. "What can do that?"

"Should we go back?" Brown asked.

"There's still five more of them somewhere ahead," Coulthard said. "And whatever is doing this is ahead as well. We'll go a bit further."

"We gotta go, Sarge!" Beaumont said. "Seriously, how can we fight this fucking—"

"Pull it together, soldier!" Coulthard barked. "Get your shit in order. We go forward for another little while and see. This tunnel has to change at some point, branch off or open out or something. I want to see what happens. If nothing happens by five kays in, we turn around."

"Five kays?" Beaumont sounded like a child. "Fuck man, five kays?"

"Move out," Coulthard said softly, his voice and demeanour a perfect example of calm.

Brown wondered if the sergeant felt anything like as calm as he acted. It seemed Beaumont was the one having a far more sensible reaction to all this. Brown bit his teeth together to stem his own trembling and walked on.

The way was still lit by the strange veins of lichen, the tunnel remained a three metre or so diameter throat down into the foothills of the mountain range beyond. They heard nothing more for several minutes.

"Stay alert," Coulthard said. "How you doing, Donkey? Feeling okay?"

Beaumont didn't answer.

The sergeant laughed softly. "Sorry, Josh, I'm only ragging ya. Seriously, you feeling okay? You were a little rattled back there."

No answer.

Sam Gladstone said, "There's no one behind me, Sarge."

"What?"

"He was bringing up the rear, but he's not there."

Coulthard spat a curse. "Beaumont!" he called out in a harsh whisper. "Fuck, surely he hasn't panicked and run back."

"Wouldn't I have heard, Sarge?" Gladstone asked.

"I don't know. Would you? Spencer, leave your tablet here and double time back up the tunnel. If you don't catch up to him in a few hundred yards, we'll have to let him go and I'll kick his fucking ass when we get back."

"Righto, Sarge."

Spencer put down his gear and jogged away. They stood in uncomfortable silence for a few minutes.

"Nervous kid," Brown said eventually. "First tour."

"Don't make excuses for him," Coulthard said. "He's a fucking soldier."

Spencer walked back towards them, holding something out. "We need to get the fuck out of here," he said. Hanging from his fingers was a chain with two dog tags.

"The fuck?" Dillman whispered.

"Beaumont's?" Coulthard asked in a tight voice.

"He's a fucking skeleton just like the insurgent fuckers we found. Nothing left but buckles and weapons and shit. He's just fucking bones, Sarge!"

Dillman began muttering and shone his helmet lamp frantically in every direction. The mood of the squad began to fracture.

Coulthard swatted Dillman's lamp off. "Stow that shit! Everyone stay calm."

"Calm, Sarge?" Gladstone asked. "Seriously, we're in deep shit here."

"Stay. Calm. Spencer, did you recover Beaumont's weapon."

Spencer shook his head. "Left it there. The strap is gone, too hard to carry. But I took his clips."

"Fair enough. Now, we need to reassess what we're doing here."

"I think we should leave, Sarge," Brown said. He tried to keep his voice calm, but heard and felt the quaver in it.

"It ain't that simple."

"It must be," Dillman said. "Fuck those guys, if they're even still alive down there. Whatever got Beaumont can get them. We'll wait outside the caves and pick off any who comes out."

Coulthard held up a hand, a pale green wave in their night vision goggles. "Chill, everyone. It ain't as simple as leaving. I'm with you. In any other circumstances I would absolutely call an abort. But whatever took Beaumont, it took him from the back."

"Which means it's behind us," Brown said, realisation like an icy wave through his gut. "Or there's more than one, ahead and behind."

"Exactly."

"Does that mean we should carry on though?" Gladstone asked. "Maybe it's only gonna get worse."

"Maybe. Or maybe there's another way out." Coulthard picked up Spencer's tablet, checked the display. "We've still got a bunch of sensors, yeah?"

Spencer dropped Beaumont's tags into a pocket. "Yeah, plenty."

"Okay. We carry on for another kilometre and see if it leads to any branches in the tunnel, any other way out. If it does, we can maybe go around whatever's in here. If not, we turn around and risk facing it. Spencer, it's unlikely but do we have any signal down here?"

The corporal pulled out his gear and spent a moment trying to get a response from Base. Then he went wide band, looking for any transmissions. He found none and no one responded to open hails. "Nothing, Sarge."

"I didn't think so. Okay, Brown, you stay in the middle. Me and Spencer will take point. I want Gladstone and Dillman on rear guard, but you two walk backwards. We move slow and you don't take your eyes off the tunnel behind us. Let's go."

They moved slowly on again. Brown felt more than a little

useless in the middle of the group, but he knew what Coulthard was doing. Protect the guy with the best chance of helping any wounded. Except it looked like whatever was in these caves didn't leave any wounded. He heard a gasp from Gladstone and turned to look.

"See that?" Gladstone whispered to Dillman.

"Yeah. There!"

Brown saw it too. He lifted his goggles to see with unfiltered eyes. A movement, more a shift of light across the darkness, like a ripple of wan blue luminescence. He caught part of a smooth, glassy sphere, a glimpse of something globular, but it pressed into the wall and vanished.

The others had stopped to watch. All five of them stared hard, but the tunnel was black as death and still.

"Keep moving," Coulthard said.

Brown walked backwards as well, eyes trying to scan every inch of the tunnel behind them.

"There!" Gladstone said sharply.

He'd seen it too. A glassy flex of movement on the ceiling about thirty metres back. Closer than before. Almost as if a giant water droplet had begun to swell and hang, only to be quickly sucked back up.

"It's fucking following us," Dillman hissed and snapped on his helmet light again.

"But what is it?" Spencer demanded. "Is it even alive? Doc?"

Brown jumped as he was directly addressed. "I'm no expert here," he said. "Whatever it is…"

His words were drowned out by Gladstone's screams and Dillman's shouts of fright as the torchlight reflected back off a huge slithering mass across the ceiling right above them. It ran and undulated like an upside down river across the rock then expanded, long and pendulous, extruding from the tunnel roof like a clear jelly waterfall. The huge, gelatinous blob unfurled itself and dropped.

Dillman leapt to one side, the deafening bark and muzzle flash of his weapon filling the tunnel as Gladstone tried to run backwards, but skidded and fell. He knocked Brown back, who

IN VAULTED HALLS ENTOMBED

dropped onto his rump in surprise and scrambled away, scrabbling for his weapon as Coulthard and Spencer aimed theirs above his head and let rip.

Gladstone's screams were bloodcurdling as the thing landed across his legs. Brown tried to see through the bursts of muzzle fire and caught staccato images like through a strobe light. Gladstone's legs, clothing and flesh alike, melted away inside the transparent blob in an instant, leaving only bones. He tried to batter it off with his hands only to raise fleshless, stark white fingerbones in horror that fell and scattered across his lap. The meat of his arms was gone to his elbows in a second. Tenticular appendages lashed forward from the globular mass and retracted like a frantic sea anemone as it filled the tunnel with its bulk. Hails of bullets from Dillman, Spencer and Coulthard slapped and sputtered into the thing with little effect. It seemed to flinch and flex away from the bullets, then surge forward again, relentless. Only Dillman's torch beam seemed to really hold it up. Gladstone's screams cut abruptly short as it reached his torso and then Brown was up and running.

He pounded down the tunnel and realised the others were with him. At least, Spencer and Coulthard were. They panted as they ran, intent only on putting distance between themselves and that foetid horror. He didn't dare look back for fear the thing was bulging along behind them, for fear he'd see Gladstone finished off or Dillman caught. He stumbled and nearly fell sprawling at one point as the tunnel floor became broken rock and one wall half-fallen, almost blocking the way. The result of the grenade they had heard earlier. Bones scattered as he kicked unwittingly through another skeleton.

A brighter glow began to fill the tunnel ahead and he pounded for it, heedless to any danger before them compared to the certain death behind.

They burst out into a dizzyingly huge cavern, skidding to a halt on a rock ledge that protruded into space hundreds of metres above the cave floor. The ceiling was lost in swirling mists far above, but a soft blue glow leaked through. The walls of the gigantic space were streaked with the strange lichen and the entire place swam in a surreal glow, almost like wan daylight leaking through tropical waters, incongruous several kilometres underground. Filling the floor and rising high into the wisps of mist was a structure clearly constructed by intelligent design – a huge spiralling tower, hundreds of metres high, with a base at least a kilometre across. Curving buttresses met smaller towers in a circle around it. Monumental, the organic-looking structure appeared to have been painstakingly carved from the rock itself. From their ledge, a mammoth stairway led down to the building's lowest levels and the cave floor. Each stair was around two-metres high and a similar width; hundreds of the giant steps leading down into haze. The air was colder and damp, smelled metallic and ancient. Everything about the sight emanated age beyond any span of history. Geological age.

"Fuck me," Spencer said, lifting his goggles. His voice held the taint of madness.

They jumped and spun at a scuffing, puffing sound from behind. Dillman staggered from the tunnel mouth, moaning in agony. His left arm was nothing but useless, dangling bone, his hand gone. Half his face was missing, teeth grinning from the exposed skull where the bubbling, bleeding skin still retracted. "Saaarrrge," he slurred, reaching out with his good hand as he fell to one knee.

Spencer staggered backwards and turned; vomited noisily. Brown hurried forward, his medical training taking over, pushing shock and horror aside for the moment. But he didn't dare touch the poor bastard. He looked closely, trying to ascertain where the damage ended. Dillman's shoulder was eaten away and still melting. The cartilage holding the whole joint together disintegrated as Brown watched and Dillman's arm bones fell to the rock with a clatter. The flesh of his neck liquefied and blood pulsed from the exposed carotid artery.

Dillman scrabbled at Brown one-handed as the medic gaped, at a total loss, even as the creep of disintegration slowed to a stop. But the damage was irreversibly done and Dillman's lifeblood pumped out. Coulthard's barrel slid into Brown's vision, pressed up against Dillman's forehead, and barked. The poor bastard flew backwards as the back of his head exploded out across the cave wall.

Spencer continued to empty the contents of his stomach as Brown sank to his knees and shook, mind flat-lining. Coulthard moved to the mouth of the tunnel from which they'd emerged and stared into the darkness. He flicked on his helmet torch and the beam pierced the black. He played it over the walls and ceiling.

As Spencer finally stopped puking, gasping short, shuddering breaths, Coulthard said, "Doesn't seem to be following us. Maybe it just guards the tunnels."

"Guards?" Brown managed.

Coulthard gestured at the impossible subterranean structure. "I don't think anyone is supposed to find that, do you?"

"But what is it?" Brown asked. "What manner of creature…?"

"Best not try to figure it out," Coulthard said. "Ours are soldier minds. That kind of question is for scientists."

"I can't believe it didn't get all of us," Spencer said.

"Out of practice maybe," Brown wondered. "It's not that quick, for all its deadliness. We only saw four insurgent bodies too. So four more got past it. It didn't like our lights, though they only slowed it."

"The flashlights were more use than the gunfire," Spencer said.

"Maybe too bright out here," Coulthard said, staring out into the wan blue glow of the cavern.

"Look."

Coulthard and Brown turned to see where Spencer pointed. Several giant staircases like the one in front of them led from the cavern floor up to various ledges around the walls. Their ledge covered a hundred metres with another staircase leading down from the far end. On that stairway, four tiny figures were clambering resolutely down. They moved as if exhausted, sitting on the edge of each high step before slipping onto the one below. One of them was being helped by the others, clearly wounded.

"Fuckers," Coulthard said. He went to Dillman's corpse, unslung the man's sniper rifle and fitted a telescopic sight.

Moving to the edge of their own top stair he dropped onto his belly and unfolded the supports beneath the rifle's barrel to aim across and down.

"Seriously, Sarge?" Brown asked, incredulous.

"We have a fucking job to do, gentlemen. I'll see that done properly, at least."

He squeezed the trigger and one insurgent's head burst with a spray of blood they could see from afar, even with the naked eye. The others became frantic, scrambling like frightened ants. Coulthard fired again and a second man went down as his chest burst open. Another shot and the wounded insurgent was hit in the shoulder and spun around to drop to the rock and crawl into the lee of a huge step out of sight. They had finally realised where the fire was coming from and the other man scrambled into cover as well.

"Fuckers," Coulthard said again. He kept his eye to the sight and lay still, breathing gently.

Spencer sank to curl up against the wall at the back of the rock shelf. His arms wrapped around his head as he rocked gently.

"Spencer's lost it," Brown whispered to Coulthard.

"I know," the sergeant said without taking his eye away from the telescopic sight. "Give him some time and see if he comes around."

"How much time do we have?"

"Who knows? Right now, that fucking thing isn't coming out of the tunnel and I'm certainly not going back in. There's one unhurt insurgent bastard down there and one with a shoulder wound of unknown severity. For now, I plan to wait them out and give Spencer a chance to get his shit together. I suggest you have a rest."

His tone brooked no further discussion. Brown moved well away from the tunnel mouth and sat down against the stone. It was cold on his back. Clearly Coulthard had lost it too, only he was dealing with it in a typically old-school military way. The big, musclebound sergeant had seen more action than the rest of them put together and he let all that training take over. Maybe it was a good strategy. If the man could divorce himself from his emotion and let his experience run him like a robot, perhaps that would actually see him out of this alive.

Time ticked by. Brown began to worry about more mundane matters like where they might sleep, how much they had left in the way of rations and water, whether there was any way out other than the way they had come in. And he certainly wasn't keen to go back up the tunnel either.

He jumped as Coulthard's rifle boomed.

"I knew I could outwait him," the sergeant said with a smile in his voice.

"Did you get him?"

"Yep. He didn't think I'd wait on a scope all that time. I've sat for longer than ten minutes, you murderous insurgent motherfucker. You're a fucking amateur, you had to peek. A dead fucking amateur now." He stood and slung the rifle over his shoulder. "All dead except the shoulder wound and I reckon he'll bleed out if nothing else. Let's go and see."

Brown stood, brow knitted in confusion. "Go and see?"

"Yep. What else is there to do?"

Brown thought hard but came up empty. The sergeant had a point. They at least needed to look around if they didn't plan to go back up the tunnel, so they might as well finish the job while they searched. It was pragmatism taken to the max, but it made a cold sense.

Coulthard went and crouched beside Spencer. "How you doing, soldier?"

"Not good, Sarge."

"Me either. But we gotta move, okay?"

Spencer looked up, his narrow face white as bone under his brown crewcut. "I got a little boy at home, Sarge. He's gonna be two next month. I'm due home in time for his birthday. I missed his first."

Coulthard patted Spencer's shoulder. "We'll get out and get you on a transport home just when you're supposed to be."

"We won't, Sarge. None of us are getting out." He pointed at the spires and tower filling the cavern. "What the fuck even is that, Sarge? We're gonna die here." He sounded perfectly calm about it.

"We're getting out," Coulthard said firmly.

"My wife always worried I'd come home with no legs from an IED. 'You won't get killed,' she said one night when we'd been drinking. 'I can feel that.' She was always what she called spiritual. Thought she was fucking psychic, you know? But it was harmless. 'You won't get killed,' she said, 'but I have a terrible feeling you're going to be maimed by a mine.' Great fucking prophecy, eh, Sarge? For all her spirituality, she certainly didn't foresee this shit!"

Coulthard laughed. "I don't think anyone foresaw this shit."

"I was supposed to go home in two weeks, Sarge." Spencer's eyes brimmed with tears.

Brown gaped as Coulthard did something he would never have anticipated. The sergeant gathered Spencer into a tight hug and held the man against his chest.

"Let it out, solider," Coulthard said, and Spencer sobbed.

Brown stood uncomfortably off to one side for a good minute while Spencer bawled. The medic wondered why he felt so calm, so cold inside, and realised he had his terror, his panic, locked up in his chest. His true self and all the emotions it harboured was in a sealed box inside him and at some point he would have to unlock that box. It frightened him to think what might happen when he did, but for now, it stopped him falling to pieces. Did that make him a better soldier than Spencer? A worse human being? For all the atrocities he'd seen, all the wounds and trauma he'd become accustomed to, surely this day's experiences should break him. He had no wife or kids like Spencer to yearn for. But the sergeant did and he was holding it together too. Maybe Spencer had just lost control of his locked box for now.

Coulthard pushed the man away. "Right. Now on your feet, son. Feel better."

"Sorry, Sarge, I just…"

"Fuck sorry, Spencer, it's all done. You ready to move out?"

"Yes, Sarge." Spencer's voice still quavered, but there was some confidence back in it.

IN VAULTED HALLS ENTOMBED

"Brown?"

The medic nodded, shook himself. "Yes, Sarge." *At least*, he thought, *as ready as I possibly can be.*

Coulthard sniffed and settled his pack. "Well, I am certainly not going back the way we came. That thing in the tunnel, whatever it is, seems to want to stay there, so we'll leave it well alone. There must be another way out. Nothing that size," he pointed at the monumental structure filling the cave, "can possibly only have one tiny tunnel leading in. Let's go."

"Sarge," Brown said, finally ready to give voice to a nagging worry that had tickled his hindbrain since they had emerged onto the rocky ledge.

"What?"

"The thing in the tunnel hasn't followed us out. Maybe you're right and it's too bright in here."

"Yeah. And?"

"Well, if it's meant to guard this place, but hasn't followed us out, that must mean something."

The Sergeant narrowed his eyes. "Like maybe there's something else in here to do the same job and that thing only worries about its tunnel?"

"Something like that."

"You have a point. Better keep your weapon ready. Let's go."

They moved along the ledge, heading for the giant stairway the insurgents had used. Brown whistled softly as they came abreast of a massive bronze plate pressed into the wall, ten metres high and five wide, inscribed with strange cursive symbols and patterns that made him dizzy to look upon. His eyes kept sliding away as he tried to make sense of them and nausea began to stir his guts.

"Over there," Spencer said. "And there."

They followed his pointing finger and saw other plaques on other ledges dotted around the cave. Small tunnel openings here and there accompanied them just like the one they had entered through.

"Any of those tunnels could have a fucking monster like the one that attacked us," Brown said.

"We have to assume each one does," Coulthard said. "We have to keep looking for something else. Move on."

Another twenty metres along their ledge gave them a vantage point past the monumental structure and they all saw it at once. On the far side of the vast cave, at the top of another giant staircase that went even higher than where they currently stood, a huge tunnel mouth yawned.

"That must be fifty metres wide," Coulthard said. "We have a fighting chance in a space like that."

"Probably where the insurgents were heading too," Brown said. "Means going through that structure though."

"Or around it on ground level."

A scream ripped through the air. High pitched and horrified, it was the voice of a man staring into hideous death and it cut suddenly short.

"Came from down there." Spencer pointed down the stairway they had nearly reached, where the insurgents had died under Coulthard's fire.

"Seems like old Shoulder Wound survived after all," the sergeant said.

"Until just then." Brown felt the lock on the box in his chest loosening.

"All right. Silence." Coulthard raised his weapon and headed for the stairs. "We have no choice but to go through, so let's *fight* our way through."

He moved to the first stair and jumped down. The riser was a few inches above his head, but he walked forward and jumped down the next. Brown and Spencer followed.

Brown's knees jarred with every drop and he wondered how long they would hold out. How long could any of them last with this kind of exertion? The insurgents were about two thirds of the way down and had looked spent, sliding off each step, staggering around.

And assuming they made it down, they would have to climb up even more stairs to get to the wide tunnel they had seen. And all the while fighting past whatever had triggered that scream. Basic training or advanced combatives, nothing prepared a

IN VAULTED HALLS ENTOMBED

soldier for this. Ready for anything? No one had ever listed this place under the heading of 'anything'.

His lock loosened a little more, so Brown stopped thinking and kept moving.

He stopped counting the drops at fifty, but after a few more Coulthard paused and raised one fist. They froze, crouched in readiness. Coulthard tapped his ear. Straining to listen, Brown heard a scratching, scrabbling noise. Distant, but getting quickly nearer. Coulthard crept to the edge of the step they were on to look down and immediately burst into action. He raked his assault rifle left to right, the reports of his short bursts shattering the quiet and bouncing back from the distant walls all around. Brown and Spencer joined him at the edge. Spencer added his ordnance to Coulthard's straight away, but Brown paused momentarily, stunned.

A flood of creatures flowed up the steps towards them like roiling black water. Only twenty or so steps below and fast getting closer, they scrambled on too many legs, black bodies like scorpions, but where the stinger should be on the end of the waving tails was a leering face, almost human though twisted somehow into something hideously uncanny, eyes too wide, mouths too deep. Those mouths stretched silently open or gaped like fish as the creatures chittered over the stone edges. Each was a metre or more long, two vicious mandibles at the front of the thorax snapping at the air as they came.

Brown brought his weapon up and added his fire to the fray. Their bullets tore into the things, shattering hard shells and causing gouts of glowing blue blood. As one fell, its fellows swarmed over it. Some staggered from shots striking their many limbs and fell from the sides of the staircase. Brown realised the things were screaming, in fear or pain or triumph he didn't know, but they had no voice and just hissed thick streams of air from those stretched and awful faces that wavered atop their segmented tails as they ran.

There was no way Brown and his colleagues would be able to scramble up the stairs ahead of these horrors, so here they had to make their stand. Coulthard plucked a grenade from his belt and lobbed it past the first wave. It detonated in a cloud of shining black carapaces and stone chunks. Spencer emptied his clip and expertly switched in a new one. He resumed firing as Brown switched in new ammo. Coulthard threw two more grenades and switched clips to resume firing. Brown threw a grenade of his own and switched in his last clip. Their automatic fire stuttered and roared, controlled bursts as training took over.

The creatures were only five steps away, then four, and ammo was running out. Brown, Spencer and Coulthard yelled incoherent defiance and raked fire across their advance. Spencer lobbed a grenade then the things were too close for any more explosives.

Three steps and their numbers finally began to thin, two steps, almost close enough to touch.

Suddenly the men were stumbling left and right, firing in short bursts as the last of the things breached their step and tried to clamber onto them, heavy, sharp mandibles snapping rapidly for limbs. Spencer screamed as one drew close, his weapon clicking absurdly loudly, empty. Brown fired three short bursts and then there were no more creatures coming. Coulthard blew two away right at his feet, turned and killed the last one right before it leapt onto Spencer.

Everything was suddenly still; their ears rang.

Dave Spencer looked up at his sergeant with a smile of relief just as Brown raised one hand and shouted, "Stop!"

But Spencer finished taking a step away from the corpse at his feet and his foot vanished over the edge of the stairway. As his face opened into an O of utter surprise, he dropped from sight.

Brown and Coulthard rushed to the edge, but Spencer was lost in shadow. He found his voice a second later, his howl drifting up before cutting off with a wet thud. Silence descended heavily throughout the enormous cavern.

Brown, on his hands and knees, began to tremble uncontrollably. "So much for his psychic fucking wife," he muttered.

Coulthard was beside him, breathing heavily from exertion, as Brown was, but there was anger in the sergeant's demean-

IN VAULTED HALLS ENTOMBED

our too. "Took the fucking radio with him," Coulthard said eventually.

He stood and yelled and screamed, kicked at the corpses of the horrible scorpion monsters all around. Brown turned to sit and watch, glad in a way that the man was finally letting some emotion out. Like a pressure cooker, he had surely been close to blowing for a long time.

Eventually the sergeant slumped back against the step above and slid down to sit. "So all we have is what we're carrying and no comms."

Brown nodded. "I've got what's left in here," he hefted his weapon, "and that's it. You?"

"Same."

"I still have two grenades."

"I got none. But we each have pistols," Coulthard said.

"Might save that for myself," Brown said quietly, and he meant it. At some point, sticking the barrel of the .45 against his temple and pulling the trigger seemed like a good option. He looked at the chitinous corpses all around. "Think we got them all?"

"Hope so. These ancient fuckers were no match for the tools of modern warfare."

"Tools which will be empty very soon if we need to use them again."

Coulthard just nodded, staring at the ground between his feet. Eventually he sniffed decisively, stood. "Right, let's go."

Brown looked up at him, stark against the backdrop of shadowy mist and the wan blue glow of the lichen. "Yeah. Okay."

They began to drop down the steps again, picking their way through the broken bodies, blue blood and shattered rock of their battle. In places, their grenades had sheered the steps into gravel slides they carefully surfed on their butts. Here and there some of the creatures still twitched, but they avoided them and preserved their ammo. After a dozen or so stairs the corpses ended. Another couple and they came across red smears on the stones and a few lumps of flesh and ragged clothing.

"A lot of blood," Brown noted. "Those things clearly enjoyed the dead as well as the one who survived. I sure hope that was all of them we killed."

Coulthard nodded and continued down in silence. Eventually, gasping, with legs like jelly and bruised feet, they reached the bottom to stand in swirls of mist.

A low moan rose, vibrating the air all around them. The stone floor thrummed. Then it faded away. As Brown and Coulthard turned to look at each other, it rose again, louder, stronger. Then again. And again. Each time, it vibrated more deeply, sounding more strained and desperate, accompanied by a heavy metallic clattering. Then silence fell and pressed in on them for a long time.

Eventually Brown said, "What the fuck was that?"

Coulthard looked towards the tall structure in the centre of the cave. From ground level it punched up high above them, wreathed in tendrils of blue-tinged mist. Brown began to dizzy as he stared up at it. The smaller towers surrounding the base, connected with curving buttresses, were each some thirty-metres high. In the base of each smaller tower was a hollowed-out circular space and in that space sat a statue. From the few he could see, Brown realised that each statue was turned to face the centre tower. They were almost human-like in form, seated cross-legged, but each had four arms with eight-fingered hands, held out to either side as though awaiting an embrace. Their bellies were distended and rolled with fat, their faces wide with four eyes – two above two. Brown moved to better examine the nearest one and the level of detail was phenomenal, disturbing. Not so much carved, as real living things turned instantly to stone. He wondered if in fact that's exactly what they were. Each was at least three metres tall and corpulent.

Coulthard's gaze was still fixed on the main tower. Brown moved to stand beside him and realised he was looking at a doorway, a dark opening in the rock wall several metres high and a couple wide. "The moaning came from inside, don't you think?" the sergeant asked.

"Who cares?" Brown said, stunned.

"I have to know." Coulthard walked towards the door.

IN VAULTED HALLS ENTOMBED

"Sarge? Seriously, let's just go. What if more of those..." Brown's voice trailed off as Coulthard approached the opening.

Soft blue light pulsed from inside as the sergeant drew near. The moan rose again, shaking everything. Brown put a hand to his chest as the deep moan sounded a second time and made his heart stutter. His feet were frozen to the spot as he watched Coulthard step through the high entrance.

The sergeant stopped just inside and his gaze rose slowly upwards. He was framed in the blue light that pulsed more and more rapidly. The groaning became a wail and Coulthard's weapon dropped from lax fingers to hang by its shoulder strap. "Chains," Coulthard stammered. He looked left and right, up and down, his sight exploring a vast area. "Giant chains right through its flesh. Through all those eyes!" He dropped to his knees, head tilted back as he looked far above himself. "This is a prison. An eternal prison!" He began to laugh, a high, broken sound that came from the root of no sound mind.

The moan stirred into a deep, encompassing voice that reverberated through the cavern. "*Release me!*"

Chains rang as they were snapped taut and relaxed again. Whatever slumbering monstrosity that filled the tower and split the edges of Coulthard's mind thrashed and its voice boomed again. "*RELEASE ME!*"

"Sarge!" Brown yelled, his stomach curdled with terror. "We have to go!"

He wanted to drag his sergeant away, but had no desire to risk seeing what the man saw. "*Sarge!*" he screamed.

Coulthard's face tipped slightly towards him and Brown took in the sagging cheeks, drooling mouth, wild, glassy eyes, and knew that Coulthard was lost. No humanity remained in that shell of a body. With a sob, Brown ran.

He raced around the tower and leaped for the first step of the stairway on the far side. He hauled himself up as the voice burst out, over and over, "*Release me! Release me! Release me!*"

Brown scrambled up stair after stair, rubbing his hands raw on the rough surface. He sobbed and gasped, his shoulder and back muscles burned, but he hauled on and on. He couldn't shake the image of all those swarming scorpion things from his mind and imagined them racing up behind him, but didn't dare to look. The voice of whatever was imprisoned below cried out again and again.

At some point, more than fifty steps up, Brown collapsed, exhausted, and blackness took over. He assumed he was dying and let himself go.

He had no idea how much time had passed when he woke again, unmolested. The massive cavern was still.

Brown dragged himself to his feet and began the shattering climb once more, step after step after step. Time blurred, his mind was an empty darkness, until he pulled himself over the top of one more step and saw a flat expanse of rock stretching out before him. On the far side, some hundred metres away, the huge yawning tunnel stood, threatening to suck him in.

Brown laughed, dangerously close to hysterical, and gained his feet, stumbled forward into the gloom. He didn't care what might be there, he just needed to leave the hideous monument and its prisoner behind.

More of the softly glowing lichen striated the walls and he dropped his night vision goggles into place. The sight before him stopped him dead, confused. A grid, some kind of lattice. He looked up and down as realisation dawned. A giant portcullis-like gate filled the tunnel, thirty metres high, fifty metres across, fixed deeply into the rock. He walked up to it and found it made of cast metal like the huge plaques they had seen, the criss-crossed straps of bronze at least twenty centimetres thick. Each square hole of the lattice was perhaps half a metre or a little more across. If he stripped off his gear, he might be able to squeeze through. Or he might very well get stuck halfway.

But it didn't matter. Beyond the gate, beyond the weak glow of the cavern behind him, uncountable numbers of clear, globular shapes moved and writhed, tentacles gently questing out and retracting again, waiting, hungry. Hundreds of them.

Brown fell to his butt and sat laughing softly. He checked his rations and canteen, tried to estimate how long he might survive, and gave up when his brain refused to cooperate. He looked

IN VAULTED HALLS ENTOMBED

back across towards the tunnel from which they had emerged. Compared to the swarm waiting beyond the gate, the one or two in that tunnel seemed like far better odds. Assuming it was only one or two. And assuming he had the strength to get back down and up again. And that there were no more guardians waiting for him in the cavern. And that whatever was imprisoned below didn't thrash free in its rage.

Lance Corporal Paul Brown, experienced medic and decorated solider, lay down and pulled his knees up to his chest. His brain couldn't work out what to do, so perhaps he would just have a sleep and, refreshed, maybe then decide which suicidal option for escape might be the best one to try.

* * *

SPECIAL COMMUNIQUE

ATTN: COLONEL ADAM LEONARD – DIRECTOR, UNEXPLAINED OCCURRENCE DIVISION.
YOUR EYES ONLY
SUBJECT – DISAPPEARANCE OF EPSILON TEAM, NORTH OF KANDAHAR, AFTER TRACKING ENEMY INSURGENTS TO UNDERGROUND HIDEOUT.
SURVIVORS – 1: LANCE CORPORAL PAUL BROWN, MEDIC.

REPORT: *After non-response from Epsilon Team for thirty six (36) hours after their last communique, a second squad was sent to investigate. They found Lance Corporal Paul Brown of Epsilon stumbling through foothills some seven (7) kilometres south of Epsilon Team's last known whereabouts. Brown was wearing nothing but ragged underwear and his helmet, raving and largely incoherent, his left arm below the elbow was just bone, no hand, the flesh stripped away presumably by acid or a similar agent. His body was covered in various other wounds, some similar to his arm (though none as severe) and others clearly made from impacts, falls, scrapes, etc. He carried no gear except a flashlight, which he pointedly refused to relinquish.*

SNAFU: SURVIVAL OF THE FITTEST

He made almost no sense except one phrase, repeated over and over: "Never let it out! Never let it out!" Current assessment by psychologists suggests Brown may never recover his faculties, but therapy has been started. His extensive injuries are being treated and are responding satisfactorily.

We're still trying to establish further facts but are preparing an incursion squad to Epsilon's last known whereabouts. Due to your standing request to be informed of any unusual occurrences, I am sending this wire. Our squad will be entering the cave at the last known location of Epsilon Team at 0800 tomorrow, the 14th, should you wish to accompany them.

Please advise.

END

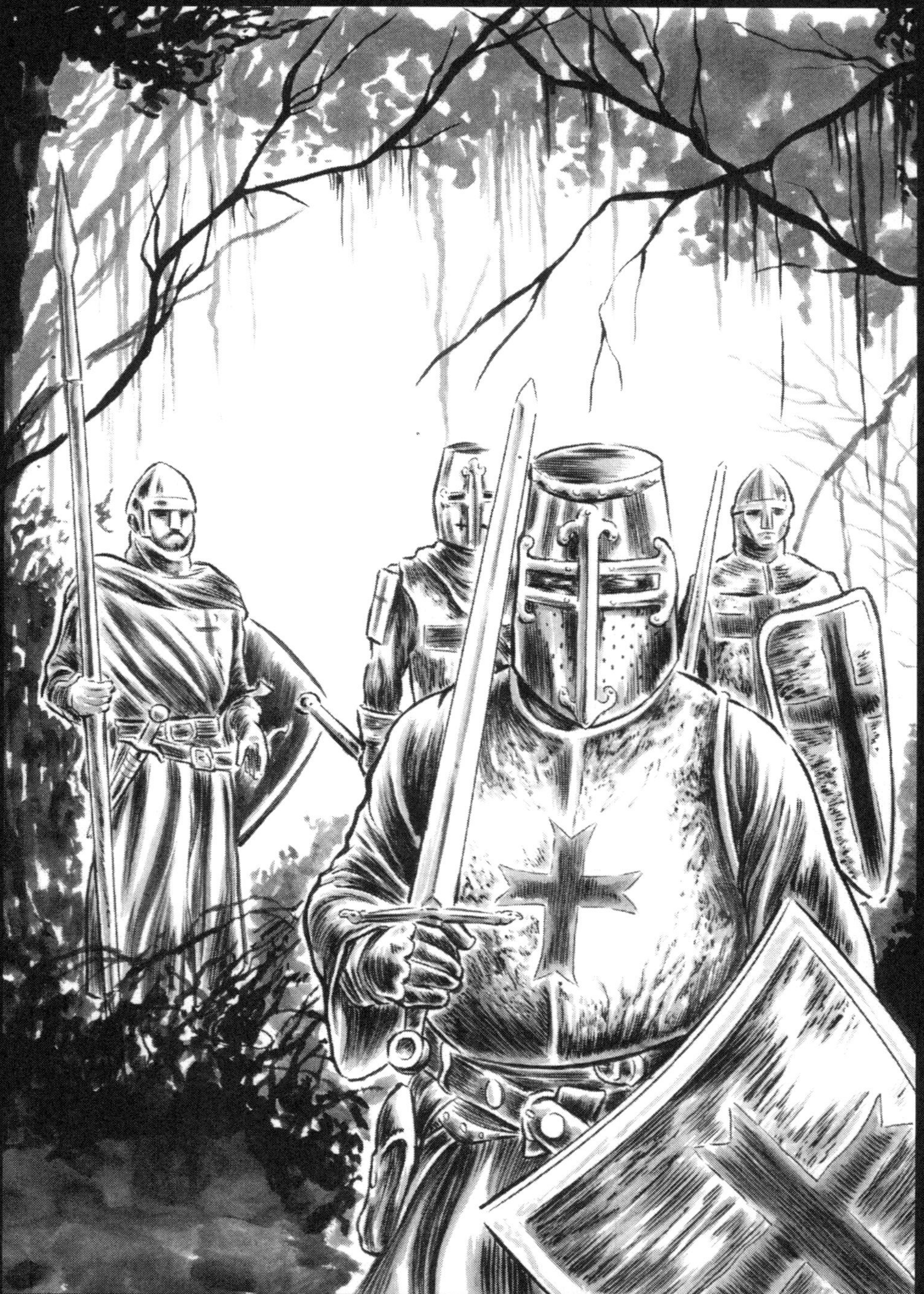

THEY OWN THE NIGHT

B. Michael Radburn

"It is only the dead who have seen the end of war"
Plato

PART ONE

The jungle has a presence. Sergeant Carl Fisher sensed it on his first tour of Vietnam two years ago. Now, nearing the end of his second tour in-country, he knew the jungle more intimately than anything back home in the States. It was a living thing, dark and secretive, a sprawling mass of ancient deep-rooted life. It can either protect, or kill, without prejudice. And it can hide things... for centuries.

It says a lot about a man who finds more meaning to life during war, than back home in downtown New Orleans. For a Southern black man, army life can be a whole lot easier than tending bar in the Blues quarter for minimum pay plus tips. Back home Fisher was nothing. A shadow; a noise; a memory. But here he was something; here he was Troop Sergeant of an armoured reconnaissance squadron, the thinking man's armour, the spearhead of the main battle tanks and self-propelled artillery units of the 1st Cavalry Regiment. Travel by night and spy by day. *Panther Troop. First in, last out.* Yeah, life here was easy once you learnt to respect the one fundamental rule.

We own the day, but Charlie owns the night.

Fisher stood in the open turret of his M113 armoured personnel carrier, his arms resting casually on the hatch rim. The APC's metal felt cool on his exposed arms; he preferred the enclosed T-50 turret to the open A-cav. 50 cal. Mount – too open to Charlie's AKs. The five-vehicle troop stood line-ahead along the deep rutted road beneath the jungle canopy, their engines idling as a calming white-noise filled Fisher's head-set.

SNAFU: SURVIVAL OF THE FITTEST

Although the jungle limited horizons, Fisher could feel the storm building somewhere ahead of them, rolling closer on footfalls of thunder through the mountains. He closed his eyes and faced its approach, his skin bristling with electricity as the sky gradually darkened. Fisher reluctantly opened his eyes again, ever aware of the suffocating jungle surrounding them, praying it would be kind to them on this bullshit mission just a day before Christmas.

"Special ops my ass," he whispered, spitting over the side as he awaited orders on the troop's next bound. He spat again, aware the taste in his mouth would never go away. It was the taste of this country, this war.

Fisher swung the turret around to see what was happening at the Lieutenant's vehicle. The LT sat on the rim of his own turret hatch, going over a map with that CIA spook, Green. *What sort of bullshit name is Sherwood Green anyway?* Fisher wiped beads of perspiration from his face with the already saturated towel around his neck.

It seemed the only swinging dick in the unit who knew where they were going and why was Green himself, drip-feeding information in short bounds. All Fisher knew for sure was that they were bombed-up to the max with ammunition, which meant there was every chance of trouble ahead. In fact Panther Troop was the vanguard for a full regiment of main battle tanks shadowing them just five miles to the rear. That much muscle this far north could only mean a world of hurt for someone. Even though mission specs were minimal, Fisher nevertheless knew how to read a map, realising being this close to the Demilitarised Zone meant breaching a dozen different conventions before so much as even firing a shot.

Fisher noticed Green fold up his map and jump down from the vehicle. He also noticed the pained look on the LT's face.

Keying the internal comms, Fisher said simply, "Heads-up boys, the spook's heading this way. Looks like we've got our orders."

"Hope he ain't planning to ride with us," said Pete Jenkins from the driver's compartment up front. "I'm not in the mood for some office jockey on board."

THEY OWN THE NIGHT

"Keep it to yourself, Trooper Jenkins," replied Fisher. "I don't care whether you respect the man, but I'll kick your ass all the way to Hanoi Jane's hut if you don't respect his rank."

"Sorry, Sergeant," Jenkins offered. "It's just that it's Christmas Eve, man. Who the fuck pulls a mission on Christmas Eve?"

"Put a sock in it, Jenkins," cut in Corporal Nathan Fry from the crew compartment below. Fry was effectively the vehicle's 2-I-C, managing the radios and Troop logistics. "I'm sure Santa will find us way out here."

Agent Green climbed up the front of Fisher's vehicle and crouched beside the turret. "I'm riding with you, Sergeant."

"It's an honour to have you aboard, sir."

"This is the last bound before our objective," he said placing his map in front of Fisher and pointing to a ridgeline eight miles ahead. "Your vehicle will lead the troop in a line-ahead formation until we hit this stream." He tapped the junction on the map with his finger. "We then follow the creek upstream through the low country until this clearing just short of the ridge where we can spread out into an arrowhead formation. You got it?"

Fisher took up his own map and drew a line along the route in pencil. "Got it," he confirmed.

"This last bound is under strict radio silence. If anyone so much as keys a handset on our frequency, I'll have them severely punished."

"I understand, sir," said Fisher, wondering what possible punishment would be worse than spending Christmas Eve in deep-J this far up Charlie's ass. He yelled down at Fry in the belly of the vehicle. "Corporal, open the cargo hatch and let our guest on board."

As the hatch swung open by Green's feet, Fisher offered his thoughts. "Sir, I believe this storm is gonna hit hard. We may need the radios to keep the troop together."

Green leered. "What part of *radio fucking silence* don't you understand, Sergeant?" He circled his arm in the air to indicate they were moving out, and each vehicle responded with a rev of their engines. "If the troop breaks up for any reason, we rendezvous at the objective's grid reference at 2200."

105

"Got it," replied Fisher, slipping his headsets back over his ears and keying the intercom as Green jumped down beside Fry in the cargo bay. "Let's roll, Jenkins," he said. "Follow this track in a line-ahead formation. We have the honour of riding point, followed by 1-2, 1-2-Bravo and 1-2-Charlie."

The vehicle lurched forward, tracks protesting until finding traction in the soft earth. The troop pushed forward, ever aware of the dying light; ever aware of the approaching storm. *Charlie owns the night*, Fisher reminded himself, glancing over his shoulder from time to time to check the LT's position in the convoy. He also checked on Green below. Constantly studying the map and his watch, Green finally keyed his intercom as the first few drops of rain hit the vehicle's armour.

"As soon as the daylight's gone, Fisher, we go to infrared. No white light."

"I figure that's about the same time this storm's gonna hit, sir. Unfortunately the IR doesn't cut through rain."

Green sighed. "It is what it is, Sergeant. IR or no IR, you get this troop to the objective by 2200 tonight."

"Will do, sir. But for the record, don't you think it's about time the crew knew what we're doing this far north? I mean, we're carrying enough ammo to take down a small city, so it's more than just a taxi service. We're just an hour or so from the RV and we still don't have any final orders."

Green sighed again, and Fisher thought he was in for a mouthful of abuse. But he was wrong.

"Okay," Green said with a little reluctance. "Your LT's got the full mission orders now, and the Delta Team travelling with Tail End Charlie has been briefed since the mission's launch point. We're bombed up because frankly we don't know what to expect, so we've prepared for anything."

"That's encouraging."

"Yeah, well, our intelligence advises that a regiment of North Vietnam Regulars are also pushing towards our objective from Hanoi."

"That explains why it's so time-critical," said Fisher. "But what exactly are we in this race for? What's the prize?"

"Okay, Fisher, I don't care how open-minded you are, so just take what I'm about to say as gospel; as the culmination of five years intelligence and well-founded ground work. Men have died getting this information to the Pentagon, and if the information is true, then we may all be about to enter the history books."

Fisher looked the CIA man in the eyes, realising suddenly just how high on Washington's agenda this mission was. He nodded his agreement just as the cool air ahead of the storm-front squeezed through the jungle in a bluster.

"There's an eight-hundred-year-old temple just inside the southern boundary of the demilitarised zone. And if intelligence is correct, this temple houses something that could not only change the course of this war, but ensure victory of any future war the United States may find itself in." Green took a moment, realising the light rain on his face was gradually getting heavier. "This temple is the source of a subterranean spring that is said to only run for the course of twenty-four hours once a year."

"Don't tell me," said Fisher, squinting against the driving rain. "Christmas day, right."

"Yeah," said Green. "Christmas day."

"So what has an eight-hundred-year-old Buddhist temple got to do with Christ's birthday?"

"The temple isn't Buddhist," Green said. "It's Roman Catholic."

"Catholic?"

"Yeah. We believe it's one of the furthest outposts of the 4th Crusade, where newly discovered Vatican documents suggest the Crusaders discovered a spring that only flows on the anniversary of Christ's birth. So now you see the absolute urgency behind this mission. It's said this spring will bestow immortality and unearthly strength to whoever drinks the water, and was said to have been used to make a super army that devastated all before it in this region. The site was promptly made sacred and secret, the Holy Roman Empire building a fortress-like temple around it in 1204."

"Don't tell me we're here to take on an army of eight-hundred-year-old Crusaders?'

Green obviously didn't appreciate Fisher's cynicism. "They call them the Guardians," he answered stony faced. "And like I said, we don't know what to expect, so we've prepared for the worst."

Fisher simply nodded his understanding then keyed off the intercom, muttering to himself, "Great. We're about to fight Charlie *and* the Vatican for the fountain of fucking youth."

* * *

"Darkness cannot drive out darkness"
Martin Luther King, Jr.

PART TWO

It sounded like a charging bull through the foliage. Even over the engine's reverberation and the constant hiss of the headsets, Fisher could hear the force of the rain-front rolling in, clawing at the jungle's face like a thrashing beast, roaring until it hit in a torrent.

Fisher lowered his seat as he keyed the intercom. "Close down, driver. You too, Fry." Fisher reached up and closed his own turret hatch, water dripping from the seals until he fastened the combat lock. "How's your visibility up front, Jenkins?"

"Near enough to zero, Sarge."

"Push-on, Sergeant!" Green's voice was distinctive over the intercom.

"What can you see?" Fisher asked his driver.

"Fuck-all, Sarge. I've got a white-out in front... The same over my right shoulder... And a whole lot of jungle slapping at my left periscope."

"Maintain that position," Fisher said, "and keep the speed steady. I've got slightly better visibility from up here, but it's marginal. If you keep the foliage against our left hull it stands to reason we should still be on the road." Fisher squinted against the forward turret window, constantly wiping condensation from the inside glass. "At this speed the jungle should make way for a clearing in about an hour or so. There we'll steer left until we find that creek line."

THEY OWN THE NIGHT

"Roger that, Sarge."

"With a little luck this storm will pass over in no time."

But it didn't. The hour passed as darkness took hold, the only images outside captured as silhouettes against each lightning strike. That's when the imagination turned on a man. That's when you saw Charlie crouching in every shadow. *We own the day...* That's when the promise of daylight was the only thing that made the night remotely bearable. *They own the night.* The hour quickly turned to two, then three, as they eventually stumbled across the now swollen creek and headed due north towards the cathedral site.

"Mr. Green?" Fisher said over the intercom. "Sir, I lost visual of the troop two hours ago, and strongly suggest we break radio silence momentarily to re-group."

"No," came Green's stern reply. "I can't risk the NVA intercepting our radio chatter, so we push on."

"But, sir, the troop could be scattered all over this fucking grid. I believe we'd be stronger arriving in force and with some semblance of organisation."

"Everyone knows their orders, Sergeant. If separated, meet at the RV at 2200. That's just ten min—"

The vehicle collided with something outside, throwing Fisher against the .50 calibre machine gun's breach and cutting his cheek. The engine revved in a violent burst as Jenkins's weight fell against the accelerator with the impact before stalling. The interior lights flickered before going out as the headsets dwindled to total silence. There was only the sound of the torrential rain on the hull until Fisher eventually broke the silence.

"Everyone okay?" he called, wiping the blood from his cheek.

"Yeah," came Jenkins's laboured voice.

"A little shook up," called Fry, "but I'll live."

"You okay back there, Mr Green?"

"What the fuck happened, Fisher? Where's the fucking lights?"

"I'd say we've knocked a battery terminal off on impact, sir. Should be an easy fix."

"Hey, Sarge?" Jenkins broke in. "You might want to see this."
Fisher straightened. "What is it?"
"I can't make out what we hit, but I think I see something moving out there. You might be better placed to see from the turret."

Fisher braced himself against the .50's breach, straining to see through the sheets of rain outside. A lightning flash briefly revealed an open landscape scattered with familiar shapes, but the multiple silhouettes also triggered a sense of denial. *"What the fuck?"* he muttered under his breath. Just then, something slapped against the turret's forward window and Fisher instinctively pushed himself away from the glass with a startled gasp. He wrenched the cocking handle back on the .50 calibre and unlocked the turret rim, his thumbs held firmly against the rear trigger as he manually traversed the turret full-circle to scan the terrain outside.

Finally, with the gun facing forward again, Fisher paused, each heartbeat resonating in his ears. Unblinking, he waited for that next flash of lightning to illuminate the land outside. Breath held trembling in his lungs, he paused to confirm the image he thought he saw earlier. Fresh forks of lightning streaked across the sky to strike the ground beyond the surrounding tree line, briefly illuminating the scattered APCs in the clearing around them, their turrets pointing in all directions, gun barrels spent and motionless. As brief as the lightshow was, there was no mistaking the remaining troop vehicles outside – immobile, strewn in every direction, and not a sign of life.

"Green," he called below. "We've got a problem."
"What is it?"
"Looks like the rest of the troop made the rendezvous point ahead of us, sir."
"How's that a problem?"
"I don't know that they're in any shape to go on from here."
"What the—"
Then the rain stopped.

It didn't peter out gradually, but rather ceased in a heartbeat, the sudden silence becoming quickly unnerving until the sound of footsteps on the hull outside caught Fisher's attention.

THEY OWN THE NIGHT

"Fuck," he spat at a whisper, staring up at the inch and a half of metal over his head.

"There's someone out there," said Green, crouching at the base of the turret space.

"Maybe it's one of our boys," said Jenkins from the driver's seat.

"No one opens a hatch until we can confirm who's who, okay?" Fisher was adamant. He considered their situation for a moment before continuing, "Jenkins, we need power back ASAP. You can access the engine's battery from the panel over your right shoulder. Reach in and check the terminals. If they've come away from the battery then hook us up again. If not, check the fuses."

"I'm on it, Sarge."

The footsteps, heavy and purposeful, continued above them.

"Fry," he said at a whisper. "Now that the rain's stopped I need you to set up the infrared imaging so I can see what we're dealing with out there before we decide on our next move."

"I'm afraid our *next move* is set in stone, Sergeant Fisher," said Green in a firm, don't-fuck-with-me voice. "Our *next move* is to secure that cathedral ahead of the NVA."

"Not until we know what we're dealing with, Mr Green! Not until I know who or *what* the fuck that is creeping around on my vehicle! Not until I know how many of our men are alive out there! We're a long way from home, Mr Green, and fountain of fucking youth or no fountain of fucking youth, me and my boys are your only way in or out of this shit fight right now, you got it?"

With a brief flash of sparks from the driver's compartment and an instinctive, "*Shiiit!*" from Jenkins, the lights came back up with a flicker. "We've got power back, Sarge."

Fisher took a deep breath, staring Green down in the process. "Let's just see what we're up against, shall we, Mr Green."

Whatever was moving around on the hull had paused a moment before trying the combat latch on Fisher's turret hatch. Locked from within, it held fast, but somehow even the inch and a half of metal didn't seem like enough armour between Fisher and whatever lurked outside. He switched from white-light to red and peered out through the narrow port window where something was moving around just left of the gun.

"Everyone at their stations," he ordered. "I'm gonna fire a few warning rounds. Jenkins, switch to infrared just as soon as I cease fire so I can see what's going on out there." He grasped the dual handles of the gun and placed both thumbs firmly on the trigger ready to fire. "Here we go," he breathed, folding down the infrared screen in front of the forward window before firing.

The sound and reverberation of the gun bounced throughout the hull as a stream of hot cartridge cases clattered to the floor plate around Fisher's boots. After a short burst he peered out through the window in time to make out the figure of a man lumbering away towards the bordering tree line.

As the cordite haze lifted outside, the IR beams unveiled a scene of devastation. The troop APCs, glistening wet from the storm, were scattered all over the clearing, no reason to their positions, no defensive tactics evident at all. If this was an ambush, then it was swift and savage. Each vehicle's ramps and combat hatches remained wide open and exposed, their engines still idling, their crews strewn everywhere, bodies contorted and void of life. Fisher slowly traversed the turret to his left as the IR beam revealed the same scene all around. The bodies closest had no bullet holes or shrapnel damage, but rather deep cuts and gouges, a number of them decapitated.

"What do you see out there?" asked Green.

"They're all dead," Fisher said.

"NVA?"

"Maybe, but I can't see any unfriendlies dead *or* alive, just our boys. What's real strange is there doesn't appear to be any bullet wounds in the bodies or signs of anti-armour damage to the vehicles. Charlie doesn't normally leave this kind of signature."

"Montegnard?" questioned Green. "Maybe one of the tribes decided to turn on us."

"The Montegnard are mountain militia," Fisher reminded him. "And besides, we're too far north for them." Fisher sighed deeply, thinking about Green's story of 400-year-old crusaders. "So much for preparing for *anything*, Mr Green."

THEY OWN THE NIGHT

* * *

"Courage is fear holding on a minute longer"
General George S. Patton

PART THREE

Less than an hour shy of Christmas, the moon – near enough to full – had risen well above the tree line surrounding the clearing. It was a hunter's moon, high and bright, casting shadows and reflecting off the damp, rain-beaten surfaces.

Having moved the APC to a suitable exit point by the creek line, Green and Fisher made the call to push on by foot to the temple while Fry and Jenkins locked-down and secured the area for their return. This meant setting up ground radar, claymores on the perimeter and maintaining contact with the main battle tanks on route behind them. If Fisher and Green could determine the enemy's strength, then perhaps they could avoid a similar fate for the MBTs when they arrived.

A mere ten steps beyond the tree line and their APC was out of sight, the jungle enveloping them in a darkness broken only by the intermittent spears of moonlight piercing the canopy above. They trod softly, carefully, for Charlie owns the night. Charlie... or whatever the fuck had ambushed Panther Troop back there.

They stumbled across a well-used trail heading north-west and flanked it from the shadows keeping about 6-feet to the left in case of trip wires or traps of any kind. It was slow going, both men conscious of time passing with every heartbeat. Then, seeing the silhouette of a man on the trail ahead, Fisher stopped and went to ground, Green doing the same as the man crawled along beside him.

"What do you make of that?" whispered Fisher.

"Look at the helmet," said Green. "Looks like NVA to me."

"The gook's just standing there."

Fisher dug through his webbing for the binoculars, raising them to his eyes as he focused on the silhouette. "It's a North Vietnamese Reg all right. But he's not gonna be any trouble.' He passed the binoculars to Green as he stood.

"Dead?" asked Green as he peered through the glass. Then, in answering his own question. "Oh, yeah. He's dead."

They stepped carefully up to the body, the only thing keeping the morbid scarecrow upright being the spear plunged down through his skull and torso into the ground.

"Jesus-H-Christ! What kinda force does it take to do that to a man?" Fisher's eyes were fixed on the tortured death mask of the NVA officer before him. "This is my second tour here Mr Green, and I ain't never seen shit like this."

"The Guardians," said Green soberly. "It's got to be the Guardians. Crusaders sent here to—" Fisher placed the palm of his hand across Green's mouth, guiding him down to their knees just as the approaching sound of heavy footfalls commenced ahead. They backed away from the trail and into the jungle, low and silent, melding with the shadows. Breathlessly they waited and watched, the only living witnesses to the Guardians' existence.

Marching in two perfect columns along the narrow track, the hunters' moon broke through the jungle canopy enough to make out details of their sunken skeletal features, the flesh of their faces like dry parchment, their eyes pale, unblinking orbs beneath their helmets and chainmail. The Guardians' tattered tunics bore multiple stains, although the broad cross of St George was still discernable across their chest plates; their armour rusted and beaten after centuries of battle damage. The absolute precision to their marching was amazing, their heads held high and facing towards the fight; shields held close to their left shoulder; broadswords clasped in their right gauntlet with one intent. To kill.

Fisher waited until the column had passed before keying his radio handset. "1-2-Alpha, this is Sunray." He waited for a replay from the APC, Green and he just looking at each other in a mix of disbelief and wonder.

"This is 1-2-Alpha, Sunray," came Fry's voice. "Sarge, is that you?"

"Alpha, yeah, it's me. Prepare for company. You have a hundred plus heading your way."

THEY OWN THE NIGHT

"One hundred plus *what* are heading this way?"

"Guardians, Fry," said Fisher. "Green's story is true, every fucking word of it, and they'll be in your location any time now. If they break into the clearing take out the second line with Claymores, and pepper the first line with phosphorus grenades from the turret launchers."

"Got it, Sarge. Anything else?"

"Do we have an ETA on the tanks yet?"

"Thirty minutes or so, Sarge."

"Then you and Jenkins fight the good fight from inside that bucket of ours until the MBTs arrive, got it? If you exit that vehicle you won't stand a chance."

"Got it, Sarge. Good luck out there."

"Sunray out," Fisher said, trying to imagine what might be happening back at the vehicle. Like the single blimp appearing on the ground radar as the Guardians broke cover. As two blimps turn to four, then eight then sixteen while their numbers multiplied before their eyes.

"We need to move," said Green tapping his watch face.

"Yeah," said Fisher. "Can't miss Christ's birthday and all."

Passing the speared scarecrow, they made their way towards the cathedral site as the pop-pop-pop sound of claymore mines firing back at the clearing echoed through the undergrowth. The jungle trail progressively became strewn with the bloodied bodies of Vietnamese soldiers, cut to pieces and making the muddy trail blood-red underfoot. A little further on they heard the .50 calibre open fire back at the vehicle; and a little further again, they broke through the jungle to find themselves standing before the Guardian's fortress.

The building was magnificent, a medieval cathedral façade carved into the towering rock face before them. The centuries were evident, with tendrils of thick vines hanging down from their hosts above the cliff above, inching their way around the twin spires, strangling each gargoyle poised along the parapet. A wide cascade of stairs narrowed at the large arched doorway, many steps occupied by dead NVA soldiers, their blood still running in rivulets.

"It looks unguarded," whispered Green.

"I find that hard to believe," said Fisher scanning the open door and parapets above.

"Hard to believe or not, the clock's ticking, Fisher. We need to get in there. I need samples, proof, something to take back. Something to save this fucking mission."

"I'd be happy to save our asses right now, but I guess we're committed." Fisher took a deep breath. "Follow me, Mr Green. You cover the door and windows; I'll cover the positions up top. Let's go."

They walked slowly, making their way around the bodies on the staircase until they stood before the open door unchallenged. Stepping inside, they could barely make out the long corridor that led to a chamber carved into the stone ahead, the dim glow from a number of flaming torches their only light. They backed up to a wall each and made their way towards the chamber where they eventually saw what they had come for. A pool of crystal-clear water. Green checked his watch as midnight rolled in, the day of Christ's birth. For a brief moment he looked concerned – then it happened.

Just as it was written, the spring-fed water began cascading down from a small cavity in the wall behind it.

"Merry Christmas, Sergeant Fisher," said Green with a smile as he took the sample vials from his map pocket and stepped toward the spring. "The tanks are coming and there's my fountain… Mission saved," he said, just as an arrow pierced his throat. He dropped the vials, all smashing on the floor as he clutched at the embedded arrow.

Fisher opened fire with his M16, spraying sporadically, uncertain as from where the arrow had come. Still clutching desperately at his throat, Green eventually fell to the floor as a second arrow entered his back, life ebbing away until his eyes glassed over with his last rattled breath.

Then Fisher saw the lone Guardian, an archer crouching in the passageway, pulling back on his bow once more. Fisher opened up the M16 again, but it was too late. The arrow flew straight and true, piercing Fisher's shoulder with white-hot pain. He staggered back with the impact as the archer loaded yet another arrow, but not before emptying his last rounds into the creature. The Guardian's chainmail shattered in places with the bullets' impact, but with little effect to the ancient warrior. The creature's way was clear now as Fisher staggered back to the edge of the spring. He watched as the Guardian pulled back on its bow; watched as the arrow sliced the air and entered his chest, forcing him back into the cool water of the spring.

He lay motionless in the shallow water as he felt his life drain slowly from his body, the pain from the arrows numbing with every weakening heartbeat. He thought about New Orleans, about the people he cared for, about his men back at the clearing. But Fisher couldn't help them now, couldn't avenge the defeat of Panther Troop.

Or could he?

Then, knowing he had nothing to lose and everything to gain, Fisher opened his mouth and let the water enter his body.

Immediately he felt something surge through his being. More than a life force rushing his body, this was power, never-ending and all-consuming. The pain was gone, and with it, an overwhelming sense of revenge, of finishing the mission he was sent on. He had their sample now. Hell, he *was* their fucking sample!

Fisher stood, knee deep in the cool spring waters, fists clenched, eyes wide, as the ancient power filled his being. The Fisher of old was no longer. The poor black boy from New Orleans; tending smoky bars; eventually commanding a recon troop here in the Nam; all gone, replaced with a power and knowledge older than the pyramids. And now, there was only the mission left. He stared into the dark voids that were once the lone Guardian's eyes, sensing it knew the balance of power had just shifted. Fisher tore the two arrows from his body without effort, each wound closing without a scar. He stepped from the spring, the two arrows raised high as he marched towards the archer with brutal intent.

"Merry fucking Christmas," he said to the creature, knowing that he would tear its parchment body apart with nothing but the arrowheads and his bare hands. "You've grown weak, soldier."

SNAFU: SURVIVAL OF THE FITTEST

* * *

"In war, the victor writes the history"
Author unknown, American Civil War

EPILOGUE

Captain Mulgrave's tank was the first to break ground through to the clearing ahead of his troop. The M48 main battle tank powered across the creek line and halted ahead of the carnage before it, tracks ploughing into the soft earth, turret traversing left and right as Mulgrave scanned the area. Each MBT fell into position beside their troop leader, Cadillac Gage engines growling like the hunter killers they were, ready to strike. *But at what?*

Mulgrave's heart still pounded in his chest as he stared through the gun sight at Panther Troop's armoured personnel carriers scattered motionless across the clearing, the multitude of bodies strewn everywhere. His last radio contact with the remaining APC was thirty minutes ago, and as he listened to the ensuing battle it slowly became evident that the lone troopers had little to no chance after defending their vehicle to the last. The MBTs spared nothing to get to the rendezvous point, charging line-ahead like the modern cavalry they were towards the besieged Panther Troop. However, after the turmoil of battle, the last transmission became abruptly calm, as if the crew were suddenly resolved to their fate.

"We're done for, Captain," came Trooper Jenkins voice. "That's the last of the ammo and now they're all over us… forcing the hatches…" There was a spasm of static before the transmission was cut, but not before a curious final statement. "What the fuck," said Jenkins. "Out there… Who is that…?" Then nothing but dead air hissing in Mulgrave's headsets.

The jungle surrounding the clearing was eerily quiet and still when they arrived, as if pausing for breath. Mulgrave continued staring through his gun sight, everything clear beneath the bright hunter's moon.

"Jesus Christ," he whispered to himself. Reaching up, he

THEY OWN THE NIGHT

unlatched the combat lock of his turret hatch and opened up, standing in the hatch ring, witness to the carnage. The moonlight glistened off the tarnished surface of the mummified soldier's armour, their bodies torn apart, scattered among the dead of Panther Troop, their weapons and shields broken and discarded.

"Je-sus," he whispered again, ordering his gunner to switch on the searchlight.

The light beam fell on Sergeant Carl Fisher's vehicle, the image strangely bizarre and surreal. Clearly exhausted, Jenkins and Fry were slumped atop the stricken APC, their arms raised over their eyes against the tank's harsh searchlight. But Fisher, an upturned Guardian's helmet in one hand, clear water lapping the rim from time to time, and a broadsword clasped tightly in his other hand, stared directly into the light without blinking. The mummified bodies of the forgotten crusaders were piled all around the vehicle, pyramiding to where Fisher stood victorious atop his vehicle.

"You're a little late," cried Fisher. He raised the helmet full of spring water above his head. "I have our sample," he said. He then brandished the sword over the killing ground surrounding him before pulling the handle back to his chest in a bizarre salute. "And so much more, Captain," he added.

As Mulgrave searched for words, each of the other tank commanders surfaced from behind their armour, their bleak expressions mirrors to the battlefield's bloodshed.

"How?" It was all Mulgrave could utter.

Fisher just smiled. "Eight-hundred years can take a lot out of a soldier," he said. "They'd grown slow, and in the end, weary." Fisher raised the sword over his head and roared, the sound echoing through the jungle. It was part challenge; part warning. *"WE OWN THE NIGHT!"*

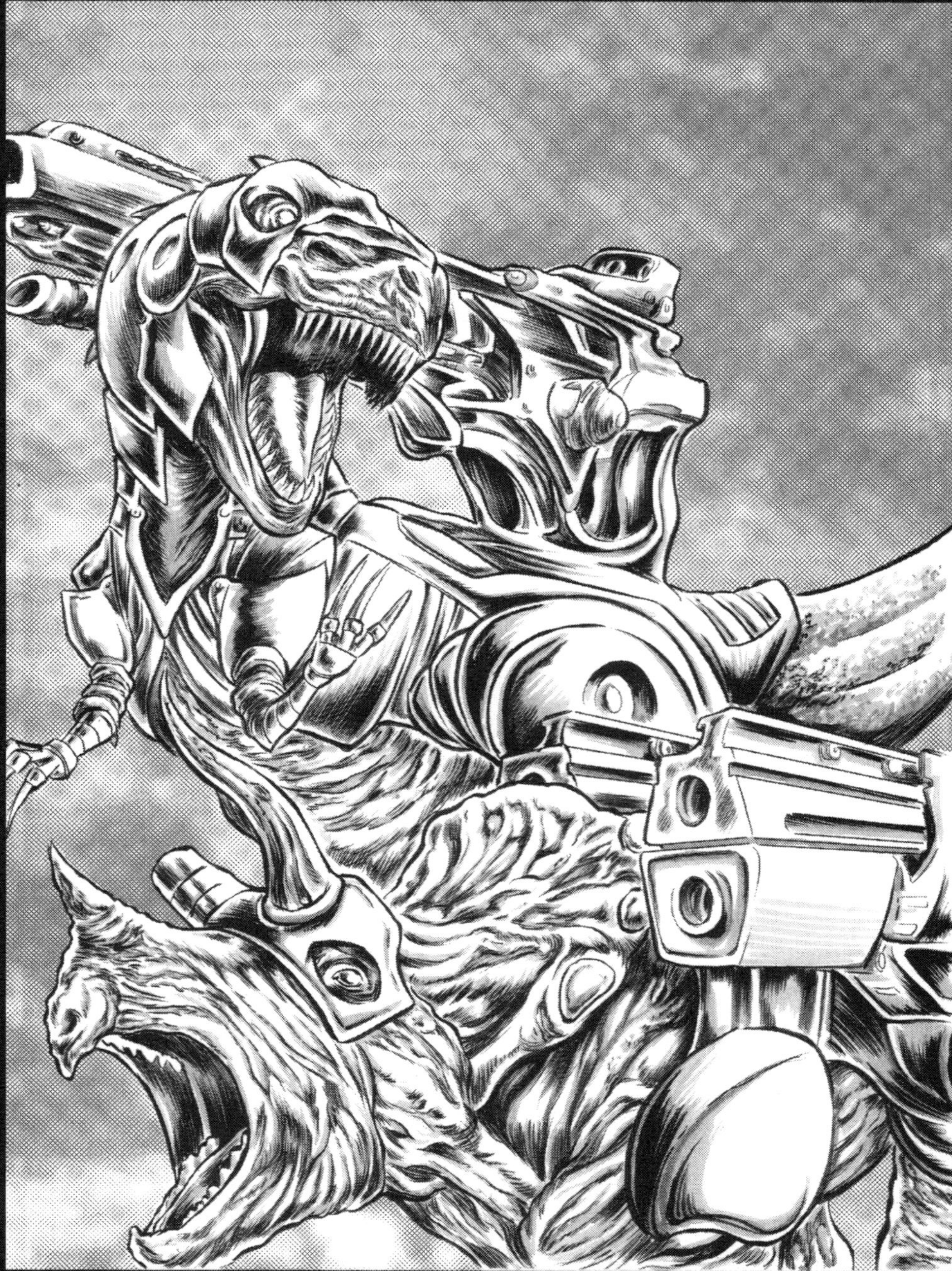

FALLEN LION

Jack Hanson

"I only recognized the solitude I lived in when I saw it in another. I only knew what 'to thine own self be true' meant when I saw it exemplified by this same Old Blood."
Marshal Ripper, By Fang and Rifle: A Memoir

The Lancer snorted and ran his claws along the composite decking under his feet, his annoyance getting a hold on him for a second. The smell of coppery blood was bothering him, made worse by the humidity in the air that was conditioned to Old Blood and Illurian preferences. Yet to the Triceratops known as Brokehorn, it only made the smell more cloying and aggravating.

If the *dhimion* leading the briefing had not been someone Brokehorn respected, he might have said something to the Bladejaw standing next to him in regard to the Tyrannosaurus' hygiene. It would, however, be poor precedent for the human janissaries standing in front of them at parade rest, sweat running down the backs of their necks into their gray battle armor. Brokehorn held his tongue.

The commander of the strike force told the troops about the planetary insertion to stop the Peace Federation raiders and rescue what civilians they could on the human colony of Libra III. The high-arching ceiling of the bay allowed a battalion-sized element to stand easily in formation, along with the addition of the two Old Bloods attached to their unit. The light in the cavernous chamber barely reach beyond the area around the haptic projection screen.

Brokehorn was somewhat troubled by the increasing frequency of these missions in the last two years. At one point, it had seemed to the veteran Lancer that this war was in its last stages, but perhaps the Naith-led coalition had pulled the other hand out from behind its back and really begun to fight. The addition of the Leitani and the Khajal, two very dangerous alien races, had certainly put iron into the spine of the Naith, and attacks on the Dominion's borders had redoubled.

"Do you think?" grumbled the Tyrannosaurus.

"Think about what?" the Triceratops asked, shaking his one-horned head. He had been lost in thought.

"About how we are to be inserted?" replied the Bladejaw.

The Lancer raked his claws along the ground once, his version of a testy shrug. "I am sure *Dhimion* Cruzah has employed us properly," he responded.

"As am I, but I was curious what your experience might lead us to believe would be the best approach for assault, as I have never worked with a Lancer before," admitted the Bladejaw.

"If you had, you would know that we don't appreciate the smell of blood wafting around us," replied Brokehorn.

"If I had, I would have the answer to my question in regards to all Lancers being so quick to whine like a hatchling fresh from the egg," the Bladejaw riposted.

Brokehorn's eyes went wide, as much at the insult as the amount of wit and rapidity it was delivered with, equal to any Scytheclaw, the Old Blood Velociraptors. As he turned to face the Tyrannosaurus, a light clap caught his attention.

"Brokehorn, Ripper. I was only able to catch your faith in my leadership, which I found heartening. Is everything alright?" the Illurian asked. His body armor was a vibrant green that clashed against pale blue skin.

"Certainly, *Dhimion*. My... *comrade* and I were just discussing matters of strategy," said Ripper, lowering his head to the level of the Illurian. The male was tall for his race, so Ripper did not need to bend as far as usual. Cruzah placed his hand on the Old Blood's muzzle in a sign of familiarity.

"You know this... Bladejaw?" asked Brokehorn. He was unable to keep the surprise out of his voice.

"Indeed I do," replied Cruzah. "We worked together during the Malbrion Incursion, and I requested him personally. I would

FALLEN LION

have said something sooner, Brokehorn, but he arrived much quicker than I expected. You have my apologies." The Illurian curved his arm inward, holding it against his middle, and bowed at the waist.

"There is no need for that," said Brokehorn, knowing the emotion he felt was called embarrassment. It was far too formal, especially with the gesture. Perhaps Cruzah had heard more of the conversation between the two Old Bloods than he was letting on. Illurians were tricky like that.

"These days, it seems like these butcher-and-bolt missions are more common than us striking into Federation territory," observed Ripper.

The slightest flicker of a frown passed over the Illurian's face, and then vanished. He tilted his head to the right then left, exposing the neural strands that passed for hair tied in a tight quirt. "The troopers garrisoned here were recalled to the inner worlds. I suspect they were used for a personal conflict, but the *djahn* insisted that the local militia here were more than adequate for defense against raids," replied Cruzah, his voice soft.

Ripper's eyes narrowed into small slits. "There are a million people spread across the land on this colony. There is no way a colony such as this could survive a protracted engagement," he pointed out.

Cruzah only gave the slightest of nods. "You are right on all counts, except for one. There are likely less than a million now. Let us hope there are some fish left after this hurricane," he replied. "I'll see you both planet-side." The Illurian saluted, making a fist and pounding the thumb side against his chest.

The two Old Bloods watched him go, and it was Brokehorn who broached the silence between them. "You've noticed as well?" he said.

"Noticed what?" asked Ripper.

"That the human colonies are the ones who suffer. I can't remember the Peace Federation daring to approach the core in quite a while," said Brokehorn.

Ripper was silent, and then nodded his head once. "Go where the janissaries and their Illurian leaders are not, of course.

The Naith call the Terrans 'terns' after all," he paused to look at Brokehorn. "It means—"

"'Killers'. It is not the original word for killers, but it has replaced the old term they used before," finished Brokehorn, beginning to walk toward their weapons bay.

Ripper followed alongside, mindful of his tail so as not to strike any objects inadvertently. "How does that make you feel? That the human colonies are the ones who are suffering?" he prodded.

Brokehorn didn't stop, but looked askance at the carnivore. "You are far too large to be of the Inner Truth, yet that's a question they would ask."

"And why would they ask that question? Why is that question considered one that someone would have to be careful who they asked it to?" Ripper pressed on.

"Because..." Brokehorn stopped, and turned to face the other Old Blood. "Why are you asking me this? Why do you care?"

"Because you seem to care what happens to the other blood of Kah, to the Terrans who fight and die for a royalty that no longer seems to value their sacrifices. So I ask again, how do you feel?" Ripper asked, his voice soft.

Brokehorn did not hesitate. "I have seen far too many of these worlds where we were too late for anything but to clean up the Naith feasts. The only Illurians were the ones who died with their human troops. The ruling caste does not care what price is paid for their suffering. You ask what I feel, Bladejaw? It is sorrow; sorrow for those who have died and those who have yet to suffer." Brokehorn stepped closer to Ripper. "And you? What is it you feel?"

"The same, but in addition my sorrow includes seeing the bright lords and ladies of Illuria consume themselves in hedonism when I remember how... noble they were at one time," admitted Ripper, shaking his head. "And surprise."

"Surprise?"

"Yes. That your willingness to speak your mind includes your principles, not just in light of your discomfort. It is a rare thing among all of our species," granted Ripper, and then stalked past the Lancer.

FALLEN LION

Brokehorn followed now, and the silence between them was more comfortable as they stepped between the pylons that would equip them with the machinery they wore to battle.

"Ripper," asked the Lancer. "Why did you ask me that question?"

"Which question?" responded Ripper as armor plates were fitted and locked into place on his torso.

"In regards to the humans."

"Because you noticed their suffering, and so few of our kind do," said Ripper.

Brokehorn grunted as he took the weight of his armor on his back, but it was more in reflex than any real burden. It sloped down his tail, along his back, and pressed up against his crest. The Lancer quickly exhaled, so no scales would be pinched as the armor swung down and locked underneath him, protecting his belly. He took a breath, then answered. "And you think that our kind should care?"

Ripper slid his arms into the massive mechanical claws that extended his reach and provided an additional melee option. "Too many of the Old Blood delude themselves into thinking their choice not to fight is without consequence. I see it as fortuitous that the Illurians gave us a choice, unlike the humans, and to say nothing of the Bhae Chaw," he said, holding still as his helmet locked into place. Twin heavy machine guns sat either side of his jaw, while his eyes were covered by an armored screen before it rose back into the top of the helmet.

There was another pause, and Brokehorn found himself mulling that comment quietly as his weaponry was locked into hard points on his armor. Electromagnetic mortars rested over both hips, and combination machine guns and flamethrowers were mounted to the front near each shoulder. A large twin-pronged fork sparked high on his torso, and a metallic sleeve was placed over the stump of his horn. A helmet resembling a domino mask was placed over his face, with the view screens descending and obscuring his eyes.

Brokehorn's visual display lit up with glyphs and iconography, much easier for the Old Bloods to comprehend, showing functionality of the weapon systems on the Old Blood's war harness. The entire rig was powered by the heat generated from the dinosaur added to thorium micro-reactors located on the Lancer's spine.

"And so what do you think our people should do?" asked Brokehorn.

Ripper stood without answering as his dorsal railgun was loaded into place. "Stand here, next to us, and fight for the humans who tend our wounds when we fall, terraform planets for us to live on, and find our every breath a marvel," he finally replied. The Tyrannosaurus waited for Brokehorn to finish his pre-battle checks, and then the two walked together toward the transport craft that would take them from the *Sea Spray* to planet-side.

"A lovely thought, perhaps," admitted Brokehorn. "But it will be the two of us saving what humans we can from the ruins of their colony." The Lancer stopped, and looked at Ripper. "Of course I have to wonder, why do we seem more prone to acting more... human to begin with? Do we empathize with them so strongly because we think and feel like them now?" Brokehorn continued walking again, and the question hung in the air for a moment before Ripper responded.

"I once read the work of a human philosopher who posited that all humanity is born bad. He described the natural state of man as 'nasty, brutish and short.' So something or someone uplifted them, and gave them a reason to do all the good deeds that I mentioned before. Perhaps that same force has worked its will on us," he said shifting within his heavy armor, settling it ready for combat. "Others call it 'Separated', meaning we are separate from other Old Bloods in that we feel more compassion for other races."

Green lights began to flash in sequence, alerting any personnel to stand back as the blast doors to the transport craft began to open. The two Old Bloods would ride down to the surface separately, even though they were being deposited in the same area of operations. If one of the craft went down – a rare event, but not entirely unheard of – it wouldn't throw the plan of attack into complete disarray.

FALLEN LION

"I hope we will be able to talk more about this after the battle, assuming we survive," shouted Ripper over the sounds of the doors opening.

Grudgingly, Brokehorn voiced his agreement. "Likewise, in spite of you smelling like whatever it was you last ate, I find the strength of the discussion overwhelms even your scent, though it is a close thing."

"It is good to know that if all of our other weaponry fails, you can still likely whine the enemy to death," said Ripper, surprising Brokehorn again and entering his transport ship, the doors shutting behind him. "'I'll see you on the ground', as the janissaries say," Ripper shouted behind him.

"Indeed you will," Brokehorn murmured as he shambled into his own dark craft. The doors hummed behind him and he stood in the dimly-lit space for a moment before the pilot spoke over the airwaves.

"Sir, it'll be about a minute to planet-side, and we drop in three minutes," said the human, instantly recognizable by his use of an honorific to address an Old Blood. It wasn't that the Illurians were rude, but they saw themselves in a much different light.

"I saw in my briefing that there was no anti-aircraft weaponry on the ground, but there's a risk of interception?" asked Brokehorn. Secretly, being shot out of the sky and falling the rest of the way was one of his fears. He had heard it referred to by some of the human pilots as 'controlled flight into terrain' with a typical sense of black humor he appreciated more every day.

"You'd be correct, sir, it being a full Federation raid. We've got a good wing of Errant fighters supporting us, though, so we'll get you to the ground in one piece," the human assured him. Brokehorn heard the locks disengaging, as the transport craft unlatched from the larger troop carrier.

The inside walls of the compartment shifted inward, limiting how much the Old Blood could be thrown around in case evasive maneuvers were necessary. Deep insertion via lander was never the preferred solution for getting Old Bloods to the battlefield. Drop pods were faster and safer in most cases, but mainly only used if the Dominion would be occupying the planet. When a beachhead was necessary, the tactical advantage was more apparent when an Old Blood was supported by janissaries arriving at the same time.

The Lancer's claws scraped at the steel grating below him as the craft sharply descended, rumbling as it made entry into the planet's atmosphere. He had begun counting down from the time of descent, and as he reached twenty felt a sudden blow rock the left side of the shuttle.

Before he could respond, the pilot had already begun talking. "Sir, we picked up a bogey on the way down. He fired some sort of energy weapon at us and disabled everything on my left wing. I can make it back to the *Sea Spray*, but I need to put you down a few kilometers away from your original drop zone. I don't think this hulk is going to make it all the way there carrying your tonnage," he explained quickly, pausing in the middle to shout something to his copilot.

"As long as you don't put me into a crater you can drop me on the other side of the world for all I care," said Brokehorn, controlling his breathing and flexing his claws. In response, the front ramp cracked, and he saw the sky flashing by, filled with stars. *Fast*, he thought, and wondered what kind of effort the crew was giving to keep them aloft.

The ramp began to yawn open, and Brokehorn saw they were descending into a besieged cityscape. The transport seemed to be aiming for an open green space. Brokehorn heard an explosion, and saw the shield flare up momentarily as they landed. The interior walls expanded, and Brokehorn bounded out. "I'm clear!" he shouted.

"Good luck!" the pilot added as his wedge-shaped transport streaked skyward without thirty tons of Old Blood weighing it down. Brokehorn didn't watch, instead turning his attention to the squad of Naith in the middle of the street a few hundred meters away, firing at the ship.

They were too far for his lighting fork, but perfect for the mortars he carried. Controlling the weapons with his eyes and

FALLEN LION

the fine movements of his face, he sent several rounds towards the green-skinned aliens. One had just reloaded some sort of rocket tube, and Brokehorn saw him raise it just as his mortar rounds blossomed fire into the center of group.

"Lancer, are you alive?" A familiar voice in his ear grabbed his attention.

"Bladejaw, you sound almost concerned," said Brokehorn, turning himself toward where the main force was landing and deploying his signals suite. He'd uplinked with the ships above, and had a map of the area along with a real-time display of troops identified as foes.

"Only because I don't wish to be responsible for all this fighting alone," Ripper said.

Brokehorn began to trot, his senses on full alert for any ambushes. Even if he was of the Separated, even though he had cutting-edge technology aiding him, he was still a dinosaur at heart, and one who had to worry about monstrous carnivores in the distant past. He'd be a fool to ignore his instincts, listening and smelling for any of the telltale signs of an ambush.

Instead of the subtle signs of a waiting attack, he heard screams to his left, and the high whine of a flechette cannon. Down the wide street, green flames began to creep up a high building, casting a rounded shadow that looked to be one of the Naith personnel carriers. It was away from his destination but the screams were what drew him. He heard another series of screams, and swung himself around wide to get a better view instead of rushing directly to the scene.

It seemed ridiculous such a massive being could be stealthy, but the enemy Peace Federation soldiers had other tasks at hand. Beside the armored vehicle, a Naith was standing beside a Khajali, and the Lancer assumed they were discussing the disposition of the humans they had bound under a pain web. Nearby, a squad of Naith stood idle. Every now and then one of the humans would shift too much beneath the wire lattice and the device would activate, sending wracking pain through the entire group.

The humans had been put to one side. The Khajali's back was to Brokehorn and seemed to be arguing with the smaller

Naith. Brokehorn assumed the Naith was female, and Brokehorn imagined she was frustrated by having to argue with a male of any species. The Khajali male was three meters tall, covered in scales that could turn a bullet and thrombium armor tougher again. He bore claws and teeth that would rend even the toughest flesh. The female would listen.

Their argument was Brokehorn's opportunity though, and he took it. As he came around the corner he used the jets positioned along the back of his armor, firing them off in sequence. His speed rose over a hundred kilometers per hour in short order and he covered the distance between himself and the enemy before they had a chance to do much beyond notice the sudden attack.

A force field shot from Brokehorn's armor and slammed into the Naith vehicle, launching it toward the two enemy aliens. The different responses of the two races showed the gulf in their mastery of war. While the Naith were standing in the middle of the road firing ineffectually toward Brokehorn, the Khajal had attempted to clear the tumbling troop transport by leaping to the side. He'd even brought his spear-cannon around, a Khajali ritual weapon known as a *rai'lith*.

If the vehicle had spun, so that it was parallel with the road, it might have missed the Khajalian. Instead it stayed sideways, and clipped him in midair. The carrier smashed into the rest of the squad and then rolled. Mangled bodies flew into the air – those that weren't hooked on pieces of jagged metal – leaving blue smears and limbs tossed about casually on the street. Brokehorn didn't congratulate himself, but instead rushed forward.

As he had suspected, the Khajali was only wounded by having a tank tossed on him. He saw the alien holding the flesh of one leg together as it rose, its half-cloak torn and rent. It turned as Brokehorn charged, and raised its *rai'lith* in one last act of defiance.

The Lancer's nose spike turned the blade, and his one good horn smashed the Khajali into the side of a building. Still, the enemy warrior attempted to rise, not quite dead even though an arm hung limply at its side. Brokehorn reared up and smashed

FALLEN LION

the Khajali under his bulk, both front feet slamming onto the alien. The thrombium armor was scratched, but not deformed. The body inside ended up a leaking bag of purple blood and crushed flesh.

Brokehorn looked down at the Khajali, and tried to think about how many of them he'd killed now. *Thirty-one?* They never died easily, or first for that matter.

"Bladejaw?" the Lancer broadcast to the other Old Blood. "I just killed a Khajali. Watch yourself."

"Watch myself? I'm surrounded by janissaries and Illurians. You're the one behind enemy lines trying to make a name for himself," Ripper said.

An Illurian voice entered the net. "Brokehorn? Are you all right? The shuttle pilot said there was some trouble on the way down," said Dhimion Cruzah.

"I'm fine, Dhimion," Brokehorn answered. "I seem to have interrupted a discussion between the Peacers in regards to the disposition of captives."

The Lancer moved toward the humans under the pain web. "I need to remove this device, but it will hurt," he told them. With surprising accuracy, the Triceratops used his parrot-like beak to grab the thick wire and haul it off the trapped humans. There was another series of short screams as it was whipped off them and hurled against a wall.

Brokehorn turned back toward the humans before him. What he saw surprised him. It was a group of young adolescents and children with a single adult female. All were staring at him in amazement.

Our every breath is a marvel to them, Ripper had said, and Brokehorn wondered if this was the first time these humans had ever seen an Old Blood in the flesh, to say nothing of one in full war chassis.

They continued to stare, and Brokehorn felt a sensation he was unfamiliar with.

What could they be looking at?

He pushed it aside and contacted Cruzan. "Dhimion, I have a number of young humans at my position. Is there any way you can send a squad of janissaries here?"

A pause, then Cruzan responded. "I wish I could. There's a Naith slaughter ship being filled with prisoners, and we're fighting towards that before they get off the ground or the Naith convince the Khajal to let them kill everyone on board. The best I can think of is you meeting up with us *en route*," said the Illurian.

It wasn't ideal, but Brokehorn knew the Illurian meant it when he said he couldn't spare any janissaries. "Send me the route you're taking and I'll do what I can with the humans," said the Old Blood, turning his attention to them. "Who is in charge?" he demanded.

"I am," said the sole adult, short brown hair slicked to her head. She was older by decades than the rest of her charges. "Who are you?"

The Lancer could see that while she was shaken by the turn of events, she was holding herself together, and he approved.

"Brokehorn, attached to an Illurian Retribution Fleet. Who are you? Do you have a vehicle available? Or, will you have to run on foot?"

"I'm Anna, and yes, there's a utility vehicle in the garage behind us we used..." she paused, and then continued in a lower voice. "I tried to explain to them that we hadn't even begun Reservist training yet, that they were no threat. These are just students..."

"As well reason with a hungry Bladejaw. If you're not a threat, you're prey," Brokehorn said, his nostrils flaring. "To one side," he commanded, and the adolescents parted for him. *Younger than I thought*, he noted.

One of them spoke up. "Mistress Anna, we can't move the rubble," said a boy before turning to Brokehorn. "We were trying before when they saw us," he explained, waving toward the Naith corpses in the street.

"I am not you," said Brokehorn, and one claw reached out, sweeping chunks of rebar and ferrocrete to one side. He made short work of the wreckage, using his good horn to rend the metal sheeting of the garage door and expose the vehicle.

Just as he was about to order them to mount up, he heard an odd, dual-pitched baying. The Lancer whipped his head

FALLEN LION

around, nearly smashing a horn into one of the humans who had gotten too close, and saw the sloping, armored forms of Naith Defenders and their hounds. The creatures making the noise were low to the ground and looked nothing more than muscular torsos with ruinous jaws full of teeth. The heavily-furred Kraka hounds would provide a screen for the Defenders and cover the distance between them and the enemy in short order.

Reflexively, Brokehorn moved forward, protecting the humans with his bulk. "Into the garage!" he demanded, activating icons on his visual display. Segments along his dorsal ridge began to glow, and the fork on his back began to spark. One of the students lost her nerve and attempted to bolt from the garage, but Anna grabbed her and pulled her back.

It was well that she did, as the fork suddenly launched a bolt of electricity, frying the first hound then jumping to the second and third and finally danced among Naith themselves, filling the air with a charred smell not unlike burnt sugar.

The Lancer shook his head to clear his nostrils, but it was a futile gesture. He stepped back from the opening and looked down the street where blackened and smoking corpses littered the ground. "Get them loaded up. We've got clicks to make across this warzone," ordered the Triceratops, and he found himself again curious about how many he had killed. Brokehorn recognized the idea as a human one, but engaged it all the same. As he peered around the corner he could hear Anna loading the others into the open-sided, rugged-looking craft from inside the hangar.

More corpses were scattered, smoldering from the energy discharge. Brokehorn realized an entire company of Defenders were dead around him. His chain lightning-fork had hopped from foe to foe to the last soldier, and the results were visible before him. It was a stroke of luck he wasn't going to question.

He turned back to the humans to find Anna driving the truck into the street. He trotted up to them, the ground rumbling only slightly under his steps as he approached. He was eye-level with the driver's open-topped compartment, and Anna looked past him to the alien wreckage he left behind before gazing at his weaponry. "That one thing did... that?" she asked.

"It did, but it won't be able to do so for a while," Brokehorn admitted. Part of what had piqued his curiosity was that the energy drain on the weapon was much higher than normal. His eyes commanded his HUD to bring up the route the task force was taking – they still had a rough trip ahead of them.

"Listen to me," the Triceratops told her, raising the screens on his helmet so she could look at his eyes. Humans always liked seeing your eyes, he had realized early on in his career. "If I engage something you need to keep heading west," he explained. "Eventually you should meet up with friendly lines."

"And what of you?" Anna asked the Lancer.

"What about me?" he replied.

"Will you be all right?"

Brokehorn snorted. "I will live or die. Nothing less, nothing more."

The human woman looked at him, and then shook her head. "You are very brave beneath the fatalism," she told him as she put the vehicle into gear.

Brokehorn didn't respond, but the comment made him wonder what she meant by 'brave'. He had explained to Ripper his reasons for fighting, but he had never considered what he did to be of that refined act the humans called *courageous*. They walked along until the vehicle shifted gear, and Brokehorn began to trot.

It was good that he had built his speed up because the Butcher tank turned smoothly as it came into the center of the road and fired its missiles. Brokehorn was able to leap forward and put his body between the weapons and the vehicle behind him.

His anti-missile systems engaged, defeating the Leitani armaments' countermeasures. Intense, narrowly-directed lasers danced off his armor and fried the warheads, causing them to explode in mid-flight. That didn't end his problems though, as two armored figures dismounted from the hull of the hovering, wedge-shaped tank.

"Get down a side street!" Brokehorn roared at Anna, returning fire with his machine guns then firing his hip mortars.

FALLEN LION

Smoke rounds burst in the street in front of him as he took his own advice just in time. Powerful energy beams from the Khajali *rai'liths* blasted craters in the ground where he had just stood, debris raining everywhere.

Turning in the tight corridor, Brokehorn calmed his breathing and waited until he heard the sound of claws scraping the asphalt in the smoke-filled street in front of him. Then he filled it with fire from his flamethrowers, spewing flaming fuel. Shields were no use against the stuff, as it moved too slow to activate them. One warrior flung its arm about wildly, trying to dislodge the adhesive stuff from his arm. The other bellowed as it sunk to its knees – it had caught both streams full-on and was now a humanoid-shaped flaming totem.

Quickly, the Lancer moved to engage the partially aflame Khajali, machine guns firing at close range. The alien's shield sprung up in response, but couldn't stop the Old Blood bearing down on him, his *rai'lith* only notching Brokehorn's intact horn before being ripped from the alien's grasp. Brokehorn activated his flamethrowers again, and turned as the Khajali fell to the ground, the corpse hidden behind the thick flames.

There was no time to watch his handiwork as his shield sprang up. The butcher tank had silently approached him in the melee, and it had been joined by another. At close range, the purple light pulsed underneath the black vehicle, the anti-gravity technology a trademark of the Leitani species. An opaque dome rose from the wedge-shaped base, where twin cannons rode either side of it, with a large anti-aircraft gun riding on the dorsal mount. The guns spun up again, and Brokehorn's shield's dropped. Pain lanced into him as shrapnel penetrated the exposed thick scales that protected his sides.

The second tank popped up above its comrade, its missile's aiming downwards toward him. The Lancer realized he had only one option, counter intuitive as it may have seemed. He charged forward and slid his horn underneath the floating tank in front of him and heaved upwards. The tank's pilot did not respond fast enough to the sudden strike and was hurled into the air. With a crunch of metal on metal the two tanks collided just as the second butcher fired its missiles.

They had not traveled far enough to arm their fuses, but instead functioned as metal spears. The range was close enough that the two powerful shields interfered with each other, and the missile wasn't turned. Instead there was a high-pitched whine as the anti-gravity engines failed on the first butcher. This was followed by a low drone as the second tank couldn't keep them both in the air, and they crashed into the ground.

Brokehorn had the good sense to retreat from the impact zone of the twin tanks in the few seconds of chaos. He had made just enough distance to save his life as the impact activated the fuse on one of the missiles. It exploded in a blossom of green fire. This combustion set off a chain reaction in short order – all the ordnance on the twin tanks exploded. Chunks of metal were hurled down the street, and Brokehorn sought refuge in another side street. All the same, one jagged piece of wreckage lodged itself into his side and he caught himself before he screamed in shock as much as pain. Another piece crashed into his armored side, and he dropped to his knees, trying to catch his breath as he shook his head.

"That last one would have killed me," he murmured. The thought of his own mortality worried him for a moment, and then he turned it aside. He had a greater responsibility than his own life to worry about, especially after his bold words to Ripper in the *Sea Spray*.

As if on cue, Ripper's voice came to life on his radio. "Brokehorn, what is going on over there? We just saw a massive explosion near your last reported position. Are you all right?" asked Ripper, unable to keep the concern out of his tone.

Brokehorn tried to catch his breath, winced, and then spoke in clipped bursts. "Two butcher tanks. Company of Naith Defenders. Three Khajali. All dead. Humans safe," he said, backing out of the side street. He motioned with his head for the humans to follow in their truck. "This way," he told them, loping down the road and ignoring the stabbing pain in his side. He did not see the wide-eyed looks the human wore as they passed the charred Khajalian corpses or the flaming wreckage of the butcher tanks.

FALLEN LION

"You're injured," said Ripper.

"I'll live," Brokehorn said, mentally chiding himself. Maybe he did whine as much as Ripper claimed.

"There are no assurances on that, but I won't let it happen because I wasn't there," Ripper retorted. "*Dhimion*, I'm going to assist the Lancer with his escort mission. He's wounded and needs aid."

There was a pause before Cruzah responded. "I heard your conversation. You have my full permission, Bladejaw. There's chatter on the enemy frequencies though. Some of the Khajal are speaking of a beast, a living tank of rage and metal that cannot be stopped, guarding a cargo of prey it took from them..." said the *Dhimion*, trailing off.

Brokehorn knew his last Khajali kills had been as much luck as his own skill. He knew he had likely been fighting lower-caste Khajal, not the elder soldiers of that frightful race. If he was being marked as a trophy that would change in short order.

"*Dhimion*, I'm attaching a Xeno Medical Squad to accompany me," said Ripper, his voice a low rumble interspersed with snorts – the Bladejaw was running now.

Cruzah did not comment on the breach of protocol, only telling Ripper, "Make sure you keep them close by. For all we know the Khajal might think you're the beast," said Cruzah.

"Acknowledged," growled Ripper. There was none of his easy wit from earlier. "Lancer, I'm a few clicks from your position. Stay tight and rampart yourself."

"Madness. They know I'm here. They'll come to claim the thrombium off their dead no matter what. I'll meet you," he managed to get out before he felt a sudden weight on his back and a piercing agony to the left of his spine. He squealed in pain and surprise. His body knew what had happened before understanding hit home, and it responded as if a utahraptor had done the deed instead of the Khajali knight that had mounted him.

Brokehorn rolled, his bulk coming off the ground for a second to body slam the offending alien into the road. The Khajal attempted to throw himself clear, but there was nowhere to go. Trapped between the building and the Triceratops, the only thing that saved the Khajal was that the structure wasn't able to take thirty tons of dinosaur smashing into it. The entire edifice crumbled on top of the Khajal, stone and mortar bouncing off Brokehorn.

Fueled by pain and adrenaline, Brokehorn staggered to his feet, the wild swinging of the Khajali's *rai'lith* scoring him across his flank. As the alien pushed itself free of the rubble, the Lancer was there. Brokehorn didn't have room for a charge or to use his bulk, but the weapon he chose was just as effective.

The parrot-like bill of the Triceratops was surprisingly strong, needing to be in order to rend the tough plants that made up the typical meal of the herbivore. Brokehorn clamped it around the Khajali's waist, holding his foe in place.

The glowing in the Old Blood's eye as the *rai'lith* charged only spurred Brokehorn to action, and the Triceratops reached the Khajali's arm with his claw before he gave a savage jerk of his head. The arm ripped free easily, and the warrior roared in pain as Brokehorn repeated the process on the other side, again flinging the useless limb into a pile of rubble. The Khajali's last act was to gnaw ineffectually at Brokehorn's nasal horn.

The Lancer's balance was off, so he shook himself and the wreckage of his lightning fork fell to the ground with a clang. "Are you... are you all right?" shouted one of the humans from the truck. Brokehorn looked over, and saw the faces were pale and wide-eyed, gawking between the Triceratops and the dismembered body of the Khajali knight.

"I'll be fine," said Brokehorn with a low grunt, smelling the hot copper scent of his blood mingling with the odor from the musky Khajalian blood. He could not see the wounds, but knew that he was bleeding quite badly from the smell alone.

"Forward! Forward," he demanded of Anna, ignoring the pain that radiated all over. He had made it this far with them, and right now he didn't care if he died – his only concern was that the Khajali were denied and the humans made it to safety.

"You're bleeding!" she shouted over to him as she punched the truck into a higher gear.

Brokehorn stumbled but managed to keep his feet. "I've had

FALLEN LION

worse," he lied, forcing air into his lungs but failing to catch his breath. There was a ringing in his ears, and for a moment he thought the screams were a hallucination. Brokehorn turned his head and spied one of the Khajal on top of the truck, *rai'lith* charging for a calamitous burst into the passenger compartment of the vehicle. Another Khajali appeared in a shower of sparks, its mirror cloak no longer.

With a roar, Brokehorn swung his head against the truck. It rolled, throwing the Khajali off balance and the shot went wide, opening a charred hole in the road several meters deep. The Khajali atop the truck had leapt clear as the vehicle rolled on its side, and shouted something at Brokehorn in its own language.

It was far too close to the humans to risk the flamethrowers, and the machine guns wouldn't puncture the thrombium or get through the shields in time. Brokehorn ignited his booster rockets, and swore he saw the Khajali's eyes widen in shock as the Triceratops' massive bulk went from stationary to hurtling.

They collided, and the enemy warrior ended up under the Lancer. A deep, twisting pain skewered through Brokehorn's belly. *The Khajali's blade.* It was no matter. Brokehorn pulled himself back as quick as he could, leaving the Khajali smeared with the Lancer's blood. Both of the alien's arms were pinned, and it snapped at Brokehorn with its jaws. Small pricks peppered Brokehorn as the Khajal attempted to bring his *rai'lith* to bear. Brokehorn drove his massive claws into the unarmored space in what little neck the Khajali had. There was a sudden, shocked croak. The alien went still beneath him, his neck so many ribbons of meat.

The world throbbed in the Lancer's vision; he was dying. The sound of footsteps. *The second Khajali.* He couldn't make out the alien's language, but the tone was not the taunting he expected. It was that of one professional saluting the dedication of another; the Khajali seemed almost sorrowful as it placed the blade of its *rai'lith* between Brokehorn's eyes and began charging the cannon.

Brokehorn fired first. The attachment over the stump of his horn came to life in a scintillating beam of white light, melting the flesh of the Khajali and leaving only singed and slightly warped thrombium among a pile of ashes as the self-contained energy weapon fired.

"One last... act of defiance," murmured Brokehorn, laying his head down and wondering why he felt so cold. There were many hands on him now, telling him not to die, but he didn't wish to hear that.

He swore that he could feel grass on his cheek, and the scent of blood that annoyed him so was replaced by that of freshly cut hay. He didn't have the strength to ask the humans if they knew which star was Sol System, so he could die gazing at blessed Kah.

Screams startled him, and he opened one eye to see another duo of Khajali walking towards them, claws pointing at the humans. Brokehorn attempted to stand, but it only precipitated his fall into darkness. The smell of grass became overpowering, and there was gold at the edge of his vision. The last thing he heard before he died was a monstrous roar, and the thought that accompanied it: *that sounds like a Bladejaw...*

* * *

White was the first color that greeted the Lancer, and even then it was fuzzy. He opened his jaws once, twice, trying to dislodge his tongue from the bottom of his mouth.

"He's awake!" exclaimed a familiar voice, and Brokehorn felt more than saw the shifting of great mass.

"I can see that," said a female voice, somewhat annoyed. "He's going to want water, and you standing up like that will likely get someone trampled and give me more work."

Brokehorn thought water was a fine idea, and thought to say as much. All that came out was a tired wheeze, his throat far too tight to make noise and activate his vox harness.

A warm hand touched his face, and he could see better now. A dark claw with a figure in white in front of him. As he focused, he saw it was a human woman who attended him. An older woman; her hair was flecked with silver, and she had many lines

FALLEN LION

around her eyes. She found a smile for him though, and placed a hose into his mouth. "Swallow as much as you can, and if some of it runs out, well it's no problem. Cleaning up is part of the job, and we certainly don't mind doing it for heroes," she told him.

He didn't register what she said, as the feeling of cool water gushing down his dry throat was a wonder that captivated him. He drank eagerly, only stopping when pain deep in his gut forced him to. Brokehorn saw the nurse's eyes squint and she nodded. "Pain?"

"Yes," he managed, his voice still rusty. "In my stomach."

The nurse nodded again. "That's to be expected. I imagine the flesh there is still healing, even though they took the stitches out a week ago," she explained.

"How long have I been out?" he asked.

"Nearly three weeks now. We... we didn't think you were going to make it when they brought you here," she admitted. "But here you are, and that's what matters."

"How bad was it?"

She shook her head. "I'll let the doctor talk about that. I don't want to get into specifics," she told him. Brokehorn had a feeling that was her final word on that subject. "I'm sure your friend will want to talk to you about it though, so you can ask him. I'm Nurse Sera, and please don't hesitate to call if you need anything."

"Is there food? Can I eat?" he asked her, trying to rise but pain forced him back.

There was a guffaw from above, and Sera looked up for a moment, scowling, before turning back to the Lancer. "I'll see what I can get for you, but it's likely going to be nutrient fluid for a bit until your gut heals up a bit more," she told him, and then turned to the other being present in the room. "You have ten minutes with him, but he needs his strength. Don't make me come in here and have you forced out again," she told the Tyrannosaurus.

"I don't think I have ten minutes of conversation in me," responded Ripper.

The nurse shook her head and left, leaving Ripper and Brokehorn alone.

141

SNAFU: SURVIVAL OF THE FITTEST

Brokehorn was able to take stock of his surroundings now. The two were in a cavernous, white room with one wall dedicated to a haptic chart of his vitals, which showed his improving medical history over different timelines. Above him hung a large piece of cloth; he couldn't make out what it was, but didn't care. Instead, he turned to Ripper.

"You just happened to be here?" Brokehorn asked.

"I did, but..."

"You were here every day?"

The Bladejaw nodded, opening his mouth several times before finding words. "It was bad. I arrived just as the other Khajal arrived and well, I finished off the two of the three survivors."

Brokehorn tilted his head at this. "I killed six. I was nearly dead when those three arrived."

"So you were. But the humans convinced themselves you killed seven, so that's what they told *Dhimion* Cruzah," explained Ripper. "They survived, though some were injured when you rammed the truck. They were very effusive in their praise of your valor."

There was another pause. "How bad was it?" Brokehorn inquired softly. This realization of his own mortality was a new thing to him.

"You died," said Ripper. "I remember the lead medic telling me that as they began working on you."

"If I died, why would they try to bring me back in the middle of an active battlefield? Especially when surrounded by Federation troops." Triage procedures of the Dominion military prohibited resuscitation.

"Maybe they decided an effort was better than answering to an enraged Bladejaw." Ripper responded.

The two Old Bloods locked gazes for a moment, and it was Brokehorn who spoke into the silence. "But why all that for a dinosaur you just met?"

"Because I think..." Ripper paused again, as though searching for the words. "We understand each other. Not just being Separated, but we understand the reasons we fight. Call me

FALLEN LION

selfish but I was not ready to lose that, not after finding it so soon. I would not have the promise of a friendship taken away from me." There was none of the light acerbic wit in Ripper's words, and Brokehorn found himself touched.

"Besides," said Ripper quickly, nodding toward the banner above them. "This is the kind of thing you don't usually see at all."

Brokehorn followed Ripper's gaze. It was a banner – gold on black. There was a lion in profile, scaling what looked like a pile of dead hyenas. Red slashes were stitched all over the lion, who seemed to be roaring, likely for the final time.

"They give that to those who died in battle," said Brokehorn, remembering what Ripper had said but speaking the words all the same.

"So you did. Your actions were heroic, believe it or not. The Order of the Fallen Lion, and you the only living member," said Ripper. "I am impressed, not just for the deeds you accomplished."

"What else would impress you?"

"That you did believe in the ideals we expressed before that battle to spend your life in pursuit of them," said Ripper.

"That was the mission," began Brokehorn.

"No, the mission was incidental. You died as true as you lived. So few beings ever do," said Ripper.

A small door opened, and Nurse Sera stood there, her hands on her hips, glaring at the Tyrannosaurus.

"I'm leaving, I'm leaving," Ripper grumbled, turning away from her and heading toward the large doors on the other side of the room.

"You'll..." Brokehorn began, and then forced himself to ask. "You'll be here tomorrow?"

"I will," promised Ripper. "Sleep well, friend."

Brokehorn watched him go, and he was left alone with Nurse Sera as she went about her tasks. He was tired, but he had slept for weeks and had questions. "Nurse," he said, and she turned toward him.

"Lancer, what can I do for you?" she asked him.

"The humans I saved, do you know where they are now?" he asked her.

She frowned, and gave a small shake of her head. "Hopefully they found their parents and are trying to recover, physically and mentally, but I truthfully don't know. Children are tough though – they bounce back faster than you think."

"That's good then," Brokehorn said, thinking of how the young humans had looked at him while he ripped apart the Khajalian. How many nightmares would that bring on?

Sera paused, visibly thinking, and then moved closer to Brokehorn. "May I ask a question?" The Lancer nodded for her to go on. "Why did you do that?"

"Because he was trying to kill me," said Brokehorn, and then realized that he had been thinking of the Khajali that he had slaughtered.

"I know that," began Sera, misunderstanding, "but you killed yourself saving human children. Why though? It's obvious the Illurians don't care – the ones who aren't fighting, that is. So why do you? You could have left them to their fate and no one would have thought less of you," she said. Her voice was soft, and she had moved closer to him, resting a hand on his crest and looking him in the eye.

There was only one answer he could give her that would be true, and to voice it would be to accept his status as Separated and no longer simply Old Blood. "Because it was the right thing to do," he said, meeting her gaze evenly. As he said it, he realized there would be no mate from the garden worlds for him. He would never be part of a herd of Lancers, and would remain forever ignorant of that which bonded his own kind.

For a second it was frightening, and then he saw Sera push tears away from her eyes, and smile down at him. "You are all so wonderful. Thank you," she whispered at him, turning away. He felt the fear vanish at her sincere expression of gratitude, and instead it was replaced by a cocktail of emotions he had no name for. The dinosaur turned his head with some pain, to look at the banner that hung above him. He had traded away easy pleasures for the hard road, but so be it. It would not be a lonely road, at least, and some would live that otherwise would not.

FALLEN LION

His last thought before he settled back down to sleep was a human one. He had no regrets.

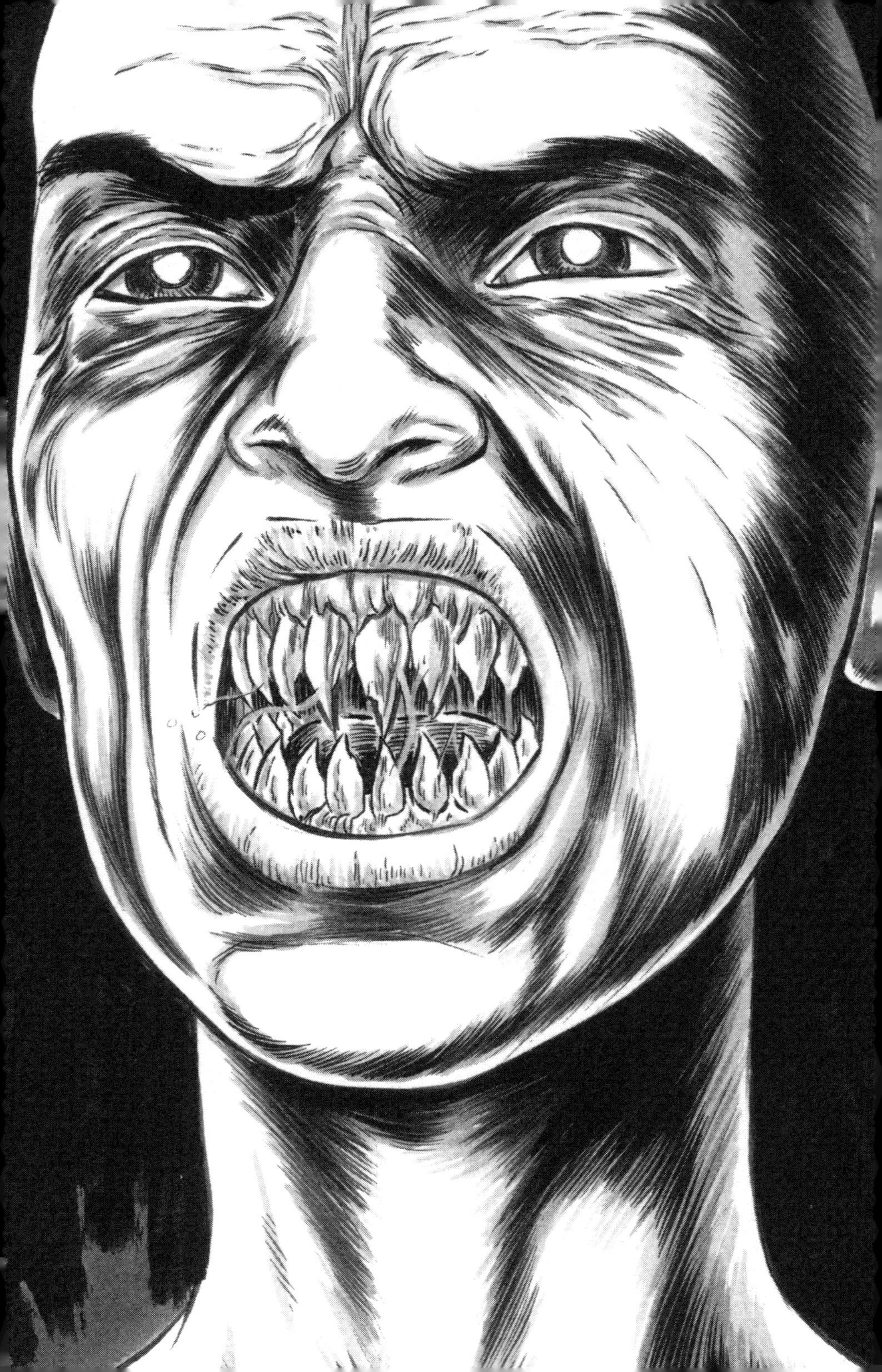

SUCKER OF SOULS

Kirsten Cross

Is that as fast as you can run? Because fella, I'm telling you right now, it ain't fucking fast enough!" Snarled from a frightened man way, *way* out of his comfort zone and desperately trying to appear in control of an uncontrollable situation so as not to 'frighten the civvy' as they stagger-ran.

Soldiers, even ex-soldiers who now got paid to babysit grave-robbing archaeologists, shouldn't show fear. Ever. Even when they were faced with an enemy that apparently had powers well beyond those that could be controlled with a quick double-tap from a Glock.

Fuck.

This was gonna be one well-earned pay cheque. If he lasted long enough to collect the damn thing, that is. What they had just witnessed had challenged Flynn's whole concept of what was worth seven hundred dollars a day plus expenses and what wasn't. And this very definitely wasn't.

"I'm sorry?" The archaeologist didn't seem to get the barely controlled desperation, panic and outright 'what the actual *fuck* was that?' tone in his babysitter's voice. Flynn was still in control of himself. Just.

When they stopped to catch a breath and take stock of their surroundings for a second, Flynn pressed home his advantage. "You bloody well will be if we don't stay ahead of... whatever the *hell* that was." The ex-soldier gave his charge a cold, emotionless smile that didn't reach his eyes.

The archaeologist peeled off a pair of round spectacles and rubbed at them with the corner of his shirt. He perched the glasses back onto his nose and pushed them up to the bridge. His hands were shaking violently. He used the mundane act to try and ground himself while his brain attempted to process the carnage they had just seen. "I'm an archaeologist, Mr Flynn, not an Olympic sprinter."

Colby Flynn turned his steely-cold, pale-green eyes onto the quivering academic, rammed home a new clip and primed his sidearm in front of the man. That always got their attention. Sliding the bolt back on the Glock 17 made that gloriously satisfying *cher-chunk* sound that all movie scriptwriters love. It acted as an underline, emphasising his determination to go down fighting no matter what. It also helped to make the archaeologist more frightened of Flynn than the thing that was currently snuffling and snarling its way towards them. And that was a good thing. Because it would mean the bolshy academic would now do what he was told for a change. "Good. That increases my chances, then."

The bespectacled, owl-like man blinked curiously at Flynn. "What?"

"It means, buddy, that while mister bitey back there is chowing down and ripping your throat out like he did with your mate, he won't be gnashing on me, will he?"

Oh no. Not again…

A snorting, snuffling sound that was so thick and black you could chew it like a piece of liquorice imposed on their momentary pause. "Seriously, will you just *fuck off*, you bastard!" Flynn abused the darkness and then emptied a volley of shots into nothing. Whether it actually made any real difference or not, he couldn't tell. But whatever was back there yelped and snarled. Flynn hoped that the swarm of hollow-points at least gave the bastard cause to pause so they could focus on running again.

Move! For fuck's sake, *move!*" Flynn spun the archaeologist around and shoved him hard. "I've got your back. As long as you stay in front of me." Flynn put his mouth next to the sweating man's ear. "And yet, you're… still… *here?*"

The archaeologist suddenly developed a surprisingly-fast turn of speed for a Cambridge academic.

Normally, Flynn wouldn't give anyone a head start. This wasn't a school egg and spoon race where the 'special kids' got to jog a few steps before everyone else set off, and it was the

SUCKER OF SOULS

'taking part that mattered, not the winning, little buddy'. This was a slime-covered stone corridor lined with spluttering, flickering lightbulbs that had been Jerry-rigged by Micky Cox – an ex-REME armed with a screwdriver, a happy disposition, and a real 'MacGyver' approach to fixing shit. Their only source of light was being produced by a wheezing, 40-year-old generator with carburettor problems combined with mile upon mile of gaffer-taped cable. And there wasn't some happy-clappy teaching assistant cheering them on. There was a five-hundred-and-seventy-year-old psychopath with a taste for blood, violence and carnage just a few turns behind them. And he – or it, whatever the hell *it* was – was playing with them, the sick, twisted little bastard.

Flynn needed the archaeologist alive. What was in professor brainiac's balding little noggin might just keep him and his team in one piece, if he could get the egghead to the safety of the citadel's old armoury that was currently doubling as a control centre for the dig. Damn it, if he was going to be paid to babysit an academic, he'd make sure the son of a bitch stayed alive.

The twisting, turning corridors were slick with algae. These dungeons and corridors were built well below the natural water table and a musky, foetid atmosphere permeated every inch of the subterranean labyrinth. Rivulets of water seeped down and followed the channels between the huge blocks of granite. There was no mortar holding these blocks together. Stone like this didn't need cement to keep it in place. These tunnels – deep under what would have been a massive, imposing castle – had thousands of tons of masonry and rock pressing down on them.

Back in the comfort of the hotel, the archaeologist had told Flynn and his team a rambling account of the supposed history of the citadel. It was, as Gary Parks had said, a 'two-bottle tale'. The bottles in question had been filled with the local hooch, a paint-stripping, intestine-melting liquor that would probably lead to blindness if you drank too much of the damn stuff. Flynn was a practical kind of guy and, right up to the point when that... *thing*... had come wailing through the door, took a pretty pragmatic approach to concepts such as the ability of true evil, despair and pain to impregnate the very walls of a building. So he listened patiently about how the stones were held together with the screams of the damned, long since dead but not necessarily buried. The archaeologist had gone into great detail about how the terror of the inmates had been etched into the stone with scrabbled, ripped fingernails and bloodied stumps. It had become as real as any painting; an everlasting memory of the evil that had happened in this dark and savage place. He recounted grisly details of how every cell had been occupied with frail, frightened prisoners, their minds shredded and tattered by the constant screams, yowls and cries for mercy that echoed throughout the underground chambers. When the guards came for them, they'd begged. Oh, how they'd begged! They crawled on their bellies. They pleaded. They called to their God – who utterly abandoned them to their fate and the whims of their sadistic captors.

The archaeologist spared no details in his story. He explained how the peepholes allowed guards who got a thrill from watching the suffering of others to observe the prisoners' slow and painful deaths as starvation and disease took hold. How they would watch as the rats started chewing on the dying when they became too weak to shoo them away, taking bets on which part of a prisoner's body the rodents would go for first. Apparently, it was always the soft tissue – the genitals, the face, the eyes. Once the body had been reduced to gnawed bones and a sticky, stinking coating of vitreous fluid on the stone floor, the door was opened and a new occupant took residence. Except one.

Like freaked-out boy scouts telling ghost stories around a campfire, Flynn and his team had leaned in. After all, everyone loves a good 'haunted castle' story, don't they? The archaeologist risked permanent sight damage by pouring himself another glass of hooch and had continued with his tale.

This cell, he explained, had no door. Instead massive stones had been seconded from other parts of the castle and used to wall up the doorway, leaving just the iron-barred peep-hole through which guards occasionally pushed a hissing, squawking cat. This

SUCKER OF SOULS

unique prisoner, brought back home to this dark and terrifying castle after rampaging for years across Europe, liked his food still kicking. So they gave him cats because it seemed to be the one thing he... it... feared. That was their torment – giving him something they knew full well he detested, but was so starved and emaciated that he had no choice but to overcome his revulsion and feed on whatever screeching titbit the guards tossed through the barred gap.

The isolation was a torment, too, especially for such a brilliant, bright and diamond-hard mind. The knowledge that the stinking, festering cell littered with the bones of cats and rats was to be his everlasting tomb – a tomb that was designed for the living, not the undead – had warped his already-twisted mind beyond evil, and beyond any form of redemption and turned it from a 'he' into an 'it'. That's why the priests had brought it back here. Even they were afraid of it; afraid of what it had become. Afraid of what it could do, especially after Death had supposedly claimed its putrefying corpse and it had reanimated, sending at least three of those same priests to early and very violent deaths.

This was the cell it had called home for years, centuries, driven utterly insane by the lust for sustenance and tormented by the hissing, caterwauling animals the guards hurled into his cell. When the citadel was abandoned and the tunnels lost to history, it went into hibernation for centuries. Occasionally, it woke and fed on any rat that wasn't quick enough to escape its clutches. Then, it returned to its state of stasis until the starvation became too great once again.

Well, that was the story. Flynn had listened, but up until about five minutes ago, he really hadn't bought any of this BS. As an ex-soldier he had seen enough horror in his life to be open to the idea of the manifestation of evil. Getting chased through slime-covered corridors by that a snarling, salivating monstrosity meant he was getting more open-minded by the second...

They'd found the cell. And behind the stones lurked a creature that had wandered the dark desert of madness for more lifetimes than it could count. When the archaeologists had unblocked the tomb it had burst forth in a howling, screaming frenzy, tearing the first man it saw to pieces. It had sucked the young man – a research fellow in the final year of his doctorate – dry, gorging itself and likely relishing the feeling of drunken power. Sated, it had slumped to the floor for a moment, laughing maniacally. The first taste awoke the hunger. Now? It wanted more.

This was what Colby Flynn and the archaeologist were running from. Not an alcohol-fuelled story. A very real, very hungry and very *angry* creature from the pit of mankind's nightmares.

But this was no simple medieval terror, released from its prison at last, and free to unleash its maddened, blackened rage once again on the world. Once, it had been a sentient, passionate young man, a visionary and military genius. But fate had been cruel to Vlad and the Black Prince had eventually been imprisoned in the stone-lined cell of Tokat Castle, a broken tooth of a citadel that towered high above the city.

The Seljuk Turks who had conquered Tokate in the 12th Century had discovered a maze of underground passages and stone-lined cells, and had turned it into their own stronghold. In 1442 they were given their most dangerous prize, Prince Vlad III. But the young boy and his brother were political hostages, not prisoners. So, during his internment the Ottomans had attempted to create an ally out of him. They taught him military strategy. They nurtured his natural ability for warfare and combat, taught him the classics, languages, geography, mathematics and science. They had given him every advantage.

But they also brutalised him, beating and humiliating this prince's son who would not bend his knee to the Turk's rule.

And that was a big, big mistake.

They turned an intelligent, bright boy into a sadistic, vicious man – a military savant whose ability to strategise played a major part in his success as a ruler later on. But his brutalised, blackened heart became darker and more infested with evil until he created a monster that would resonate through the centuries.

Dracula.

The Impaler.

The devourer of children and sucker of souls.

SUCKER OF SOULS

This was to be his prison – firstly in life, and later, when the monks of Comana had brought his bloated corpse back from their monastery to the one place on earth they knew would hold him.

And it had held him. The monks' plan had worked – right up until the moment when well-meaning academics with no understanding of true evil and a firm if totally misguided belief that knowledge would be their shield, had torn down the stones that kept Vlad from unleashing his unique brand of horror on the world.

To modern minds, especially those belonging to academics and military specialists that had indulged in the local hooch for a couple of hours, vampires were nothing more than a myth. One that had been responsible for some of both the best and the worst literary endeavours, and that echoed down through the ages to become sanitised by Hollywood into sparkly vampires with sickly complexions, beloved of swooning and incredibly stupid teenage girls. All of the archaeologist's tales were merely that. Just tales. Stories. Pseudo-romantic embellishments of the history of an otherwise ordinary Ottoman castle.

Yeah. Tell that to the ragged, bloody remains of a twenty-five-year-old research fellow who had been Vlad's first real meal in over five hundred long, long years. He had taken the full brunt of Vlad's maddened rage. Flynn and the archaeologist had watched helplessly as a whirling maelstrom of hatred, blood-lust and utter fury swirled around the screaming student, tearing and shredding his skin, ripping it from his face and spraying blood in an arc around the corridor. It moved too fast to see clearly; just a tornado of rage that dismembered the student in a heartbeat.

And then?

Silence.

For a few fleeting seconds, a lull had descended on the corridors, allowing the echoes of the research student's screams to fade into the stone and join the entombed chorus of thousands of other victims locked into the granite blocks for eternity. But then slowly, after the savagery and the silence, came a growing, rolling, maniacal laugh that reached out beyond the walls that had entombed the monster for so long. In the nearby village, the not-quite-so-ignorant-as-everybody-thought peasants who had grown up on fireside stories of the demon that was entombed in the citadel's secret tunnels, bolted their doors, pulled the shutters closed and huddled together, gripped with an ancient fear that their ancestors had passed to them in their very genes. They knew. They knew that Vlad was free. The Dracul, the Black Prince, the Impaler. He was *free*...

* * *

Flynn had been the first to snap out of the terror trance and realise that they weren't dealing with some damn fairy story here, but a real threat. A real *nasty* threat that was just about to turn its attention onto Flynn and the one remaining and utterly freaked out archaeologist. Flynn didn't care whether this monster was the real Vlad, some crazy, inbred village idiot or the damn Devil himself. So he'd reacted in the only way he knew how. Natural or supernatural, this son of a bitch was flesh and blood. So a Glock should have an effect on it, even if it was only to slow the fucker down for a few seconds and give them that chance they needed to put more than twenty feet between it and them. He emptied an entire clip into the thing and watched as its body twitched and danced.

The blood-daubed creature recoiled for a few seconds and then stopped its snapped-marionette-string dance. It smiled, white teeth emphasised by the gore-covered skin. It stood, unfurling and flexing taloned fingers.

"Oh, shit..." Flynn grabbed his charge by the shoulders and screamed one word at him. *"Run!"*

Whatever that thing behind them was, it kept pace. Flynn got the distinct impression it could quite easily overtake and overwhelm them. But it was toying with them like a cat would play with a mouse. It was watching how they reacted, determining how well they knew the terrain. It was assessing them, learning their tactics, and letting them draw it along. Flynn had the distinctly unpleasant feeling that the little the archaeologist had told

SUCKER OF SOULS

him about the legend of the Black Prince being a military genius was just the tip of a blood-soaked iceberg. His skin prickled. Back in Afghanistan there had been this one Taliban chieftain that had made all the others look like complete amateurs. He had had that cold, detached way of disciplining his men that revolved around 'making examples'. The examples were bloody remains left swinging in trees in the savage winter gales that swept through the Tora Bora caves and the White mountains between Afghanistan and Pakistan. He had mounted an IED campaign so successful that it had claimed the lives of twenty regulars and seven Special Forces troops. He had been known for his extraordinary ability to pre-empt when and where the SF teams would go in on a 'flush out', and vanish like a wraith into the mountains, forever one step ahead. He had retained that arrogant, smug smile and defiance right up to the moment Flynn put two bullets between his bloodshot, hate-filled eyes.

Flynn then had to run for his life as the man's two radicalised and equally insanely-violent sons pursued him and his team through the badlands, promises of revenge screamed in Pashto ringing in their ears. He learned then that when you cut the head from the Hydra, two more grow back. Evil is never conquered. It's merely subdued until a greater evil comes to take its place. He had seen that same evil in the eyes of... whatever the fuck that thing was when it paused in its bullet-dance, dropped the mushed-up, ruined heart of the research fellow, and locked its gaze with him. An evil allowed to fester in a dark, vile place for centuries had become focused into a singularity that, when unleashed, would sweep everything before it. And Flynn's Glock17 was going to do fuck-all to stop the bastard, no matter how many clips he emptied into its emaciated, putrefying body...

* * *

Vlad watched the soldier and his charge scuttle away down the corridor and smiled a chilling, venom-filled smile. Cold. Calculating. A military strategist like no other before or since.

Stalking its prey at its leisure. It had waited hundreds of years. It could wait a few moments longer. Blood was only half the meal. It wanted to savour the fear as well. It wanted to hear their hearts pounding in anticipation of the terror that was about to befall them. It relished the futile attempts of a little man with a pop-gun trying to comprehend the evil he faced. That sweet, satisfying moment when the man realised that there was no escape. There was no fate other than the one the Black Prince had chosen for him. The Black Prince smiled a virginal white smile. Soldiers rarely operated alone. So there were more. So he would make sure the little soldier with his useless gun stayed alive long enough to watch any comrades he may have devoured in front of him. The anguish, the rage, the pathetic howling and screaming as he watched the Black Prince's teeth rip into the throats of men he loved like brothers would be almost as delicious as the blood itself.

'Lead on, little soldier. Lead on...'

* * *

Flynn and the archaeologist pelted down the slippery corridors that twisted and turned under the citadel and carried them deeper into the labyrinth. A line of gaffer-taped cables acted like a trail of breadcrumbs leading them back towards the sanctuary of the armoury. Without that advantage they would have become completely turned around in the myriad of tunnels that weaved and meandered beneath the ruined towers and crumbling walls. A wrong turn would take you into a dead end. And a dead end had a very literal sense when you were being pursued by an insane and bloodthirsty monster.

As he shoved the archaeologist again in the small of the back, Flynn pulled out a radio and pressed the squawk button. "Micky, get ready with everything we've got ordnance wise. We're coming in *fucking* hot!"

"*Don't tell me those boffins have gone rogue on your arse? Coo, there ain't nothing worse than a cocky egghead, fella!*" Micky Cox's cheerful voice crackled out of the hand-held and bounced off the stones.

SUCKER OF SOULS

"Don't fuck about, Micky! I'm serious! *FUBAR*! FUBAR like you wouldn't fucking *believe!*"

"Fuck... copy that." Micky's light-hearted tone instantly changed.

Flynn felt himself losing step as the archaeologist, not the fittest of academics, started to slow. The adrenaline was wearing off and panic was starting to take hold. Flynn knew from experience that he had seconds before the bloody fool froze up and probably went foetal on him. He reached out and grabbed the man's shirt, overtook him and ignored the protestations as his coaching method changed from snarled encouragement and threats to brute-force dragging. "Move! We've got a few more turns before we get to the control room. I'll lay money that your bitey friend back there won't be able to get through that door once we've locked it, right?"

The archaeologist gasped as he tried to keep pace with Flynn. "And once we're locked in with nowhere to run, what do you suggest *then*?"

"I'm not thinking that far ahead right now, fella. Priority number one is to stay away from Count Chompula, okay?" He yanked hard at the archaeologist's multi-pocketed waistcoat, hauling him around another corner and a few steps closer towards safety.

They were close.

They were so damn close...

Flynn and the archaeologist rounded the next corner and skidded to a halt, flailing wildly to try and keep themselves from tumbling into the waiting arms of the Black Prince. It stood stooped and filling the corridor, disproportionately long arms full of muscle and sinews ending in talons that would rip through flesh and bone like it was paper. White teeth shone in the flickering light. Unlike those dopey movie vampires, this vicious fucker didn't have two slightly longer canine teeth and a mouthful of perfect orthodontry. It had a whole mouthful of dazzlingly-white points bathed in saliva and dripping with toxins. It opened its maw and hissed like an angry cat. Eyes fixed on the two stumbling men, eyes filled with insanity, hatred and a raging hunger beyond anything Flynn had seen during his humanitarian missions to Sudan. *"Shit!* Back! Back! Back!" Flynn shoved the archaeologist backwards, trying to twist him around. The academic, unaccustomed to any physical activity more strenuous than reaching for a book on a top shelf, lost his balance and collapsed in a heap directly behind Flynn's legs. Flynn toppled backwards, and the archaeologist and CPP bodyguard became entangled in a mess of flailing arms and legs.

Flynn extracted himself and rolled backwards, coming up and drawing the Glock in one smooth move. He knew it wouldn't stop the laughing, blood-smeared monstrosity, but at least it might slow the fucker down a bit again.

The archaeologist had gone foetal, curled up on the floor, whimpering like a baby with bellyache.

'Fuck him. Focus on the target.' Flynn's eyes narrowed and he squeezed the trigger. Two shots rang out and the monster twitched briefly. Then on the third squeeze the Glock, normally a stalwart of reliability, did nothing other than issue a mocking 'click'. "Shit!" Memory gave him a hard slap in the face. He'd emptied most of the clip into the bastard back in the corridor earlier. Damn, damn, *damn!*

Most people would have railed against fact that the clip was empty and pulled the trigger again and again, as if the action would magic some spare ordnance from out of the sky and into the weapon. Flynn had spent six years in Special Forces. He'd spent more time behind enemy lines than the enemy had. So he knew better. The clip was empty; don't fuck about trying to deny the bloody obvious, just reload, prime and fire. Flynn jettisoned the empty clip and fumbled in his vest pocket for a new one, ignoring the old magazine as it clattered against the stones. Normally, he'd be able to reload, prime and start shooting again in a split second. Put him up against a bunch of howling Afghans armed with AKs, bad personal hygiene and angry intent and it would have been a walk in the park. But this? This guffawing, cackling monstrosity? It had him rattled.

So he did the unthinkable.

He dropped the damn clip.

SUCKER OF SOULS

Time demonstrated that whole 'fluidity' concept in glorious technicolour, and decelerated to a crawl. Man and monster watched the clip fall in slow motion, fleeting, flashing glimpses of the jacketed hollow-point bullets emphasised by the matt black of the clip. It hit the ground end on, bounced and spun through three-sixty in mid-air, spewing one bullet off at a right-angle. The clip and stray bullet clattered back down, shuddered and finally came to rest. The errant JHP rolled away into the darkness, lost in the shadows.

Flynn tore his gaze away from the clip and refocused on the grinning face of the monster. He knew, didn't he? The smarmy, grinning motherfucker! He just damn well *knew* that was Flynn's last spare clip. He fucking *knew*.

Flynn was determined to go down fighting. He stuffed the Glock17 back in his belt and pulled out his trusty Blackhawk blade from the drop-down leg holster it liked to call home. No self-respecting SF squaddie would be caught dead without one of these black beauties. The six-inch symmetrical blade was precision ground D-2 steel. It would cut through skin, bone, and flesh, and didn't differentiate between the dead or the undead. Flipping it around so the blade w edge-on against the inside of his forearm and hidden from the monster's line of sight, he smiled back at the monster like a man with nothing left to lose but his life. "Wanna dance, fuck nuts? Huh?" He beckoned with his outstretched left hand. "C'mon, you ugly fuck! Let's do it, let's fucking *dance!* C'mon!"

He knew it was hopeless.

He knew he was going to lose. And that losing meant dying. Badly.

He knew that as soon as that cackling, guffawing bipolar son-of-a-bitch flip-flopped back into black fury and bloodthirsty rage, he'd be facing an enemy whose savagery was beyond all comprehension. Savagery of that level made an opponent practically invincible. He'd seen how fast the thing was when it launched itself out of the cell. Nothing Flynn had ever encountered moved that quickly. His only consolation was that while mister bitey here was getting busy with him, it would give the archaeologist a chance to get out of danger, at least for a few moments. But it might just be enough.

Flynn may have appeared to have scant regard for his charge, but he was a good man. And good men care about those who can't fight for themselves...

* * *

The monster stopped its insane cackling. The hunger was burning in it once more. And this time it lusted after the blood of a warrior, not that of a screaming, pissing boy. It wanted blood filled with passion and fire. Blood that had been spilled on the battlefield. Blood that sang out to him like a war trumpet. The blood of a soldier.

It could sense the man's heart beating, a slow, steady rhythm, not the usual frantic pounding that its victims normally demonstrated. Ah, *delightful!* A true, battle-hardened warrior. They were always the most satisfying, especially at the very end when they knew they had lost their final conflict.

It would also give the Black Prince an insight into modern combat tactics. It knew it was capable of tearing the soldier to pieces as easily as it had devoured the screeching boy earlier. But it wanted to 'dance', as the mocking soldier said. It wanted to see just what kind of a 'dance' these modern warriors engaged in, and how things had changed in the five hundred years it had been locked away in that stinking cell.

But the hunger was also strong. It filled the creature. It consumed every fibre of its being.

Time to feed...

The Black Prince coiled, ready to spring. The soldier was certain to land a few blows before he succumbed, but the brief glimpses of fleeting pain would remind the Black Prince that it was alive. Free. And would be *feared* once again! The beast flexed its taloned fingers. Long, yellowed nails tapered into savage points. The knuckles were pronounced and gnarled, like the knots in a tree trunk. Sinews like cords snaked across the back of its hands and up his arms. It spread its arms, threw back its head and roared – a scream of defiance at those who would incarcerate and starve it for all these years. They were gone. Mere dust and ashes. Corpses for the worms. But Vlad? Ah, Vlad. He was here. He had survived! And now he could feed once more on the blood of a soldier. He lumbered towards his opponent, a low snarl grumbling in the back of his throat cut short when another sound intruded – a soft mewing. The creature stopped in its tracks. Its bloodshot eyes widened in horror and it screeched – a sound so piercing it made his human opponent recoil and cover his ears. The screech went on and on, reverberating around the corridors and echoing through the citadel, folding and doubling back on itself.

A small, calico cat sat serenely in the middle of the corridor, casually studying him. The skinny creature was one of the hundreds of feral cats that inhabited the citadel. For as long as the stone walls had stood, the cats had been there. They served a practical purpose in that they kept rats and mice under control. But the villagers seemed to have a special reverence for the mangy creatures, leaving out food and milk for them and chastising anyone who might feel the temptation to kick one of the creatures in passing. Cats, in this part of Turkey, were almost sacred.

Vlad hated them. They represented its madness, its incarceration, its humiliation. Every time it had fed on one of the screeching beasts, the creature's insides felt as if it had swallowed acid. For days afterwards Vlad would writhe and scream in agony as the cat's blood burned through its body. For Vlad, this tiny, mewing calico cat represented all the torment, the agony and the rage that had turned a man into a monster. What once had been a brilliant young mind had degenerated into that which terrifies mankind the most – a physical manifestation of the darkest evil that we are all capable of becoming…

Vlad recoiled in horror, inching backwards away from the calm little cat. Paying the vampire scant attention, the cat cleaned its paw, a tiny pink tongue darting out as it licked the fur smooth. It stood, stretched its back and legs, yawned and sat back down again, curling its tail neatly around its feet.

SNAFU: SURVIVAL OF THE FITTEST

* * *

Flynn watched as the little cat studied Vlad with that casual interest felines have when they're mildly distracted. Then, it got up, waved its tail in the air and walked towards the creature, purring happily and blissfully unaware that its misplaced show of affection was tormenting the beast.

Vlad screamed again and vanished down the corridor. The cat, baffled by the reaction, stopped and sat down.

Flynn looked at the cat in disbelief, amazed that such a tiny little thing could do what he couldn't – repel a monster. "Well, fuck me."

"He hates cats." The archaeologist had uncurled from the foetal position and stood, supporting his shaking body by pressing his palm against the slick stones that lined the corridor. "Hates them."

"You don't say." Flynn scowled, and put the knife away and pulled out his gun. He stepped forward and rescued his dropped clip, deftly flicking the clip into the butt of the gun before scooping up the cat. "Okay, kitty, you're coming with us." He turned to the archaeologist, Glock 17 in one hand and scrawny cat in the other. "Wanna get out of here before that bastard decides he's more hungry than he is scared of a little pussy?" He nodded towards the darkened end of the corridor. "Straight ahead. Follow the cables. Don't worry. Me and puss here are right behind ya."

The archaeologist stared open-mouthed at the cat for a second, turned, and trotted away down the corridor, slightly crouched and ready to backpedal furiously if Vlad did his 'surprise!' tactic again around the next corner.

Flynn scratched the little cat's head affectionately, and let the agile little critter clamber up onto his shoulder. The deep, rumbling purr felt like a massage cushion on his shoulders. He gave the cat one last affectionate pat and ran after the disappearing academic.

The cat turned and looked back, narrowing its emerald green eyes at *something* in the shadows. Its ears flattened against its skull and it hissed...

SUCKER OF SOULS

* * *

"Shut the door! Shut the damn door!" Colby Flynn dived through the opening and into the armoury. As he tumbled through the air he jettisoned a small calico cat from his shoulder, rolled and came back up on one knee facing back out into the corridor, the Glock17 up and ready. He stared out into the gloom. Shadows crowded in, advancing towards the armoury as one by one the Jerry-rigged bulbs Micky Cox had strung like Christmas lights along the corridor flickered, popped and died. Each section plunged sequentially into darkness, allowing the thick blackness to jump ever closer to the place Flynn hoped would be safer. Flynn knew that if the darkness reached them before Micky got the door shut, they'd all die in that room…

Micky slammed the heavy oak door into the frame and turned the key in the lock. There was no rusty squawking or atmospheric creaking from the hinges. Micky was ex-REME, a Royal Electrical and Mechanical Engineer, and a damn good one. He hated any piece of machinery that didn't work as it was supposed to, no matter how seemingly inconsequential. So the hinges and lock had been cleaned and oiled. They worked perfectly, and the reassuring *click* as the tumblers fell into place was the best damn sound Flynn had heard all day. Micky slid the top and bottom bolts back into their housings, providing additional reinforcement to the lock. He turned, grabbed a thick plank and dropped it into the cradle with a deeply satisfying and wooden-sounding *clunk*. The huge armoury door was now shut – *properly* shut.

Flynn lowered the Glock as Micky leaned against the door. Never point ordnance at your mates. Kind of a rule, really.

"Mind telling me what the actual fuck?" Micky turned and frowned at his boss, his vivid blue eyes narrowing. "Also? What's with the cat?"

"Little Rupert here saved our hides, fella."

"Rupert?"

"What's wrong with Rupert?"

Micky's frown deepened. "Okay, let's gloss over the fact

that you've called some mangy, flea-infested moggy Rupert, you weirdo. And just so you know? I'm allergic to cats."

"Trust me, Mick, you'd be a damn sight more allergic to the thing it stopped from chowing down on our arses, mate. I'd put a week's pay on that." Flynn stood and ran his hand through his dirty blonde hair.

Micky shrugged. "I take it that's what the FUBAR's all about?"

Flynn glanced down at a heap in the corner. The weeping academic had gone foetal again. Flynn sniffed sharply, grabbed a handful of archaeologist and hauled him to his feet. "Upsy daisy, fella." He shook the man like a rag-doll. "Oi! Stop now with all that yodelling and tell us what that thing is, and how we can kill it." He deposited the frightened man on the corner of a table and shook him again. "Because right now, our situ is not good, son. All that's stopping some insane, bloodthirsty creature from tearing you, me and my boys apart is a five-hundred-year-old door and, for some reason, a bloody cat." Flynn glanced at the cat, which was winding its skinny body around Micky's legs and purring loudly. Micky looked decidedly distressed.

"Which damn question do you want me to answer first, Mister Flynn?" The archaeologist sniffed indignantly.

"How 'bout you work through them in order, mate?" A hard cockney voice snapped angrily from the corner and Gary Parks, a hulk of a man with a passion for blowing things up loomed from the shadows. His deep brown eyes shone out from mahogany skin and he raised a quizzical eyebrow. "Boss?"

"Waiting for Poindexter here to enlighten us, fella." Flynn focused on the cowering academic. "Well? There's four of us—"

"And this bloody cat!" Micky sneezed violently. "See? Allergic. Fucking allergic."

"And the cat, yes, thanks Mick. Take an antihistamine. There's some in the medipack."

"Couldn't we just chuck the cat out?"

"The cat stays, Micky. It stays. Okay?" Flynn jabbed a thumb at a pile of supply boxes. "Antihistamine pill. Now. Get it down your neck, you tart." He rolled his eyes. "Allergies. Seriously.

Who the fuck ever heard of a member of the Regiment with allergies?"

"Damn near got him returned-to-unit, boss, remember?" Gary grinned at Micky and flicked him the finger.

"Bollocks, Parks, you 'roided up wanker."

"Focus, you pair of reprobates." Flynn stared hard at the academic. "So. Wanna fill in the gaps, little guy?"

"Mister Flynn, I don't think you realise the seriousness of the situation."

Flynn glowered and slapped the man hard across the mouth. "Really? You think? You think I don't get the fact that whatever that thing is out there has just ripped your mate to pieces and eaten his fucking *heart?*"

"Wait, *what?*" Gary and Micky stared open-mouthed at their boss.

"Or that I emptied two clips of hollow-points into the fucker and all it did was dance a little jig?" Flynn slapped the man across the mouth again. "What part did I miss?"

The archaeologist recoiled from Flynn's raised hand. "Stop hitting me, damn it!" His shaking hands tried vainly to ward off another slap. "I'll tell you, just... please, *stop* hitting me!"

Flynn dropped his hand. "Okay. Start at the top."

"Vlad. It's Vlad."

Gary Parks frowned. "What, as in the Impaler?"

"Isn't that a type of car?"

"That's an *Impala*, Micky, you idiot!"

"Yes, as in the Impaler. The 'Dracula' of legend. Only he's very, very real, believe me." The academic ignored the scowling, sniffling Cox and focused on Flynn and Parks. "Remember that story I told you last night? It's true. Believe me, I'm as surprised as you are. I expected to find nothing but bones, Mister Flynn, I swear!"

"Yeah, well that didn't pan out, did it?" Flynn sighed. "Seriously. Look, sorry about your lad, by the way. That was bad."

"So let me get this straight. We're being laid siege to by *Dracula?* Are you serious?" Micky Cox's voice was filled with incredulity. "Fuck off! That's a myth!"

"Trust me, Mick, that thing out there, whether it's actually Dracula or not, is no damn myth. So let's ignore the fact that we've been dropped kicking and, in the case of Professor Braniac here, screaming into an episode of the Twilight Zone and figure out how we kill that fucker and get everyone out of here in one piece, copy?"

"Copy." The two ex-soldiers nodded. Everything else was irrelevant. Myth or not, the identity of their opponent could be argued over later. They needed to focus on the reality of the situation. This was now a simple matter of survival.

"Right. So what's the state of play with ordnance, Gary?"

"Not particularly tickity, to be honest. We weren't expecting gunfights with angry vampires, boss. We've got two boxes of ammo for the Glocks and the three P90s are stocked up with subsonic rounds, with two spare magazines each. Other than that?" Gary shrugged. "I got some C4, if that helps?"

Flynn stared at his friend. "Why? Why do you have C4, Gary, *why?*"

"I thought it might be useful. Ya know. If we had a cave-in or something. And had to blast our way out. Hey, look. I don't feel right if I ain't got at least a little bit of Play Doh to bugger about with, okay?" Gary's explanation tailed off into a mumbled, petulant mutter.

"Normally, I would be gently taking it off you and calling the men in white coats. But today, you crazy fucker, you might just have convinced me that your presence on this op hasn't been a total waste of a plane ticket." Flynn grinned at his friend. "Good. So we've got C4, some P90s and Glocks, and seriously limited ammo."

"And that bloody cat."

"And Rupert, yes, thanks, Micky." Flynn snapped his fingers at the calico cat and it immediately stopped tormenting Micky and leapt back onto Flynn's shoulder.

"It's not enough," a voice broke in.

All eyes focused on the archaeologist.

"What?" Flynn glared at the man.

"I said, it's not enough. You're not dealing with some Taliban terrorist here, gentlemen. You're dealing with an ancient evil that has defeated whole armies and laid on banquets where his minions feasted on the hearts of his enemies!" The man's voice was hitting the hysteria button pretty hard. "Once it gets through that door? I promise you, none of us will survive!"

Flynn grabbed the man's collar and snarled in his ear. "Not helping, fella, not *fucking helping!* You're upsetting my lads, mate! So enough with the 'we're all doomed' shit, okay?" He tossed the man aside.

"I got a salami sandwich if that's any use?" Micky held up a brown paper bag.

"How the hell would that be of any earthly use whatsoever, you tit? We're up against some denizen of unmitigated fucking evil, not an angry deli counter server!" Gary cuffed his friend across the back of his head.

"Hey! It's got garlic in it. Vampires hate garlic, right?"

All eyes turned again towards the archaeologist. He shook his head.

Flynn shrugged. "Right. So how about sunlight? Don't they burst into flames or something when sunlight hits them? If that's the case, then all we have to do is wait until dawn, old chompy out there has to retreat back to his cell, and we can get you and us out of here, seal up the doors and get the fuck out of Dodge, right?"

Again the archaeologist shook his head. "We're underground, Mister Flynn. It could be midday and it wouldn't make any difference."

"Fine. So our options are we either blow the fucker into pink mist with Play Doh, or die of boredom and bad rations locked in here. Well, honestly boss? I didn't expect to go out like this." Gary Parks glared at the door and picked up a P90, winding the webbing strap around his arm and priming the stubby gun ready for action. "But whatever happens, at least we can go out shooting, right?"

"Reserve your ammo, big guy. Don't get too trigger happy, okay? I've emptied two clips into this bugger and it didn't even flinch. We need to find anoth—"

A massive impact made the door vibrate in its frame. Particles of masonry floated down. A second impact made the door judder again.

"Shit! How big *is* this fucker?" Micky turned and indicated at the ordnance box. Wordlessly and with the fluidity that comes with years of training, experience and working together, Gary grabbed an FNP90 out of the box and tossed it to his friend. Both men took position, stabilising their stance by dropping down to one knee and tucking the P90 hard into their shoulders. They sighted on the door, ready to fill anything that came through with hollow-points. The P90s held 50-shot magazines, so they were pretty sure they could at least dissuade Vlad from simply waltzing in and turning the armoury into an abattoir in short order.

"Wait out..." Flynn gave the order to stand by to engage as soon as the ancient door gave way. A third impact sent tremors through the wood. All three men primed their guns in unison and waited.

A fourth impact. The door flexed – but it held. Just. From beyond the iron-hard blackened wood came a primeval snuffling and snarling. Clawed fingers scrabbled at the wood, sliding ineffectually over fibres that had long ago hardened into the consistency of steel ropes. The snuffling and snarling became frenetic, the sound of scrabbling nails more frenzied. The beast let out a howl of rage and launched a barrage of attacks against the door. A final scream of pure fury rang through the granite corridor then silence. The last few motes of mortar dust floated down.

"Fuck, fuck, *fuck!* Has it gone?" Micky Cox's voice was an equal balance of hard-core 'bring it on, you fucker!' and just enough concern to ensure the element of self-preservation kicked in.

"Doubt it, Mick. Probably just buggered off up the corridor to take a good old run up, mate. Eye's on." Gary Parks' eyes flickered briefly from the door to Flynn. "Now what, boss? Another battering like that and that door's coming down."

"Stand fast." Flynn shifted his grip on his own P90 and waited. "Okay, Professor, suggestions? Because we can't hold this thing off forever."

SUCKER OF SOULS

"I... sir, I'm an archaeologist, not a damn strategist!"

"Fella, I'm an ex-soldier, not Buffy the fucking Vampire Slayer, but you don't see me crying in a corner, do you? Now *think!* Use that brain of yours to try and figure a way out of here!" He jerked his head towards the table. "There's a map of the citadel tunnels on the table. Find us a quick way to the surface. Because Gary's right, that door ain't gonna put up with another battering like that. Mister Bitey out there is coming through on the next assault, and I want to be ready for him."

The archaeologist scuttled over to the table and started poring over the map.

"Boss? I could set a charge if you like? When Sir Chompsalot comes through I could vaporise the bugger, no probs."

Flynn shook his head. "As much as I like the sound of that, it would bring the whole damn chamber down on top of our heads too. Kinda a lose-lose situation, wouldn't you agree?"

"Nah. I can use it like blasting cord. Loop a line of Play Doh around the door frame and direct the explosion inwards. It would contain the blast, wouldn't compromise the chamber ceiling, and give Chompy out there one hell of a headache. If nothing else, it would at least buy us some time to make a run for it. And to be honest? I don't like the fact we're effectively cornered in here."

Flynn looked at his friend. "I agree, mate. Look, are you absolutely sure?"

"Yep."

"You're *sure* sure?"

"Boss, your doubt in my ability to blow shit up in a controlled and refined manner wounds me!"

"Gary, I have no doubt that you can blow shit up. I just don't want you blowing *us* up at the same time." He glanced at Micky. "Mick? You're our engineer. You concur?"

"Do-able. As long as the Play Doh is put on the very edge of the frame it should do exactly as Gary says without compromising the roof. But dude, you better be pretty sparing near the apex of the door arch. If that central keystone block comes down, the whole lot follows it."

Gary nodded. "Duly noted. Boss?"

"Do it."

Gary immediately put his P90 down and turned to the ordnance box. Flynn flickered his eyes away from the door and towards the professor. "Professor? How's it coming? Got a green route out of here yet or what?"

"I may have something…" The professor spun the map around and stared intently at it. "Yes… yes! There's another way out!" He looked up and smiled a hopeful, slightly hysterical smile. "That door is obviously the main exit route, but there's another egress marked here. It drops us into a corridor and then out into the main passageway."

"Aww, bless! Listen to you, fella! Egress!" Micky laughed sharply. "We must be rubbing off on ya. Anyone else would've said a 'secret door'!"

"Leave the man alone, Mick. Right. Where's this 'egress' point, Professor?" Flynn nodded at Micky. "Don't take your eyes off that door, Cox."

"Copy."

Flynn focused his attention back on the academic. "Okay. Show me."

"This is the armoury. This is where we are."

"Well, shit. Thank you for pointing that out to me, professor. I thought I was on the third level at Bluewater fucking Shopping Centre! Door, fella, where's the damn *door?*"

"I… yes, sorry about that. It's supposed to be here." The academic stabbed a finger at the map.

"*Supposed* to be?"

"Well, I'm assuming that's what this symbol means, yes."

"And you know what they say about 'assume' being the mother of all fuck ups, right?"

"Um, boss? We got snuffling over here…" Micky Cox shifted his grip on the P90. Outside the door came that stomach-churning snaffling and scratching. The Black Prince was back and worrying at the timbers.

Flynn walked to his friend's side. "What d'ya reckon he's up to, Mick?"

SUCKER OF SOULS

"Weakest point of any door is the hinges. My guess? If he's smart he'll go for them. But another few shoulder barges and it's going to be a bit of a moot point, boss, because that door is on its last legs. Look." He pointed at the central plank. Bright, fresh wood that had been buried under ages of grime and blackened layers could clearly be seen. The plank was splitting.

"Oh, he's smart, Mick. Believe me." He jabbed a finger at the archaeologist. "Professor, find that trap door or whatever it is. Find it *right* now." Flynn turned. "Gary? We ready, mate?"

"Two minutes."

"We may not have two minutes, big guy." Flynn took up position with Micky. He stared at the door and frowned. "Mick? I've got an idea. You're not gonna like it."

"O-kay?"

"We open the door."

"Fuck off!"

"No, hear me out. If he starts battering that door again, it's gonna give and we'll be wide open with no way of stopping him from coming through full tilt. Trust me, this bugger moves *fast*. So we open the door, fill the bastard with two clips worth of twenty-eights, shut the door again and by then Gary should be ready with his Play Doh and the professor will hopefully have found us a way out of here by the back door."

Cox's eyes widened. "You're insane!"

"You got a better idea?"

"Oh, I dunno, how 'bout I try clicking my heels together three times and say 'there's no place like home'?"

"So that's a no, then?"

"I've found it! The door! I've found it! The professor grunted as he pushed against a massive stack of shelves laden with old boxes. "It's... behind here!" He grunted again.

"Take the damn boxes off, you idiot! Then you'll be able to move the shelves." Flynn looked back at the door. "Okay, fuck that, plan B."

"Good. 'Cause you're bang on, boss, I didn't like plan A."

"We'll do exactly as I said and put the welcome mat out."

"Oh, c'mon, *seriously*?"

Flynn ignored Micky's protestations. "We fill Chompy with ordnance, shut the door bloody damn quick, and then you, me, Gary and the professor get the hell out of here through the trap door. Gary? Don't worry about being all delicate with the Play Doh, mate, put the whole lot up. Everything we've got, just slap and go, okay? We let him think we're still in here, he comes barrelling through the door, trips the detonator and brings the entire bloody castle down on his head. Meanwhile, we're exiting stage left sharpish. Any questions?"

"What about the cat?"

"Rupert comes with me." Flynn looked at the cat and winked. Its green eyes lit up and it started purring loudly again. "All clear?"

"Copy."

"Professor?"

The academic grunted a response and tossed another dust-covered box into the corner. "Um, copy?"

Flynn grinned at the man. "Adda boy! Okay then. On three, Mick."

"Not liking plan B at *all*…"

"One." Flynn heaved the cross beam out of its cradle.

"Two…" He slid the bolts back one by one.

"THREE!" He flicked the key, grabbed the handle and turned, pulling the door wide open. Flynn dropped to the floor so that Micky could fire over the top of him. He angled the P90 up so that anything running towards them would get a belly full of bullets at 45 degrees. He didn't care how 'undead' you were, that would do a *lot* of damage.

Micky aimed into the darkness. "Incoming!"

The Black Prince came howling towards them, venom-laden saliva spraying from his open maw. There was none of the cackling laughter this time. Just a crazed scream that resonated like savage bells from the granite walls, ringing and echoing through the entire citadel.

"Fire!" Flynn depressed the trigger and the P90 spat bullet after bullet at the monster. The P90 could fire nine hundred rounds per minute, so Flynn knew they only had a few seconds before the fifty-round magazine was empty.

SUCKER OF SOULS

Above him a swarm of bullets from Micky's P90 buzzed. The noise was deafening as one hundred rounds focused a colossal amount of kill-power into one soft body.

Blood sprayed the walls of the corridor. Vlad had just fed, so his stomach was full of the congealed remains of his victim. The bullets ripped open Vlad's belly like a piñata. His own guts and those of his latest victim spilled out onto the floor and he screamed. Scooping up his own intestines with one taloned hand, he stuffed them back into his stomach cavity and roared at the two men. He slithered back into the shadows, burbling and spluttering, fresh blood flowing from the dozens of wounds on his body.

"Door! Shut the door!" Flynn rolled out of the way and Micky reacted instantly, slamming the door closed once again and re-securing the bolts, lock and cross beam.

"Gary, you're up!" Flynn scrabbled to his feet, jettisoned the empty P90 clip and replaced it with a fresh one.

Gary sprinted to the locked door and slapped two blocks of C4 on either side of the frame. He inserted a detonator into one, stretched a thin trip-wire across the door frame and into the second detonator on the opposite side. He flicked a switch on the nearest block and a small red LED light started to flash. "Door's live. I strongly suggest *not* being around when it opens."

"Okay." Flynn helped the professor give the shelves one last shove and they toppled over. Behind was a barely visible door, coated in layers of grime and filth. Flynn looked at the door – and the very large and very shut lock. "Okay. Key? *Key?*"

"No key."

"Fuck. Gary? Got any more Play Doh?"

"A little bit."

"Blow the lock."

"Okie dokie." Gary pulled out a small piece of C4, rolled it into a thin sausage and inserted it into the keyhole. He pushed a detonator in and waved everyone back. "Fire in the hole!" He pressed the detonator button and turned his head away, cowering from the small but deadly explosion. The lock, made brittle by years of rust and decay, shattered and the door swung open into a cobweb-infested corridor.

"Go, go, go!" Flynn pushed Micky, the archaeologist and Gary into the passageway. He took one last look at the door. Behind it he could hear the beast snuffling and snarling again. A slow, nasty smile spread over Flynn's face. "Come on in, fella, come *right* on in!" He glanced down at the cat and nodded. "You ready, Rupert?"

The calico cat stood, stretched and mewed softly. His stripy tail lifted into the air and he leapt with one bound onto Flynn's shoulder. "Let's get out of here, shall we, little guy?" Flynn turned and followed his friends into the corridor.

* * *

The Black Prince felt pain. Pain that he had never experienced before. These metal projectiles were very different from the firearms of the fourteenth and fifteenth century. They spat bullets faster than bees erupting from an overturned hive. Vlad smiled. They would be a useful addition to his new army's arsenal. Behind the weakening oak door was not only more living food to help his body repair from its injuries, but more of these weapons too. Time to take ownership of both. He would feed on the small man with the spectacles. The others were soldiers. He appreciated their usefulness. They would be turned, infected with the venom that dripped from his mouth, to be forever compliant servants. He looked at the door, ascertaining its weakest point. The cracked central plank indicated that one more hard impact would shatter the ancient timbers. He let out a scream of delight and ran at the door.

The wood exploded and the Black Prince stood in the fragmented remains of the doorway.

A flashing red dot caught his attention and he peered at it, curious. What new experience was this? Vlad looked closer at the muddy brown block stuck to the stone arch. Inserted into its centre was a metal cylinder and the torn end of a wire.

The light stopped flashing…
* * *
Further into the tunnel a muffled 'boom!' and a shower of debris

from rotting walls and crumbling ceilings caused the four men to stop, crouch and cover their heads with their arms. Stones and lumps of mortar clattered down and the men balled up tighter, pressing their backs against the wall.

Flynn was the first to uncurl. "Sounds like matey's found our little gift. Let's not wait around to find out if he's gonna send a thank-you card. Move!" He hauled the archaeologist to his feet. "C'mon, fella, let's get you back to the hotel for a nice hot bath and a couple of bottles of that local shit."

"Which way?"

"Follow the cat." The four men trotted after the little calico cat out into the main passageway – and straight into the waiting arms of a crowd of shuffling, snarling vampires.

These were Vlad's most trusted lieutenants, whose own tombs beneath the armoury had been cracked opened by the explosion. The cat stopped, flattened its ears and hissed like an angry kettle.

Flynn brought his gun up to his shoulder and swore passionately. "Oh, you have *got* to be fucking kidding me…"

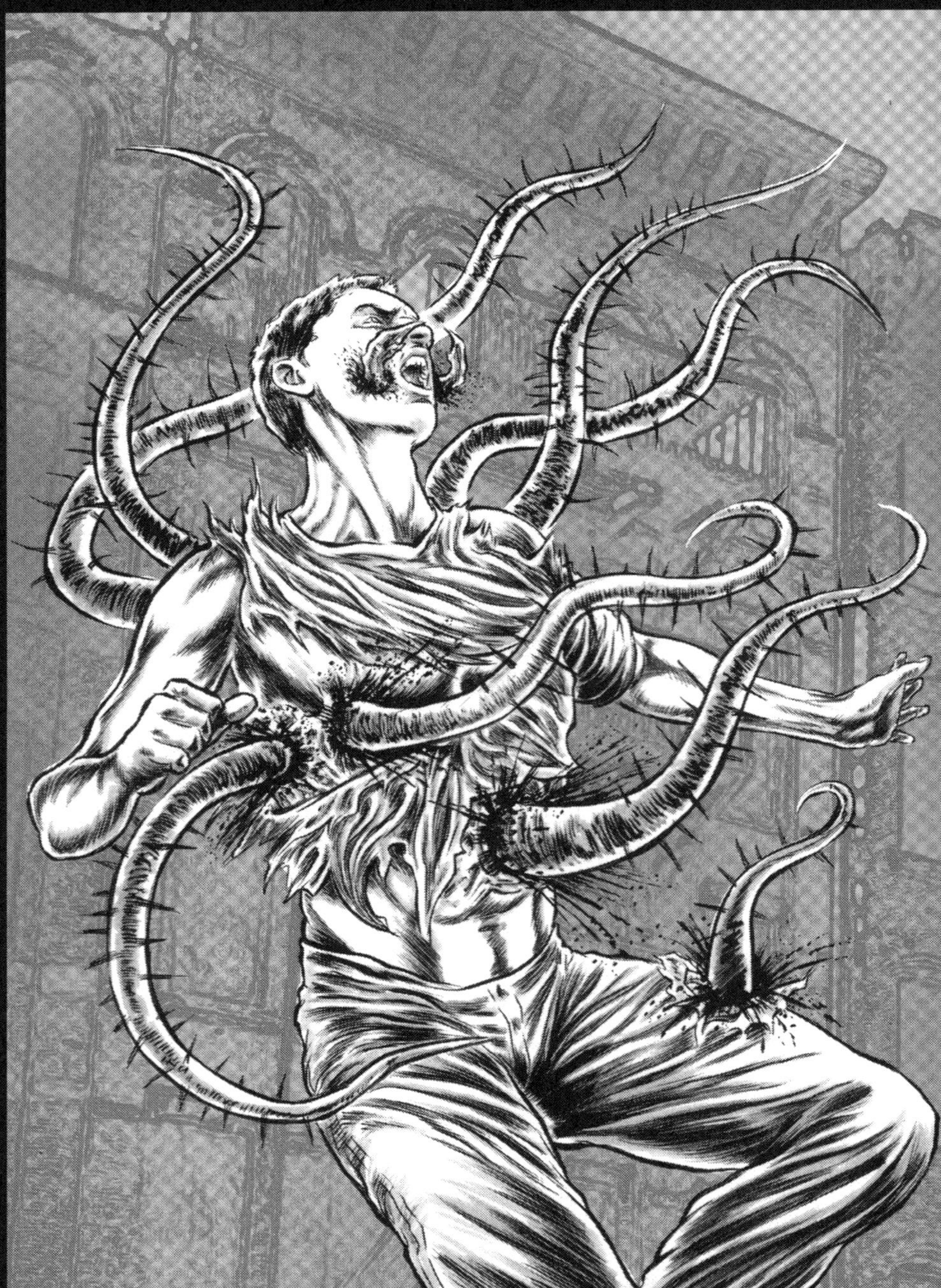

AFTER THE RED RAIN FELL
Matt Hilton

Minutes Ago...

I should originally have been on point, but I'd been given the task of breaching the locks on the doors so "Duke" Dickinson went in first, and Duke died instead of me. I'd be a liar if I said a small part of me wasn't thankful. Duke was no slouch, he was an experienced soldier, and he was armed with an M4 that'd tear new arseholes in an entire roomful of men, but the poor sod didn't even get off a shot.

Our six-man team was stacked, ready for dynamic entry. I was the dedicated breacher, armed with a Remington 870 with a pistol grip and 12.5-inch barrel, and protected from any flying debris by a helmet, Oakley M-frames and breaching gloves, as well as an anti-ballistic vest over my battle fatigues. I aimed the shotgun at a downward angle at the lock, standing the requisite safe distance away, breathing slow and steady as I listened for the go. Cameras mounted on our helmets relayed live footage of the op back to a control vehicle where our officers counted down. I probably looked cool and collected but my butt-hole was twitching in anticipation.

Greenlight.

I pulled the trigger.

The shockwave from the Hatton round pulverised the locking mechanism and bolt. I ducked back against the jamb, allowing the shotgun to swing on its shoulder harness, and brought up my own M4 as Sgt 'Hooky' Johnson yanked the door wide and Duke powered inside. And that was it for him. A split-second of thunder as he brayed out a challenge that echoed through the warehouse, then steaming chunks of him splashed the threshold. Hooky was only a beat behind him, and he skidded on a slick tubular worm of Duke's intestines. He went sideways, his shoulder rebounding off the doorjamb before he righted and lurched inside. His boots sucked at the splash of bloody guts on the concrete floor and he cursed loudly, but then the rest of us were charging past.

Things had happened so quickly that none of us realised there'd been no detonation, no drumroll of gunfire, that had ripped Duke to pieces, and we were already inside that gloomy space before I recalled that this was going to be no normal sweep and clear operation. Not by any stretch of the imagination.

The team was one man down and had no clear idea of what we were up against.

But we had an objective from which we wouldn't back down.

We had to sweep and clear the building, each of us with an area of responsibility to secure with overlapping fields of fire, immediate, near and far zones. With Duke torn to shreds, it meant the responsibilities shifted for team members, but we were experienced enough that we could flow with the shifting circumstances. Hooky was now point man, and he cleared the immediate and near zones with one blistering hail of bullets while the rest of us formed a stack alongside the first corner we came to. While I crouched there, ready to proceed again, I looked for hostiles, dead or alive, but there were none.

So what the fuck had killed Duke?

Something shifted in the darkness ahead.

Hooky fired, his M4 lighting the corridor beyond with sporadic flashes.

"What the hell was that?" he said.

"Whatever it was," snapped Jack 'RP' Wilson, "it got Duke. We aren't leaving this place 'til I'm wearing its fucking skull for a hard hat."

RP moved past Hooky, sliding along a wall in the darkened corridor, his carbine seeking targets. Hooky signalled the rest of us to move while he covered from the corner. I glanced at him as I passed, and saw that he was chewing his lips. He blinked at me. "I put half a clip into that fucker and it didn't go down. Stay frosty, Muppet."

Hooky wasn't insulting me. We'd all gained monikers that had stayed with us since basic training. My real name is Bill

AFTER THE RED RAIN FELL

Grover. Think of that blue puppet with the red nose from Sesame Street and you'll understand why I got stuck with 'Muppet'.

"I'm icy, Sarge," I promised him. No way would I admit to almost shitting myself, even though we all were.

Then RP was in full reverse and his machine gun roared.

The two guys in front of me – 'Brainpan' and 'Twinkle' – made target acquisition at much the same time. Their M4s screamed in unison as brass rattled on the floor at their feet. Flashes and sparks lit the corridor, and beyond the drifting smoke I watched the shadows surge and contort, glimpsing reaching hands, and heads lolling on malformed shoulders. Many of their rounds struck walls, floor and ceiling, but as many bullets found their targets. The solid smack of projectiles through flesh was a drumroll that sung to my heart. I raised my M4 to join in with the chorus.

But then Brainpan edged back, his eyes rolling as he glanced at me. Twinkle yelled something animalistic, a split second before he was yanked bodily into the surging wave of inhumanity that swept towards us. There was the briefest attempt at fighting back, Twinkle's carbine snapping off a short burst, and then the timbre of his yelling changed to bleats of terror. His last scream was ripped in two along with his body.

"Twinkle's down," I yelled, and propped my M4 to my shoulder, filling the gap he'd left with a hail of rounds.

Brainpan was still backpedalling. "Get the fuck out, Muppet! There's no stopping them."

He was right. For all that my rounds punched into bodies, scattered gobs of bloody meat and bone in all directions, the tsunami of bodies advancing along the corridor came on as if untroubled. For the first time I got a clear view of the mass of limbs and torsos through my Oakleys and knew I'd be as well trying to hold it back with a pea shooter.

"Fall back!" Hooky's order was rhetoric; I was already backing up alongside Brainpan. We fired, but we were wasting rounds.

"Shoot them in the fucking head," Hooky commanded.

I did, but it was advice he'd gleaned from watching too many B movies, and was woefully misinformed. I blatted skulls, one after the other for all the difference it made, because the insidious things just kept on coming and coming. Chest shots didn't stop them either. The only thing that slowed them was to render their limbs to stumps, but that was only momentary because they still flopped and squirmed, worming their way across the ground with singular intent. You might think an eviscerated torso harmless, but that wasn't the case. These things didn't need teeth to gnaw or fingers to rip, when even their jellied flesh consumed.

There were dozens of them, maybe even hundreds, because it was too dark to tell beyond the sporadic flashes of our weapons. The darkness surged and moved, and I was sure that those we could see were only the leading trickle of a tidal surge.

"Where the fuck did they all come from?" Again Hooky was shouting questions for questions' sake as he laid down covering fire. None of us knew. All we'd been briefed on was that there was a small cell of infected holed up inside the warehouse, and we'd been given the order to go in and clean them out. Nobody told us to expect a horde.

Maybe it was something to do with the hive mind these things were suspected of having. Once assimilated, you became part of the larger organism. Maybe their cell had reached out and called more of their kind. Whatever. All that was important now was getting back out again with our arses intact.

Four of us.

Minutes ago we'd been six. A third of our force down already, and our chances of making the exit door were getting slimmer with every expended round and yet another failure to drop any of those things.

"Fire in the hole!" Brainpan was growing desperate. Using grenades in the corridor was as likely to kill us as it was the shambling mass surging towards us. But what was done was done. I turned, crouching, ducking my helmeted head as if that would save me. The grenade went off within the mass of limbs and torsos so the detonation was dampened by the pile of flesh between it and me. The sound was like God's loud clap, and then I was pummelled by raining chunks of meat and bone. Some of the sharper clumps rattled off my helmet or stuck in my fatigues. Thankfully a spearing rib fragment lanced into my antiballistic vest and not in my throat. Blood spray was all over my Oakleys. I didn't try wiping the smear away, just yanked off the M-frames and threw them aside, even as I lurched up and ran back to the first corner we'd initially cleared.

Brainpan wasn't named for his high IQ.

"Crazy fucker," I snarled at him. "You almost took me out with that grenade. Next time a heads-up would be appreciated."

"If it comes to it, I'd rather go out to a grenade than torn limb from limb by those things," Brainpan replied. "Promise me, if they're gonna get me, you stick a frag down my pipe first."

RP smacked a gloved hand across Brainpan's helmet. "Don't fucking tempt me," he snarled. "I might just as well do it now as later."

Shaking my head, I checked on Hooky. The blaze of the sergeant's carbine told me where he was in the opposite corner, and only his covering fire had given Brainpan and me a moment to chat. There was no more time for talk, just saving our butts.

We backed into the entrance vestibule. The shuffling, creaking and bubbling noises of our enemies filled the space as Hooky's shooting fell silent. He jerked his head at the door we'd so recently blown open. "We can't let them get out," he said. "If they do that, and in these numbers, they'll be all over town like sweat rash on a crack addict's arse."

He was correct. We thought we'd only to deal with a small bunch of infected people, not a horde. If they escaped the warehouse – an easy egress through the demolished door – their numbers would spread like wildfire once they got among civilians. We had to deny them escape, but I didn't see how our guns, or even frag grenades, were up to the task.

But I guess that was what we were being paid for.

"When the fuck did I sign up for this shit?" Brainpan moaned.

"The same time the rest of us did," I said, "after the red rain fell. Now suck it the fuck up, Brainpan. I don't intend joining the flock, but neither am I going to let these bastards out if I can help it."

SNAFU: SURVIVAL OF THE FITTEST

"The world's already gone to hell," Brainpan reminded me. "Why fight it?"

"Because we can," I said, full of shit. "No, because we must."

My understanding of the plague is at a layman's level, but here's what I know. Back in 2009, after sending up high-altitude weather balloons, the Indian Space Research Organisation discovered three types of bacteria living in the extreme conditions of the upper atmosphere, at heights of more than forty kilometres, hailing them as proof of extra-terrestrial life. Debate was lively among scientists, some claiming that the bacteria could have originated on Earth, thrown into the upper atmosphere by volcanic eruptions, rather than having arrived there from outer space. Regardless of where the bacteria originated, it had to contend with conditions deadly to terrestrial bacteria. The UV rays alone were intense enough to kill them, let alone the extremes of temperature, lack of organic matter and sparse air particles, yet they flourished. Those were only the first of many discoveries concerning new life forms over the next few years, though nobody deemed them a threat to humanity. How wrong they were.

Intense solar flare activity, unprecedented weather patterns, and the shifting of the air currents all conspired against mankind, and in true Biblical fashion deluges from the heavens brought with them other uncategorised life that fell in gobbets of scarlet jelly-like lumps throughout many regions of the Earth. These scarlet globs were colonies of bacteria, and they responded robustly to the kinder conditions of the Earth's surface, propagating wildly, and largely unchecked. Within days the simple bacterial forms had mutated into something more akin to parasitic amoebas. They weren't picky about what they infested. Though they had no interest in the planet's flora, everything else they contacted was fair game. All animal life was under threat of infestation, and the major culling of livestock and household pets wasn't enough to stop the advance of the plague spreading throughout the world. How did you cull the wildlife, the vermin, or the insects, that continued the spread at exponential rates?

Throughout history there have been many major extinction

AFTER THE RED RAIN FELL

events, most famously the one that wiped out the dinosaurs, and people began fearing that we were on the verge of the next and greatest extinction event the Earth had faced. But they were wrong. This wasn't about extinction, it was about transformation. Infected creatures didn't die, they *became*. Parasites require hosts to survive, and they need a manner in which they can continue to propagate their species. The mutations they caused were as wildly different and numerous as the creatures they infected. Seeing a beloved pet dog sprouting insectile mandibles and writhing tentacles armed with thousands of stinging needles can kind of throw you a loop, but seeing your fellow man transform into something equally unrecognisable, a walking delivery system for the alien species, can seriously fuck up your day.

There was a rudimentary intelligence in these new beings, one with singular focus. To spread their kind. It wasn't about killing – apparently humans held the monopoly on that intent – but they weren't beyond protecting themselves, and anything they deemed a threat was responded to with devastating consequences. Take Duke and the way he'd been torn to shreds. A similar fate was on the cards for the rest of us who'd the temerity to attempt stopping their progress. But as I'd just told Brainpan, we must.

The infected poured into the room. Literally *poured*, like thick lumpy soup from an overturned cauldron. It was easy to see now why our guns were proving ineffective against them, because they had truly assimilated their hive mind now only one conjoined thing about them. Their jellied flesh and contorting bones had merged and moulded together, so that instead of hundreds they had become one immense writhing mass of mutated inhumanity. The pulpy mass was enough to engulf and drown us, before we too would become one with it, but the creature felt threatened and wished only to see us destroyed. It had sprouted spines and claws, and huge scythe-like protuberances, and without thinking too much on it I now knew what had minced Duke Dickinson.

RP said he'd wear its skull for a hard hat. Well, he had the choice of dozens, because the heads that once belonged to living, breathing human beings were now bobbing and weaving on thick tubular arms, and in those warped faces the eyes bulged and glared, and again without too much thought, I knew that the monstrous creature could see through them all at once. The heads swivelled on those tubes like crab eyes, simultaneously fixing all four of us under baleful stares. It weighed and judged us, and made its own target acquisition. A barbed tentacle shot from the mass, the tip formed of something like hardened chitin, and it cut through RP's chest armour like it wasn't there. He barely had time to croak out his agony, before the tentacle spasmed and he flew off his feet, suspended in the air a moment before he was slammed against the ceiling, then the floor, his body was a sack of broken bones. The monster wasn't done with him though. The spear tip must have parted down the middle, because it scissored open, and the upper half of RP landed wetly at my feet while his legs flew over the mass, where other snatching claws tore them into bony fragments.

"Fuck me..." What else could I say?

Now our team was halved. And with RP that was stating the obvious.

Brainpan screamed. But give him his due, he funnelled his horror into rage and he fired, unloading on the vicious tentacle weapon and ripping it to fragments. But it was hardly respite, because half a dozen more tentacles writhed overhead, and the creature had picked the next man to die.

Me.

Lance-tipped, one of those writhing tentacles exploded towards me. I threw myself down, and the tip struck the wall instead of my body. It jammed in the plaster, before the creature yanked free, but by then I was scrambling for my life. The lance scythed overhead by inches and again I just threw myself bodily away. I went down flat on my face. A second lance-tentacle snapped into the floor inches from my eyes, and gritty concrete peppered me. I scrabbled sideways, finally got my M4 up, and fired off an arc of rounds. Whether I hit anything of importance or not I'll never know, because by then I was back on my knees, then my feet, and then hauling arse away from the next sweeping tentacle.

Something snagged my collar.

I hollered, battering furiously backwards with an elbow.

"Watch it! You nearly broke my fucking face!" It was Hooky, and he had a hold of me, propelling me towards the door we'd so recently entered by.

"Sarge, where's Brainpan?" My words were a breathless wheeze.

Hooky thumbed backwards.

I looked, but my vision was filled with grit and tears and I could make nothing distinct out of the writhing mass now filling the vestibule area.

The harsh detonation of a grenade hinted at where our pal was. But it was followed seconds later by the ripping and tearing of flesh, Brainpan moaning as each chunk of him was torn away.

"Should have held on to that grenade, Brainpan," I said as I slammed my shoulders to the wall alongside the doorjamb.

"Hold that door, Muppet." Hooky was braced against the other doorjamb. His carbine flashed.

I fired too, but the mag fell empty after a short burst of rounds. I grabbed at a full mag even as I dropped the empty one, rammed in the fresh ammo. Before I could hit the arming bolt my M4 was snatched upward. A hand – human-like – but on the end of an insectile arm with too many joints, wrenched my gun up and away. Another one grasped my throat, even as a third punched me in the groin. Only my armour saved me, but I still experienced the dull ache in my nuts from the impact. A lance speared for my face. I ducked out of instinct, my chin mushing into the jellied flesh encircling my throat, and the lance-tip careened off my helmet and sank into the doorjamb with a crack louder than a gunshot.

I fought to get free of the hand choking me. But I went down, and now the insectile arms rose up and the hands transformed into wicked hooking talons. They raked down on me, not to rip me apart but to ensnare my clothing and drag me towards the pulpy mass now rearing over me. Hooky swung in like a barbarian warrior, his M4 empty, but still a club. He batted at the arms dragging me, breaking fragile limbs that at once reformed, growing needles that hardened into giant thorns. Something akin to a giant thresher arm ripped sideways through the air and hit Hooky in the chest. He flew out of my vision, and if I'd to be totally honest, out of my immediate concern. I tore away from the grasping limbs, and fell out of the door.

How many minutes had passed since I'd gone inside?

It'd be under three, but it had felt like an eternity.

Five heavily armed soldiers had died in less than one hundred and eighty seconds. What did that mean for the rest of humanity? I was never very good at math, but even I could add up our chance of survival if this thing was allowed to continue unchecked. If it were only about halting this one mass then perhaps the human race had some hope, but this was only one of millions of outbreaks already reported. Though this was the first where the individually infected had been known to come together in one massive conjoining. Was that the plague's eventual intention, to become one entity? A world-wide mass formed of a singular living organism? Fleetingly I imagined a planet wreathed in a reddish pulpy mass, the only signs of terrestrial life the trees and bushes, all animal life consumed – no, combined. It was a nightmarish snapshot, but it was enough for me to rage against it.

"Sarge?" I yelled. "Hooky! Where are you?"

The chatter of his gun told me he was still fighting for his life.

I looked back to where our command and support team was entrenched. There should have been a dozen armed troopers, vehicles, and a 50-cal machine gun. They were no longer where I'd last seen them. I saw the back end of a truck – troopers stacked in the rear – burning rubber for a nearby underpass.

"What the fuck?" As usual my question was rhetoric. I knew what was wrong. Our ill-fated assault on the warehouse had been observed via our helmet-cams, second by second, and death by violent death, and our officers had given the order to fall back from a fight they knew they couldn't win with conventional weapons. They thought both Hooky and I were dead, so I could partly forgive them for abandoning us, but they should have made sure. You didn't leave anyone behind, not ever.

That thought galvanised me, because I'd all but abandoned Hooky to his fate, so who was I to judge? I immediately turned to the open doorway. My Remington 870 still hung on its sling from my shoulder, and I'd regular ammo in the chamber – once the Hatton round was fired, you needed a backup plan in case the breach man came under immediate assault. I swung it up into play, and went back inside.

The amorphous creature now filled the vestibule area, a writhing mass of limbs and protuberances less identifiable. Heads on tubular arms swung towards me. One of those malformed faces was still identifiable by its twinkly blue eyes, the defining feature that had given him his nickname during basic training. There was no hint of recognition in Twinkle's eyes as they swivelled towards me. His mouth opened in a soundless snarl and his teeth were wicked barbs.

"Sorry, Twinkle," I whispered.

I blasted his head to mince.

"Muppet? Muppet!"

Despite the odds, Hooky was still alive. I looked at where the creature seemed to be focusing and saw the vague form of Hooky barricaded behind an overturned desk. He was out of ammunition for his M4, and down to only his sidearm. Rather than waste bullets, he was using his revolver's barrel to bat away the questing hands reaching for him, but other thin, pulsating tendrils had wrapped his arms and one leg. The creature seemed to understand that he was no longer much of a threat and had chosen to assimilate rather than rend him to pieces.

"Get it the fuck off me!" Hooky roared.

I racked the Remington, fired, racked and fired.

Chunks of protoplasmic jelly flew, splinters of chitinous stuff crackled on the floor. The bulk of the creature swung towards me, but those tendrils kept a firm grip of Hooky, tugging him up and out of hiding. He fired at close range with his pistol, to little effect.

"Muppet! Do something!"

"I'm trying, I'm trying!"

Racked and fired.

"I've one round left. I'm not gonna waste it!" Hooky promised.

"Don't! Let me…"

Too late. Hooky placed his gun barrel under his chin.

Our gazes met, both our heads shaking in denial.

Hooky squeezed the trigger.

"Fuck!" he yelled. "I miscounted. Muppet, you'll have to do me. Don't let this thing have me."

"Can't, Sarge," I said.

"Fuck you, you can. Just fucking do it. That's a *bloody order!*"

I fired.

But not at Hooky. I placed the shot into the nearest claw bearing down on me. I'd tried to count my rounds too. How many left? I racked and the spent shell clattered at my feet. It caught my eyes as it bounced, and only then did I see the squirming tendrils that had wormed across the floor to latch around my ankles. I turned the Remington on them, but the gun clacked empty. I used the stock as a club, mashing the tendrils into the floor, kicking and dancing free. When next I checked, Hooky was suspended in the air, and now it wasn't only tendrils that had him, but four of the insectile arms. In desperation, Hooky had yanked out his knife, his final recourse to cut and slice.

"Muppet! You coward! Just fucking do me."

I threw away my shotgun. Pulled out my sidearm.

Deeming him more trouble than he was worth the creature lanced Hooky through the gut, the tip spearing out of his lower back, dripping with his viscera. Blood flooded his mouth, but he turned to me, his eyes pleading. *You can do it*, his expression said.

OK, Sarge, mine said.

I shot him in the face.

The creature must have sensed his instant demise, because it suddenly whipped half a dozen lances into him and they scissored, chunks of bloody flesh and splintered bones flying overhead. Then those lances whipped towards me.

I tripped, but good job, because my fall took me back out of the door and I slid down the short incline to the pavement. Before I'd got my arse under me, the monster was forcing its gelatinous bulk out of the doorway, reminiscent of the way an octopus can contort and constrict to negotiate seemingly impossible places. As its compressed form cleared the doorjamb, it grew exponentially, almost flooding the ground around the exit with barely recognisable shapes. The heads had absorbed into the mass, but now they began popping out on those stalks. Rolling eyes searched for and then fixed on me. Sitting there, I fired, and my rounds took some of those faces, some of those bilious eyes, but for each one I obliterated a couple more oozed out of hiding.

It began pouring towards me, and those waving arms that came through the door reached out. But they didn't snatch at me; they simply wavered overhead, the fingers moving like an impatient pianist's.

I didn't run.

Why bother?

Something squirmed in my chest and I knew.

I allowed my handgun to slip from my fingers and reached down to fasten it over the splinter of rib bone that had pierced my vest when Brainpan let loose with that first grenade. The bone was red with gore as you'd expect, but the red was too jellified to be human. I pushed down on the rib and felt a corresponding scratch against my own sternum.

Sonofabitch...

The bone had punctured my vest, got through my fatigues to the skin beneath, made a shallow groove in my flesh. The wound was so inconsequential that it hadn't really registered when I'd expected to be torn to ribbons by the detonation. Shit, at the time I'd only been thankful that the rib hadn't sliced through my windpipe. Now I wasn't as sure.

The squirming was in my throat in the next instant, and in my gut and groin. I felt as if I needed to shit. I did pee; there was no controlling it. I rolled back my head and peered up at the hands above me. They now gestured, coaxed me, soothed me with their gently waving motions.

Now...
I am becoming.

Bill Grover is a memory, one that will be forever lost, forgotten, no more. Muppet barely exists anymore. I can't recall the names of my teammates. They aren't important. They were a threat but they have been dealt with. I shouldn't be troubled with their memories. *They... are... no... more...*

I look to the greater part of me. Those welcoming hands, those faces that are me, those lancing spines that will protect me, and I reach up to accept.

A noise.

Some dim recollection tells me what it is.

Something called an 'officer' once watched me.

Abandoned me.

Called in this rocket strike.

I don't know what a rocket is any more.

I don't even recognise these final words that play through my fleeting conscience, but I know they are dangerous.

Offsuuu... I moan in warning to my beautiful brethren.

Rohcutt...

My words lose meaning.

I am become.

White and heat and burning...

I am...

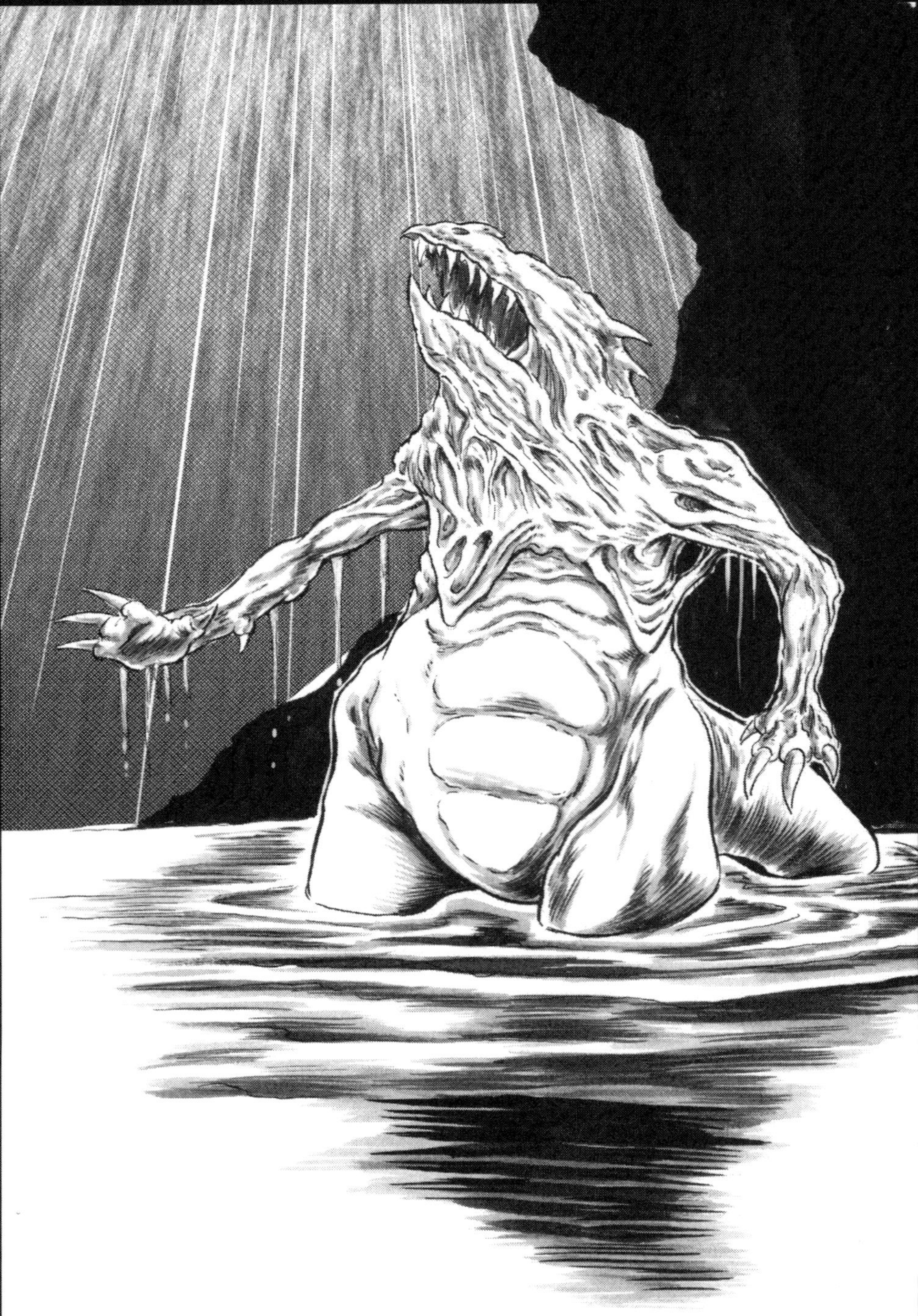

THE SLOG
Neal F. Litherland

Vietnam smelled like an off-season slaughterhouse. It had been washed by rain and perfumed by flowers, but even after Mother Nature scrubbed and polished the sprawl it was impossible to forget what was underneath. Impossible to forget the sharp tang of cordite and the fresh shit smell of bladders and bowels being emptied. The jungle had blood on its breath, and once that abattoir stink got in the nose you never forgot you were in a cattle chute.

They all coped with that the memory of that smell in different ways. Baxter stripped and cleaned his 60 from belts to barrel every night, his hands assembling and disassembling the pins and latches like it was a lethal rosary. Hawkins read and re-read his letters from home until they were smeared and smudged, tattered around the edges like he'd sucked all the well-wishes out of them. Big Billy Watts built card houses in the moonlight, and before he rolled into his fox hole he knocked 'em down like a kid with building blocks. They brought their rituals and their talismans, their whispered prayers and their good luck charms. They didn't really believe those things would keep them safe, but they needed something to hold fast to when the sun went down and the shadows grew bold.

"So there I am, one big bastard on either arm, my hands cuffed behind my back, and my dick still hanging out of my fly," Johnny drawled, carefully arranging the crown of royals in his helmet band from Jack to King. "They haul me in, and dump me on the bench like a sack of taters. I drop right on my nuts, and for a minute I swear I can hear bells ringing and angels singing."

"Must have been a lucky drop," Jenkins said, running the razor edge of his Bowie knife down his left cheek. He had a dozen scars attesting that blade shaving hadn't always been so easy for him. "Ain't much of a target to hit."

SNAFU: SURVIVAL OF THE FITTEST

"When my eyes uncross the chap's staring down at me, his greens pressed and his little collar on," Johnny continued, wiping his florid face on his sleeve and ignoring the commentary. "He tells the monkey patrol to take the bracelets off. Problem is my hands are still numb, so I'm trying to tuck myself back in still half a sheet to the wind and I can't even bend my fingers."

Simms was rolling up his poncho from the night before, Gardner was scraping the rest of his MRE between his yellow teeth, and Cooper was going through a last check on his med kit before slinging it over his shoulder. Nobody was really paying attention to Johnny; he was a radio with one station. He faded into the background more often than not, but his stories about what he did once his pretty Susan broke up with him were still better than silence.

"Finally I get my gun holstered, and the chap's giving me that hellfire and brimstone look." Johnny turned down the corners of his mouth so they cut deep grooves in his sweaty cheeks, and narrowed his eyes so his forehead wrinkled up. The expression added thirty years to Johnny's face, and made him look like the chaplain's red-headed younger brother. That got a chuckle out of some of them.

"The old man say anything?" Luke asked. His back was against a tree stump, and he was rolling a smoke just as thin and dark as he was. A smile played around the corner of his lips, like he'd heard it all before and still found it just as funny the second time around.

Johnny folded his arms across his chest, and like magic the twang was gone from his voice. Instead it was low, deep, and serious. "Is there something you want to confess, my son?"

That got some real laughter. Johnny grinned, and he was himself again. A few more ears turned, but the soldiers' eyes stayed busy on the jungle. Luke touched his tongue to the paper, and dug out an old steel lighter. He flicked it, and touched the flame to the tip of his smoke.

"So I says to him 'no sir, I can't think of anything I've done that I need to confess.' He puts his hand on my shoulder, leaning over me like he's about to give me the facts of life, right? He looks me right in the eyes, and he says, 'John, you need to confess before you go back out into that jungle. If you don't there's no telling what might happen.'"

"So what did you say?" Luke asked, the words dribbling up from his lips in a blue mist.

"Well I thought about it for a minute," Johnny said, screwing up his face like he was trying to remember what year he needed to be born to buy a beer. "And I said to him, 'Father, are you telling me I might end up in the Slog?'"

Gardner choked on his last swallow of runny eggs. Jenkins' blade stopped, poised just under his jawbone. Even Simms looked up from his meticulous rolling and tying with a nervous, piano-wire smile on his face. Luke let smoke trickle out of his open mouth, dragging it back in through his flaring nostrils. The wind died down, and the trees leaned closer; as if the jungle was curious to hear the rest of Johnny's story.

Everybody had a story about the Slog. A grunt in Baxter's old squad said it was a ghost town set up by CIA spooks somewhere deep in the shit. The way he told it the ghosts took deserters, protesters, draft dodgers, and VC fighters, then did something to their heads. The spooks fed them dope, and poked around in their brains until all they could say was "yes sir" before turning them loose in the jungle with no fear, no pain, and a fully loaded M16. Baxter always shook his head and laughed, but he wouldn't look anyone in the eye when they asked if he believed it.

Jenkins was getting drunk in a bar one night when he heard a couple of non-coms tossing back rice whiskey and talking tall. One of them got real quiet before he told his buddies he'd heard from a green beret that the Slog was where all of the special forces had bivouacked deep in the jungle. He said the greenies had taken over some half-rotted stone temple all covered in red stains and letters nobody could read. According to him the greenies took VC prisoners, staked them out on top of the tallest stones, and cut them up one piece at a time. They let the blood flow, and howled out the old names that wind, rain, and the jungle damp had spent centuries trying to erase from the walls and floors of that unholy place. What they did after was worse though, and when his drinking buddies prodded for more the storyteller tossed back another shot and refused to talk about it anymore.

Luke had been sitting up keeping watch with Cooper one night when the medic had started shaking. Before his teeth had finished chattering Cooper told Luke about his first week on patrol. It had been a routine nature hike until a kid named Frankie Prince had found a booby trap the hard way while walking point. The kid had lost a leg, half his face, and most of an arm, but Cooper had kept him alive. They called in an evac but it didn't come. Frankie had been lying there moaning and twitching, slipping in and out of consciousness. Cooper was half-nodding when the kid's good eye shot open, and he grabbed the medic's arm hard enough to leave week-long bruises. Frankie said they were all dead, dead and rotting in the Slog. He said he'd be dead too if he didn't get out. He took two more deep breaths, and then whatever was still holding on inside Frankie let go. Cooper said it was like watching someone's soul drown. Ten minutes later the medic threw up in the latrine.

Gardner had been chasing the dragon in a chop-down tent while some guy two puffs away from floating out of his skin babbled about screaming trees, and something pale and blind swimming down out of sight in the swamp water. Simms had been down in the brig trying to ignore a shiner he'd gotten for taking a swing at his sergeant while the guy in the next cell muttered about ghosts coming to drag him down into the mud. According to the guard the guy had been the only survivor of his unit, and he'd tried to desert twice right out of the hospital. Whatever it was he saw out there had scared him bad enough he was less afraid of a court martial than staying in-country for one more day. In the end he chewed off his own tongue, and choked on it. Even Johnny, with his freckles and carrot-colored high-and-tight wore a hard grin when he said the name of the place out loud. Like those two words might be enough to call up the devil.

"Well," Luke said, blowing his two-stroke smoke back out through his nose. "What did he say?"

THE SLOG

Johnny gave Luke a you-aren't-going-to-believe-this-shit head shake. The redhead opened his mouth, and the right side of his head exploded like his skull had sneezed. Half a second later lead rain poured through their little camp, accompanied by the distinctive, clacking chatter of Kalashnikovs. Men dove for foxholes, snatching helmets with one hand and rifles with the other. Luke rolled, sucking in breath and choking on his smoke as a nine-pound sledge slammed into his back and sent him tumbling. He crashed into the bottom of his foxhole head-first, and his teeth snapped shut like a spring-loaded trap. Lights blossomed behind his eyes, and he felt wetness around his thighs. Dirt showered down on him, and he had enough time to wonder if he'd pissed himself before he went under.

* * *

Luke came to with cold mud cupping his balls, and harsh light slanting the wrong way into his hole. He tensed, then slowly relaxed. He took shallow breaths that barely filled his belly, and listened. He didn't hear anything. There were no voices, no squelching footsteps, and no groans of pain. There was no wind, and if the jungle was still up there nothing moved in or through it. The constant drone of mosquitoes, like the high tension wires in the backyard you forgot about until there was a blackout, was gone.

Moving like a man underwater Luke felt for his rifle. He dragged it close, and probed blindly for his helmet. He hung the dark green half-turtle on the end of the barrel, and slowly raised it. No shots rang out. Nothing moved. He lowered the decoy, and raised it a moment later. Still nothing. Skin pebbling and muscles tensing he put his muck-smeared helmet back on. Luke checked his weapon then coiled his legs under him. He took a deep breath, kissed the silver crucifix his mama had given him, and stuck half his head out of the hole.

Nothing had changed, but everything was different. The jungle was still there, but in the flat light its deep, rich green was two licks from black. Simms' bedroll was half-undone, sodden with mud like a bad memory of some forgotten summer camp. Jenkins' mirror hung from a low branch, swaying and flashing as it swung in and out of shadow. The King of Hearts stared at the sky, his placid face covered with fat, red spatter and tiny chunks of gray meat. Three sheets of notebook paper with ragged edges fluttered from underneath a root like crippled birds. There were no other holes.

Luke's brain tried to process what he was seeing. A hundred synapses fired in a thousand directions, trying to shine a light on the answer. Luke's legs decided it would be a question better considered from a distance, and his heart agreed. His lungs fell in line, and in less than three seconds all of him was into the trees and away.

He didn't run like a soldier, with his eyes up and his ears sharp. He didn't run like a civilian either, bulling through anything that got in his way. Luke moved like a swamp rabbit, panting as his arms and legs pumped in a perfect rhythm. He leaped over outstretched roots, swung around skinny trunks, tucked down under clutching branches, and vaulted over dead falls without thought or hesitation. It was graceful, even pretty in a desperate sort of way as he defied gravity to put the unnamed terror behind him.

He stopped running when he came to a blasted tree. The thing had been a cypress once upon a time, until God had laid it low. Black and twisted, with gnarled fingers severed at the second knuckle, the tree sat alone like a woodland pariah. Words had been carved into it by a hundred hands, and they were written in nearly as many languages. Luke saw English and French, Vietnamese and Dutch nestled side by side in ways their mother countries never had been. He saw short, choppy characters he didn't recognize, and letters that made his eyes hurt to try and follow them. Poetry, profanity, and the worst parts of the bible ran helter-skelter over the tree's lightning-struck skin, blending into a cacophony of carpentry. In the bloody light of late day it looked like the Maypole at a devil's social.

Luke took one step into the no-man's-land that surrounded the blasted tree. His nostrils flared, and he silently mouthed the words he could make out. Closer to the tree the smells of char, damp, and rot lingered in the air. There was something else, too; something sharp and tangy, like a sock full of pennies accidentally thrown in the wash. Luke socked his rifle to his shoulder and took a careful, quiet step around the tree. On his third step he found the source of the smell.

The body still wore the black pajamas of a Viet Cong soldier. The cloth was shredded, and it hung like a tattered flag at a hobo's funeral. Beneath the cloth the flesh had gone bloated and sallow, sagging off the bones like the corpse had been a hundred years old when someone put him out of his misery. The legs were gone at the knees, and only a grisly shard of red bone poked out of the remains of the left sleeve. A colony of beetles nested in the stump of the neck, and the noises as they ate sounded like wet radio static. The ghastly sack of flesh was nailed to the tree, and its one remaining arm pointed off into a thick wall of unbroken tangle. In big, bold letters where the head should be were the words *Checkpoint Charlie*. Above the hand, little more than a bony puppet held together by strings of gristle was carved one word: *Slog.*

Luke stood there with his mouth open, and the sour taint of the decaying road sign sitting heavy on his tongue. His guts clenched, and his rifle lowered, but those things seemed far away and unimportant. He stared transfixed at the mangled effigy while mud soaked through the vents in his boots. A centipede as thick as his middle finger and nearly as long as his forearm burrowed out through the hollow of the throat. Charlie sighed, and a rush of thick, black blood burbled down his skinny chest.

Luke turned his head, and vomited. It was thin and yellow, like polluted river water. He heaved three times, hands on his knees and his asshole puckering every time his belly knotted up. Cold, greasy sweat ran down his cheeks, and dripped from the tip of his nose. He wiped his mouth on the back of his hand, and spit. When he looked up, he saw what Charlie was pointing at.

The jungle had parted her legs, and in the thick tangle Luke saw a hole. The edges dripped dampness, and thick musk wafted from it. The smell was a miasma; new life growing fecund in a womb filled with teeth. It stank of black water in stagnant pools, overgrown toadstools blooming from the mouths of dead things, and the slow, serpentine life that fed and bred in the shadowy places of the earth. To Luke it smelled like home. He looked back the way he'd come, and the twisted trees stared back at him with sunset eyes. The shadows reached for him, and a flock of birds burst into the sky no more than three klicks back. Something was headed his way.

Luke took stock. He had his rifle, two full magazines, a sidearm, an M-7 bayonet, a brush knife, a canteen, and a dirty handkerchief. He had a compass, an old lighter, makings for two or three more smokes, a dirty helmet, a pair of wet boots, an entrenchment tool, a torch with a cracked red lens, and a couple packs of stale crackers he'd been keeping in his breast pocket. What he didn't have was a radio, a map, or a clue. He was four days' out, off of any and all trails he knew, and he had to get back to friendly territory. That meant dodging patrols, avoiding the locals, and conserving as much ammunition as he could. He glanced up at Charlie again, and watched as one beetle chased another down the dead man's shoulder to fight for a particularly succulent chunk of throat meat. He looked where Charlie was pointing, then down at his compass. The needle wavered, but it seemed pretty sure that Charlie was pointing in the direction Luke needed to go. Whatever was down that way was no friend to the Viet Cong. Even if the enemy of his enemy was his friend though, a man would have to be crazy to go down that path in the dark. Another man would have to be even crazier to follow.

"Anybody else comes this way, you never saw me," Luke said, his usually deep voice an octave or so higher than normal. The rotting neck bobbed slightly, as if Charlie was trying nod. A laugh burbled in Luke's throat. He choked it back, turned, and ran for the hole before he lost his nerve.

* * *

Luke swept his torch over what little path there was, looking for trip wires, snares, or signs of recently disturbed earth. He

THE SLOG

glanced up every half-dozen steps or so, clearing his three, six, and nine o'clock positions. There was the usual animal chatter, splashings and crashings in the dusk-clotted brush and high up in the dim tree tops, but there was nothing big enough or close enough to warrant his attention. He was fifty yards in when he raised his head; what he'd thought was just another vine was staring at him with flat, dead eyes the size of croaker marbles. He gasped, and fangs as long as bass fish hooks clicked off his helmet. He squeezed the trigger, and his rifle hacked a round into the underbrush.

Luke dropped onto his heels, and brought the M-16 up to catch a blow that never came. The snake swung like a busted door spring, spinning slightly as it arced through the air. Luke swallowed until his heart was back where it belonged. He stopped the fleshy pendulum with the barrel of his weapon, and raised his light.

It was a python, and the goddamn thing was big enough to swallow a six-year-old and still have room for her little dog too. It had a shovel head big enough to dig a grave with, and in the red glare its hide was a dull, rubbery black. It had been stapled to the tree by its tail with wooden stakes, and thick, viscous fluid dripped from the jutting jaw. Something snapped with the wet pop of a sodden rubber band. The mouth bulged, distended, and a pale sack of meat fell out. It plopped into a puddle of the serpent's dribbling decay, and spattered Luke's boots. It looked like a leather purse with the lining pulled out. He let the snake go, and kept walking.

There were others. A toad the size of a dinner platter hammered down a broken branch where it had popped like a balloon full of moldering guts. A marbled cat strapped to a skinny trunk with a web belt, all four feet and its tail cut off for good luck. A family of crucified rats watched him pass without so much as a squeak, and a gibbon's head grinned at him good-naturedly like they shared some private joke.

That wasn't all. Whoever had left the bloody blazes marked the trail in other ways too. Some of it was smudged and smeared, written in pencil, pen, blood, or shit by the smell of it. Other messages were clearer, dug deep into the bark with knives or burned in with careful patience. *I volunteered because I wanted to defend my country*, one trunk proclaimed. *I married a girl I hate because I knocked her up*, another said. *I bought drugs for my brother so he'd spend more time with me*. After a while Luke stopped reading; the confessions made him sick in ways the gutted signposts never could.

The path decayed along with its markers, meandering back and forth like a drunk with a sextant had plotted the way. What had been a trail grew wild and bent-legged, jogging over hillocks and dipping into ditches. The earth grew wet and spongy until it was like walking over a dead man whose skin was starting to give way to corruption. In places it opened up, and dark water gaped beneath the ground. Flies buzzed in the blackness, eating away the mangled bread crumbs until there was almost nothing left. The clouds parted for Luke's lamp, and closed in a curtain when he'd taken his light and moved on.

He'd gone nearly twenty yards with no sign of something dead when the air opened up. It was like stepping from a narrow narthex into a vaulted cathedral. The hum ceased, and somewhere nearby water lapped at muddy shores. Far above was a faint click-clacking sound, like bats roosting. Luke held his light up high, but still couldn't see more than a few yards in any direction. Thick grass shushed against his knees. He turned left, then right, skin prickling on the nape of his neck. The torch flickered, and Luke smacked it against the heel of his hand. It juttered, then steadied. He unscrewed the red lens with careful fingers. White light bloomed, and Luke nearly dropped the flash.

Towering trees stood in a wide circle, their hoary branches and scarred trunks thick and strong. Bones hung from those branches, swaying on twine tendons with every breeze. Femurs clacked against scapulas like wind chime xylophones, and finger bones conducted a symphony of swaying spines. Beneath the bones a lagoon swallowed the land, but eight little islands reared out of the murky pool. Across the expanse, no more than forty or fifty yards away, two trees embraced each other like conjoined lovers. Martyred above the arch like a meat gargoyle was another torso. Black rags and flayed skin dangled from scored ribs, and something was carved in sloping, idiot letters above the carcass.

"Golgotha," Luke muttered, sounding out the legend written in yard-high letters. The word fell into the quiet, hollow as a lie told in a confession booth. "Jesus Christ."

Luke stepped closer to the water's edge, shining his light up at the macabre mobiles. They reminded him of the gator bells his uncle put up every spring. They'd ring in the wind, but people in the parish looked for the brass baubles even if they couldn't hear them. They knew if there was a bell hung in a tree it was there to let everyone know to keep their hands on the throttle and their fingers on their triggers.

Something splashed in the water, and Luke swung his beam over the pool. Ripples skipped and bounced, turning the surface into a melting spiderweb. Luke thumbed his rifle's selector switch with his right hand and cozied his finger around the trigger. His knees bent without conscious input, and he tracked his light from one end of the water to the other. All he saw were the waves, and seven little sandbars.

Luke was already moving when the water surged. He made it two steps before the little lake burst like an infected sore, showering his back with warm, brackish wet. His ankle turned, and he went down hard. His flash bounced away in a crazy kaleidoscope of light and dark, and something went after it. Something the size of a diesel tractor that hissed like July rain on a hot top. Luke swung his rifle up with clumsy, half-numb hands, and fired. Three rounds made flat, slapping sounds, and the shape grunted. The torch stopped rolling, and the creature turned toward Luke.

It looked like something that had crawled out of the bottom of the barrel after the six days of creation were over and done with. Its hide was a pale, quarried gravel stretched over a too-big frame. Its massive chest dragged the ground, but its belly sloped up and back to pair powerful hindquarters. Meat hook claws tipped the end of massive feet, tree trunk legs churned the mud, and a lashing, scaly tail dug great gouges in the earth. It had too many legs, too many teeth, and a face that was nothing but a pale, eyeless shelf of bone above a double line of gaping, snuffling holes. The blind behemoth hissed, and charged.

It was fast. Fast enough that Luke barely had time for one more burst before it was on him. He rolled, and the thing thundered past. The tail smashed against Luke's helmet, turning his roll into a spin as the chin strap gave way and the steel cap sailed into the darkness. He slammed into a tree hard enough to shake dew from the leaves. The bones overhead beat out a dinner-bell boogie.

The ground shook as the thing wheeled 'round and came again. Luke didn't have time to roll out of the way. He jumped, grabbed a branch, and swung his legs up just as the sightless freight train rammed the base of the huge tree. The tree swayed, and Luke's grip went queasy. He hooked his legs around the branch, gritted his teeth against the pain in his ankle, and hauled himself up. The thing hit the tree again. Then a third time. It paused, head cocked like it was listening for falling fruit. When nothing fell it walked around the side of the tree with its head held high in the air. It took a step and snuffled. Then two more. Then a third. Luke stood slowly, arms out for balance until he had his back against the trunk. The thing wasn't sure where he was, but Luke was sure it would find him if he didn't figure something out fast.

He drew his M-7 and slipped the muzzle ring over the barrel. He held his breath then clicked it into place. There was a pause from below, then the damp snuffling continued. He took a firm grip on his rifle and pressed on the ejector clip with his thumb the same way he'd pushed in the spring lock on his door when he'd been a teenager. The tension built, and it clicked like a tiny twig breaking. The creature paused again, holding its breath. Luke did the same, and after fifteen seconds it started walking and sniffing again. He pressed in the fresh magazine but if the creature heard it around the tree it gave no sign.

Luke shifted his grip on the rifle and waited. The whatever-it-was came closer, circling around the other side of the trunk. It rose up, clawing and sniffing at the lower branches. Luke cocked his arm and let fly. The half-empty magazine sailed through the air and struck a hanging skull with a hollow crack. The skull rebounded, banging off a set of leg bones, which jived along half a dozen ribs. The thing dropped low, pointed itself at the other tree, and Luke jumped. His boots slid on the creature's skin but he brought his rifle down bayonet-first into the back of its neck. The steel caught against something hard, and turned just as Luke's boots skidded off the back plates and his ass hit hard enough to make his tailbone go numb.

The creature roared, and the sound reverberated over the water. It shook and bucked, whiplashing back and forth across the broken shore. Luke held on, jerking and twisting the six-and-three-quarter inches of steel embedded just south of the base of the skull. When he didn't come free, the thing turned back toward the lagoon and started running. It managed three lumbering steps before Luke pulled himself onto his knees, and squeezed the trigger.

A bomb went off in the creature's neck, and pain raked Luke from crotch to crown. The behemoth spasmed and threw him off. Luke hit the dirt hard enough to jar his brain, skidding through the mud in a graceless ballet. The creature swayed like a drunken prize fighter, blood and ichor pumping from its mangled neck. Its knees gave out slowly and it collapsed with its snout in the water. Blood pooled, pouring into the lagoon and turning it a darker shade of black. Luke watched the thing twitch and scrabble, but he stayed where he was until the creature's bladder let go in a stream that reeked of battery acid. When he was sure it was dead he levered himself to his feet, collected his light, and went looking for his rifle.

He found what was left of his M-16 half-in and half-out of a mud puddle. The stock was cracked, the carry strap had pulled loose from the front mooring, and a thick clot of muck dribbled from the inner workings. The firing pin had blown through the rear workings, the hammer was bent back like a crippled gymnast, and the barrel ruptured like a rusty sewer pipe. The M-7's handle was locked in place, but the blade had sheared right off. Luke ejected the clip, unsnapped the strap, and sat on a rock where he could watch the water along with its recently deceased resident.

Luke flexed his ankle and swore. It hurt, but nothing was torn or broken. He took off his boot, wrapped the ankle with the carry strap for support, then laced his boot back up. It still hurt, but he could probably run on it if he had to. He stripped off his jacket, grunting at all the little slivers that had blown back in his face. There were fewer of them than he thought there were, but still enough that it took him some time to pluck them all out. A few of the cuts bled, but not enough to worry about. He put his jacket back on, and ate his crackers while he looked for his helmet. He didn't find it, but he did find the half-used clip he'd thrown at the bone chimes. A fair trade. He took out his compass. The cover was busted, and the needle was bent up at a useless angle. Luke swore then gathered a couple of big stones.

Keeping an eye on the corpse Luke panned the water and counted. There were seven little sandbars, each with a tuft of thick grass growing on them. He bounced a rock in his hand, and threw it. It landed on the first island with a dull thud. He threw the others, plopping a few lobs into the water for good measure. Nothing came roaring out of the depths. No mysterious ripples broke the surface. Luke nodded, and built himself a smoke. He took care not to spill any of his tobacco before putting it back in the little pouch that kept his makings dry. He flicked his lighter, and heat lightning lit up the treetops. Luke waited for thunder, but it never came.

He considered his situation. He was hurt, and a little shook up. He had no way to keep his direction straight. He was running out of light in a hurry. He could bed down where he was and hope he made it through the night, or he could keep going. He took a look at the dead thing and imagined what would have happened if it had found him in the dark. His lips writhed. Luke looked back the way he'd come, toward the clouds of flies and the bloody trail they were eating away to nothingness. No one was coming, but if he went back that way he'd be no better off than he was now. He checked what was left of his gear to make sure everything was buttoned up and strapped in.

"After a while, crocodile," he said, flicking his smoldering roach at the thing that had lived and died in the Golgotha. Luke drew his pistol and started picking his way around the rim of the water.

He paused below the arch and looked up at the body. It was older than the first one, and it had rotted faster. It had both arms, and they were spread wide in welcome. Either that, or it was getting ready to drop on him when he wasn't looking. Luke pursed his lips, and took a long drink from his canteen. There was another legend scratched into the left tree, faint enough that he had to lean in close to see it.

"Abandon all hope, ye who enter here," he read. He looked back over his shoulder, then back at the dark doorway. He crossed the threshold.

* * *

Luke found the first stone with his bad foot. It was the size of a brick, and cocked at an angle like a sinking ship. It was the color of hospital sheets, and jagged cracks ran the visible length of it. Rounded and pounded by wind and rain the stone stood defiant; the tip of some buried pyramid lost and forgotten for centuries. Luke limped past, barely giving it a thought except to remember to pick up his feet.

He found more. At first there were only one or two, but they grew into clumps of a dozen or more. The clumps grew more frequent until he was on something that resembled a road. The trees parted, and Luke picked his way over the undisciplined-soldier course beneath a sky as black and empty as a Sunday chalkboard.

Nothing moved. No birds scuttled through the trees, and no snakes slithered after them searching for tasty eggs. Nothing stalked through the empty spaces, or pawed through the dead leaves carpeting the ground beneath emaciated bushes. Ragged cobwebs the size of burial shrouds hung from skeletal branches, and wrapped sacs the size of severed heads hung like sticky, tumorous pendulums. The road was dead, and its corpse was unquiet beneath Luke's feet.

He smelled the river before he saw it. On top was the musty scent of stale rain, but beneath there was something else; a sharp tang like spoiled eggs in a burn bin. It crawled up Luke's nose and squatted there, adding a touch of brimstone to every breath and making his eyes water if he sucked in too much air. The trees thinned and twisted, thinning like an old man's hair. Ancient slabs of stone leaned against each other, fringes of thatched roofs still clinging to a few of the lean-tos. Scrimshaw sigils half-erased by time and the caustic air decorated some of the buildings as well, and shifting shadows lived behind their broken lintels. The darkness watched as he passed, and Luke picked up his pace.

The road ended atop a rise between two decaying stone columns. The eroded stumps were each two feet taller than Luke, and wide enough that his whole squad couldn't have held arms around one of them. Tiger grass grew knee high, and hieroglyphics faded to near-invisibility spiraled over their surfaces. Beyond the leaning towers was a land of mist and darkness that glowed with witch fire. A red moon rose over the horizon, painting fingers of land in scarlet, and the slow-moving water a deeper, darker crimson.

The place was wrong. It looked wrong, it sounded wrong, and it smelled wrong. There were no sulfur swamps in their patrol area. There were no rivers big enough to make a clogged drain like this one for at least a hundred kilometers in the opposite direction. No one in the area had reported stone landmarks to the map crews, and nowhere in the entire fucking country from bombed out tunnels to defoliated drop zones was ever this fucking *quiet*. It was like a library, in a church, in the middle of a graveyard, on Mars.

Luke flicked off his torch and belly-crawled over the rise. His ankle pulsed like a parade-ground hangover, and his canteen was nearly empty. His skull felt naked, and his eyes throbbed as he tried to see through the murk. The skin between his shoulders puckered, and his gut wouldn't unclench. Everything in him said there were eyes out there, and whoever owned them was none too friendly. He glanced back the way he'd come, but saw nothing but darkness. When he turned back he saw something scrawled over the stone below the grass line. Luke held his kerchief over the torch to cut the glare, and leaned in for a closer look.

THE SLOG

Now Entering Spook Central, the stones proclaimed in letters that had been written in an unsteady hand. Below that, the printing slanting the other way, was the missive *Kilroy was here*. Luke touched his tongue to the pad of his thumb, and ran it over the last *e*. It smeared, and when he sniffed his thumb there was no doubt about what the words had been written in. They were fresh, but not that fresh. A gunshot rang out somewhere in the darkness, and Luke's shoulders twitched. He remembered Baxter telling him once that if you heard the shot you weren't dead yet, and that if you weren't dead it was time to get a move on before you were. Forward or backward, Luke couldn't stay where he was.

The world came in flashes. Luke was halfway down the hill, scooting on his ass like a little kid and trying to look everywhere at once. Then he was at the bottom of the hill, bent over like a runner getting ready to put his feet in the blocks. He was scuttling through the grass, breathing through his open mouth, trying to hear something other than the slamming of his heart. He zigged and zagged over the open land, keeping his head down and his eyes wide open in the dark. He felt with his feet and his fingertips, slithering and scrabbling over ground he could barely see. He used the torch sparingly, kept its flashes brief, and managed not to run into anything. The fourth time he flicked the switch there was a crack in the near distance, and the torch exploded.

Luke dropped the flash, and rolled to his right. Three more sharp barks followed, and gray grit flew as rounds buried themselves in the dirt around him. Luke let out a moan, and coughed. He let it trail off into silence, going limp in a patch of scrubby grass. His left hand felt hot and wet. He spider-walked his right hand to his hip, making the muscles in his arm relax. He waited. No one approached. There was no more shooting, either. A minute went by, then a friend came to join it. The clock party had just gotten started when he heard whistling.

The notes were flat, tone-deaf things; the ghosts of murdered music. At first Luke thought it was the wind, but the sounds were too regular. Too human. The atonal dirge drifted, and something moved in the mist; a skinny shadow with its weapon held at port arms. Luke drew and fired, squeezing the trigger twice. A firebrand burned the back of his right shoulder, and the figure went down with a sound like laundry being dumped on a concrete floor. The whistling continued, but there was a wet, wheezing quality that said it no longer came from a mouth. Luke stood and approached, weapon leveled.

The shooter was lying on her back. Her frizzy blond hair stuck out like a halo in the dimness. Ugly, puckered worms of scar flesh squirmed at her temples and along the shaved sides of her head. She had a junky's tan, and the skin around her nails was cracked and jaundiced. One or two of the nails still had chips of yellow paint on them. Her lips writhed over pale gums filled with loose teeth, and her breath hissed through the hole the copper jacketed slug had torn in her chest. She wore busted sandals, cut-off jeans, and beneath the mud and blood her tee shirt was stamped with the letters for Ohio State. She raised empty hands, and squeezed a trigger that wasn't there. The whistling stopped, and her hands flopped in the dirt like dead starlings.

Luke didn't recall sitting down. One minute he was standing over the girl, staring into her dead, hazy eyes, and the next he was on his ass. His face was wet, and clear snot dribbled from his right nostril. He flicked his Zippo, and noticed several, deep gashes along his left hand. Shards of plastic stuck out of a few of them. He pulled them out, grunting with each chunk.

He turned his attention to the girl. She had a spare clip in her back pocket, a wad of used chewing gum covered in lint, and a handful of pennies. Luke exchanged his pistol for his brush knife, and cut her shirt into strips. The tearing cloth was like a scream in the silence, and it brought him back to himself. He wrapped a long strip around the knife, and ran the Zippo back and forth over it. The cloth hissed and huffed, but eventually let the flame climb on. That was when Luke noticed the folded piece of notebook paper jutting out of the girl's bra. He plucked it out and unfolded it.

It was a garbled mess. There were confessions to gods whose names Luke didn't know, pleas for mercy, and cryptic

THE SLOG

nursery rhymes that reminded him of the stupid, endless tricks teachers had written on the board to help him remember facts and formulas. He read it twice, lips moving in silent repetition in the wan, wavering light.

Her name was Susan Griffith, and she was a sophomore. She'd been at a protest against the war, and someone had hit her on the head. After that was a series of white rooms, where people gave her pills and patted her arm reassuringly. She was flying, but she didn't know how she got on the plane. She wasn't alone, either.

She was taken to a cell to wait in silence and darkness. Then her food had come; a tray of sweet, salty mash with a bitter taste she couldn't identify. The first three times she refused to eat, but the fourth time she gave in. It was the best meal she'd ever eaten, and she'd fallen into a stupor. She dreamed of men in white coats telling her everything would be all right. Saying her family loved her, and she was away at camp. She woke to whispers in the vents, and the cold, rhythmic echo of gunshots. The devil's choir didn't make sense at first, but in time she learned to love their words. To love their words and to hate the light.

They gave her Toto, a sleek, black thing that barked when she squeezed him, and stayed warm in her hands. She cleaned him, loved him, and when they'd grown inseparable the doors opened and she could go. She still thought about home sometimes, and about her boyfriend Paul. She thought about how she was going to fuck him after the protest, but never got a chance. She always found new friends though, and Toto would bark in the dark and put out their lights. The lights that hurt her eyes so much. Across the bottom of the page, written in tiny, smudged letters were the words *All roads lead to Midian*.

Luke was about to start over at the beginning again when he heard the moaning. It was flat and dull, like a busted church organ that only remembered one note. A high-pitched humming joined it. Teeth chattered in the mist like hungry castanets, with no rhyme or reason. A tongue clucked monotonously, like the owner was calling for a dog whose name he couldn't remember. Shadows shambled out of the mist, drawn like blow flies to the dying fire in Luke's left hand.

The first bullet spanged off the knife, twisting the metal out of true. The second tore through the meat of Luke's little finger, snapping the bone and leaving the digit dangling by a thread. The third and fourth shots hit the knife just above the cross guard, sending it flying out of Luke's hand. There were others, more than he could count, but they followed the burning brand as it tumbled into the dry grass. Luke leaped away, clutching his left hand to his chest and crouching near the dead girl who'd once been called Susan.

The spooks kept shooting, but the fire wasn't made of flesh. It grabbed hold of the dry grass, and grew brighter. They kept shooting, but the hot lead passed straight through. The spooks reloaded, moving with a jerky, mechanical quality that was still faster than human hands should have moved. By the time they emptied their second magazines the fire had become a blaze, rearing like a dragon. It ate one of the shooters, who kept humming long after his clip went dry. The others fell back, chattering and clicking like a swarm with a dead queen. Light poured into the darkness like an ink stain, puddling around the borders of the mist. Luke turned, and that was when he saw the bridge.

It was an old bobbing Betty. She was held together with rusty chains, and the slick, moldy boards didn't look overly reliable. The half-deflated pontoons sagged like an old woman's dugs in the slow-running current. The span shot straight into the mist though, and Luke knew if the old sow was busted she'd have been pointing down river. He sucked in a breath and forced his feet to move.

The bridge was old, and she ducked below the water in a few places, but she held long enough for Luke to make it across. He fell twice, and almost went over into the river, but he managed to limp onto dry land. The bridge calmed. After a few minutes it started to bob again. In the middle distance something cracked. Someone did a poor imitation of an owl, asking the same nonsense question again and again. Luke snatched the shovel off his belt, and brought the edge down on the bridge. Boards splintered, and the pontoons beneath sighed as they dipped down the rest of the way. Luke crashed the shovel into the chain hard enough to send shivers up his arm, but it held. The bridge bobbed more vigorously, and a chorus of barks and howls joined the questioner. Something stirred the mist, and a bullet clanged off the shovel head. Luke let it go, drew his pistol, and fired. The chain snapped, along with the supports holding it in place. The bridge shuddered, shimmied, and hung on for three more heart beats. Then the second chain gave way with a metallic sigh.

Luke stood with the smoking gun held tightly in numb fingers, and watched the bridge float away into the mist. He heard splashes, but no one came toward him. No one shot at him. The expended .45 shell bobbed in the water like a small boat. Luke watched until it vanished, wondering for a moment just where the fuck it was going. He wished he'd had the presence of mind to snatch Susan's rifle.

A rope creaked, and Luke turned. A black ash stood tall in the center of the little island, its dead roots anchored in dead soil. A dozen busted pieces of wood were nailed to the trunk, and strips of ragged canvas hung from the branches like a mummy's wrappings. A fraying, hemp rope hung from a top branch, and a rocking chair dangled from the end. Luke sighed. Seated in the chair and dressed in dusty black scraps, was a headless body. Hanging from the foot rest was a bent, dented number plate with rust around the edges. Written on it were three, simple words; *Welcome to Hell*.

Luke shook his head slowly. He coughed, wincing as he moved his left hand. He flexed his remaining fingers, gritted his teeth, and snapped the string holding the tip of his pinky on. Luke wrapped the warm, wet nub in a cloth, and put it in his pocket.

"Don't mind me," he said to the dead man. "I'm just passing through."

Charlie nodded, bobbing his hollow neck in a wind Luke didn't feel.

* * *

The tree was a directory of the damned. One set of splintered boards pointed toward a plank bridge anchored to the ground with steel stakes. In that direction were Gehenna, Tartaros, and Limbo. Another pointed to a stone trestle that stretched onto a shadowy patch. It said Viti, Butcher Field, and the Stalking Grounds were that way. An arrow pointed at nothing, but when Luke looked closer he saw the water was broken by rounded stones the color of infected teeth. The splintered sign claimed Sheol was down that path. Scratched into the bottom of every sign in jagged, palsied letters was the word *Midian*.

Luke seared the worst of his wounds, then wrapped them in the cleanest strips of cloth he had. He drank all but a mouthful of his water, and found his shovel lying in the dead, dry weeds. There was a pockmark in the blade, but it was still serviceable. He stood next to the tree, and listened. He didn't hear anything except the dead man's creaking rope and the shushing water all around him. He tried to orient his direction. He looked up at the moon, but it sat high in the sky with no stars anywhere to be seen. In the end he chose the rope bridge, carefully notching the post before setting off across the planks.

Luke shifted his weight slowly at first, keeping his good hand on the rough-spun rope. It prickled his skin, and after about ten feet he tied another strip of cloth around his palm. That was better, but gripping the rope still felt like he was bare-hand fishing in a nettle jar. Down in the water fairy lights bobbed like the souls of drowned children. Luke reached a pair of heavy, wooden pylons. The left said *Look*, and the right said *Don't Touch*.

The second span dipped lower, a few of the slats nearly kissing the water below. Luke focused on the boards, and on putting one foot in front of the other. His shoulders hunched, and the cords in his neck stuck out. He was gritting his teeth, but couldn't make himself stop. Step, creak, wait, breathe became the stuttered rhythm of his life. The rhythm broke without warning as a board snapped, and Luke's left foot plunged into the water.

It was like stepping on a stove. A hiss, followed by a sublime moment of nothing. Then lightning coursed along his leg, and slammed into his head. Luke tried to scream, but only managed a high, mewling sound like a dog whose lungs had been crushed by a car. He threw himself forward, and the bridge shuddered under his horizontal weight. His foot came out of the water, but kept burning in his boot. Luke snatched his canteen, and dumped the remaining water over his foot. There wasn't much, but smoke rose from Luke's leg as the cool stream turned his boot from soaked to sodden. He fell back, breathing in little sobs as he waited for the pain to retreat.

It did, eventually. Luke moved his foot experimentally. The skin felt taut, swollen inside its leather casing like an overcooked sausage. He wiggled each toe, and felt it move even if there was a delay from his brain to his foot. He rolled onto his side, and that was when he saw it; the sleek, black stock of a standard-issue M-16. Luke blinked, but the stock stayed there, standing straight up not two feet from the bridge.

Luke was flat on his belly, peering at the stock. There was a deep groove along the right side, and one screw seemed a little loose, but it looked serviceable. A ball chain ran through the sling clip, and a single dog tag trailed in the water. He wondered how long it had been submerged, and if it would be possible to dry it out and get it working again. He wondered if the bayonet was still in one piece. He ran his tongue back and forth over his teeth. He tasted blood, and he couldn't place when that had started. He swallowed hard, and reached. His fingertips were half an inch from the rifle butt when the bridge shivered. Luke froze. He looked down, and something looked back up at him.

The kid had been handsome. His hair looked like black silk in the water, and the strands billowed out to reveal a face that was all hard planes and sharp features. He had a straight nose, a strong jaw, and a single, dark eye like a polished agate. The other eye was gone, swallowed up by a black hole in the side of his skull. White bone jutted up through an alien landscape of melted fat and seared skin. He was missing a leg, and most of an arm. The rifle was driven in through his heart, pinning him down like a moth on a cork board. The eye blinked, and the mouth opened. He reached for Luke, and Luke snatched his arm back so fast he was sure he'd tip the bridge and spill himself over the side.

The mist shifted. Upstream the scarred stock of an AK-47 stuck out at a 45-degree angle. The distinct, heavy butt of an M-1 Garand rose like the mast of a sunken ship, straight and true with the broken bowline of its strap bobbing to and fro. There were more, many more, in uneven, staggered lines up and down the wide river. They shifted, shook, and occasionally a few fingers broke the surface. They scrabbled at the weapons, fingernails leaving gouges and grooves, but none of them came free.

Luke turned his eyes away, and pulled himself to his feet. He ignored the pain the ropes cut into his palms, and the protest from his missing finger. He rejected the outrage from his swollen foot or twisted ankle. He took deep, chest-stretching breaths, and looked straight ahead. He didn't run, but only because some distant part of him knew that if he did he'd go down to join the dead men all around him.

The bridge ended, and Luke collapsed onto solid ground. He coughed and wheezed, cried and shuddered. He heaved, but nothing came up. Something burst in his boot, and thick fluid sloshed in his sock. He contemplated staying where he was until something came along and put him out of his misery. Or doing it himself. He stroked his hand along the .45 then froze. He pulled his hand away from the gun, got up, and started moving again.

Luke toured islands of madness in a quiet, uncaring sea. He passed through an orchard of gallows trees, where meat had been hung piecemeal from vines that pulsed and quivered like spider veins. He saw a place where cleavers were buried in salted stumps like axes awaiting the grinder. Another was covered in stone plinths, leaning against each other in some places, standing tall in others. Some bore dark stains, and the wind howled like the rocks had bitten it bloody. He followed mismatched footprints through gray dirt on an isle where nothing grew, and felt eyes on his back even though there was nowhere to hide. He crossed over stone arches, chain suspension bridges, twisted trees that grew from one bank to another, and made his way over fallen stones where the river gurgled and whispered with drowned secrets. He saw shapes in the shadows; hunched, bent things that watched with wide, yellow eyes as he passed. Twice they ran when he pulled his pistol. The third time he fired, and something screamed. He kept moving.

The moon was kissing the horizon when Luke crossed the final bridge and came to the walls of Midian. They were old and worn, crumbled in a hundred places. They seemed held in place by the weight of years more than by mortar. The buildings inside the city were boxes of stone smoothed by time. The windows were open sockets, and their doors slack, stupid mouths. They were stacked a dozen high in some places, like piles of skulls at the entrances of crypts. Dusty tarps hung over some of the doors, their jungle green dusted to a colorless gray. Bent, rusting antennae jutted above a few of the roofs, and a pair of boots sat next to one doorstep like forlorn puppies. There were no voices but the mute ghosts of abandoned things.

"Hello?" Luke croaked, licking a split in his bottom lip. "Is anybody here?"

No one answered. Luke's throat tensed up, and as dry as the rest of him was, tears welled in his eyes. His legs wobbled like sprung springs and he started to pant. He patted at his belt absently, like he couldn't quite remember what he was looking for. That was when he looked up and saw the light. It blazed over the rooftops; a burning beacon that could be seen for miles. He approached, breath hitching in time with his steps.

He walked until the detritus of the one-time occupiers was behind him. He crossed ancient aqueducts, and stepped past dried-up fountains filled with flat stones. He turned down crumbling boulevards and ducked between the shadows of the too-close ruins. He continued until the city grew humble, with the eaves cut at sharp angles so the houses bowed toward the center.

The heart of Midian was a colossus that dwarfed the rest of the city. Built of the same stone as everything else, it was a tapering pyramid that brushed the low-hanging firmament. The plateau of the lowest level was higher than the tallest of the surrounding structures, built from blocks bigger than they had any right to be. They were cut with short, narrow stairs. He saw no other way up, so Luke started climbing.

The stairs were deceptive. The first dozen went by easily, and he barely noticed the dozen after that. They seemed designed to strain the ankles and torture the feet of climbers though, and they were cut at such an angle that Luke had to lean into them like a man in a high wind. Sweat streamed down his skin, burning like battery acid as it cut through the dirt and seeped into his wounds. He stepped wrong and almost fell, pin-wheeling his arms as he tried to reclaim his balance. His shovel slid off his belt, clanking and spinning off into open air. He crawled from that point on.

Dragons guarded the first landing; huge, serpentine things with hollow eyes and empty mouths full of sharp teeth. They reared out of the walls like they were trying to escape the stone. Ball chains had been hooked around their jaws, and dozens of dog tags swung below their maws like grisly souvenirs. Luke stared at them, trying to get his breath back. Slowly he pulled his tags off, and took them apart. He hung the long chain on the left, and the short chain on the right. Then he started climbing again, looking back every few steps to be sure the dragons weren't following.

There were others. Graven demons with no eyes; carved forests with men's faces along their branches; and giants who stood the full height of several blocks. Some of the guardians hurt Luke's eyes to look at; creatures who seemed to be made of light with thousands of eyes that lived inside ever-dancing flames. He left his spare magazines, his empty canteen, his pistol, his equipment belt, his shirt, his boots, and even the stump of his little finger behind as he marked his own, bloody trail up the side of mountain.

In time he reached the summit, shaking and shivering like a newborn. A fire burned brightly, but it gave off neither heat nor sound. It was like someone had torn a hole in the night, and the light that lived behind the sky was looking in. Luke stared at it until his muscles ceased trembling and his breath came clear again. He stared until his pains quieted. Then he looked up, and nearly fell back down the way he'd come.

Something sat on the other side of the fire. A shroud covered its face, the threadbare cloth imploding as it breathed deep, and billowing as it breathed out. Ichor dripped from its chin and pooled in its lap. Two legs were crossed under it while the other two sat splayed out. Its cock dangled, barbs glistening with something too thick to be sweat. Antlers and horns curled above its distended head, framing it like a predator's smile. It sat on a throne of meat that heaved and breathed, sweated and shitted. It dragged talons over the shivering cushions, and chittered as the blood ran from the pulped, palpitating flesh. Luke's chest cried out, and his vision went pale as he clutched at his chest. His hands came away bloody, and the thing laughed a hissing laugh. Its breath smelled of corruption and cordite.

It had many names; Lord Flatline, King Cancer, Old Man Darkness, Mourning Glory, The Great Beast, Baphomet, The Pale Rider, and others. There were more, many more, but they didn't matter. Luke had heard them whispered at family funerals, and in evac choppers, in med tents and on burial duty. Every man was born with a death, and one day he'd have to look it in the eye. Luke stood, and stared. The thing lifted its veil. Luke pulled his cross over his head with his bloody hand, and kissed it once. He threw it at the king's feet and it tinkled like a broken bell. Luke took a single step forward, and fell into the fire. He had enough time to wonder if he'd pissed himself, and then he was gone.

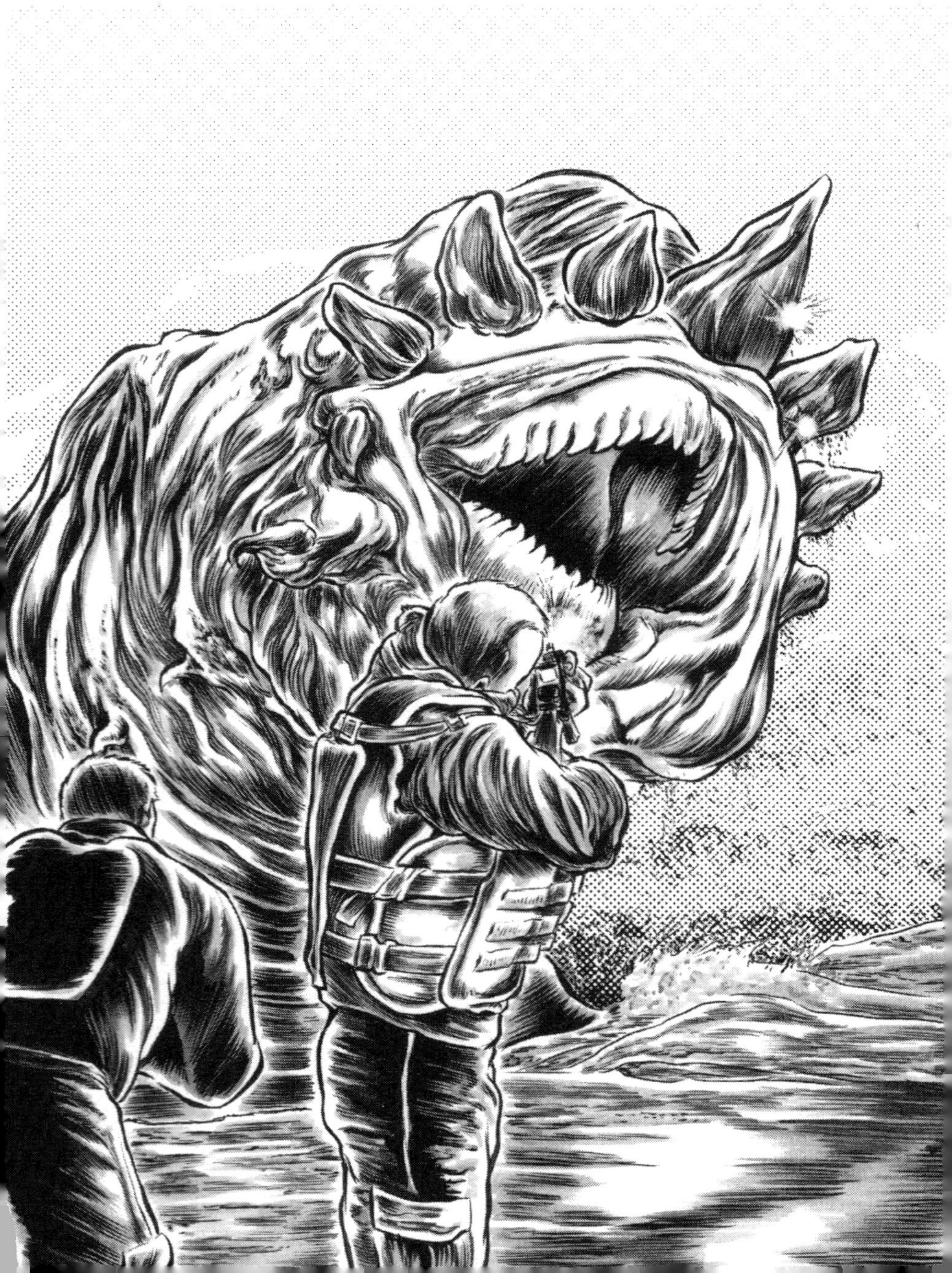

SHOW OF FORCE
A Jack Sigler / Chess Team Novella

Jeremy Robinson & Kane Gilmour

"Show of force operations are designed to demonstrate resolve. They involve the appearance of a credible military force in an attempt to defuse a situation."
– Joint Publication 3-0, *Joint Operations*

1

The helicopter set down a half mile from the raging storm, which made the desert look as if it were being sucked up into space. A twisting cloud of dust, sand, dirt and snow spiraled into the sky and covered a region that stretched for miles, engulfing most of the so called 'Great Gobi B Strictly Protected Area.' Six bodies slipped from the rotary-winged vehicle and began a fast march toward the howling blizzard.

The region had been set aside as an International Biosphere Reserve in 1991, but in practice, that just meant there was very little there. Mongolia had agreed to the classification of the rarely-used land in exchange for developmental aid. Stretching over 3000 square miles, the place was a combination of drab-colored desert steppe and low, craggy, arid mountains.

The paramilitary team arrived at the leading edge of the storm, and was swallowed by the blinding whiteout conditions. Bursts of sand and ice particles, propelled to 100 mph by roiling winds, blasted across the landscape in thick, nearly solid slabs, buffeting their bodies. Unwavering, the soldiers pressed on. The radio earpieces and speakers inside their helmets, hidden beneath hoods, blocked external audio unless they were switched on. Without that block, they wouldn't have been able to hear each other over the mechanical, high-pitched whine of the rampaging weather.

When the gusts of the storm periodically cleared, they could see each other in their full-body, white environment suits, trudging across the patchy scrub-grass-coated ground. The suits looked like the bastard children of environmental hazmat suits and yetis. With full-plate face masks, and tight, fur-coated hoods, they might have easily been mistaken for small polar bears missing their snouts – polar bears with plastic-coated automatic weaponry. The synthetic fur on the exterior of the suits repelled the sand and snow. Each member of the team also wore a tactical climbing harness that covered chest and pelvis, which could be used for rappelling or climbing, but more often was used for attaching equipment to the body. Underneath the outer suits they wore gel-heated full-body wetsuits to help maintain a comfortable internal body temperature.

Outside the environment suits, the mercury would be hovering around -40 degrees Fahrenheit, without the wind chill. Scrubbing filters could provide exterior air if their self-contained tanks ran out, but they anticipated being on the ground for less than twenty minutes.

The land was barren rock and jutting hardy grasses – until unexpectedly, it wasn't. The hard ground gave way to treacherous sand dunes, and then just as seamlessly merged back into more crumbly rock and clumps of pale-green vegetation.

"Charming. Like New Hampshire in the spring," one of them said, breaking the silence on their internal comms.

"Nah," the burly man in the lead said. "Spring is mud season. It would be like this, but we'd be caked in mud, too."

The slightest of the group groaned and said, "Golf alpha romeo." It was shorthand for 'get a room.' It was a common thing for the man and woman to bicker while in the field, but the other team members all knew how they really felt about each other.

"Hold up here," the slim man in the rear said. He squatted, and the others paused in their march without protest, dropping into similar crouches. They all held specially-designed, plastic-coated FN SCAR rifles, capable of withstanding the grit from extreme sandstorms. Even the weapons' muzzles were covered in a thin layer of plastic that would be ripped away once they opened fire, should it come to that. But they expected it wouldn't. This mission would be a cakewalk compared to what they normally faced.

The slight man, carrying a simple M-21 sniper rifle, also wrapped in white plastic, approached the thin man who had called a halt. He squatted and brought his weapon up in the direction his leader was looking, straight into the thick maelstrom. "King, you see something?"

The team's leader, King, stayed motionless for another full minute, before he replied. "No, Knight. Sorry. Just getting used to the complete lack of visibility and exterior sound. We don't know what's out here, so everyone stay sharp." Jack Sigler, callsign: King, stood up and headed out, into the howling storm.

Named for pieces on a chess board, each of the other members – designated Chess Team – stood and followed. The team was formerly with the US Army's 1st Special Forces Operational Detachment – commonly known as Delta. Then, for a time, they had operated as part of a freelance organization, Endgame, stopping threats that politics and time constraints prevented other Delta groups from engaging. Now the Chess Team were fugitives from the US government, but they still fought the good fight across the globe. Each member of the team played a different role, and their callsigns designated those positions.

The burly man in the front of the group, Stan Tremblay, callsign: Rook, was their heavy weapons and ordinance specialist. He had armed the team for this mission with a special weapon that operated like an underwater spear gun, but what it fired were short javelins with radio-controlled explosive rings around the shafts. They could be fired from a distance, arcing into the ground, and then detonated later from a safe distance. In addition to a rifle and a spear gun, he also lugged an M240B machine gun.

Behind Rook in their line-up, as they penetrated the storm, was a woman, callsign: Pawn. Anna Beck had formerly been the team's security specialist, when they were a part of a larger organization. Now she functioned as a spotter for the team's one-eyed, Korean-American sniper, Knight. She also held her own in a fight either with her FN SCAR or in hand-to-hand combat.

Shin Dae-jung, callsign: Knight, moved up beside Beck, and kept pace with her. After an injury in Africa had taken his eye, he'd learned several tricks to deal with the loss of depth perception, and he had even briefly used an artificial, computerized implant, but the thing had given him sizzling migraines. While the implant was still there, it was turned off. He was using old-school techniques until the pain-causing kinks were worked out. Pawn was always by his side, to prevent his limited vision from causing him problems. She spotted for him when he was sniping, covered his back during incursions and held his hand in their down time, as his lover and friend.

A few paces behind them, another small figure trudged through the howling snow and ice. At just over 5'6", Bishop was the second of three women on the six-person team. Asya Machtcenko, a former Russian soldier, and King's sister, hauled spare drums of ammunition for the M240B Rook carried. The huge weapon was also covered in plastic, although the vents on its barrel assembly were covered with a thinner layer, which could be quickly punctured with a pin, should the shooting need to start. The weapon needed to vent its heat. Bishop and Rook would take turns using it, if there was a need.

"It had to be during a *Zud*," she said.

"A what?" Queen, the final member of the team, asked. Zelda Baker was the team's medic, and also its most deadly hand-to-hand combatant. She stalked through the storm just behind Bishop, carrying yet another FN SCAR rifle, and several more ammunition canisters for the big gun.

Before Bishop could answer, the team's handler, a man named Lewis Aleman, who communicated remotely with them from a hotel room in Beijing, replied, "She means the winter. It's a Mongolian term for a particularly bad one. Entire herds of livestock can perish when these Siberian anti-cyclone storms keep temperatures plunging to forty below." Aleman, callsign: Deep Blue, orchestrated matters from afar, providing whatever satellite intel he could for the team's missions, although their resources were not what they used to be.

SHOW OF FORCE

"This gorilla suit is keeping me plenty comfortable," Rook said.

"Pretty sure she meant the lack of visibility, numbskull," Queen retorted.

"It's going to be hard enough to find this terrorist base," King spoke up, "with them being dug in underground somewhere."

"Sorry I couldn't get you better intel, guys," Deep Blue's disembodied voice replied. "All we know is the Bright Tomorrow cell is operating out of the area. Military sat coverage didn't show anything, so they must be concealing heat signatures and working out of a tunnel system or a cave or something."

"We'll find them," King said, determination filling his voice and lending the others hope.

"I don't think that's going to be a problem," Rook said. "I think my Aunt Mabel's half-blind dog could find them."

The others reached Rook's position, where he had stopped in his tracks. As they looked up, another hard gust of wind blasted into them from the north, pushing away a wall of grit and white, extending their view to over a hundred yards and revealing what appeared to be a huge castle.

2

"Can you believe this, Blue?"

"I can't see it, King," Aleman reminded him. While Aleman was used to having a video feed, on this mission he did not. The others quickly described the structure to him.

"Okay, you're right. I don't believe it. There was nothing on sat scans. Nothing on Google Earth or half-a-dozen geographic aerial photos."

As Aleman spoke, the others melted back into the edge of the storm cloud behind them, until the building was no longer visible, and they were concealed from any prying eyes on the tops of the battlements, the style of which reminded King of the Great Wall of China. The sloped walls, constructed from rammed-earth, brick and stone, had crenellated tops, all supporting four corner watchtowers. He had glimpsed it only for a moment before moving back into the cover of the raging storm, but that was enough for him to question his location, since the nearest segments of the Great Wall should have been almost 400 miles to the southwest.

"Are we at the right coordinates, Blue?" King asked.

"That's confirmed. My best guess would be that the Mongolians built it to be modeled after the guard tower sections along the Great Wall, which they would have been familiar with. Why? Beats me. The top must be painted in local camo patterns to conceal the structure from sat photos. And the area is covered in clouds or outright storms, like you're dealing with, for much of the year. It's still amazing nothing showed it being there."

King settled flat on the snowy ground with the others. If the particulates in the air were swept away by another gust, their suits would camouflage them somewhat. All of them kept their weapons trained toward the strange building in the desert. "Sounds like the perfect place for Bright Tomorrow to operate out of. But I wonder why none of the other teams found it."

Aleman had tasked the team with finding the terrorist command camp after several attempts by US and joint European teams had failed to locate the headquarters. Most of the special forces teams sent into the stormy region of desert had simply not returned. Those who had come back alive complained of supernatural creatures in the sand that had killed or eaten entire squads of men. The stories had been conflicting and unbelievable – exactly the sort of thing Chess Team faced on a regular basis.

Although the team had been surprised by the sight of the building when they had been expecting caves, King was already strategically assessing the situation. "Bishop, take the 240 and break right. One hundred yards, and set up there. Crawl forward until you can just barely see the building. The edge of the storm probably won't hold here, but you should have some cover."

Bishop collected the big gun and slipped away into the white gloom.

"Rook and Queen, break left." King didn't need to elaborate any further. "Knight and Pawn, the back. Find a way in. Those towers look like good overwatch."

SHOW OF FORCE

"Visibility would be crap from up there, but we'll find something," Knight replied. He and Pawn were up and following Queen and Rook to the left. They would then circle around the left side of the structure to the back. That left King to cover the front of the building – a hundred yard long wall with a massive twenty-foot high set of banded wooden doors in the middle, closed against the rage of the storm.

He crawled forward in the blinding snow and sand, noticing for the first time that the grit scraping across the full faceplate of his helmet was actually scratching the plastic. If this went on too long, they would be blind, even when the wind cleared the air. Another of a thousand small variables he filed away in his head for later.

"Blue, how long until you can get us infrared coverage?" King asked Aleman.

"Another twenty minutes – and that's if I can get in. It's a DARPA satellite, and their encryption is crazy."

"Do what you can. I'd like to know if someone's coming up on us from behind, before they actually step on me."

"It's not that bad," Knight mumbled.

King recalled a report from a mission Knight had been on in Uganda, where a soldier had actually been standing on Knight's concealed sniper position – had actually been standing on Knight's arm, completely oblivious to the danger he was in. If that was the only time that ever happened, King would be happy.

He felt a twitching sensation at the back of his neck, and quickly whirled around, scanning the swirling white and tan haze. The base looked abandoned, but King's instincts told him it wasn't. Not being able to see or hear in the field was as limiting as wearing a bag over his head. With the helmet keeping in heat as well, he couldn't even smell an attacker sneaking up on him. The only thing the team had going for them *was* the weather. It was unlikely any Bright Tomorrow security would be outside in this mess – and the building looked pretty sturdy against attack. Between its remote location, the camouflaged roof and the extreme temperatures and low visibility, they probably had their forces set up inside the outer walls of the building. It would be enough. That's how King would have done it.

"Knight, are you in position in back?"

"We're up top, in back. Place is totally deserted. Looks like no one has been up on these walls all winter." It didn't surprise King that Knight and Pawn would have taken the initiative to scale the back wall without reporting on the lack of posted guards. They all knew each other's strengths and played to them.

"North and east are clear," came Bishop's thick Slavic accent.

"South is... wait. Do you feel that?" Rook said.

King was about to reply when he did feel it. A tremor in the ground. Aleman had briefed them about the region, which was prone to mild earthquakes and aftershocks. After a second, the rumbling sensation faded. "Just a quake. Moving on the door. Watch me."

King stood in a low crouch, waited for a strong gust of wind and then sprinted forward, toward the looming doors of the big building. He zigzagged as he ran, hoping to throw off the aim of any guards Knight and Pawn might have missed. They were at the back of the square, castle-like base, and the length of each wall was over 100 yards, so even with Knight's keen eye, they might have missed someone in the front. But with Rook and Queen on one side of him, and Bishop on the other, King felt safe in making the dash to the wall.

When he reached the sloped surface next to the looming doors, he turned his back to the stone, sweeping his SCAR back toward the snowstorm. If there was a threat above him on the fortress wall, Bishop would have him covered. He was far more concerned about the concealment the storm afforded anyone circling behind the team. And if he was honest, the rumors of supernatural creatures had him on edge – he'd faced things that shouldn't have been possible on more than one occasion.

He turned and faced the door, prepared to plant one of Rook's explosive spikes in the dirt in front of the threshold, but at the last second he had an idea. The doors had massive circular iron rings for handles, about the size of dinner platters, hanging at King's shoulder height. He guessed most of the much shorter

Mongolians would have had to reach up for the handle. King just reached straight out and grasped the ring in his gloved hand.

He tugged, and the door opened, as if its hinges had been oiled at least sometime in the last week – otherwise all the grit in the air would have jammed them up.

"The place might look abandoned, but someone's here."

3

Knight hurried along the edge of the crenellated wall, running his hand along the edge of the parapet for balance. He knew Pawn would be on his blind side, doing the same. The wind was worse up on the forty-foot tall wall, and the snow and sand blew so hard that he couldn't see more than a few feet.

They had been lucky to get one of the gusting bursts that had cleared the air temporarily, so they knew they were alone on the top of the wall. As they raced to the nearest corner watchtower, they stayed low, but speed was now more essential than stealth. With the snow untouched on the walkways along the walls, and on the pagoda-like central building inside the outer wall, anyone even glancing out this way during a clearing in the storm would see the new footprints.

"This feels all wrong," Pawn said, speaking directly to Knight on a separate sub-channel they had between them, for additional communication. It was another subtle tool they used to compensate for the loss of Knight's left eye, but they rarely needed it for that purpose. Instead, they used it to talk privately, away from the ears of the others. The system was set up so that if anyone spoke over the network, they would hear the exchange in their left ears. If Pawn and Knight wanted to speak exclusively to each other, they would hear the replies in their right ears. A toggle switch allowed them to choose on which network to broadcast. So far, they hadn't mixed up the channels.

"I agree. I know it's brutally cold out here, but they don't even have any cameras," Knight said, as he reached the doorway into the corner tower.

"Sand would probably scour the lenses on the first day," Pawn observed.

"Front door's open. Going in," they heard King report from the front of the building. "Stay frosty. The hinges have been oiled recently."

Knight felt the need to get deeper inside the building than King, and faster. He knew it wasn't necessary to compensate for his injuries with his actions, but being sneaky and fast was something he had done even before the loss of his eye.

Pawn didn't need him to explain the plan. They had become like one human in two bodies over the last few weeks. She would anticipate his moves, learning his style and his intentions from simple gestures. Pawn was fast enough to anticipate what he would do, and to keep up with him.

He grasped the door to the tower, and tugged on it. It opened a little stiffly, as if it, too, had been oiled, but grit from the blowing storm had still found its way into the frame and the iron hinges. Pawn covered his entrance, then they leap-frogged positions into the unlit stone stairwell. Knight pulled the door closed after them, plunging them into darkness.

"Blue, do you copy?" Knight asked.

"Crystal clear," came Aleman's reply.

"We're inside the southwest tower. What's the temp in here?"

Their suits, which Aleman had appropriated for them on the black market, had temperature sensors inside and out, allowing Aleman to monitor their bodies in the frigid climate, but also so they would know if the temperature outside the suit warmed up enough for them to remove it.

"Ten above," Aleman said after a brief pause. "It'll be chilly, but you can remove the helmets."

"'Bout damn time," Pawn groaned, slipping the helmet off over her head.

Knight did the same, and instantly he heard the roaring of the wind outside the thick wooden door. The sound was somewhat muted, so he was able to listen for sounds in the darkened stairwell. Convinced they were alone, he donned an AN/PVS-14A night vision monocular, and Pawn did the same. The devices were strapped over their heads, amplifying the available light.

SHOW OF FORCE

In this case, there wasn't any ambient light, so Knight activated an extremely dim LED at the sole of his boots. The light was so slight and diffuse that an unaided human eye could see it, but not be able to pinpoint its exact location. That wouldn't help them much while in the confines of the tight stairwell, but once they were down at ground level, the space would open up, and they would be able to hide in the darkness. Also, at the first sign of contact, Knight could douse the dim light, switching it to a pulse mode. It allowed both he and Pawn to see the walls and the steps of the twisting spiral stone passage, and he quickly descended, looking for tripwires or other security devices as he went. So far, he was disappointed in the security, but terrorists weren't known for their adherence to norms, and he supposed with the remote location and the climate, they really wouldn't need too much to dissuade visitors.

"There should at least be a guard dog, or something," Knight said softly, over the open comms.

"Perimeter report," King asked.

"All clear, Boss," Rook said.

"Nothing," Bishop added.

"We're approaching the ground level," Knight said.

"Warmer inside, but still no tangos," Pawn said. "This doesn't feel right."

"Agreed..." King said, and then he lapsed into silence. Knight could tell from the way he had said it that he was considering calling the operation off. It wouldn't have been the first time King had done so, and he tended to be the most cautious of the team now. Knight continued down the steps, waiting for the call.

It didn't come.

Oddly, neither did the ground floor.

The stairs kept circling down, and Knight was sure they had descended close to sixty feet now. The ground level would have been at forty.

"These stairs keep going down, King. We're investigating."

"Roger," King said. "I'm checking the main floor, but it looks deserted here, too."

As Knight and Pawn descended, they noticed the shades

of green in their monocles brightening. Knight switched off his boot LED and found he could still see. "Light source," he whispered, speaking only to Pawn. She made a soft grunting noise he knew to be an acknowledgment.

After a few more steps, the stairway opened up onto a catwalk in a dimly lit, wide open space. The lights were far below, but bright enough that Knight removed the monocular entirely. They stayed in the shadows of the doorway, stowing the assistive devices, before Knight belly-crawled to the edge of the metal catwalk, and peered down into the chamber forty feet below him.

"Shit. King," he whispered on the team network. "This looks like a bio-weapons lab. All bright white walls and glass down here. We're forty feet below the surface level. I'm seeing large glass vats with nuclear green liquid and bio-hazard symbols on them. A few people milling around in white lab coats."

"Deep Blue?" King asked, irritation audible in his voice.

"Everything we have says it's a simple terrorist command center. I have no intel on labs or chemical weapons."

"The brief is the same," King said. "Plant your bomb-spikes. We get out and blow the place sky high. No matter what they're cooking up here, the remote location will prevent it from spreading and the sands will cover this place up."

"Damn, remember those guard dogs you wanted, Knight?" Rook's voice came over the net. "We've got a roving patrol here. I don't think they've spotted us. Looks like six men. They're all bundled up like hairy brown pillow turds."

"Still nothing on this side," Bishop added. "I can't see anything."

Welcome to my world, Knight thought, still rueful over the loss of his eye.

Then he saw a dozen men, armed with AK-47 rifles, come rushing out onto the floor of the lab below. He crept backward across the metal suspended floor, toward the door to the stairwell. Pawn was already there in the shadows. She raised a finger, pointing at the far side of the catwalk that surrounded the entire lab space. Over eighty yards away, on the opposite wall, was another doorway, most likely to another guard tower.

SHOW OF FORCE

Eight men rushed out of the doorway, their boots clanging on the metal catwalk. They were bundled up in what looked like rags and furs, and they were each armed with a rifle. The men circled the catwalk, heading right for Knight and Pawn's doorway.

4

Queen slipped through the snow like a wraith. While Rook attempted to cover her position from where they had been keeping an eye on the south and eastern sides of the building, she followed close behind the roving patrol of men as they moved along the south wall. She briefly switched on the audio for the outside of her helmet, listening for any noises over the howl of the storm, but all she heard was the constant, roaring whine of the wind.

Feeling confident in her approach, because the storm would cover any noise she made, Queen rushed toward where she'd last seen the men, before they disappeared into the blowing ice crystals. The whiteout was thick, but she pressed on blindly, hoping to catch the men and dispatch the entire patrol before anyone was the wiser.

Instead, she ran right into a wall.

Of fur.

In the split second it took her to realize that the men on patrol had performed a 'Crazy Ivan' technique, suddenly turning to ensure no one was following them, the man she had run into, covered in rags and furs, and carrying a fur-wrapped AK-47 rifle, began to raise his weapon. Queen's wasn't in position. Her rifle was angled off to her left after the unexpected impact. So she lunged upward with it, the side of the SCAR smashing into the man's gauze-covered head. She figured he could barely see through the layers of cloth anyway. After the weapon impacted his head with a dull thud, the coverings were displaced upward, blinding him.

She didn't know if a gunshot would be audible over the screaming wind, but she didn't want to chance it. She dropped her SCAR, and it swung down to her side on its sling. Her hand came up with a SOG SEAL knife instead. The blade was seven inches long, making it a monster of a weapon. She normally preferred a shorter 4-inch blade, but in this environment, where she expected any opponents to be wearing thick layers of clothing, she had thought it best to go with a longer knife. As the blade rammed home into the man's throat, and continued straight back to sever his spinal cord just above his second thoracic vertebrae, she congratulated herself on the choice. The wide man, looking like an overstuffed brown pillow in his thick clothing, tumbled backward. She held tight to the handle of the knife, and it sluiced out of the guard as he went down.

She was just starting to turn, to keep her own system of Crazy Ivans in the blinding white, when she saw the barrel of an AK-47 emerge from the white fog to her right. With no time to fully turn, she lunged her whole body in that direction, mashing the barrel of the weapon away from her, even as it lit up, spewing 7.62mm death in an uncontrolled burst. She only hoped the man, whose finger had clenched in surprise, managed to mow down some of his fellow guards. Then she and the man were tumbling down toward the ground.

Moving the fight to the rocky soil was a bad enough turn of events, but just as she and the second man hit the hard, frozen ground, something worse happened.

The wind abruptly stopped.

And the blowing snow and sand that had been obscuring her from view, vanished with it.

* * *

"Fight or flight?" Pawn asked, sheltered in the shadow of the doorway.

Knight waited a beat before replying to her. "Option 3. Rook style." He dove forward, rolling out onto the catwalk. As he went low, Pawn came out behind him, aiming high and firing at the oncoming team of guards. Her three-round burst hit the first man, spinning him, and her second burst hit the next man in line. As the two victims fell sideways, the third man on the narrow catwalk was revealed, and a second later, he was impaled.

SHOW OF FORCE

Knight had fired one of Rook's tailor-made spear gun-like bomb-spikes. The compressed-air weapon was strong enough to send the metal spike across the catwalk to drive itself deeply into the man's chest. Pawn could see the small red LEDs on the ring of explosives around the shaft were lit already, indicating that the bomb was armed. As the man fell backward into the others still standing, Knight and Pawn took off running the other direction along the catwalk.

The remaining three men opened fire on them, bullets pinging off the metal catwalk near their feet as they ran. Suddenly the wall to their left began sparking from additional bullet impacts, and Pawn swept her SCAR over the railing to her right, firing several blind shots down at the floor of the lab, where she assumed the other guards were standing. She knew there was a risk of hitting the vats of fluid down there, and she had no way of knowing what they contained. But since the mission was essentially to *break everything*, she figured it would all work out okay.

As Knight reached the corner of the catwalk, and another doorway to their left – most likely to another watchtower, he darted inside, holding his arm up to show her that he held the transmitter for the bomb-spike. He was going to flick the switch.

Pawn darted into the doorway, just before the pressure wave ripped along the metal floor, nipping at her heels. As soon as it was done spewing shredded fabric and shattered, blood-stained chunks of rock their way, she darted back out onto the catwalk, which was now mangled and on fire at the end. She leaned over the railing and fired a bomb-spike from her own spear gun down into the lab. The spike implanted in the ground right next to the largest vat of lime green fluid. Pawn then pulled back and swept her SCAR up to cover Knight. He had reloaded his own spear gun and leaned over the rail, as she had done, firing his spike to a far corner of the lab's floor. They took turns, laying suppressive gunfire and launching their deadly cargo, until Knight had loosed four of his seven remaining spikes and Pawn had fired all eight of hers.

Wordlessly they turned to ascend the darkened stairs of the new tower, hoping there would be an exit, because the space behind them was about to erupt in a fireball of chemicals, pulverized stone and slivers of metal and bone.

* * *

"What in the name of Michigan J. Frog happened to the friggin' storm?" Rook asked, scrambling to his feet and racing toward the distant brawl between Queen and one of the patrolling guards.

With the air suddenly clear of ice and grit, he could see she had already taken one of the men down, but while she grappled with another, there were four more men. Two had turned already and were rushing toward their fallen comrades.

Rook loosed a controlled burst of fire from his FN SCAR, dropping one of the men, and winging the other. He kept running toward them, firing again as he got closer. He dropped the second alarmed guard, just as Queen plunged her huge knife in the chest of the man she had on the ground. Rook kept advancing and was pleased to see the last two guards hadn't even turned yet.

Queen climbed to her feet. Rook was still half-a-dozen yards from her position and heading for her at a run. He was about to fire on the last two guards, when one of them turned and the other simply dropped. Rook raised his weapon to fire on the turning man, but he dropped as well.

Queen felt the ground trembling again and then saw Rook heading her way, aiming past her. She turned back and saw the last of the guards fall down. Then she and Rook both understood what had happened to the men.

King, approaching from the back of the building, he had taken both men down with single shots from his rifle, as he'd come around the corner.

But something was wrong. He was running toward them, and moving full out.

"King, what's—" Rook started to ask.

Then Rook noticed the vibration beneath his feet. At first he'd written it off as another of the tremors Aleman had mentioned. But it was stronger now, and the ground was bucking and jumping, as if this earthquake was going to be a huge one.

Then the source of the quake became clear, as a monstrous thing followed King around the corner, hissing and frothing.

5

King ran faster than ever before, but it still wasn't enough.

Once he'd heard there was a bioweapons lab concealed underground, he'd planted four bomb-spikes – one in each corner of the ground-floor courtyard inside the outer wall, then he'd headed out a rear gate. That was when the trembling had begun. He'd sensed that it was closer than the rumble they had experienced the last time, and that its force was increasing at an exponential pace.

He had wondered if it was something Knight and Pawn had set off underground, but then the wind died. He could see. A hundred yards behind the building, the soil had erupted, as if a mole twelve feet in diameter was burrowing up from underground. He had thought of the giant 250-foot-diameter sinkholes that had opened in Siberia months earlier.

But the thing that fired out of this hole like a breaching whale was no mole, and the hole had not been a sinkhole, but a tunnel. The creature was ten feet in diameter, and rose up out of the hole straight into the air, at least twenty feet high. It had shiny, wet skin, blood red and covered with cascading rains of dirt. Its long, tapering body was ribbed into segments, and the front end of its tubular shape opened into a huge gaping maw.

It's a worm, he had thought. *It's huge!*

And then the mouth had opened wider, and a plume of purple vapor shot out, making the rocks and soil that it hit steam with wavering fumes.

And... King had thought, *Time to go.*

As soon as he'd started running for the southwest corner, the massive thing had begun to chase him. He reached the corner and took down two guards, but he didn't slow.

"King, what's—" Rook was starting to say.

King had no time to answer him, and the man would get an eyeful in just a second. "Bishop! Going to need that 240, southwest corner. Coming in hot!"

Rook and Queen were already turning to run as he approached them.

"Why am I not surprised it is you who started the big rumbling?" Bishop replied from the other side of the building. She hadn't said so, but he knew she would be hauling the machine gun to the location he had specified.

"Yeah, count on him to find the one thing out here bigger than a damn rabbit. Knight, Pawn. We're leaving in a hurry," Rook said, running side by side with King.

"We're already on the roof. What the hell is that?" Knight said.

Then King, who had opened his exterior microphone, heard the small man take three shots at the pursuing worm with his sniper rifle. "Didn't even slow it," Knight said.

"Slow what?" came Aleman's disembodied voice. "What are you dealing with?" He was used to being able to see everything the team saw through high tech lenses and video feeds, and he was clearly at a loss with no visuals.

"Seen Tremors or Dune?" Rook asked.

"A giant worm?" Aleman said, disbelief coloring his words.

"Yep, but redder than a Doberman's wanger."

Queen had taken the lead in the sprint and was veering toward the corner of the building, just as Bishop rolled on the ground from the opposite direction, coming to rest prone and planting the 240B on its bipod legs.

Queen nimbly leapt over the long weapon and Bishop, and she rounded the corner of the structure. Rook was right behind her, and hopped over Bishop, too. King dove to the ground, next to his sister, just as she opened up with the chugging big gun. He added his FN SCAR to the process, unloading a full magazine at the giant slithering thing heading their way. The ground trembled slightly as the monster approached. King assumed the full-on earthquakes were from it tunneling under the soil and rock.

"*Kakova hera,*" Bishop swore in Russian – *What the fuck?* – while pounding the approaching worm with a withering torrent of 7.62 rounds, highlighted with the occasional tracer shot of brilliant orange, so she could adjust her vector of fire. The concentrated fusillade chewed a ragged hole through its side, just to the right of its black, gaping maw, but the beast's approach wasn't halted or even slowed.

"Pick up," King said, buttoning out his magazine and quickly inserting another before blazing away at the worm again.

Bishop scooped up the machine gun and ran. King turned to follow her around the corner of the building, just as the rumbling thing spit at him again. This time a burst of the purple liquid arced forward out of the cloud of vapor, dashing against the side of his environment suit. He saw his left arm start to smoke, but he didn't slow down his pace.

Bishop, Rook and Queen had all set up at the northeast corner of the building, past the big, wooden front doors. While Bishop inserted a new drum into the machine gun, the others were firing above King's head at the pursuing creature. The worm had continued well past the corner. It clearly couldn't turn effectively, and King was grateful for the brief reprieve.

"Boss, your suit's smoking, like it's gonna melt," Rook said.

Bishop opened fire on the creature, this time able to strafe the worm's full forty-foot-long side, as it slowly arced around the open desert floor.

"It sounds like a Mongolian Death Worm," Aleman said over their comms.

"Oh that's helpful," Rook said. "It couldn't be the Mongolian Fluffy Rainbow-Pooping Worm?" He dropped a magazine and slotted a fresh one into his SCAR, but then let the weapon hang. It wasn't doing any damage to the giant ribbed creature. He'd wait until it closed the distance, and then he'd try his 'Girls' – a pair of IMI Desert Eagle Mark XIX Magnum .50 caliber semi-automatic pistols. He'd had several pairs over the years, some getting lost in different skirmishes. He hadn't yet come across anything, no matter how big, that wouldn't feel a few slugs from the handguns at close range.

"He has a point," King said, perturbed. "How to kill it would be better than a name."

"It's a mythical cryptid. Supposed to be about four feet long," Aleman said.

"Bigger," Queen said. "Much bigger. Twelve-foot diameter. Forty feet long."

King pulled free his KA-BAR knife, a 7-inch blade like Queen's, and slid it into the boiling, formerly fur-covered sleeve of his environment suit's fabric, slicing it open, then he dropped the smoking knife on the ground. He'd tried to cut away the burning part of the suit, but had failed. "Rook."

It was all he had to say. As he flipped off the helmet and hood of the suit, breathing in the freezing air, Rook moved forward to grab the outer fabric of the suit in places where it hadn't been coated in the creature's deadly venom. He pulled the fabric taut as King disentangled himself from the outer garment, being sure to lean as far from the smoking side as possible.

Rook instantly saw King's breath add a cloud of vapor to the already rising ribbon of steam from the cooking fur on the ruined suit.

"It's supposed to be able to spit venom," Aleman continued.

"Think we can confirm that one," Rook said.

Queen fired a sustained burst with her SCAR as Bishop reloaded the machine gun. The creature had finished its wide loop and was homing in on the team, at their new location.

"We need a plan," Queen urged.

"There's nothing about how to kill them. No one has ever even had a confirmed sighting of one..." Aleman sounded frantic.

"Then give me some other intel," King said, his teeth beginning to chatter. "How long do I have in just the wetsuit in temps like these?" He had shed the outer garment, now smoking on the ground like a dead animal on a charnel heap. He wore just the under-suit, which was a special gel-heated neoprene, and he had been able to salvage his boots and the furry gloves from the outer suit.

Rook thought he looked strange in white, fur-clad boots and gloves, but a black body suit and hood. Like some kind of snow bunny at the Winter games, but this one had an automatic rifle and was collecting the bomb-spikes for his spear gun from the pile of quickly discarded equipment.

"Your suit? Oh crap. Um...if you keep active, any part or

your skin that's exposed might be able to withstand frostbite for... around ten minutes. Maybe less."

King turned to see the approaching worm was just a few yards away, and it was beginning to rise up in the air, like a cobra poised to strike.

6

"There!" King pointed the barrel of his SCAR and fired an unrestrained, fully automatic burst, holding down the trigger. "Under its neck."

The others instantly saw what he was targeting. Just under the rim of the creature's black mouth, which lacked teeth but had short one-foot-long wriggling tentacles, like insect feelers or kelp waving in an undersea current, was a small metal box affixed to the creature's crimson skin. It looked to be the size of an old metal lunchbox, and King's bullets pounded the can, pinging off of it. Then Bishop opened with a sustained burst from the 240, and the box, as well as the slick, wet-looking skin below it, disintegrated.

The giant worm dropped down from its attack position, its heft slamming into the ground and sending a shockwave underfoot. Then it turned and headed away from the building, and the surprised team.

"Control mechanism?" Queen asked.

"Possibly," King said. "Blue, we need a pickup, ASAP."

"They can't, King." Aleman's voice was apologetic. "The chopper is still on the other side of the storm. It's no longer blowing where you are, but it still stretches for forty miles. No way for them to get to you. You'll have to hump it out to the LZ."

"Knight?" King asked.

"Proceeding. We'll catch up."

Knowing he had to keep moving, and even then his time was limited, King made the decision. "Move out."

The team picked up and headed toward the distant cloud that marked the edge of the storm, back the way they had come. The wind had stopped blowing in their location, but they could still see a far off wall of white and swirling brown. They double-timed it for the raging storm, keeping an eye on the receding worm, as it wandered aimlessly south and then west again, back from whence it had come.

The team made it halfway from the castle to the edge of the cloud when the rocks around them pinged with the ricochets of missed rifle fire. They each dropped, and rolled to the sides, then faced back toward the strange brown fortress. But the shots hadn't come from that direction. They were coming from a small team – maybe ten strong – of additional guards to the north. They were still a few hundred yards away, their rifles only just inside the effective firing range.

Queen glanced at King and saw that he wasn't reacting as quickly as she would have expected. His lips hadn't turned blue, but they had lost their color, and his face looked pale against the black neoprene hood lining. "Rook, Bishop. Take this. I'm getting King to the LZ."

Rook raised his SCAR and fired off a few rounds at the approaching men. The weapon had a much longer range, but at the distance, any kills would be simple luck. "Watch out for the Jumbo Fire Turd."

"Nice," Queen said, grabbing King by the arm and starting to run with him toward the nearby wall of the storm. "You kiss *me* with that mouth, remember."

"Only because you ask me to—" Rook started to say, before his body was violently flung to the ground. Bishop had opened up on the approaching guards with the machine gun, but she stopped immediately and turned to Rook. The left arm of his suit's fur was a deep maroon. "Shit in the milk carton! That stings like bastard."

Bishop started opening a portable med kit they each carried, which was strapped to their stomachs, over the environment suits, but as she unzipped it, Rook spoke again.

"Just a through and through," he growled. "I'll be alright."

Bishop lunged back to her trigger, trusting Rook's self-assessment. They had all taken minor grazes from bullets – or worse – at this point in their careers. She laid down a suppressing fire that had the new group of guards diving for cover or simply dropping dead with tufts of crimson mist staining the white clouds around them. She counted ten men, but their number was dwindling under her constant stream of automatic fire.

Rook rolled over, pulling up his rifle and adding his bullets to hers. They had the guards, all of them wrapped in their brown furs, pinned just behind a small ridge of rock. But then two things happened at once.

The wind picked up again, the storm having shifted enough to cover them in waves of sand and snow. Their visibility was lost completely.

Then the building, so reminiscent of China's greatest architectural accomplishment, detonated. The chemical reaction made the explosion far stronger than the bomb-spikes should have done alone.

A howling burst of flame ripped horizontally across the ground, with a pressure wave so strong that it rolled Rook's body across the rocky ground, crushing him into Bishop's prone form, and the two of them slammed into a low ridge of crumbling rock. The wall of flame came next, flashing across their bodies and whipping across the fur coatings on their environment suits until they were singed clean. The shrieking wind carried the rest of the destruction away.

"I think I just got a tan," Bishop said, shoving Rook's body off of her.

"You got off light," Rook complained. "I think I just lost my nut hairs."

"Aww, both of them?" Bishop said. She started to look for the machine gun, but found the barrel had been coated in small pebbles and sand, the grit having invaded the open gas ports. Attempting to fire it now would result in a misfire at best or another explosion in her face at worst. She left it, and hauled Rook to his feet. As she did, a huge wall of red flashed by on her right, just where she had been lying.

The death worm had returned.

The massive creature worked its way past them like a shark blitzing past its prey. It was so close she could reach out and touch it. It blurred by like a subway car if she had been standing too close on the platform. She could see the ragged gouges and holes in its scarlet hide, where she had riddled it with the 240 earlier.

The blasting wind slowed, and she could see once again in the direction of the small group of pinned guards. She wished she couldn't. The worm ran straight for the men, snatching one guard up with its black tentacles, and flipping him into the air. The beast rose up again, close to twenty feet straight up in the air, like it was performing an old Indian rope trick. Then it grabbed the man before he reached the apex of his flight, and swallowed him down in one gulp. Again, Bishop was reminded of a shark.

She saw one of the other guards banging his heavily gloved fingers on an oversized remote control with a three foot long silver antenna. It reminded her of the controllers she had seen boys in Russia use on remote controlled toy cars. "They *are* controlling the worms."

But then the worm flopped down onto the man, mashing him and two of his fellow guards into the ground, before another gust of wind obscured her view with a river of white snow. The gust curved down toward the ground and then straight up into the sky, like a geyser.

"I've got nothing you can fight them with," Aleman said over the comm, "short of immense doses of electricity or dousing the region with chemicals from above – things we don't have. Get out of there, Bishop."

"We have one more thing that can do the trick," Knight yelled, as the ground rumbled.

Rook turned in time to see – and then side-step away from – another giant worm. This one looked fatter, but shorter than the first. Twenty feet at the thickest part, just past the head, and then tapering down to ten feet in diameter, over forty feet away, down by its tail end. It was a darker, richer red than the first. Not as shiny, and without as many defined ribs. This one also had another unusual feature.

Knight was hanging from its side.

With one hand, he clung to one of the bomb-spikes, which he had manually impaled in the creature's side. The worm was moving fast, and Knight was fifteen feet off the ground, as the creature rushed past, spiraling higher, so that Knight was lifted up and on top of it.

7

Anna Beck raced after the runaway death worm and its precious cargo. The thing was moving at a good clip, and the ground – covered with random clumps of hardy vegetation or craggy rocks – made for treacherous footing.

The plan had been simple. Knight had raced after the second worm, bomb-spike in hand. He hadn't had a chance to load it into his launcher, and instead had run on foot toward the side of the massive creature. He should have impaled it and dropped away, so she could detonate the bomb once he was clear. Instead, Knight had held onto the spike, and been hoisted for a ride on the top of the charging worm.

"What the hell are you doing, Knight?" she asked, huffing, as she ran full out behind him. "You were supposed to spike it and get off, not go all rodeo."

She knew the transmitters for the detonators on the jury-rigged spikes had a limited range, so she needed to be close enough to the creature to kill it, but she needed to get Knight and herself far enough from it that the blast didn't injure them, too.

"Getting elevation," he said. "There are more of them."

She heard the distinctive crack of his sniper rifle go off, over the howl of the wind on her exterior speaker. Then she turned her head and saw a third worm – this one a mottled brown and white – suddenly veer away from its previous course. Knight had just shattered its control box. If he hadn't, she never would have known it was pursuing her until it was too late. Now the brown creature made a lazy turn heading back toward the destroyed lab.

"How many more?" Aleman asked in her ear.

"Enough," Knight said, his voice terse as he concentrated on firing again. Beck knew his voice well enough to tell when he was aiming.

"Team, if you can kill those things with the bomb-spikes, you need to do it," Aleman said, hesitating as he said it, as if he were doing three other things on the computer at the same time.

"King said to bug out, Blue," Rook said over the comms. "Bish and I are already moving toward the LZ." Everyone knew that King made the final calls when the team was in the field.

"Those things already have a taste for human flesh, if the guards have been using them for security. If even one of them survives, it could rampage across the countryside, devouring nomads – or worse, it might pilgrimage to a population center like Beijing."

"Blue is right," King's voice came over the comms, his teeth still chattering. "We're nearly at the chopper. I'll be fine. Sending Queen back for support."

"I'll take the brown one, then," Pawn said, changing direction and pursuing the large mottled worm. As she ran, she mounted one of the two bomb-spikes Knight had handed her into her spear gun. She planned to chase the thing into range and then simply fire the weapon at it, but the lumbering creature turned instead of continuing straight. It performed a slow loop back to the north, and then in the direction Knight had gone, riding on the back of the brick red worm.

The ground shook with each leaping step she took, and she found it easier to run in the patches of loose sand than on the vibrating rock. As the thing changed direction again, cutting across her path, her distance to it was shortened, and she soon got within spear-gun range. As she loosed a spike from the weapon, the visibility increased yet again, and she saw the brick worm, Knight squatting on its back, charging straight for her mottled brown worm. The two would either attack each other, or pass right next to each other, like speeding trains. Unsure of which it would be, and what Knight would need, she continued racing for the collision site.

As she ran, she saw Knight stand up.

Then at the last second, the two speeding worms altered direction just slightly, and she could see that they would pass right next to each other. Knight leapt from the reddish worm to the brown one, rolling on the back of the latter. Pawn altered her trajectory to follow the brown worm. As the red worm's tail cleared the brown's tail, Knight activated his transmitter, and the speeding red beast's front end exploded in a gout of thick white fluid and chunks of brick-red skin. Much of the obliterated head was involuntarily swallowed by the hollow, fast moving cylinder of its body, before the creature ran out of steam and seemed almost to deflate, finally stopping its momentum.

Pawn chased the brown worm as it fled into the storm with Knight now surfing on top of it. "Brick-red one's down. That leaves the brown one Knight's on and the one you guys filled with lead," she announced on the open channel. "What next, Knight?"

"Run alongside," Knight told her. "I'll lower a rope."

"Why not just get down?" she asked, frustrated that he didn't get off the thing. How could she blow it up, if he was still in range?

"This one is going our way."

"The first one is still out there," she pointed out. "We need to get them all."

"Nah," she heard Rook's voice say, followed immediately by a resounding boom. "Queen and I just took care of Chuckles, the Swiss Cheese Worm. That just leaves yours, Knight."

Pawn ran as fast as she could, but she didn't think she would catch the fleeing brown worm and the man riding it. The ground rumbled hard under her feet, making every leap and hop treacherous. Her boots had slid more than once, and she was afraid she would turn an ankle. She was also starting to sweat and overheat in the warmed suit.

"Guys, I'm seeing a much bigger Richter pattern than before. The seismic readings suggest a full on earthquake is coming. Maybe all the tunneling from the worms?" Aleman sounded uncertain. "I think you should bail. You can re-arm and come back for the last worm."

"Shit," Knight blurted.

"What is it?" came King's voice. His words no longer stuttered from cold, and Pawn assumed he had reached the helicopter and a spare environment suit.

"It's turning," Knight replied, and just as he said it, Pawn burst through a cloud of swirling snowflakes and grit that gusted so hard it almost knocked her backward. She saw the brown worm turning. It would cross her path if she didn't hurry. Getting stuck between it in front of her and an earthquake behind her, with the helicopter on the other side of it did not appeal to her. She poured on the speed, intending to run past its head, like racing a train, and continue through the storm. She had already seen the thing was slow to corner, so she wasn't worried it could change direction at the last second and maul her.

"Time to get down, Bronco Billy," she said, as she raced past the thing's black-tentacled mouth. As she passed it, she saw Knight slide down the creature's ribbed side like it was a playground slide. Until its curvature stopped at its widest spot, a good ten feet off the ground, and dipped back under the fast moving beast. Knight dropped those last ten feet into a sand dune and rolled in the dirt, his furred suit flinging a spray of grit in the air like a car's tire spinning in mud.

Pawn veered toward Knight, but he was already rolling to his feet and running toward the distant helicopter on the other side of the storm's whipping frenzy. He wasn't waiting on her to catch up, so she forced herself to sprint faster.

When she felt they were far enough from the receding brown worm, she activated her transmitter, and the sky behind them filled with an orange ball of flame and smoke, billowing from the last worm's split open center. The massive creature rolled across the ground, out of control.

The ground shook hard, and Pawn realized it wasn't from the explosion, but from the earthquake Aleman had mentioned.

"Don't look back, Anna," Knight called. "Just run!"

Her eyes grew large inside her faceplate as she realized what he was saying.

It wasn't an earthquake.

She really didn't want to know how big this one was.

She really didn't.

But she looked.

8

"Report," King's voice came over the comms.

"Umm," Rook said, taking aim with his spear gun. He pointed it up in the air like an English longbowman, and Queen, to his side, picked up on his intent and did the same with hers.

SHOW OF FORCE

"Knight and Pawn are being chased by the biggest friggin' large intestine you can imagine."

With that description to King, he fired, and Queen did likewise. The twin bomb-spikes arced through the air and over the heads of Pawn and Knight, who were running toward them full tilt. Behind them was a massive death worm. This one dwarfed the others, with a diameter at the head of forty feet. As far as Rook could see, the thing's body trailed behind it a hundred yards.

The spikes implanted themselves in the top of the thing's neck, and Rook loaded another spike. Then he turned to run toward the edge of the storm, where King and the helicopter pilot, a retired Marine named Woodall, waited ready to take off at a moment's notice.

"We'll be coming in hot with the giant shit garage on our six."

"Taking it too far," Queen said, berating his disgusting description, while twisting in the middle of her run to fire another bomb-spike backward in an arc. This one implanted in the creature's back, ten yards further down from the first two. Then she continued her twist until she was facing forward. She kept running.

Knight and Pawn were catching up to them, and the megaworm kept twisting through the storm on their heels. It was so large that even when the gusts of snow blew through the air, mostly obscuring Knight and Pawn, Rook could still see the bright, shiny red of the thing's skin and the dark waving tendrils at its mouth through the blizzard.

Knight pulled alongside him, as Rook bunny hopped clumps of pale grass and stunted shrubs growing from rocky patches in the ground where they had sunken roots deep and found a source of water. Looking over, Rook saw that Knight carried a rope bag in his left hand and an empty spear gun in his right.

The bag held a neatly coiled 11mm climbing rope, and it was designed so the tip could be pulled out one end, and the rope would keep feeding out of the bag without tangling. The team carried two such rope bags. Knight had one and Queen wore the other strapped across her back. Rook wondered if they could lasso the giant slithering creature, but he quickly discarded the thought and poured all his energy into running for their one and only escape route.

As a larger, heavier man than the others, Rook was a slower runner. Pawn and Knight soon pulled in front of him, and he could no longer even see Queen in the distance. He glanced over his shoulder at the massive oncoming freight train of tendrils, the mouth of the worm yawning open like a dark cave that was chasing him. He found a second wind and began stretching out his strides.

"Hurry up, ma puce," Queen said over the comms. "We need to leave. The pilot says the storm is getting worse. If we don't take off in the next two minutes, the engine might get borked from the sand."

Even with the new burst of speed and Queen's encouragement, using her pet name for him, Rook didn't think he was going to be able to make it. Each step he took rattled his bones, as the pursuing giant worm shook the earth. He didn't even know if the few bomb-spikes they had planted in the thing would be enough to stop it. This one was twice as thick as the last one and many times longer.

What if the bastard splits in half from the explosion and turns into two worms?

Then he burst out of the boiling cloud of snow and sand to find he was running across clear, open, sandy ground. The sudden lack of wind resistance almost pitched him forward onto his face, but his legs awkwardly pinwheeled until he regained his step.

Two hundred yards away, the helicopter's rotor was already spinning up to speed. The pilot wore an environment suit like the team, so he could keep the side door open and waiting. Pawn was tossing her FN SCAR rifle into the interior and clambering up. Knight was right behind her, slinging his rope bag and empty spear gun inside. Queen was aiming another spear gun in Rook's direction, but at an upward angle. King, wrapped in a spare, white environment suit, was reaching down to haul Pawn into the doorway.

SHOW OF FORCE

The sight of his teammates gave him hope, and Rook found yet another burst of speed, his legs beginning to burn, and a cramp forming in his side, just above his right hip.

At one hundred and fifty yards, Rook saw Queen launch her bomb-spike, and then scramble to load another. King was hauling Knight into the open bay, and Pawn was fumbling to load another spear gun.

It was the frantic handling of the weapons that made him look back.

The ground vibrated and rippled beneath his feet, as Rook twisted to see the pursuing creature. The Mongolian death worm raised its head up as it came, looking like a huge, fast-moving wave of surf, ready to crash down on him. Its mouth was a gaping black void around a brilliant, scarlet skin that glistened in the sudden sunlight at the edge of the blowing storm behind the thing.

The creature, like all the others, had no visible nose or mouth. It was just a long, ribbed tube with a dark tendrilled opening at one end and a tapering diameter at the other end. But this worm was so big that the spaces between the ribbed segments on its sides were so deep, Rook thought he could stand inside one without the sides of the segments touching him. He tentatively planned to try just that if it came down to it.

He faced forward and threw the last of his energy into a final press of speed toward the helicopter, which was just beginning to hover. In his quick look, Rook had seen that the storm was closing almost as fast as the giant, hungry cylinder.

The ground shook so hard that rocks the size of baseballs skittered across the jagged landscape. He didn't have to look behind him to know that Mighty Joe Worm was gaining on him. The fact that all five of his teammates were firing spear guns over his head now was all the indication he needed that his time was almost up. When the pilot raised the helicopter another foot, and started to bank the craft even further away from his frantic dash, it underscored the point for Rook.

When he glanced back one more time and his boot caught on an unforgiving shrub, he felt himself pitch forward, overbalanced. Rook knew it was the end.

9

King saw that Rook was going down. He leapt out the still-open helicopter door and raced to meet the man. Rook had almost made it, before he had tripped, just thirty feet away. King cleared half that distance before Rook actually hit the ground. Either to his credit or due to his sheer momentum, Rook continued forward on the rocky soil, rolling forward on the ground, even as King skidded to a halt next to him.

Together, they got Rook to his feet and ran the last of the distance toward the black helicopter. To the pilot's credit, he had angled the vehicle closer in, toward the men, the pursuing hell worm and the raging whiteout wall.

King simply dove head-first into the belly of the cargo area, willing Rook to follow him. He slid across the floor of the angled craft and his hand grasped a cargo strap, just as someone else's hand latched onto his wrist to hold him in place.

The helicopter banked away, still rising off the ground. King was worried that the tips of the vehicle's blades might scrape the rocky soil at such a steep angle of departure, but the pilot was top-notch.

When he turned to look back out the open side door, King saw the massive worm was just below them, but rising up off the ground, pursuing the rising helicopter. The pilot was gaining altitude, but only at a slightly faster rate of gain than the death worm. The black maw followed them into the sky like a pirate ship intent on doing them ruin.

Rook had indeed made it into the craft, and he was now sitting with his back against the bulkhead. He'd formed a figure eight knot on the end of the rope from Knight's bag and was clipping it to the front of his harness with a black, anodized aluminum carabiner. King expected he would clip the other end of the rope onto the body of the helicopter for safety, but he never got the chance.

As the helicopter began to pick up vertical speed, the worm fell farther from the open door until Knight judged the distance enough. He flicked the switch on his transmitter, holding it up so everyone could see him deliver the coup de grâce.

SHOW OF FORCE

Nothing happened.

"Son of a bitch," Rook called. "Try this one." He reached out the hand of his bloodied arm and slapped the switch on his own transmitter, which was attached to the front of his gear harness.

Again nothing happened.

"We're too far away from it now," Queen said, reminding them all that the devices had a limited range. She called to the pilot. "We need to drop altitude a little."

"Screw that," Rook said, standing and pulling his twin Desert Eagle pistols. "Somebody get the friggin' rope."

With that he leapt head first out the open door, and toward the still rising void of the death worm's mouth.

Five sets of hands scrambled for the rope bag and the black climbing rope that rapidly unspooled from its depths.

* * *

Rook sailed straight down through the air, head first toward the oncoming ring of waving tendrils. He could see that the creature had raised almost half of itself straight up off the ground, chasing the rising helicopter with unrestrained hunger.

He had no question in his mind that the others would secure the rope, preventing him from falling to his death. Instead he worried that his plan to get close enough to the bomb-spikes that the transmitter would work might be flawed. He couldn't do the math quick enough to determine when his plummeting body would meet the rising worm. He'd always hated those kinds of problems in school.

Instead, he focused on what he knew how to do best.

Time to break shit.

He fired his huge pistols at the inside of the worm's mouth, blowing huge chunks of skin apart, even from that distance. Then the rope caught taut above him, jerking his descent to an abrupt stop, and he felt the last meal he'd eaten, hours ago, try to leave his body through the top of his head. Then his body flipped upside down, because the attachment point on his harness was in front of him. He was now hanging in the air with his back facing the lunging creature and his stomach facing upward at the bottom of the helicopter.

As the vehicle swung him over the edge of the worm's mouth, he twisted in his harness, looking down at the outer side of the beast. He could see one of the bomb-spikes implanted in its flesh. He figured he was close enough to the creature now. He slapped a hand still holding a Magnum against the switch of the transmitter on his chest, but the bombs still refused to explode.

"Monkey fucker-noodle!"

A boiling cloud of purple vapor bellowed out of the creature's mouth, and Rook knew they had just a few seconds before the death worm spewed a stream of poison at him and the helicopter. The edge of the storm had found them, too, suddenly whipping the rope, and Rook's dangling body.

He raised both pistols and fired both magazines dry at the single bomb-spike he could see on the side of the worm's slick body. He quickly ejected both magazines and slotted in a single new one for the pistol in his right hand. He took a single steadying breath as the raging wall of white began to cover up the creature's body, just feet below the silver of the bomb-spike's surface. The purple cloud coming out of the creature's mouth was billowing back past the creature, as its mouth still rose into the air. The thick viscous fumes further obscured the explosive spear nailed into the worm's hide. He started to worry that the acidic nature of the fumes could incapacitate the detonators on the bombs, but then he let the thought fall Zen-like from his mind as he aimed, released his breath and squeezed the trigger.

The effect was instant.

Although the explosive compound in the spears was hardy enough to take a shot from a bullet without exploding, the small detonators on the spikes were not. The bullet impacted the detonator, and the smaller explosive it contained went off, taking the larger explosive with it. The bomb-spike's explosion then activated the others embedded in the creature's thick hide, all over the front half of its body. The entire upper half of the giant beast turned into a maelstrom of orange fire, black smoke, purple venom, red skin fragments and white swirling snow and ice.

The helicopter rose abruptly, tugging Rook with it, but his suit still got splattered with gore. Smoke rose from parts of his formerly white covering, melting from the viscous goo that now coated him.

"I'm gonna need a new suit fast," Rook said over the comms. "And an aversion therapy doctor with a gallon-sized bucket of sour gummy worms."

"Copy that," Aleman said. "Are you clear?"

Rook looked up as he was tugged from above. The team pulled him up as King looked down for visual confirmation of Rook's situation. Rook gave a thumbs up. "Aside from the melting, we're golden."

"We're done here," King said. "En route to the safe house."

"Actually," Aleman said. "The safe house is compromised."

"Admiral Ward?"

"Uh-huh." Aleman said in almost a groan. "Better come to me instead."

"Will do," King said, adding his muscle to the rope pulling effort. "But then we're going to have a chat about what to do about this thorn in our side."

Thanks for reading *SNAFU: Survival of the Fittest*.
We really hope you enjoyed it, both for the brilliant efforts by our authors and for the wonderful artwork by Monty Borror. We're proud to present what we consider the best military horror/sci-fi we can find.
Geoff Brown and Amanda J Spedding

READ ON FOR AN EXTRACT FROM SNAFU: HUNTERS

www.cohesionpress.com

Extract from 'Bonked' by Patrick Freivald, featured in
SNAFU: Hunters

* * *

Flynn jerked his thumb toward the back. "You want me to get the trunk?"

Matt shook his head. The REC-7 carbine and Auto-Assault 12 combat shotgun could stay where they were, in the trunk under lock and key. If worse came to worse he had his personal Glock 9mm in the glove box. But it wouldn't. They'd been made as cops in a no-go zone, but hadn't done anything to justify a murder, even from a gang as vicious as the Camino Reals.

They blew through two red lights, the jeeps swerving and honking behind, but as they passed from one turf to the next the pursuit broke off and didn't return.

"You sussed those out pretty fast. Precog, yeah?" Flynn asked.

Matt nodded without taking his eyes from the road.

"Brilliant, brilliant. They wouldn't clear me for it, said I'd had enough. I'm thinking what's the harm, right?"

"The harm is you go bonk and kill everything around you until other people like you put you down."

Flynn chuckled. "That's what I mean, right? The side effect is 'fun.'"

"Just keep your pants on."

"Aye, Sergeant."

Ten minutes later they rolled past the Marquee, a modern glass-and-steel structure at odds with the dilapidated neighborhood. The fading day washed the neon lights to a pale glow but did nothing to hide the ultraviolet paint across the front windows, a cartoon shark swimming through a golden crown that would be invisible to unaugmented eyes.

"See that?" Matt asked.

Flynn nodded. "Fancy. You think the Shades don't have blacklights?"

Matt shrugged. "One cop in fifty might have augged vision, maybe. Not like the Mako Kings don't know the police know where they hang out, anyway. As long as they think we're just cops, we'll—"

Flynn popped his handle and stepped out, the car still rolling at fifteen miles an hour. He hooked a parking meter with his right hand and used it to spin himself around, stopping with a flourish with his toes balanced on the edge of the curb. As Matt slammed on the brakes and swore under his breath, Flynn took a bow to the wide-eyed onlookers. Flynn waited behind the car for Matt to pull over, put on the brake and get out.

People milled the streets, heading home from work or out for a Friday on the town. As one they gave the car a wide berth, eyeing both newcomers with open suspicion or naked hostility.

Matt stepped up to his friend with his jaw clenched in frustration. "Dammit, Conor, we're supposed to be scoping the place, not painting bullseyes on our heads."

A seven-foot tall bouncer, rippling with muscles impossible through normal exercise, eyed them from the front door across the street. Taking in the sea of Hispanics, all either staring or trying too hard not to stare, Flynn ran a hand over the stubble on his pasty scalp. "See, we fit right in, sunnies and all." He put on his shades and sauntered across the street.

Music trickled out behind the double-doors, Latin horns over a hip-hop beat, death-metal Spanish growling from a microphone. They approached, cop-casual, Matt two steps behind. The bouncer moved to intercept them. His voice rumbled an octave lower than a normal man's, his accent a blend of Mexican and south Florida. "Can I help you gentlemen?"

"Yes," Matt said. "We—"

"Looking for a drink and twirl is all." Flynn spun, an elegant pirouette that ended in a curtsey. He held the pose and looked up under his brow into the bouncer's eyes. "Heard the Marquee had it happening, am I right?"

"You're not our target clientele, *ese*." The bouncer put his hands on his hips so that his massive frame blocked most of both doors. Matt winced as Flynn's eyes flashed, an almost imperceptible twitch that showed not the slightest hint of fear. The bouncer put his hand on Flynn's chest, fingers splaying almost to his shoulders. "You're going to have to leave."

"What, because I'm white? You discriminating here? You think the Irish haven't faced—"

Matt put his hand on Flynn's shoulder. "We're not here to pick a fight, Conor."

"—their share of discrimination, you racist prick? Why don't you make me leave, big guy?"

To his credit, the bouncer didn't take the bait. Much. He extended his arm, slowly, forcing Flynn several steps back on the sidewalk. "Move along, little man. This isn't the place for you." He extended his fingers and Conor stumbled back two steps.

Matt moved between them and Conor rebounded off of his back. "We're sorry, sir. We'll be on our way." He stepped back, bumping Flynn toward the street, then turned and backed him off the curb and into the road. Through gritted teeth he mumbled, "The point was to maintain surprise, moron."

Flynn almost frolicked toward the car, locking eyes with anyone and everyone who dared challenge his right to be there. "Nah, there's no fun in that, and he thinks we're cops or feds or something anyway. The point was to size that meathead up. You see what I saw?"

Matt recalled the scene, his eidetic memory enhancements bringing to crystal-clear focus details he hadn't seen in real time. "Tracks?"

"Right is right. He's on the H, not just Jade. We follow him home, wait for him to snow out, bangers and mash," he mimed tossing a flash-bang grenade, "black bag over the head, voila. New toy for the intel department."

Matt tried not to smile as he gunned the engine. "Call it in."

* * *

READ ON IN *SNAFU: Hunters*

Printed in Great Britain
by Amazon